JAMES

Other books by Trudy J. Morgan-Cole

By the Rivers of Brooklyn

Daughters of Grace

Deborah and Barak

Esther: A Story of Courage

Esther: Courage to Stand

God's Positioning System

Lydia: A Story of Philippi

Sunrise Hope

The Wise Men

Yosef's Story

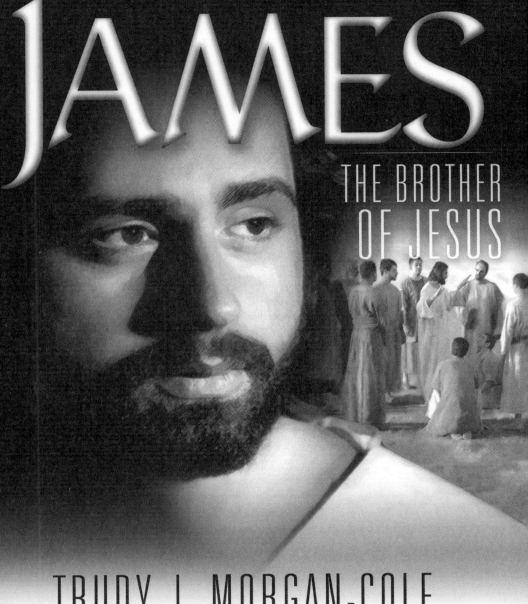

JAMES
THE BROTHER OF JESUS

TRUDY J. MORGAN-COLE

Pacific Press® Publishing Association
Nampa, Idaho
Oshawa, Ontario, Canada
www.pacificpress.com

Cover design by Steve Lanto
Cover design resources from istockphoto.com/sermonview.com
Inside design by Aaron Troia

The author assumes full responsibility for the accuracy of all facts and quotations
as cited in this book.

You can obtain additional copies of this book by calling toll-free 1-800-765-6955
or by visiting http://www.adventistbookcenter.com.

All Scripture quotations in this book, unless otherwise noted, are from the THE
HOLY BIBLE, NEW INTERNATIONAL VERSION®, NIV®. Copyright ©
1973, 1978, 1984, 2011 by Biblica, Inc.™ Used by permission. All rights reserved
worldwide.

Library of Congress Cataloging-in-Publication Data:

Morgan-Cole, Trudy J., 1965-
James : the brother of Jesus / Trudy Morgan-Cole.
  p. cm.
ISBN 13: 978-0-8163-2512-2 (pbk.)
ISBN 10: 0-8163-2512-X (pbk.)
1. Jesus Christ—Family. 2. Bible. N.T.—History of Biblical events. I. Title.
PS3613.O7487J36 2011
813'.6—dc22

                                                                    2011026816

11 12 13 14 15 • 5 4 3 2 1

Contents

Chapter One

This is the worst thing I know about myself, my darkest confession. When I heard Jesus was missing, I thought he was dead.

And I was not sorry.

Not glad, of course, but not sorry. I felt no real regret. Mary's face looked up into mine, a blur of worry and fear. "Have you seen him, James? Was he with you?" Seeing her panic, I thought, *He has wandered away in the city streets; he is lost; he is dead.* And I felt no sorrow but an empty space almost like relief in my chest.

I hadn't realized, till that moment, how much I hated him.

Of course, I let none of that show in my face. Indeed, I would not admit such feelings even to myself. Age has made me more honest about the kind of man I was in my youth. But then, I was still young, and I knew enough to know that when a frightened, worried mother asks if you have seen her missing child, you show nothing but concern.

"I have not seen him all day, or yesterday, Mother," I said. I called her Mother, out of respect and because it pleased my father, although she was only four years my senior—my father's wife, mother of my half-sisters and half-brothers, including the incorrigible Jesus.

He had, in his usual thoughtless way, gone missing in Jerusalem during Passover. Thousands of pilgrims pouring into and out of the city from every Jewish community in the world, and that reckless boy could not even take enough thought for others to keep within sight of his mother and father. *If some evil has befallen him, it serves him right.* But that thought, too, I quickly smothered.

"Let me find Father," I said quickly. "I'm sure the boy is with him, or some of the other men. You mustn't worry."

"I've already seen your father!" she said, her voice rising quickly to impatience. "He thought Jesus was with me and the other women, and I thought he was here with you men. Joseph has gone to spread the word among the other travelers from Nazareth. If we can't find him among the caravans, we'll have to go back to Jerusalem."

"Of course." I forced my voice to echo her concern. "Have you spoken to my uncle?" When she shook her head, I went on, "No doubt he is with them, if he is not with you or with Father. I will go look for our kinfolk, and see if Jesus is with them."

He might be, of course. He could be walking along with my uncle's family, chatting with some of the younger cousins. It would ease Mary's mind to think so. What I did not say, as I moved away from her into the crowd of travelers now making camp for the night, was that Jesus could just as easily be traveling with a group of complete strangers. He might be talking to a crowd of Greeks bound for Sepphoris. He could have joined a group of Alexandrian Jews and decided to go back to the country where we had all lived so many years ago, when he was just a baby. He could have been pressed into carrying a Roman soldier's pack and be trotting happily along, thinking it a great adventure, so busy talking to the soldier that he went past the allotted mile and carried the pack all the way to Jericho. The boy was capable of anything.

My father and stepmother seemed to think this a rather charming quality of his. I thought as I'd thought for years: he was a nuisance.

I had tried. Give me credit; I'd tried as well as a boy of eleven could do when I was presented with a new stepbrother. Even though Jesus' birth had meant a complete upheaval in our life—departure from our comfortable home in Nazareth, the long journey to Bethlehem for the census, then that panicked flight into Egypt and the strangeness of a new city and a new country. Even though, with all that change, the worst thing was that I'd lost my father, lost that special bond that had existed between us in the years of his widowhood. I lost him to his new wife and new son.

Later, other children came. A second family. They blended well enough with my younger siblings, Jude, Sara, and Leah. Mary's children were Jesus, Rebecca, Simon, Joseph, and Naomi, the baby. Nine of us in all, and by the time we were all settled back in Nazareth, Jude and I working beside Father as carpenters, we seemed like one family. The dividing lines between first family and second existed only in my divided heart.

I didn't mind the younger children, and I showed Mary the proper respect due to my father's wife, always. But in my heart I saw her, her and Jesus, as the interlopers. The ones who had changed my world, taken my father from me, uprooted my life.

I shook myself, as a dog shakes off water, trying to free myself of those thoughts. It was preposterous. I was no longer a boy to sulk at the arrival of a stepmother and a younger sibling. I was a young man, returning home from a year of study in Jerusalem with the rabbis, returning home to the bride my father had chosen for me. I was a man ready to begin his life, and a twelve-year-old brother with a gift for drawing attention should have been the least of my concerns.

I moved quickly through the little groups of travelers heading north toward Galilee. I wound my way between tethered donkeys, small cooking fires, and bundles of belongings, stopping here and there. "Have you seen my brother? My brother Jesus?" I asked of everyone I recognized. If they seemed unsure who I meant, I would explain further, "Jesus, the son of Joseph and Mary from Nazareth." Then they would smile in recognition. It was me they didn't know; Joseph's eldest son they had forgotten. No one who had met Jesus ever forgot the boy.

But, though they smiled, they all shook their heads. "No, we've not seen him today. We thought he was with his mother—with his father—with his cousins. We thought he was with you." Nobody had seen Jesus today. They would have remembered.

"I spoke with him this morning, didn't I?" my cousin Samuel said, looking at his oldest son, a boy of Jesus' age, for confirmation. "Remember how he had us all laughing with the story he told—"

"No, that was yesterday," the boy corrected him. "Before we left Jerusalem, wasn't it?"

Samuel nodded. "Of course, of course it was. No, we've not seen Jesus today. But he must be somewhere about, with some other family. A boy like that won't be lost for long. He can't be!"

As word spread, others joined in the search. By the time dusk fell, as I rejoined Mary and Father at our campsite, Mary was in tears. No one had seen Jesus all day. Though our friends and relatives had looked far and wide throughout all the caravans on the north road, no one had found Jesus.

"Hush, hush, Mary," my father Joseph said, resting her head against his shoulder. "If he's not on the road with us here, then he must have been left behind in Jerusalem. We'll go back at first light to find him."

"But where would he stay? He knows no one in Jerusalem," Mary sobbed.

A faint smile crossed my father's face. "He knew no one in Jerusalem when we arrived, wife. Knowing Jesus, he doubtless has firm friends there now, friends who have invited him to share their hearth and bed until we return for him. Let us sleep a little now, and as soon as dawn comes we will go back to find him."

She did not want to wait, but even she could see the folly of setting out to travel at night. I do not think she slept that night, but then neither did I. I sat staring at the dying embers of our fire, thinking how once again that boy had thrown my plans out of order and brought upheaval to my life.

In Jerusalem the following evening, after another frantic day's journey, my parents had no idea where to begin looking for their still-missing son. The busy city streets still teemed with festivalgoers, for though Passover had ended, not all travelers had yet left the city.

I suppose I need not have gone back with them. Father had even said as much, encouraging me to continue on to Nazareth with the rest of our extended family from the village. "Go home, my son. Your brothers and sisters will be anxious to see you, after such a long time away," he pointed out. Only Jesus had made the journey to Jerusalem with my parents this year, having just reached the age of manhood. I had no doubt, knowing him, that he had tormented them with begging and pleas for months and months till at last they had agreed to take him along.

Our family was too poor to bring everyone to Jerusalem every year for Passover, but the plan had long been in place that Father and Mary would come for the festival this year and accompany me back home for my marriage. It was just like Jesus to make himself part of the plan, whether my father willed it or not. Everyone said what a good boy he was, how charming, how pleasant. I often wondered if I was the only one who could see his iron will and how he made everyone in the family a captive to it.

I led my parents through the winding, narrow streets to the house of my teacher, the rabbi who had been like a second father to me during the past year. Rabbi Eli had allowed me to live in his house and learn from him as he learned from his own teacher many years ago—and his teacher had been a disciple of Rabbi Shammai himself.

It was an honor indeed for a young Galilean like myself, son of a carpenter, to learn at the feet of a master Pharisee. If we had stayed all my childhood in Nazareth it might never have happened; I might have grown up to be a carpenter like my father with no greater ambitions. But when circumstances drove us into exile in Egypt, we found ourselves in a world very different from our simple Galilean village. I made the transition from childhood to youth there in Alexandria, among learned Jews who recognized my eager mind and readiness to learn. Mary—I must give her credit for this much—urged my father to allow me to be taught the Scriptures and writing, thinking I might perhaps aspire to become a scribe. We had a friend there, a Persian scribe who had somehow become entangled with my parents in those strange times after Jesus' birth, who taught me my letters, while an old rabbi who lived in our street guided my study of the Torah.

So it was that after our return to Nazareth—I was about sixteen then, when we made the long journey home—I found the life of a village carpenter somewhat narrow. I worked along with Father, but I also kept up my studies with our village rabbi, though truth to tell I knew as much as he did and more. It was he who finally suggested to my parents that if money could be saved, I might go to Jerusalem to sit at the feet of learned men and further my studies.

This I had done for a year now, and I was eager to learn more, but first I must take another step toward manhood and marry the girl my father had found for me. I found myself eager for marriage, though I barely remembered Rachel. In my mind she was one of a dozen similar village girls her age in Nazareth, but I trusted that my father had chosen wisely and I was ready to meet her as my wife, to begin this new stage in my life. I was impatient at the delay that brought me back to my mentor's house looking for another night's lodging for my family. Yet I could not leave my father and Mary to face Jerusalem again alone. I knew the city better, and besides, I already had an idea about Jesus and where he might be found—if he was not, indeed, dead or run away.

"You rest here," I told them, for I could see they were both weary from the day's journey and sick with their worry and fear. "I will speak to some people."

"Do you think he is still here in the city?" Mary asked, her dark eyes shadowed with darker circles beneath them. How she loved that boy! It was natural, perhaps, to love her own children better than the stepchildren, though she was kind to us all, and my sisters Sara and Leah adored her as if she were their mother. But I could see—I had always seen—that Jesus was more special to her. Not just more special than my siblings and I, but more special even than her own little ones. She cared for us all, and I think truly loved us all, but when she looked at Jesus it was as if she had given him a piece of her heart to carry around, and would never get it all back.

I had my own suspicions about why that might be.

My teacher's wife and son were in the house, and his wife graciously allowed us to unroll our bedding in front of their hearth for another night. But she had seen no sign of the boy Jesus.

"Where is my master?" I asked.

"I have not seen him since the noon meal," his son Simon told me. Simon was about my own age, an able scholar who had become a good friend of mine in the year I had studied under his father and lived in their home. "Do you think he might know something of the boy?"

"I intend to find out," I said grimly, leaving my parents there to share an evening bowl of stew while I headed out with Simon into the darkening streets.

Two days earlier, waking in that same house, Jesus had begged me to take him with me to hear the rabbis teach, to hear their debates. He had gone to worship at the Temple with our parents, eaten the Passover meal, but he still thirsted for more of Jerusalem, more of the Temple, and he thought I was to be his key to enter that world.

"Not a chance," I told him. "My master and the other rabbis have no time for ignorant boys interrupting their study."

"But I would not interrupt! I would be silent and listen and learn," Jesus promised, his bright eyes turned to mine, that same appealing stare that seemed to transfix everyone who met him. It did not charm me. "Besides, I am a man now," he added, as if he had just remembered the passing of his twelfth birthday.

"Barely a man," I said. "And when have you ever listened quietly, without interrupting?"

He grinned, not hurt in the least, knowing I spoke truly. "Well, I would try!" he promised. "Please, James? May I come with you? Just to sit on the edges, with the master's disciples?"

I refused him. Now, no matter how many scenarios presented themselves to me, the one that came to mind over and over was that that willful, headstrong boy had somehow found a way to get what he wanted after all. He always did.

I did not find him that night, but I found another Pharisee, from the school of Hillel, who told me that he had heard a rumor of a clever young boy—"from Galilee, like you, no less!" he laughed. "Have they begun breeding clever Galileans all of a sudden?" It was not a kindly jest: this man was no friend of mine. "I heard this lad was questioning the rabbis and teachers in the Temple courts. I don't know his name or where he is lodged, but perhaps if you go there tomorrow you'll find him."

That was all I needed. I went home and reported to my parents that in the morning we would find Jesus in the Temple court.

And so, indeed, we did. Through the busy throng—less crowded now than at the height of the festival, but still as busy as any great marketplace—I threaded my way; Father a few steps behind me. We entered the Court of Women, where Mary grabbed the sleeves of everyone who passed, describing her son, asking if anyone had seen him. Father and I went on to the pillared porches where small groups of rabbis, scribes, and students gathered, discussing the Torah and the Prophets.

I heard him before I saw him. His was still a boy's voice, high and clear, not yet fallen to the deeper tones of manhood. As I moved toward the area where my master and his disciples always sat to dispute and discuss the Law, I heard the voice rise above the low rumble of the men's conversation. "But does not Moses say in the Torah—?"

My father's head lifted; his eyes brightened. "Isn't that him?" he said. "Doesn't that sound like Jesus?"

His whole face was alight with joy and relief; he picked up his pace to move toward the group of men. And of course it was only natural that he should be joyful. His son had been lost and was about to be found: What father would not rejoice at such a moment?

Why, then, did my heart darken with the thought: *He has never worn that look of joy for me? Never once has any word or deed of mine brought that brightness to his eyes.* Village gossips had whispered for years that Jesus was not even my father's own son, but the son of another man, and I thought there was likely to be truth behind that rumor. Indeed, my father had admitted as much to me, though the story he told me was not one I could believe. My father was not a man to dishonor his bride before the wedding; surely Mary had tricked him into accepting Jesus as his own, I thought. But none of Joseph's trueborn sons ever delighted him as Jesus did. I was sure of that.

"Jesus!" my father called out now, his voice bursting into the disputation of those learned men. I could see the boy now, standing in a little cleared space in the middle of the seated men, his hand upraised as if he were teaching. "Truly, cannot all the laws be summed up in this single law of love to our neighbor?"

"You reason like a little disciple of Hillel!" one of the men replied. Jesus raised his eyebrows.

"I have not heard of this Hillel," he said. "Is he a rabbi too? It seems he has much wisdom, if he, too, sees the law of love written on every line of the Torah."

Snorts and murmurs all around the group now, for my master and his disciples followed the school of Shammai, Rabbi Hillel's great rival. But still, they looked at this boy, answered him, listened to him, as if he were a man of learning. This village boy not yet old enough to grow the first shadow of a beard!

"Jesus!" my father shouted again, and this time, the boy looked up.

Half a dozen expressions chased themselves across his young face as he turned, shaking dark curls out of his eyes. Surprise—shock, even, at being interrupted. A sudden awareness that might have been guilt, at the realization that my father must have been looking for him. Annoyance, the impatience of a boy interrupted in the midst of a game that interests him. Then, quickly erasing the others, that huge smile of his, warm with welcome. The smile that charmed everyone.

"Father! You found me! But I supposed, James told you I must be here. I've had such an interesting time."

Father and I drew closer to Jesus now, pulling him out of the circle of men, for even though he must be chastised, I had no desire to play out this family scene in public, before the eyes of my elders and mentors. Perhaps I did not want them to see how little control my father and I had over this clever, wayward boy.

"Jesus, what were you thinking? Do you know how your mother and I have worried? We traveled almost as far as Sychor before we realized you were not with us, and we came back to Jerusalem. We have been searching . . ."

"Come then, let's find Mother and put her mind at rest," the boy said, already a step or two in front of us, already leading the way. He turned back for a cheery wave to those dignified men to whom everyone spoke with such reverence. "Farewell, teachers—perhaps I will come and talk with you again someday!"

And those grave men laughed—a few of them did, anyway—and one called out, "I hope you do, young rabbi! I expect we will be hearing of you again!" With a start I realized the voice was that of my own teacher, Eli, he who doled out his praise and approval so cautiously, who had questioned and tested me for months before finally offering a word of approval. He sounded merry—he had never sounded merry before—as he bade farewell to that younger brother of mine, who was almost dancing as he walked ahead with Father, telling about his adventures in the city, about all the subjects he had discussed with the rabbis and all the things he had learned and seen.

And then we were out in the women's court, and Mary was there, rushing into Jesus' arms. He was as tall as she was now, I noticed with a start, though she was a small woman, so that was no great feat.

But he was growing up. If he had been insufferable as a boy, what would he be like once he started fancying himself a man?

She drew away then, as mothers will at such a time, her relief overcome by her indignation. "Do you know what we've been through, these last three days?" she challenged him, her voice growing shrill. "How worried I was, how frightened, how we looked for you—"

"Father has told me," Jesus said. "He made it very clear, how much worry I caused you by staying here. But truly, I didn't think you had left the city yet—I thought you would have come to look for me in the Temple. Surely you knew I would be in my Father's house, doing my Father's business?"

Joseph glanced sharply at him when he said "my Father," but Jesus wasn't even looking at Joseph. He and Mary shared a glance filled with meaning, and I knew without a word said what they were thinking. His Father. God, his heavenly Father. Joseph had spoken of it only once to me—Mary's firm conviction that Jesus was a miracle child, birthed by God's own Spirit. I had come away from that conversation saddened—sad that my good, kind father could have been so duped by a woman. I never wanted to speak of it again. And now here was Jesus, cheerfully unrepentant for all the trouble he had caused, a boy giddy with excitement about his first great adventure, hauling out that old slander into the light of day as if it were nothing at all.

"Enough of this," I said abruptly. "Let us go back to my teacher's house and gather our belongings. It is not yet noon, and we can be on the road and cover some miles before nightfall. I have a bride waiting for me in Nazareth, and you, little brother, have delayed me long enough."

Chapter Two

I thought of that day often in the years that followed, thought how it summed up everything I disliked and the few things I loved about my younger brother. I could see that for him that trip to Jerusalem had marked a turning point, a step into manhood, into a sense of his own importance and purpose. And this was a child who had always had a healthy sense of his own importance! The proper humility of a child had never become Jesus well. The picture of him there, a boy among learned men, disputing with them as if he knew as much as they, surprised me not at all. It was how he had always been.

His charm too—that was there, of course. That was how he had won the attention of the rabbis in the first place. Not just his intelligence—which, I am compelled to admit, was fierce and quick—but his personal charm. When he turned on that brilliant smile, when those big dark eyes sparkled, people were drawn to him. That same charm made our parents forgive him for his thoughtlessness, made them believe his repeated story that he had simply lost track of time and assumed they were still in the city somewhere. That charm even drew the sting from his casual arrogance when he said, "Didn't you know I would be doing my Father's business?" Any other child would have been whipped for such insolence, and perhaps he should have been. But he never was.

The journey to Jerusalem and back the second time revealed another thing I had known for years: the way in which our family's life revolved around him. I have already said that both my father and Mary loved Jesus more than the other children. I never heard any of the others complain of this bias, but it was obvious to me that they viewed him as special, set apart. The circumstances of his birth should have placed him under a cloud of shame, but it was, instead, a cloud of glory, as if everything that happened to him was a little more important than what happened to the rest of us. If one of the other children became sick, Mary would use all the home remedies that every village wife knew to lower a fever and ease pain until the sickness passed. If Jesus so much as coughed, she would take a few coins from her meager supply and pay for a doctor to come. It was a good thing he was rarely sick.

Even that return journey from Jerusalem to Nazareth, once we finally found Jesus, was marred for me. It was to have been my homecoming, my triumphant return as the carpenter's boy who went away and studied with the learned rabbis. I would be married as soon as we returned, and I dared to hope that this one time, at least, I would be allowed a little share of the family's attention, that my accomplishments would be praised as my marriage was celebrated.

But now it was no longer the homecoming of James; it was the homecoming of Jesus, their precious boy who had been lost and was found, their brilliant child who had been debating with his elders like a man. Rather than being shamed and punished for his disobedience as he should have been, Jesus was praised for his cleverness, and they rejoiced that he had been found safely. The story was told over and over—even at my wedding feast—until it entirely overshadowed anything else of importance in our family.

You will think that I am jealous. It's a charge I have heard before, and perhaps it is a fair one. Was I jealous of Jesus? It seems like folly for a grown man to be envious of a boy of twelve. Why did I imagine myself competing with a younger half-brother? It wasn't that I wanted the attention and acclaim that seemed to follow Jesus everywhere. Rather, I wanted each of us to be in our own proper spheres. I wanted Jesus to be appropriately quiet, humble, and obedient, as a child should be, not to draw attention to himself. I wanted to be recognized for my own accomplishments, to be seen as the eldest son of the family, a credit to my parents.

They went through the motions, of course. On my wedding day, my father kissed me on both cheeks. "James, you have a lovely bride and a bright future ahead of you," he said. He looked around the courtyard of our home, where the wedding feast was being celebrated, and his eyes misted with tears. "I remember when you were just a little lad, following me around the yard, pulling along planks of wood bigger than you were. I thought then you'd be a fine little carpenter! But I see now that you were meant to be so much more . . . I am so proud of you, my boy."

"Thank you, Father," I said, as was right and proper to say. We had shared such a close bond when I was a boy, Father and I, in the years between Mother's death and his marriage to Mary. It galled me, I suppose, to see the boy Jesus trotting at his heels as I had once done, helping him with his work, learning to take the other end of a saw or swing a hammer. Perhaps, in time, it would bother me when the littler boys, Mary's younger sons, did the same, but I doubted it. There was something about Jesus that unsettled me, that always had.

Nor did things get better in the years that followed my marriage to Rachel. My brother Jude married as well and went to live with his wife's family in a nearby village. Her mother was widowed and had no sons, so Jude became the man of that family, working their small farm. He liked tilling the soil and found himself better suited to it than to the work of a carpenter that my father had done all his life. One of our sisters, Sara, also married and left home. Rachel bore me a son we named Benjamin, and we continued to live in my father's house.

I divided my time between laboring alongside my father and

studying the Torah. I knew that the latter was my true calling, that if I could follow my heart's deepest inclination I would be a rabbi and a scholar. But we were poor folks, and it was a blessing I had been able to gain even as much learning as I had. My hope was that when our village rabbi was finally laid to rest with his fathers, I would be able to fill his role. But even then, I would need to labor for at least part of the time, to provide daily bread for my wife and children.

Jesus, too, worked with our father Joseph during those years. We all worked at the simple carpentry jobs required in our own village, but those were never enough to support a large family like ours. We regularly traveled to the cities nearby to work for our Roman masters and the wealthier class among our own people. Great houses and public works existed there such as one would never find in a village.

We went to Sepphoris one autumn to work on a new palace for the city's governor. The city was Herod's capital, though there was talk that he planned a great new city at Tiberias, which would mean plenty more work for laborers like us. My second child, a daughter, had just been born a few weeks earlier, and though I was as passionate as ever about my Torah studies, I was more keenly aware of the need for paid daily labor to keep my family fed.

Jesus would have been sixteen or seventeen that summer. He came along with Father and me to Sepphoris. Our brother Simon, who was a few years younger than Jesus, came too—his first time joining us on such a trip.

We were four of dozens of men working on that project. Throughout the morning the air rang with the sound of axes, hammers, and picks. I worked beside Jesus, both of us stripped to the waist and gleaming with sweat. Say what I will about the boy—and I am trying to be honest here—Jesus was always a good worker. He never shirked; he worked as hard as I did, and his work was always good, even on a task such as this that required little craft or skill.

"Does it make you angry?" he asked me abruptly as we worked.

"What, an honest day's work? Why should that make me angry?"

"Is this an honest day's work? Building a huge villa for a Roman official? A palace that will be trimmed in gold and silver, while all around are Jews living in poverty, some even begging for their bread? In this same city, when we were children, the Romans drove out our people and sold them into slavery. Does it seem right to you that we are building their villas?"

"Right or not, it's how the world is," I said. "Our world. We live in the world as it is, not in some world of dreams."

"Don't you care, then? For the poor, for our own people?"

"Of course I care for them! But God ordains that we care for the poor by giving alms, sharing food with the hungry, sheltering widows and orphans. All that is part of our faith, as the Law says. We do not honor God or our own people by trying to overthrow our masters. No matter how little we may like either Herod or Rome, God does not call us to overthrow them by violence. Vengeance belongs to the Lord."

Jesus stared at me oddly. "I know that, James."

"Well, be sure you remember it."

I feared he might become a Zealot. He was so impulsive, so full of big ideas, and sadly lacking, I thought, in prudence or caution. He was not a violent or angry boy, had never been in a fistfight as far as I knew. Yet I could, for a moment, imagine him crouching in an alleyway in Sepphoris with a dagger in hand, ready to kill a Roman soldier for the cause of God's people.

We worked from dawn till midday, when the sun was at its height and all the men paused to eat and rest in the shade. It was during that rest time that I noticed Jesus was missing, not just from our small family group but from all the groups of laborers around us. Father said not to worry, that Jesus would no doubt be back in good time, but when we picked up hammers to begin work again, he was nowhere to be found.

We worked for another hour, and still no sign of Jesus. Finally I laid down my tools and went in search of him.

He was nowhere on the work site. I wandered through the streets till I came to the marketplace. Few boys or men of Jesus' age were there; most were working at this hour of the day, and it was women, children, and the elderly who visited the market stalls. But as I passed a fishmonger's stall, I heard a babble of young male voices, among them one that I recognized.

"Jesus!" I called, and he turned away from the others. It was like that scene in the Temple all over again, except that these were no learned rabbis he was keeping company with. He was with three boys his own age. They were all speaking Greek, not Aramaic—Jesus, like all of us, knew enough Greek to carry on a simple conversation—and I could see at once that his three companions were not Jews, but Gentiles.

"James! You didn't have to come searching for me; I was on my way back to the site." In his voice was the aggrieved note of a young man annoyed at being treated like a boy just at the moment when he is acting most like one. "I came to the market with these fellows to get something for the noon meal, and while we were here, one of their friends, Philip, took sick, and we brought him back to his house. You needn't worry—I was going to let the foreman know at the end of the day that I missed two hours' work. I wouldn't have taken pay for work I didn't do." He saw that I looked no happier, and added, "I'm sorry you'll lose time by coming to find me—though, I'll tell you again, you needn't have come. I was in no danger."

One of the Gentile dogs called something to him, I couldn't pick out the words in his accent, and Jesus called back cheerily, "You go on without me; I'll walk with my brother! Tell Philip I hope he's well tomorrow."

He fell into step beside me as the others ran off toward the work site. He looked as relaxed and easy as I'd often seen him with his own friends in Nazareth, laughing and talking. It was beyond belief.

"Are you such a fool that you truly don't know those fellows are

Gentiles?" I said finally, when I could trust myself to speak.

"Of course I know they are Gentiles, James. What do you take me for?"

"I hardly know," I said. "You spoke to them? Ate with them? Went inside one of their houses?"

"They are men, James. Like you and me. They're interesting enough to talk to."

"Interesting!" I spat the word. "Is 'interesting' enough of a reason to defile yourself with those who are unclean? Truly, Jesus, I have no idea what to think of you. This morning you're talking like a rebel, and I'm afraid I'll look around and see you sticking a knife in some Roman's ribs. Then I find you laughing and talking and eating with Gentiles as if you're King Herod himself, as if you've no idea what it means to be a Jew."

"What an interesting question, James! What *does* it mean to be a Jew?" It was just the sort of philosophical question he loved, and to tell the truth, I did too. Half the time I would let him drag me into a discussion about Scripture that would tear my attention away from what I was meant to focus on. But not today. Glancing at him, I saw the corner of his mouth quirked up in a smile and knew his question had been framed to disarm me, rather than to draw me into a debate.

I saw, too, that all my scolding and berating had made no impact on him at all, not even the reminder that he was now ritually unclean for having entered a Gentile house and eaten food with them. The proper respect due to an older brother, to the Law, to the code of purity—he lacked that respect entirely.

As we walked back to the work site, I pondered that other time I had searched for him through city streets. When he was a boy, I had found him in the Temple among rabbis, daring to speak to them as an equal. Now I found him in the market with Gentiles, treating them as if they were his equals. For him, neither encounter seemed stranger than the other. Whereas I and everyone I knew saw the world in carefully structured hierarchies, with respect due to one kind of person, contempt due to another, Jesus seemed to move through a world where those boundaries did not exist. He hated our Roman rulers for enslaving our people and making them poor, yet chatted with Greek boys and Roman soldiers as if they were children of God like we were.

I shuddered to think what would become of him.

Chapter Three

W hen tragedy struck our family, it came so swiftly and decisively that I hardly had time to absorb one disaster before the next fell. It was a fever sickness that went through the entire village, as happened some years. People would wake in the morning feeling perfectly healthy, be sick in bed by noon and, in some cases, dead by nightfall. Not everyone, of course. Not even most. Most recovered. But many did not. Every family, it seemed, lost someone. We were less fortunate than most in Nazareth that year. We lost three.

The children were the first to fall ill, and of course we worried most about them, for with such fevers, the very young and the very old were the most fragile. My own two children were both under five years old at the time, and I feared for their lives. They were ill, and so were Mary's younger children. The mothers nursed them through the fevers and were the next to fall ill, lying down beside their still-fevered, still-coughing children. In our whole house, only Jesus did not get sick, though Simon and I had only mild fevers, and we joined Jesus in trying to care for the very sick, keeping them cool and bringing water, cleaning up after them.

I felt weak myself, in those strange days, my head aching and my throat raw and dry as I crossed the courtyard carrying a water jar whose weight would have been nothing to me at one time—though carrying water was normally a woman's work, of course—but which now seemed to weigh as much as a huge bundle of bricks. All around, from the sleeping quarters of the house, came coughs and cries from the sick women and children, from our father Joseph and our youngest brother, also named Joseph. I thought with terrible clarity: *They are all sick; they cannot all survive. Who will be taken? Who will be left?*

I saw Jesus cross the courtyard in the other direction, carrying a pile of soiled rags to the firepit to be burned. He looked sober, but not weary as I did, and I wondered why he was the only one of us not to fall ill. It really did seem sometimes as if Heaven favored him, just as everyone in the family did.

"Who needs water first?" I asked him.

"Father, then the little ones, I think," he said. "I'll go down to the well and get more, so we will have it for later."

Despite how I resented his health and energy, I knew he was bearing the greater share of the work, and I felt compelled to say so. "You have done well, caring for everyone," I said, the words sounding grudging even to my own ears. "I hope you will not fall ill too."

Jesus shrugged a little then met my eyes with his own dark ones. "Sometimes I think this is what I was born for," he said.

"Oh, you fancy yourself a physician now, do you?" I couldn't keep the sharp edge from my tone, and then he was gone across the courtyard, and I was off to care for the sick.

Our sister Rebecca, who was sixteen, growing into young womanhood, was the first to die. Her death was a hard blow to everyone, especially to Jesus—she was the closest in age to him, and they loved each other deeply. But before I had time to grieve for Rebecca, my wife, Rachel, coughed out her last breaths in my arms.

I went from Rachel's bedside to find my children, not knowing how or what to tell them, fearing they were dead, too, though I knew they had been recovering. I found my son Benjamin in the arms of his uncle Jesus, looking comfortable curled on his lap. "His fever's broken," Jesus said. Then he looked more closely at my face, stood up, and gave the child to me. "Rachel?" he asked, mouthing her name silently, and I nodded.

The next day, when most of the sick were beginning to show signs of recovery, Jesus came to me as I sat with my two children. They were too young to comprehend what it meant to lose a mother; they both seemed to think Rachel would come back soon. I wished with all my heart they could be right.

"Father is calling for you," Jesus said.

I got up swiftly, and Jesus moved to take my little ones; all the children came to him naturally and happily. "He must be better then, if he is talking."

Jesus frowned and shook his head. "I thought so, too, but—his fever is still high. I could do nothing to bring it down. I prayed with him, and that seemed to calm him some, but he insisted he talk to you."

I went to my father. Even in the midst of my own grief, I was shocked by how wasted and ill he looked after only a few days of the fever. But he was the oldest in the house, nearly sixty years of age, and such things, as we knew, were harder for the old to bear.

"James. My firstborn," he said, his words coming out something between a croak and a whisper.

"I'm here, Father."

"If I die . . ."

I wanted to contradict him, to tell him not to speak of death. But death was all around us, in our house and in the village, and he was an old man with a gray beard. At least his death, if it came tonight, would not be untimely like Rachel's or Rebecca's. If it were time for him to be gathered to his fathers, then I would be shirking my duty as eldest son not to say farewell, to listen to his last words.

But it was such a struggle for him to say any words at all. The cough took him again, and then he turned this way and that on his sleeping mat as if trying to escape something. His eyes darted around the room wildly. Only his hand, gripping mine hard, seemed to anchor him to this earth. "My son," he said again, his eyes finally find-ing mine.

"Father. I'm here. You don't need to fear."

"You will . . . you . . ." He could get no more words out, and I began speaking in as calm and measured a tone as I could manage. "You need not worry, Father. I will care for Mary and the children when you die. I will be the head of the family; I will make sure no harm comes to them." Bitter words, when my own wife and my little sister had died in the last forty-eight hours, when any of the others might still slip away from us. But that was the will of God; I could not protect them from that. "I will do all that I can. They will not go hungry or be in want." That much I could promise.

He nodded, his eyes still holding mine, and I thought he was fol-lowing my words. If he was going to die, I wanted him to be at peace. "You have been a good father to me," I told him, searching for some words to convey that overwhelming love I felt, stretching back to the days when I was a little motherless boy trotting around the work yard. "You have done all that a father should do for his family. I will try to do as you have done." With my own little children, motherless, too, now as I and my siblings had been; with my half-brothers, with my stepmother Mary. I would be the patriarch of the family and care for them.

"Jesus," he croaked.

For a wild moment I thought he was confused, that he thought I was Jesus. Then, with great effort he said, "Look . . . to Jesus. His life . . . will be hard." He coughed again, then whispered, "Care for him."

His eyes closed, and he fell into a fevered sleep, and spoke no more. He died before dawn, the last of our family to succumb to the plague. And his dying words to me, his dying thoughts, were, as they had always been, about Jesus.

Still, I was the man of the family now—a shattered and dimin-ished man, in those days as the family slowly recovered from the sickness. It does not shame me, now, to admit that I was lost and broken and alone after my wife died and my father passed to his ancestors. I knew the tasks I had to do, to get through each day, but I went through them like a man only half-alive. The care of my children fell to the surviving women of the house, as they recovered. It pained me to think my children would not even remember their mother.

We recovered from our losses, after a fashion, as people do— carrying on, yet always carrying the memory of those we had lost. Mary, when she was fully recovered, took over the daily tasks of caring for my two children along with her own younger ones, and that seemed to help her heal, a little, from the loss of her daughter and husband. I was lonely without Rachel but would not give in to despair. My own father had been left a widower with young children at about the same age. Life was difficult, and hardships were to be borne. With Father dead, most of the burden of working to support our family fell to myself, Jesus, and Simon, as Jude was busy with his wife's family.

And so the years passed, our lives falling into a routine to which we were all accustomed. My sister Leah married and left our home. My youngest half-brother, Joseph, grew old enough to do a man's work, and with four of us men working now, Mary and the children were well provided for.

The biggest change in my own life, in those years after the plague summer, came when the old rabbi—who had been the leader of our synagogue—died, and I took up his tasks, as we had planned for so many years. Calling the faithful to prayer on Shabbat, reading the Scriptures, and tutoring the little boys took me away from work as a carpenter, but I realized as I watched Jesus, Simon, and Joseph that they did not really need me anymore. I was free to spend hours in study of the Torah, which I loved. Though I would never have the life I had dreamed of, studying in Jerusalem with the great rabbis, I could do God's work here in the village. I longed for Rachel to share that joy with me, but despite my loneliness I was glad for this change in my circumstances.

"You should marry again," Jesus told me one Shabbat afternoon when he sat in the courtyard with me after the service. "People like it when their *hazzan* is a married man."

His tone was light, almost teasing, but as always I distrusted what might lie under his words, and my distrust—be honest, my dislike— sharpened my tongue. "You are a fine one to talk about being married," I said, for Jesus was well into his twenties by then and should have been a husband and father. I had suggested several times to Mary that we try to arrange a match for Jesus, and there were families in the village with daughters of a suitable age who would have been happy to be joined to ours, despite the taint of scandal still attached to Jesus' birth. Yet he told me he had no desire to marry, and Mary, despite my urgings, had said to respect his wishes in this.

"And you're a fine one, too, to talk about what people like in the leader of the synagogue," I went on. "Do you know what people like? A *hazzan* whose brother doesn't cause scandal."

"Have I been causing scandal again? I'm sorry if it means trouble for you," Jesus said.

"But not sorry for anything you've actually done, are you?"

"What am I supposed to have done?" he asked.

"Most recently? A group of men called me aside to tell me their wives were concerned; you were seen consorting with an immoral woman."

"An immoral woman? Are there even any immoral women in Nazareth?" Jesus asked, his voice still disconcertingly light. He never took things as seriously as I thought he should.

"Not here. In Cana."

"You mean Anna, the daughter of Hammai? That poor girl. She and her baby are starving, James."

"Yes, because her family have cast her out for the immoral life she lived in Tiberias. She married a Gentile dog, and when even he wouldn't have her anymore, she sold herself to any man who would have her. Then she crawled back home to have her child—do you really expect her father to feed her and give her a place in his house?"

"What kind of father is he, if he does not?" Jesus countered. "Is the law about purity, or about compassion? Scripture says we are to care for the poor, the orphaned, the outcast."

"Don't lecture me about compassion! You know that no one believes in caring for those in need more than I do—but not those who bring misfortune on themselves by their own sin! And if you go out to that hovel where she lives to visit her, you know what people will say—there's only one reason a man would go to see Anna!"

"Is there?" Our pleasant conversation had turned ugly so quickly. Just a moment ago we had been sitting side by side and now we were both on our feet, face to face, Jesus' burning eyes just a few inches from mine. "Is that what you think of me, brother? Do you believe the village gossip?"

I was so angry I could have struck him, but honesty forced me to say, "No." I had known Jesus all his life; and he was exasperating, frustrating, independent, and unwilling to listen to the wise advice of his elders. But he had never been immoral or wicked. "No, I do not believe it. I believe you went there because you saved up what coins you could from your own earnings and bought food for her and the child, and brought it to her. That's right, isn't it?"

He said nothing, but his level gaze met mine and he nodded slowly.

"But what you never seem to care about is how things look to others!" I went on, wishing I could make him see sense. "By even associating with such a woman, whether it's out of compassion or not, you defile yourself in the eyes of the village, and in—"

"In the eyes of God? Is that what you were about to say?"

I stopped short, paused for breath. "The Law says not to associate with such a woman."

"But the Law also says to feed the hungry and have compassion on the poor. Which is the higher law, James? How do you decide?"

"I decide as men have always decided, by listening to the guidance and counsel of those who are wiser and more experienced, who have studied and debated the Scriptures! I listen to my teachers, my elders, the voice of the community! And what do you listen to? The voice of God, speaking in your own head?"

Jesus turned away abruptly. "Perhaps. The Spirit of God."

"Can you not see your arrogance, your folly, to believe that God's Spirit speaks to you alone even when you go against all those around you?"

"Boys!"

Only one person would call us boys. We were men, but Mary, Jesus' mother and my stepmother, still saw us as squabbling boys who would someday make peace and get along. That, at least, was her hope. The strife between us had always disappointed her, and that disappointment was clearly written on her face as she crossed the courtyard to come speak to us now.

"Can we not enjoy a Shabbat afternoon in peace without another quarrel between the two of you?"

"Forgive us, Mother," Jesus said at once, but I frowned.

"I am sorry for disturbing the peace of the Shabbat," I said after a moment. Truth to be told, I thought Mary was as much to be blamed as Jesus himself was for his headstrong ways, for now that he was a man grown, she indulged his foolishness just as she had when he was a boy. She was the only person he ever seemed to listen to; I had urged her time and again to rein him in, counsel him to behave in a more seemly manner, not to arouse gossip and disapproval in the village.

"Jesus is who he is, James, who God has called him to be. He has to follow his calling," was all she would ever say.

Now, seeing the warm smile that passed between the two of them, I knew she would never rebuke him, never keep him in line. And it was too late, anyway—the time for a parent's guidance had passed. Jesus' path, whatever it was to be, was set now, and I knew that as a man he would no more listen to his older brother than he would to any other authority.

"Pardon me," I said, and turned back toward the house. "I am going into the house to study Scripture. I will see you for prayers at sunset."

Chapter Four

One of the best days of my life—that part of my life, anyway—was the day Jesus told me he was leaving Nazareth. My emotions were hardly simple or uncomplicated, but relief was foremost. He had given me so much trouble these past years that I couldn't help but be glad he was going to take his questions, his challenges, his everlasting new ideas, somewhere else.

I had no idea, of course, that he'd cause so much trouble away from home that eventually I'd be begging him to come back to Nazareth.

He should have asked my permission rather than simply informing me he was going. As elder brother and head of the family, it was my place to make, or at least approve, such decisions. But when did Jesus ever do things properly or appropriately? I had arranged the marriages of his brothers, Simon and Joseph, and was negotiating a good match for his sister, Naomi. He had done nothing to interfere with those decisions, had allowed me my authority. But when he came to me and announced that he was leaving Nazareth, leaving Galilee altogether to go to Jerusalem, I saw that the only reason he had respected my authority in those matters was that he had not greatly cared to whom his younger brothers and sister were married. When it came to anything that mattered to Jesus, my opinion counted for nothing.

"Just going, are you? Nothing more to say to anyone?"

He shifted his weight from one foot to the other but didn't drop his gaze under my challenge. "I've spoken to Mother," he said.

"You should have spoken to me first."

He shrugged a little—not enough to be rude, just enough to imply, *I've done what I've done; what are you going to do about it?*

I suppose I could have tried to forbid him from going, but what would that have accomplished? He surely wouldn't have obeyed me, and even if he had, that would hardly have been in my interest. I wanted him out of Nazareth. Yet I couldn't let him go without at least going through the motions of playing an older brother's proper role.

"What will you do in Jerusalem?"

"Find work, I suppose, enough to live on, anyway. But I want to learn more about the Scriptures, talk to people, see more of the world. I think there's—God has work out there for me."

"Do you expect a rabbi to take you on as his disciple?"

He laughed. "How would I do that, without a recommendation from my own learned brother rabbi?"

"I might give you such a recommendation." *If only to stop you causing too much trouble,* I added silently.

"I don't want it. I'm sorry, I don't mean that to be rude, but I don't want to study under a rabbi. Talk to them, perhaps, but—I don't feel God is calling me to be anyone's disciple."

"Perhaps he's calling you to gather disciples of your own," I said. A joke, of course. I intended it as a joke. I certainly never meant to put ideas in his head.

"I will go where He leads me," Jesus said.

"Fine words, but you need some kind of plan."

"Mother has kinfolk in Judea. She had a cousin who used to live in the hill country there. The cousin and her husband are dead now, but they have a son, John, that I've never met. Perhaps I'll stay with him for a time."

Now it was my turn to shrug. His plan was as flimsy as a butter-fly's wing, but if he chose to leave home, family, and village, and strike out among strangers, what was it to me if he ended up begging his bread in the streets of Jerusalem or Jericho? Likely he would do fine. He could work, after all, and had a trade. If he were out of Galilee, he would be less trouble to me.

"I don't like to leave Mother," he added. "But she is well cared for, with you and Simon and Joseph all working. I needn't fear she'll go hungry."

"Of course not. She may not be my mother by blood, but you know that I will always care for her, even if her sons were unable to," I said. "You can trust me with that much, at least."

Jesus smiled, the kind of smile he bestowed so readily on others but rarely on me. "Oh, never doubt I can trust you, James. You're the most trustworthy man I know."

The day he left, his few belongings packed in a small cloth bag over his shoulder, I sat by Mary on a bench in front of our house after she said Goodbye to him. He went off on foot, alone, on the road south, not waiting to travel with a caravan. Some family and neighbors had gathered to say Goodbye and were now in the court-yard, eating and talking together. Mary sat alone, watching.

I sat down beside her. "He was sorry to leave you," I said.

"I know. He told me. But he felt God calling him to go, and I would never have had him ignore that call. He has been waiting for it his whole life."

She had always had such dreams for her eldest son. But what had they come to? He was nearly thirty years of age already. He had not married nor had a child; he had worked as a laboring carpenter in Nazareth and the nearby cities his entire life. Now he was off to seek some fortune I didn't pretend to understand. He was obsessed with God and the idea that God had some special plan for his life, but he was completely unprepared to study under a rabbi, so what future could God have for him?

I said none of this aloud, not wanting to be harsh with Mary. She had worked hard, all these years, raising my mother's children as well as her own. She deserved her dreams, her illusions.

"God will look after him," I said as gently as I could, laying a hand on her arm. "And we will look after you."

She brushed her eyes with the edge of her veil and struggled to smile. "Thank you, James," she said.

Even with Jesus gone, our house was a busy one in those days. The girls, save for Naomi, were all married and gone to their own homes, and Jude still lived with his wife's family, but Simon and Joseph and their young wives lived with us, and Simon had two small children already. My own children, Benjamin and Tabitha, were growing quickly; Mary cared for them, filling the role of the mother they would never know. Simon and Joseph continued taking carpentry jobs whenever and wherever they could, sometimes working in the village and sometimes going to Sepphoris or to Herod's new city of Tiberias for work.

I worked alongside them some of the time, but I was kept busy with the work of the synagogue—studying the Torah, leading worship, teaching the village boys. I enjoyed the work and the respect it earned me from my fellow villagers. It was not the scholar's life I had dreamed of when I was a student in Jerusalem, but it was a good life. The men of the village sometimes called me James the Just, for they respected my judgments, my fairness when they asked me to arbitrate their quarrels, and my knowledge of the Scriptures and the way I applied them. I was pleased with that small honor. My life was full and busy, and I will confess that in the months after Jesus left us, I did not give much thought to what had become of my wayward younger brother, though Mary waited avidly for any news of him that a traveler from the south might bring.

News from the south finally came, though not of Jesus. I heard it at the synagogue one Shabbat, as the men stood around after the service discussing the Scriptures.

We were talking, as we often did, of the hated Romans and the even-more-hated Herod—for the Romans at least were known to be outsiders, while Herod ruled over us as if he were our own king, which made him even more reviled.

"It is our own fault these foreign overlords come upon us," one of the village elders said. "It is as the prophets said in the time of the Exile, if we would turn our hearts back to the Lord, He would have mercy."

"But we do not worship idols as in the days before the Exile!" said another. "We worship only the Lord our God! Why should He punish us?"

"Outward worship is not the same as a truly committed heart," I said. "Bowing before the statue of a Greek god, or an image of the emperor, is not the only kind of idolatry. We can worship God in outward form, but be far from Him in our hearts."

"Spoken like a true Pharisee, Rabbi," said a man I had only met that morning. His name was Aaron, and he was a merchant, kinsman to Uri the potter. This Aaron had recently traveled into Galilee from Jericho. He was staying in Nazareth with his people for a while, conducting his business with the Gentiles in Sepphoris.

I did not respond one way or another to being called a Pharisee. On some men's lips, it was a term of praise; on others, an insult. I had no way of knowing how this man felt about Pharisees, although coming from Judea, he would have been more aware of parties and factions among rabbis. My old teacher in Jerusalem had been a Pharisee of the school of Shammai. As I followed his teachings, and was certainly neither a Sadducee nor an Essene, I would have worn the label "Pharisee" with pride in my Jerusalem days. But after so many years in a remote northern village, leading simple people in their prayers, I felt far removed from the Jerusalem rabbis and their intricate debates over the Torah. I was a Jew, leader of the synagogue in Nazareth: What more label did I need than that?

"What do you say, then, that we should do to turn our hearts back toward the Lord?" the Jericho merchant asked me, seeing that I made no response to tell him whether I was a Pharisee or not.

"Be holy, even as He is holy," I said. "Keep ourselves pure, separate from the world and its temptations. Obey the Law and show justice and righteousness to all, especially the poor, orphans, and widows. In doing so, we honor Him who is just, righteous, and holy in all that He does."

The men all nodded and stroked their beards thoughtfully, including the Judean. But I heard another voice, like an echo in my mind: that brash, young, challenging voice that had haunted me for so many years. *"And what do we do, dear brother, when the demands of purity and of justice clash with one another? Are we called to show love even to the unclean—at the risk of becoming unclean ourselves? Do we bring bread to the home of the harlot and her children?"*

I almost said aloud, "Be silent, Jesus!" as I'd said so often when he was a know-it-all boy, speaking out of turn among his elders. But, of course, he was not there. I had listened to him for so many years, without even wanting to, that his voice had become lodged in my head.

"We stand by the principles the prophets taught our elders," I said, raising my voice slightly, though no one else was speaking at the moment. Probably I was trying to drown out Jesus' imagined voice in my mind. "Let justice roll on like a river, and righteousness like a never-ending stream, as the prophet Amos told us," I quoted.

"Rabbi, in the time of exile, the Lord sent us prophets, and for the many hard years after that. Yet now, when our need is greatest, why does He send no prophets?" one of the village men asked.

"The time of prophets is done," said another.

"You may think so, here in Galilee," said Aaron the traveler. "You might not think so if you were in Judea and heard John the Baptizer."

"Who is John the Baptizer?" I asked. I had not heard this name before.

"Some think he is a new prophet," Aaron said. "He preaches by the Jordan River, tells people that God is about to judge Israel and that we must turn aside from wickedness and devote ourselves to doing right. If people say they repent of their sins and desire to live right, he immerses them in the waters of Jordan—like a *mikveh*. He calls it a baptism, a new beginning."

"Perhaps he is not a prophet, but our promised Deliverer," one man suggested.

"He says he is no Messiah, but that he is to prepare Israel for a prince who is coming, one far greater than he," said Aaron.

This was becoming interesting indeed, but a few of the men, talking among themselves, began to laugh. "Rabbi, we must go," one said. "My boy is here with a word from my wife, that if I do not come soon for the midday meal, it will be fed to dogs!"

We all laughed then, for every man there—except for myself and, I suppose, the traveler—had a wife waiting at home, and some things are more important even than prophets or Messiahs. "Go to your homes and your dinners," I said. Then to Aaron and Uri I added, "I would hear more of this John the Baptizer and what he teaches. Will you come to my home to dine, and afterward we will talk more of this matter?"

They were not free to join us for the meal, but said they would come later in the day, and so they did. It was still the hot season, and the Shabbat hours provided a welcome rest for men who otherwise labored in the heat of the afternoon. Shabbat was a time to sit in the shade and talk about the mysterious purposes of God. And there was much mystery in the tales he told of this John the Baptizer.

"He sounds like one of the Essenes," I said after Aaron described how John lived in the desert as a hermit, clad in rough clothes, emerging from his solitude only to preach to the people who sought him out, the crowds who came to hear him on the banks of the Jordan.

"He sounds to me more like a new Elijah," said my younger brother Simon.

"Well, he is no Essene, though some of what he preaches sounds like their talk. He lives apart from the world, but he does not call others to forsake the world, only to forsake their wicked ways. And as for Elijah—well, you would not be the first to have called him that. He does not claim it for himself, but he does not deny it either."

" 'See, I will send you the prophet Elijah before that great and dreadful day of the LORD comes,' " I quoted Malachi. "But who is this Baptizer? Where does he come from; who are his people? What rabbis has he studied under?"

The traveler shook his head. "He's studied under no rabbis, has no time for the synagogues or their learning. He does come from a priestly line. His father was a priest named Zechariah, from some little village in the hill country. But he's turned his back on all that, Sadducees and the Temple and everything, as if he gets his messages directly from God."

Something tugged at the edge of my memory then, but I didn't chase it down until later, when the guests had left and our women-folk joined us for the Shabbat prayers. Afterward, Mary asked me what news the traveler from the south had brought.

"Nothing about Jesus," I told her. I had described my brother and asked the traveler if he knew anything of a Jesus bar Joseph from Nazareth, and of course he did not. "We spent most of the time talking about a new prophet who has arisen in the Jordan region. He calls himself John the Baptizer."

As I told Mary what I had learned about this man John, her eyes widened with interest. When I mentioned that he was the son of a priest named Zechariah, she gasped. "James, that is—it must be—my cousin Elizabeth's son! Elizabeth's husband was a priest named Zechariah, and their son was named John. Zechariah was told by an angel before John's birth that he would have a special work to do, to be a messenger from the Lord."

I nodded, trying to look patient. It was much the same as Mary's stories about Jesus' birth—angels, heavenly messages, a special mission. *This sort of thing must run in her family,* I thought, *if her cousin has the same foolish ideas.*

"There must be hundreds of men named John in Judea," I pointed out.

"John bar Zechariah? Did the traveler say how old this prophet was? An old man, or—"

"I don't know—no, he said a young man," I remembered, knowing this would only confirm her fantasies.

"Just about Jesus' age," she said, nodding. "Elizabeth and I were pregnant at the same time, but John was born first. Oh James, I'm sure it must be the same John! And perhaps Jesus is with him."

"It could be so," I said. The prophet was as likely to be her kinsman John as any other John in Judea. And whether he was a kinsman or not, I had no difficulty imagining that Jesus would be drawn to some madman who imagined himself the new Elijah.

"I'm sure he and Jesus will have a great deal in common," I said. I had hoped Jesus would stay out of trouble and out of my way down in Judea, but I now realized, as I said Good night to Mary and crossed the courtyard to bid Good night to my own children, that I did not even mind very much if he stayed out of trouble. Let him and his cousin John get into as much trouble as they liked down there on the banks of the Jordan—as long as none of it reflected back on us here in Nazareth. It was a long journey from the Sea of Galilee down the Jordan, and I hoped no bad news would travel upriver to disturb the peace of our village.

Chapter Five

My son, Benjamin, was fourteen years old, stepping forward into manhood. He was a bright boy, clever and curious without being bold or brash. He was dutiful, with a keen, quiet intelligence. His sister Tabitha, a year younger, was more under the care of Mary and my brothers' wives than my own care. But I went out of my way to spend more time with Benjamin, beyond simply teaching him to read the Scriptures, as he grew up. He was the only person in the household I felt truly close to.

"He reminds me of you, when you were a boy," Mary said to me one day.

"He does?"

"Very much. You were quiet and thoughtful, as he is, never quick to speak, but I always knew those still waters ran deep." She smiled fondly, though to tell the truth I cannot remember her doting on me as a child. Her motherly impulses were spent on my younger siblings and, of course, on her own children when they came along. But thinking of what she'd said about Benjamin and me, I guessed that I might not have been the kind of child to encourage caresses and fond words. He was a self-contained boy, reserved, I suppose, and seeing him now as a reflection of my younger self, I wondered if I had pushed my young stepmother away, if the formal relation between us was as much my doing as hers.

"What else do you remember?" Mary looked amused, but pleased, as if she had been waiting years for me to ask these very questions. I would not indulge in memories for their own sake, but if the past could provide me with a key to know how best to raise my own son, I would be glad to have such a key.

"You were very close to your father, just as Benjamin is to you," she said. "For the same reason, I suppose—so many years alone without a mother, and you were the only one of the four children old enough to really remember her vividly. You carried that loss inside you in a way the others did not, and it was something you shared with your father—not in words, I mean, for neither of you spoke often of her, but in your hearts. You spent a great deal of time with Joseph when you were little. Your father's sister cared for the younger ones, but you always wanted to be in the work yard with your father, toting around wood and learning to swing a hammer."

Her words warmed me, just as coming into the courtyard on a cold winter night I might be warmed by the fire blazing merrily there. "I did not have the learning Benjamin has, at such a young age," I said.

"No, you knew only your alphabet and a few simple words when I first married your father, but you learned very quickly after we went to Alexandria. Growing up in such a place, among such people, the years we spent there—I think that shaped the man you became, taught you to think as something more than a village carpenter." She paused. "Every time I go to the synagogue and see you at the front, reading from the scroll, I think how proud your father would have been of you, James. He loved you so very much."

Her words were like water to my thirsty heart. How little anyone had ever spoken of love to me! And how often had I ever told Benjamin I loved him? It was important to me that he grow up to be hardworking, obedient, God-fearing, and educated. That he should also feel loved by his father had not occurred to me. Like my own father, I suppose, I had assumed he would simply know it without the words being spoken aloud.

"I know it was difficult for you, when I married your father," Mary said softly. "Then when Jesus and the others came along, and we had a second family to care for, I often worried that you felt— pushed aside. I think Benjamin might struggle much the same way, if you were to marry again—though he was much younger when he lost his mother than you were, and he does not have the same memories of her. Still, while he allows me and his aunts to care for him, he does not accept anyone in his mother's place. I think that is what makes his bond with you so close and so special."

I shook my head briskly, as if to clear away cobwebs of sentiment. "That's no matter. I've no thought of taking another wife." This was unusual for a widower, especially one who was a synagogue leader. Many of the men in Nazareth had made it clear to me over the years that their daughters or sisters would be honored to accept my proposal. But I had never been seriously tempted, and besides, my children were half-grown now—Benjamin almost full-grown. He hardly needed a stepmother now, and for Tabitha I should soon be seeking a husband rather than a stepmother. Soon enough it would be time to start thinking of my children's marriages rather than my own—an altogether easier and more pleasant task. But before that time came . . .

"Benjamin is well past twelve years of age," I said to Mary. "I had thought of taking him to Passover this year." It was a custom in our family as in many others to take a child for his first Passover visit to Jerusalem when he reached the age of manhood. I had gone when I was thirteen, when we were still in exile in a foreign land. My father and I had joined the mass of Alexandrian Jews going to Jerusalem for the festival, leaving Mary and the younger children in the care of our friends back in Egypt. Those were turbulent times, those days during the rule of Archelaus, when riots and uprisings in Jerusalem during Passover were common. My father went that year partly to learn firsthand how things stood in his homeland, with a thought to bringing his family back home. But he also wanted to take me to see the Temple, to observe that rite of maturity; and he was willing to risk the journey and even the possibility of violence to take me there. After returning home to Nazareth, we had made the pilgrimage often; we could not afford it every year, and it had been several years now since I had gone, but this year I wanted to take Benjamin.

"We should all go!" Mary said. "Well, not the little ones, perhaps. Ilana could stay home with her children, and keep Tabitha with her, but wouldn't it be grand if the rest of us could go? It's been so long since we all went to Jerusalem for Passover."

She sighed happily, and I knew what she was thinking. If she went to Jerusalem, she might find out some news of Jesus, might even be able to see him there—though how she expected to find him, in all that vast city swollen with festival crowds, I had no idea. She had lost him there when he was just a boy; now, as a man grown, he could hardly be easier to find.

But she was growing older, and it had been many years since she had been to a festival. With all Herod's new building projects in Tiberias, it had been a good year for work, which meant that we could afford the journey. So after discussing it with my brothers, I said we would all go to Jerusalem. It turned into quite an exodus—once Jude and his sons, and Leah and her husband, and half a dozen more relatives and neighbors, all decided to join us. Simon's wife Ilana chose, as Mary had thought she might, to stay home with my daughter Tabitha and her own young children. The rest of us set off in a large, slow-moving caravan for the south, and arrived in Jerusalem just as the Feast of Passover began.

Chapter Six

Ihad not, up till that time, spent much of my life in cities. I lived for a few years of boyhood in Alexandria, and as a younger man I had gone to labor in Sepphoris and later Tiberias, but I had never lived there. I knew what cities were like—the crowds, the noise, the smells—but I was a man more at home in my small village, surrounded by simple daily tasks and a circle of familiar faces.

Ah, but there is no city like Jerusalem. I had lived there for a while as a young man, and I suppose the fact that I was doing what I loved while there—studying the Torah, sitting at the feet of learned rabbis—colored my memories of the city. But where all cities are filled with the presence of men—voices, faces, shrill hawkers' calls in the market, soldiers tramping the streets to keep order, thieves weaving in and out of the crowd trying to upset that order—Jerusalem is the only city where the presence of men is overwhelmed by the presence of God. How could it be otherwise, with the Temple at its heart, that great building dedicated to the worship of God, to sacrifice and praise? How could it be otherwise, when so many devout and learned men gather in this place to read and discuss the Scriptures? God's Spirit is everywhere, I know, but it is in Jerusalem as in no other place on earth.

I tried to convey some of this in words to my son Benjamin as we streamed through the Damascus gate with all the other festivalgoers. But he was only half-listening, his attention pulled by all the strange sights and sounds that attract a country boy on his first visit to a big city. I had never taken him to Sepphoris or Tiberias: he was not yet old enough to work on construction jobs in the cities, and there was no other reason to bring him to those pagan breeding grounds. None in our family except the working men ever went to the Gentile cities. But Jerusalem—that was different. Jerusalem was our city.

We had no kin in the city to stay with, so after walking through the streets and markets and taking Benjamin for his first glimpse of the Temple, we pitched our tents outside the city walls, in one of those little temporary cities that sprang up outside Jerusalem at each of the major festivals. There, among our fellow pilgrims—our own family and neighbors from Nazareth, and others from Galilee who camped near us—we kept our Passover. We bought our lamb at the Temple and slaughtered it with all the others in the great ceremony, then brought it back to our campsite to prepare it for the seder meal.

We stayed in the city after Passover itself, throughout the Feast of Unleavened Bread. On the first day of the week, after Shabbat, the women went to the markets to look for fine cloth and trinkets we would never get in the north—not that we could afford much, but there was a little money set aside for these rare luxuries. My half-sister Naomi, youngest of Mary's children, was going to be married soon, to a young man in the neighboring village of Cana. Mary, Leah, and Joseph's wife, Abigail, took her along to the market looking for some fine fabric to make her marriage robes and some jewelry to complete the outfit.

While the women shopped, I took Benjamin with me to the house of my old teacher, Rabbi Eli. Had it been nearly twenty years since I had lived here as his disciple, studying the scrolls, dreaming of a life of dedication to the Torah? Ah, well. That had not happened, but I had put my learning to good use, nonetheless, and I was anxious to see if the man who had once taught me still lived so I could thank him again. I had seen him once or twice since, on other festival visits to Jerusalem, but even those visits were long in the past now.

I was reminded of the relentless passing of the years when I found his house occupied by strangers. A neighbor told me that my old master had died five years earlier, and that his widow and son had moved to the town of Bethany, where the rest of their family lived.

I remembered the son, Simon, about my own age. He, too, had been studying the Torah with his father, and I had not seen him on any of my visits in the years since, though we had once been good friends. That night when our family talked around the campfire about when to depart for Galilee, I suggested I might take an extra day to go to Bethany and look up my old friend and pay my respects to his mother if she still lived.

"We could make good use of another day in the markets here," Abigail said.

"I would be glad to stay another day," Mary put in quickly. Ever since our arrival, Mary had been asking everyone she could find if they had heard of Jesus from Nazareth. She had heard no sign of him— though many people were talking about this John the Baptizer, whom she still thought might be her cousin's son. I knew she wanted another day or more in the south to continue her quest, and while I would have been impatient at the delay ordinarily, because I had my own calls to pay, I decided we would stay in the area of Jerusalem a little longer.

Bethany, where Benjamin and I went the following day, was a quiet and pleasant village, not unlike our own town of Nazareth. There was an air of refinement, though, even among the working people in the villages, that was lacking in Galilee. I suppose the proximity to Jerusalem had something to do with it: people in a place like Bethany had many opportunities to go and worship at the Temple, to hear learned men talk about the Scriptures. There were more educated men in such a village, a better quality of debate in the synagogues, a sense of being close to the pulse of things, rather than being out on the fringe of the world and surrounded by Gentile dogs, as we were in Galilee.

I found Simon the Pharisee, as everyone in Bethany called him, living in one of the better houses in town. He was sorry to inform me that his mother had passed away the year before, but we were able to sit in the shade of his large and comfortable courtyard and share memories of his father and the time I spent living with them in Jerusalem. Benjamin sat beside me, listening silently as befitted a boy of his age, learning from our conversation.

As the afternoon shadows grew long and we shared the evening meal with Simon and his family, a few other men gathered in the courtyard. Simon introduced them as his kinsmen. There were three or four of them, I suppose, though the only name I remember is that of Lazarus, because he was the one I came to know well, and our lives were to be entwined in ways I could not have guessed then.

Lazarus was a younger man than Simon or I, about Jesus' age. He was no scholar like his cousin, but a laboring man, one who specialized in plastering the walls of fine dwellings. As the evening drew on, we found ourselves in a lively discussion of Jerusalem politics, how our nation stood with its Roman overlords, and whether a new King of Israel—a true King, who could restore our nation—might someday arise out of all the rebels and rabble-rousers constantly springing up.

This last topic—new kings and messiahs—was as much discussed back in Galilee as it was here, but I was impressed that the men of Bethany seemed to have a better grasp of how the world worked, as well as a good knowledge of the Scriptures, underlying their talk. They could compare the prophecies of Daniel and Isaiah; discuss what views the Pharisees, Sadducees, or Essenes might have on a particular question; and consider how the Roman governor might view the whole problem. I felt like I had been in exile all these years in the north, isolated from the kind of men who should have been my peers. It was the life I was meant to live. God help me, I tried not to be bitter, to resent the path my life had taken. If my family were wealthier, if my father and my wife had not both died when they did, if the Lord had arranged events a little differently—well, I would have lived a different life. No need for regrets; everything was according to God's will. Still, it was good to enjoy a day like this, in such company once more. Who knew when the chance would come again?

I was preparing to leave, telling Benjamin the way back to our campsite, when someone said the name that caught my attention.

". . . all very well to talk of turning the nation back to God, but John's habit of speaking bluntly to those in power, especially Herod, is going to get him in trouble soon," Lazarus said.

"John? Do you mean John the Baptizer?"

"Yes. You've heard of him, even up in Galilee, I suppose?"

We had heard of him. News of the hermit-prophet's ministry drifted north from time to time, since the first time I had heard his name. Now I said, "My stepmother thinks this John might be a kinsman of hers and that my younger brother may be with him. Do you know anything about John's followers?"

"A little," said Lazarus. "I've gone out to hear him speak once or twice, as most everyone around here has done. Quite impressive, both the things he says and the crowds he gathers around him."

"Have you ever heard of a man named Jesus bar Joseph, from Galilee, among John's disciples?"

Lazarus raised his eyebrows. "Jesus? Oh, I know of him. I've never heard him use the name 'son of Joseph,' but he is definitely from Galilee, and he is close to John. John baptized him several months ago. I wasn't there, but I heard it was quite an event, for many people claimed to have seen signs and wonders on the day of his baptism. The Baptizer himself said to several people that this Jesus was his appointed successor, the one who was coming after him. Now Jesus still follows John, but he has gathered his own little group of followers, I think, from among John's disciples."

My heart sank. This was worse than I'd imagined, but I couldn't doubt for a moment that it was our Jesus he was talking about. Signs and wonders? John naming him a successor? Jesus gathering disciples? It didn't seem as if his delusions of greatness had gone away with his move to Judea.

I almost considered, for a moment, not carrying this news to Mary. Did she really need to know? But she worried so much about whether he was alive and well—and besides, Benjamin was sitting right beside me, taking in every word. I could hardly go back to Mary and lie that I had heard nothing about Jesus. Wherever any of us went, whoever we talked to, she always wanted to know if anyone had had word of her beloved son. Now, finally, I had news to share.

"His mother is back at our camp and is most anxious to see him again," I told Lazarus.

"Of course, of course. I thought Jesus was in the city for the festival, but he may well be back with John now. John never comes to Jerusalem. If you wish, I could take you and the rest of your family to find John tomorrow, and you could hear him preach. If Jesus is there, you'll have the chance to see him. If not, well, you'll at least have had the chance to hear John, and that's an opportunity that should not be missed."

Chapter Seven

The crowd on the banks of the Jordan was so large that the arrival of our family group created no stir. I wondered if John the Baptizer always drew such large crowds, or whether the group had been swelled by those attending the festival. Looking at the faces and voices around me, I guessed that many of the listeners were festival-goers who had decided to add a visit to the riverbank prophet to their Passover itinerary. It was as if, having sought God's blessing through the official channels of worship and sacrifice, they now looked for an added blessing, a little more contact with God from a wilder source.

Wild was certainly the word to describe John. I could see him in the distance from my perch on a small rise of land. He stood hip deep in the Jordan's muddy waters, and he was indeed, as I'd heard, clad in a tunic that looked as if it were made from animal skin. His hair and beard were wild, unkempt, and untrimmed. I couldn't see his eyes at this distance—people had told me they burned with a strange, passionate fire, and it wasn't hard to imagine. He spoke to the crowd with one arm upraised, his powerful voice carrying to everyone, even though there must have been two hundred people or more on that riverbank.

"Repent!" He flung out the word like a battle cry. "You with your comfortable lives, your holy rituals! You come to Jerusalem for Passover thinking that the Temple will save you, that a priest will save you, that a sacrifice will save you! But the sacrifice God demands is the sacrifice of your hearts! Flee from the wrath and judgment that is coming! If you do not repent of your sins and turn from wickedness, you are a nest of snakes, a brood of scorpions. And when the Lord brings judgment upon this land, you will be destroyed!"

"It's not hard to see why people compare him to Elijah, is it?" my brother Simon said. "He looks like one of the prophets of old, and his message is the same."

"Surely that's no accident," I said. "He deliberately makes himself the image of Elijah so that people will grant him a prophet's authority."

"Why are you such a skeptic?" Simon asked. "He tells people to turn from their sins and follow God. What fault can you find in that?"

I motioned him to be silent because I wanted to listen—but he was right, I was not listening to John with an open heart, ready to be convicted. I was ready to criticize. I have never trusted wandering rabbis and would-be prophets, men who claim their inspiration comes directly from God Himself. Such men, it seems to me, are rarely well versed in the Scriptures: they claim to have messages from God but do not spend years studying the books in which God has revealed Himself. And they place far too little emphasis on the Temple, the sacrifices, the priesthood—all the ways that God has ordained for men to come to Him.

Even as I thought this, I saw people streaming down the riverbank to meet John in the water. One by one, he took them and plunged them into the stream.

"What is he doing?" Benjamin asked me.

"He calls it baptism—that is where he gets his name, John the Baptizer. I think it is meant to wash a man clean of his sins, just like the *mikveh* does when a man is about to enter the Temple. The Essenes have a daily *mikveh*, but John's idea seems to be that this ritual cleansing needs to happen only once, to signify repentance and a new life, and that it can be done anywhere, even in the river Jordan. This is not part of our tradition. This is a new thing, a fashion among fanatics."

Seated beside me, Simon laughed. "You should hear the tone of your voice when you say the words 'a new thing,' James. You sound like another man would sound when he says 'a half-rotted fish.' "

Even my son Benjamin snickered at that. I ignored my family's mockery and turned my attention back to John the Baptizer. For a moment, Simon reminded me of Jesus, and I remembered that he, too, was a son of Mary. Perhaps there is something in that whole branch of our family that makes them admire the new, the exceptional. What I value are our traditions, the customs that our people have handed down since the time of Moses. The Law that has made us what we are.

When John had finished preaching and baptizing for the day, the crowd dispersed. Some headed back on the road toward Jerusalem; others went to campsites like ours to prepare a meal. A smaller group of men gathered around John, and I guessed these were the disciples who lived with him and studied his message.

"Can you go talk to him, James?" Mary urged. "I need to know if he really is Elizabeth's son—and if Jesus is here with him."

I sighed, but as the others returned to our camp to prepare a meal and a place to sleep, I walked down the riverbank and joined the knot of men around John.

When I finally got to speak to him, he was everything I might have expected from his public delivery—rough, uncouth, not given to social pleasantries. "Yes, my father was the priest Zechariah and my mother was named Elizabeth," he said. "What does it matter to you?"

"My stepmother, who travels with me, was a relative of Elizabeth's," I explained. "She wished to meet you."

"I have no time to chat with women about family matters," he said. "My parents are both dead, and I have business from the Lord. The time is short. Give your stepmother my blessing, and tell her to prepare for the Day of the Lord."

I nodded. I wished the man could be more gracious, but I agreed with him: there was no need to prolong this encounter on the basis of a kinship between Mary and his long-dead mother. "There is another matter, however," I said. "My stepmother, Mary, is concerned for her son Jesus. He left our home in Nazareth some time ago, and we have heard nothing of him. We thought he might be among your followers."

At the name of Jesus, John's whole demeanor changed. "You are one of the brothers of Jesus?" he demanded. "Why did you not say so? Of course he is with us!" He looked—I cannot say, exactly. Excited? Could that be it?

If it was hard to pinpoint the change in John's mood, there was no difficulty interpreting the expression on the face of one of his followers. It was clearly resentment, as he said, "With us? I would not say so. Jesus of Nazareth was a disciple of our master, but he has since gone his own way, teaching his own message, gathering his own little band of followers."

"Silence, Micah!" John snapped. "Anyone would think there were two different gods, the way you and Jesus' disciples go on! We preach the same message—prepare for the Day of the Lord. The One Lord. God can use more than one messenger. I am a mere messenger, but Jesus is something quite different."

"An upstart," I heard the same disciple mutter, but under his breath. John had at least enough tact to pretend not to hear as he went on, "It is true that my kinsman Jesus has begun to preach his own message. The Spirit of the Lord is on him in a mighty way."

My heart sank, but I kept my face calm as I said, "Where might we find him?"

John scanned the crowd. "He was in Jerusalem during the feast, but perhaps someone here knows where he is now. Andrew!" he called out to a man who was standing a little distance away. As he turned toward us, John asked if he knew where Jesus was.

"Not far from here—if someone wishes to meet him, I can bring them to him," the man named Andrew offered. He was a man a little younger than I, about Jesus' and John's age, and as soon as he spoke, I knew he was a Galilean like ourselves.

Indeed, when he led me to Jesus and his friends, I noted that the air was full of Galilean accents. Jesus had come all the way to Jerusalem to find a group of men much like those he had left at home.

Then I heard Jesus' voice—his accent, too, speaking clearly of Galilee, but the voice unmistakably his own—filled with authority and confidence that should never be heard in a voice not softened by old age. "But why are you worrying about such things?" he was chiding someone, his tone two notes removed from laughter. "What matter if we don't have money to rent a place to sleep? What's wrong with sleeping here on the good earth? Look at the birds!" I saw him now, gesturing toward the trees. "Do you see them worrying about where to sleep, or where their food comes from? They trust God to care for them, and so should we!"

"Birds put a good deal of effort into building their nests, I notice," I said, loudly enough to be heard, as I approached the circle of men sitting around a campfire on the ground.

Jesus looked up at once, his face lighting up. "That voice, and such a sensible sentiment, could only come from one man." He scrambled to his feet. His robe, I saw, was threadbare and dirty, as if he'd been living in it for weeks, probably sleeping out on God's good earth, as he had said. He came toward me with arms outstretched, as if we were the best friends and the closest brothers in the world. "James! Good to see you! Come, meet my friends!"

I was introduced to them—Andrew bar Jonah and his brother Peter, fishermen from Bethsaida who were living here in Judea for a time. Andrew had been a disciple of John the Baptizer, even before Jesus had arrived on the scene. With them was another man from Bethsaida, Philip, and a Judean named Nathanael, along with a few others whose names I did not catch.

I sat with them at their fire for a while, but soon I had had enough of these friends of my brother, sitting around and listening to his every word as though he were another new prophet. Prophets! Men like my brother Jesus and John the Baptizer seem to think we need more prophets, when what Israel has always needed is more faithful men who will heed the words of the prophets we already have.

Though Jesus had welcomed me warmly, he had not asked about the purpose of my journey or who was with me nor even about the rest of the family. He and his friends continued on with their discussion, until I finally interrupted, to say, "Jesus, your whole family is back at our camp. Your mother is longing to see you. Will you come back with me, so that she knows you are alive and well?"

Again that happy light filled his eyes, as if he was glad to be reminded of his mother but would never have thought of asking after her on his own. He seemed, as he always had, to live so completely in the present moment that all other concerns were pushed to the edges of his mind.

"Of course, of course," he said now. "Who else is with you, besides Mother?" Waving a cheery farewell to the other men by his campfire, he walked with me along the river toward our camp.

It was a good long walk, more than half an hour, which gave me plenty of time to quiz him on what he had been doing since coming south. He was vague—he had spent some time, he said, just drifting from place to place, talking to people, but did not list the places he had drifted or these people to whom he had spoken. He had come to the Jordan to hear John and was baptized by him—he made no mention of miraculous signs or heavenly voices accompanying this event—and had then gone away, spent some time alone in the wilderness, before returning to the Jordan region.

"And what are you doing now? John's disciples seem to think you're something of a rival to him, taking on your own disciples, preaching in your own right."

He shrugged, in that way so characteristic of him. "I talk; some people listen. I don't seek to take anything away from John. Indeed,

I don't think I could. His mission is unique; mine is a part of the same thing, but separate from it."

"And what is that 'same thing'? Some kind of religious revival? Or a revolution to overthrow the Herodians and drive out the Romans?"

Jesus grinned at me. "The kingdom of God, James. That's what it is."

"I wish I knew what you meant by that," I said.

"I wish you did too," he said.

We were approaching our family's campsite now, and the women were sitting by the fire. I called out to Mary so she would be prepared; immediately she was on her feet and coming toward Jesus. He took her in his arms and then turned to all the others with kisses, embraces, laughter, and rejoicing.

He stayed with us all that night, talking late into the night. Mary urged him to come back to Nazareth, but I was relieved when he laughed and shook his head.

"Someday God will call me back to Galilee, Mother, I'm sure of that. But not today. There is more for me to do here in Judea. The time for me to return to Galilee has not yet come."

"Even for a visit?" Mary protested. "Come home for Naomi's wedding." We had already told Jesus that his sister was to be married to Omer, from Cana, after the wheat harvest. Now he smiled.

"My friend Peter is going back to Galilee for his own wedding in the summer," he said. "His family sends word they have found him a wife in Capernaum, and he and Andrew are returning home. Perhaps when they go, I will come for a visit home and be there in time for Naomi's wedding."

Chapter Eight

The wedding at Cana was a disaster.

I suppose not everyone would agree. Naomi and her new husband Omer no doubt thought it was a great success. After all, their marriage was celebrated, and one might argue that was what it was all about. At least, that was what it should have been about.

Omer's family thought it was a great success, too, no doubt due to being able to impress their guests with lavish hospitality. And Mary thought it a great success—though, predictably, not so much because her youngest daughter got married as because of what her eldest son did. She was as bad as she'd been when we were all young, thinking the sun rose and set over Jesus, leaving the rest of us in his shadow.

The wedding was a modest affair, for neither family was wealthy. Still, every village wedding is important to the village and to the families involved, and each of the weddings in our family had been lengthy affairs, with feasts lasting all day and trickling into the next. This would be the first time we would stay with the groom's family in a neighboring village—my sisters Sara and Leah had both married young men from Nazareth. Omer's family was hosting the feast, but Mary bustled about just as much as she had for my wedding or those of my brothers. She packed up baskets of food to bring along and spent hours with Naomi, sewing and decorating the bridal robe made with the precious fabric from Jerusalem.

She waited, too, for Jesus to arrive. She was so certain he would come, though his promise had been so casually given that I was sure he had forgotten it and would remain on the banks of the Jordan—as, indeed, I hoped he would do.

Finally I persuaded Mary to stop waiting about for Jesus, who might never arrive, and prepare to take Naomi to her bridegroom's home. We all traveled to Cana, where we unrolled our bedrolls in the courtyard of the bridegroom's uncle's house. It was here that Naomi waited with her three maidens—my daughter Tabitha, and two other cousins—dressed in their best, for the noisy procession of the bridegroom and the other young men who accompanied him to claim his bride. While it might have been picturesque for him to come all the way to Nazareth to get her, it would hardly have been practical.

We made a noisy parade through the streets of Cana, everyone clapping and singing, little children running along on the sides of the road. When we reached the home of the bridegroom's father, it was my honor to say a prayer of blessing over the young couple. I was truly fond of Naomi, thinking of her almost more as another daughter than a sister, since she was so young. Indeed, as I looked at my Tabitha among the attendants, I thought how in just a few years I would go through this as the father of the bride.

How quickly life passes! I thought then, joining the hands of my little sister and her young husband, that my tale was nearly run its course. I thought I knew what my life was about, that I was James bar Joseph of Nazareth, carpenter and village rabbi, a man who lived a simple life with few surprises.

I could not have been more wrong about that; but the surprises, of course, were all due to Jesus—who surprised us, almost as soon as the ceremony ended and the feast began. He arrived with his group of ragtag friends in tow, causing both Naomi and Mary to shriek with delight and run across the courtyard from the women's side to the men's to launch themselves into his arms.

The men from Bethsaida, Peter and Andrew and Philip, were with him again, and a few others, some Galileans and some Judeans. The Galileans quickly found people they knew, or whose relatives they knew—it's a small world, here in the north—and joined the party. The Judeans stood apart, watching the festivities, which I'm sure looked very provincial to them. None of them seemed to be wealthy men, but they carried themselves with that air that Judeans in Galilee often do, as if they think they are a little better than we are. And while I will admit to envying them their learning and culture and easier life, still it is never pleasant to be the one looked down upon.

As I came up alongside Philip and Nathanael, Philip nodded toward me and said to Nathanael, "See, here is another learned man from Nazareth—a Pharisee, I believe? You remember Jesus' brother James, don't you?"

I greeted them, and admitted I ruled the synagogue in our village and that I had once studied the Torah with a learned Pharisee in Jerusalem. "You see?" Philip said again. Turning to me, he explained, "When I first introduced him to Jesus, Nathanael said, 'Can anything good come out of Nazareth?' He's very prejudiced against the Galileans, but like most prejudice, it's based on ignorance. This is his first trip north of Samaria."

Nathanael laughed in apology. "Forgive me," he said. "If I didn't know better before, I certainly do since meeting Jesus; clearly there are many wise men in Galilee. But you live so close to Gentiles here—forced to mingle with them so much. Even intermarrying with them, I've heard."

"Not here!" I said, looking around the courtyard: we had investigated Omer's family closely before promising Naomi to him in marriage, and I knew they were not tainted by Gentile blood. But the same could not be said of every family in Cana, or in Nazareth for that matter.

"It is true," I admitted. "But there are faithful Jews here in the north, just as there are in Judea, and we do not mingle with the foreign

63

dogs." Strange to find myself defending Galilee, but I suppose every man is like that about his homeland.

"Yours must be a devout family indeed, to produce two rabbis," Philip said, and after a moment's confusion, I realized he was talking about Jesus. Was Jesus styling himself a teacher now? I remembered what he had said—he spoke, and people listened. But what more than that did it take for a man to be called Rabbi? All it took to be a teacher was to begin gathering pupils, and Jesus clearly had begun to do that.

He hardly looked the part of a learned rabbi now, in the thick of the guests who were dancing, laughing, eating, and drinking. He wore a slightly cleaner version of his old, travel-worn robe. Ah well, at least he was not off consorting with women of dubious reputation; I remembered Anna from Cana, many years ago, and the trouble Jesus had caused me by helping her. That was one Cana family not invited to the feast today, one I had no desire to ally our family with.

"Still it must be difficult, Herod building his new city here, making everything as Greek and Roman as he can," Nathanael said. "We in Jerusalem may have the Roman governor, but there's no doubt it's a Jewish city—more than anyone can say for Tiberias."

"We rarely go to Tiberias," I said, "and most of us do not waste much loyalty on Herod."

"Nobody in the south is fond of him either," Nathanael said. "Though few are as outspoken as John the Baptizer."

"Really? He has criticized Herod?"

"Openly, for his many sins, especially for taking his brother's wife as his own. Many people wonder how long John will continue to evade the authorities. He may be preaching in Judea, but he's very close to Perea, which is Herod's territory, and Herod has great influence in Jerusalem. Jesus wonders whether John might be arrested."

"That would be . . . unfortunate," I said carefully. My one encounter with John had not made me a supporter, even if there was a distant family connection between us. But I had no wish to see any

Jewish teacher, no matter how unorthodox, imprisoned by Herod simply for speaking aloud what everyone said in private.

As Nathanael, Philip, and I continued our conversation, I saw the father of the bridegroom beckon to me, and excused myself to go speak to him. "What a wonderful feast," I said politely. "We are honored that you celebrate the joining of our families in such grand style."

"Thank you, James; we are honored to have Naomi join our family." Then, the polite words out of the way, he grimaced. "But perhaps the style is a little too grand; we had not counted on quite so many people, nor on the celebration lasting so long. I only hope we do not run short of food and drink."

"Oh, surely not," I said, assuming this was a meaningless pleasantry, a show of humility. He glanced away, and I realized this might be more than just talk.

"Are you truly in any danger of running short of food?" I asked quietly. "We will do whatever we can to help."

Omer's father made a small dismissive gesture with his hand. "Ah, food, not so much. Wine, now, I thought we had enough, but I'm beginning to doubt."

A wedding feast with not enough wine would certainly make the bridegroom's family look bad—it would reflect the fact that they were poor, or perhaps just ill prepared. Nobody wanted to look like a bad host.

I went around quickly to the members of my own family—except Jesus, who was in the thick of the celebration and whom I did not really think needed to be concerned with family matters—warning them that Omer's father was concerned about the supply of wine and that they should all drink sparingly. "And perhaps eat sparingly too," I suggested, thinking that if he was about to run out of wine, he might also run out of food, despite his protests.

Mary was the most concerned and went off to talk to the women. When she returned, she pulled me aside. "They've just brought out the very last jug of wine," she said. "What can we do?"

"I hardly know what to say," I said. "It's not as if I have a jar of wine in my baggage. Could we offer to find a wine merchant and buy some more?"

"I don't know if we could afford that," Mary said, her forehead wrinkling below her veil. "And there may not be a wine merchant in Cana." Working people in a village the size of Cana, as in Nazareth, drank and ate what they or their neighbors had grown. Our family traded wooden tools, tables, boxes, or benches that we made for things like wine, flour, fish, and most of the other staples of life.

Mary and I stood talking near the house while the wedding guests milled about the courtyard, the men on one side and the women on the other. Small dancing circles spun around a group of musicians playing flutes and drums, women in one circle and the men in another. Mary scanned the courtyard crowd keenly for a moment then plunged into the men's side of the party, seeking out Jesus.

From a distance, cradling my empty wine cup, I watched as she approached him. He was surprised to see her, I could see, almost irritated as she pulled him away from the people around—who were, as usual, hanging on to his every word. How he hated to leave that kind of attention to listen to his mother trouble him with a trivial problem! I couldn't imagine why she would even discuss the matter with him, though it was clear from her expression and gestures that she was trying to interest him in the shortage of wine. What did he have to do with the feast? He certainly had neither wine nor money to offer.

Jesus must, for once, have agreed with me, for he shook his head. Mary turned away, looking disappointed, as he turned back to the group of men around him. Yet a few minutes later I glanced over again and saw him looking thoughtfully off into the distance.

I would not have imagined that the lack of wine at a family wedding would have mattered to my brother, who was so convinced of his great mission in life. But I watched as he excused himself from the people around him and made his way over to the house, where Omer's mother and sisters and a few servants hired for the occasion were busy filling platters with food and cups with drink—for as long as that last jug of wine lasted. Even as I watched, I saw the bridegroom's mother shaking her head as a servant girl approached with a tray of empty cups: there was nothing left to fill them.

Jesus stood quietly for a moment, watching the scene, and I followed his gaze toward several large water jars that stood against the courtyard wall. He pulled one of the menservants aside and spoke to him briefly. The man shook his head; he seemed to be questioning Jesus, perhaps arguing with him, as Jesus had with Mary a few moments before.

But Jesus persisted, so focused and sure of himself that I couldn't help but move closer. My natural desire to be as far as possible from any trouble Jesus was creating warred with my curiosity. What could he be doing?

The servant went back to his mistress as if to clarify his orders, and suddenly Mary was there too. Had she been there all along, working beside Omer's mother? I was no longer certain. The party swirled all around us, talk and laughter and music and dancing, but this quiet, intense scene drew all my attention, even though nobody except those involved seemed to notice.

Mary said something to her daughter's new mother-in-law then spoke to the servants, nodding vigorously. The manservant and one of the women hefted several empty jugs and left the courtyard, heading toward the well just outside.

I moved over to stand beside Jesus. "You sent them to get water?"

Jesus was watching the servants with the water jars intently; at first I didn't think he had even heard me. He had a faraway look in his eyes, and his lips were moving just slightly, as though talking to himself or perhaps even praying.

As the servants began making their way back into the courtyard from the well, Jesus nodded and turned to me. "I'm sorry, James, what did you say?"

"I just wondered why you had sent them for water."

He smiled, not his usual broad smile but a quiet, preoccupied smile. "Wait and see," he said. We watched for a few moments, and then the servants returned and began filling the large stone jars from their smaller jugs. As soon as they had finished, Jesus gestured to the jugs again. "Please keep filling them until all the jars are full," he said.

The servants glanced at each other—I actually saw the girl roll her eyes—but they turned obediently and went toward the well again. Jesus strolled over to the water jars, glanced inside one, and wandered back toward me, still with that preoccupied look on his face.

When the servants had made their last trip back from the well and all the large stone jars were filled, Jesus told the manservant, "Now fill a jug again from one of these jars. Take this to the man in charge of the feast, and pour out a cup for him."

"A cup of water, sir?" the man asked hesitantly.

"Yes. Just pour out a cup and offer it to him."

The man in charge was, of course, Omer's father, and I could not imagine what Jesus hoped to accomplish by pouring him a glass of water fresh from the well, but I followed the servant over to where the bridegroom's father sat on a bench against the wall. He looked deflated and ashamed; some of the guests had already noticed that there was no more wine, and he knew the complaints would soon begin. His house was shamed, not just before our family but before the entire village and the guests from Nazareth too.

He looked up curiously as the servant took up his empty cup and lifted the jar to pour. "No, I don't need any wate—" he began, but then stopped. He looked as shocked as I did. The servant was shocked, too, and as a result he forgot to stop pouring when the cup was full. The liquid inside splashed out of the cup and over the man's hand— not clear well water, but good, dark red wine.

"Where did this come from? Did a neighbor lend us some?" Omer's father asked. "Is it any good? Why is it in a water jug?" Spluttering with questions, he raised the cup to his lips, and a look of even greater surprise crossed his face. "Well, this will be a shock—most people serve their best wine first. This stuff is far better than I was able to afford. Where did it come from?"

He looked from the servant, to me, to Mary, who had also followed the servants. Her eyes were glowing with excitement. The one person missing from the scene was Jesus, who seemed to have wandered off before the wine was poured, not waiting to see the effect of his—what? Conjuring trick? Miracle? I couldn't wrap my mind around it.

"Sir, I cannot explain it," the servant said. "It was water from the well. I drew it up myself." He beckoned to the servant girl who had accompanied him to the well, and she came up with her water jar, nodding to corroborate his story. This time I held out my empty cup, and she filled it. This jar, too, was filled with rich wine. The scent of the grapes filled my nostrils as I raised the cup to drink. And, of course, it was the best and finest wine, just as Omer's father had said.

"Just well water!" the manservant was insisting. "This man told us to fill the six big jars, and we did, and—and it was ordinary water, sir, I saw it myself. It didn't change until—until we brought it back. I don't know what he did. I never saw him touch the water or do a thing with the jars, but when we poured it out—go, look in the other jars!" he ordered the other servant. And she did, and of course every one of them was filled with wine.

"Who was this man? Who told you to fill the jars?" Omer's father demanded. The servants didn't know who Jesus was, but Mary was there, quick to step forward. "It was my son—my son Jesus. Look, there he is."

Jesus was found and brought before the bridegroom's father. By this time quite a little circle of people had gathered, mostly from our two families, though a few of the other guests had heard of the miraculous wine and were curious. Most were just glad to have their cups filled again as the servants quickly made the rounds, sharing out the new wine.

Jesus was uncharacteristically quiet throughout all this, resisting every effort to get him to explain. "There was no trick to it," he assured

Omer's father, when the man pressed him for an explanation. "I'm not a magician. I just asked my Father—He who made the grapes in the first place. Don't you think He has power to turn water to wine?"

Of course no one doubted that God had the power to turn water to wine if He so chose; what nobody could believe was that Jesus of Nazareth, the carpenter, had the power to call on God to do such a thing. "It is like the miracles of Elijah and Elisha," one of Omer's brothers said.

"He is a disciple of John the Baptizer, isn't he?" someone else said. "But even John does no miracles. He is truly like the prophets of old—remember how Elijah made the widow's oil and flour last forever? And how Elisha paid another widow's debts with a cruse of oil that never emptied?"

"But even they could not have turned water to wine! Could such a thing really happen?"

"It did, it did! I drew the water myself; it was ordinary water from the well," the manservant insisted. He was becoming quite the center of attention, telling the story over and over, while Jesus stood apart from it all. For once, he did not seem to want glory and attention, at the very moment when he had finally done something to deserve it.

But, of course, he was the center of attention anyway, whether he wanted to be or not. No one could stop talking about the miraculous wine. Everyone had to taste it and comment on how good it was; everyone had to hear the servants tell the tale over and over. In the end, neither the bride nor the groom was the center of the wedding: it was all about Jesus and the miraculous thing he had done.

Nobody but me seemed upset at this: Naomi threw her arms around Jesus' neck and thanked him a dozen times for coming, for making the feast so wonderful. He seemed glad to accept her thanks, kissed her, and wished her and Omer all happiness. Omer's family all thanked him, too, for he had saved their feast from disaster and shame. Nobody seemed to mind that they really had run out of wine and would have been disgraced if not for Jesus; everyone was laughing, thanking Jesus and thanking the hosts, and having a wonderful time.

I could not help remembering my own wedding, how the triumph of my return home and my marriage had been overshadowed by Jesus' disappearance and rediscovery in Jerusalem. No matter what happened at our family, even when he had moved away, he was at the center.

We left Cana the next day. Jesus and his disciples were going to Capernaum for Peter's wedding, and some of our family chose to go with him. "So you have another wedding to attend," I said to Jesus as we parted. "Will you make wine for them there?"

He was very serious now: his moods were so changeable I could not predict how he might react. "Don't make light of it, James. I know you don't like it, but this is the beginning of something."

"Are you going to make a habit of performing miracles now?"

"I don't know!" He sounded irritated. "I didn't plan this, you know. Mother asked me. I wanted to help—but this wasn't the way I intended things to begin."

"What is beginning, exactly, Jesus?"

He met my gaze steadily. "I'm not sure yet, James. But God is calling me to something. You must know that—I've known it for years."

"You cannot live here now, in Nazareth or any other town in Galilee, as an ordinary carpenter. Not after this," I warned him. "But then, you never wanted that, did you?"

"I don't even want to come back to Galilee," he said. "Not right now, at any rate—there is more for me to do in Judea. God has work for me there. When the time is right for me to come back to Galilee, I will know. But I have to return to Judea now, after I say Goodbye to Peter and Andrew."

"I think that is a very good idea," I told him. "Go back to Judea. We need no more miracles around here."

Chapter Nine

For months after that we heard no news of Jesus, which suited me well enough. Our lives went along in their usual routines, though every so often in the synagogue someone would ask me about the wedding at Cana and the miracle my brother had performed and what it all meant.

"God's ways are mysterious," I usually answered. "Miracles can still happen in our day, though they seem to be rare, not like in the days of the ancient prophets. We cannot tell why God might choose to perform a miracle; we can only be grateful when He does."

"But your brother, Jesus," one man persisted, not willing to accept my polite dismissal of the subject. "I visited my sister in Capernaum, and there is a man there—a fisherman called Peter bar Jonah—who knew Jesus in Judea. He says Jesus is a mighty prophet, that God has given him power to do all kinds of things."

I wished Peter—who had struck me, on the two occasions I'd met him, as a boisterous man who spoke before thinking—would keep his mouth shut. I sighed. "Friend, you know Jesus. You knew him growing up here in Nazareth. What would make you think him a prophet? The words of a fisherman from Capernaum?"

"But the miracle? The water turned to wine—you saw it yourself!"

"God was pleased to perform a miracle, it's true. I cannot tell what it means, but I hardly think it means my brother is the new Elisha."

"They say John the Baptizer is the new Elijah, and after Elijah comes Elisha, so why not?" the man suggested.

"If John the Baptizer is the new Elijah, he should start praying for his chariot to come from heaven soon," added my brother Simon, who had been listening quietly to all this talk.

"Why?" I asked.

"Have you not heard? They spoke of it in the marketplace at Sepphoris—that John has been arrested and put in prison."

"By Herod?"

"Yes, at Herod's fortress in Machaerus."

Everyone was interested in this news. John, whose fame had by now spread through the entire land, had little to do with us here in Galilee, but Herod was our tetrarch, little as any of us liked him. The fact that he would arrest a popular Jewish teacher did not sit well with many of the men who attended my synagogue in Nazareth.

"These Herods, they set themselves on thrones as if they are kings of David's line!" a man muttered as the news was discussed and one bit of gossip added to another. "All they are is Idumenean upstarts with Roman soldiers to back them! If we had a true king of the house of David, he would whip the Herods and the Romans and all the Gentile dogs out of all Israel, and make us a nation again!"

The man spoke with the force of someone calling men to battle, and others shouted agreement. They conveniently forgot, at moments like these, that there was no king of David's line for them to rally around. If such a man had appeared, these men would have been willing to fight and die for him in a moment, though I doubted any of them even owned a sword.

I spoke above the babble, calming them with the tone of my voice as much as with my words. "The Lord has promised us a Deliverer. When His Anointed One comes, we will know Him and we will follow Him. Until then, we bear our lot with patience."

"Not everyone has your patience, James," my brother Simon said. I silenced him with a look, and as the other men began to disperse, he fell into step beside me, walking toward our home.

"I wonder what this will mean to Jesus," Simon mused.

"What, John's arrest? I hope he'll have the sense to lay low and avoid trouble." Even as I spoke the words, I knew what a futile hope that was where Jesus was concerned. "I suppose he's still connected with John in some way."

"He preaches in the same area, and doesn't set himself up as a rival to John, though some of John's disciples see it that way. The authorities are likely to think of him as one of John's followers. I imagine they'll be watching him pretty closely after John's arrest."

I looked sideways at Simon. "How do you have all this information on Jesus? I've not heard a word since he went south again after the wedding."

"Of course you haven't, James. You haven't heard a word because you haven't wanted to hear. You don't want to know what Jesus is doing, so you don't ask questions. Judea isn't exactly as far as Rome, you know; people travel all the time, and if you ask the right questions of the right people, you can find out quite a lot."

"And I suppose you're friends with some of his friends here in Galilee?" I knew this to be the case, in fact. Simon was friendly with the fishermen Peter and Andrew from Bethsaida, though Peter now lived in Capernaum with his wife's family. They fished on the Sea of Galilee along with a man called Zebedee, whose wife was Mary's kinswoman. Galilee is a small world, and there are many threads tying our villages together. The friendship Simon had formed with these fishermen was just one more such link, tying us all together, reminding me that whatever foolishness Jesus got up to in Judea was not nearly as far from home as I'd have liked it to be. Better if he did go to Rome or back to Alexandria or east to the Parthian lands.

Instead, he came home. And I wasn't surprised that it was Simon who brought me the news. He had gone to Capernaum one day to work on a building job there and returned with the news that Jesus was back in Galilee.

"He's been there a week or two, it seems," Simon said. "Decided to get out of Judea after Herod arrested John—things were getting a bit uncomfortable."

That showed more prudence than I'd given Jesus credit for. "I don't know if coming back to Galilee was the best idea, though; this is Herod's own territory, the place where he has authority."

"Of course, but even to Herod, Galilee doesn't matter compared to Jerusalem. You can get away with preaching sedition and treason in Galilee because nobody's paying attention." Simon laughed.

"Sedition and treason! I hope that's not what Jesus is talking about."

"No, but neither was John—unless you count it treason to say that Herod Antipas is a sinner, not worthy to rule over God's people, and that we wait for the Lord to send us a true King and Deliverer."

I grimaced. "Whether I consider it treason or not is hardly what matters. We don't need Jesus stirring up trouble so close to home. And speaking of home—were you talking to him? Why did he go to Capernaum instead of coming to Nazareth?"

Simon shrugged, looking a bit like Jesus himself as he did so. "He came up with some of his friends—Philip from Bethsaida and that Judean, Nathanael, and a couple of others. John was with them too—Zebedee's son. He went down to Judea awhile back, mostly to meet Jesus. I suppose that because John and his brother James and their family live in Capernaum, and Peter and Andrew are there now, it was a natural place for Jesus and the others to go. And Jesus seemed to feel he might not be—entirely welcome at home."

Simon glanced at me, then away. We were sitting in our family courtyard as the women worked and the children played around us. Joseph, our youngest brother, sat nearby, listening but saying nothing. "He asked about Mother, of course, and all the family—including you," Simon went on. "But when I asked him if he was coming

75

home to stay, he said, 'My Father has business for me to do—and my brothers may have their own reasons for wanting me to stay away from Nazareth.' "

Well, that was as clear a message as he could have sent me. "Does he intend to settle permanently in Capernaum, then?"

"I don't know if he intends to settle permanently anywhere," Simon said. "He was already talking about moving on to another village, perhaps back to Cana or to Bethsaida. But James, there's more news—and you're not going to like it."

He was right, I didn't. And I might have passed off Simon's stories of Jesus' miracles of healing as just the exaggerations of a man who clearly admired his older brother if I hadn't begun to hear similar stories over the next few weeks from all kinds of people with friends and family in Capernaum. Apparently, Jesus was not only preaching and gathering disciples, as John had done, he was also performing miraculous healings of people with all kinds of illnesses.

The stories kept coming to me, and, of course, people came to me to ask if my brother, the carpenter Jesus they all knew so well, could really be doing such things, and if so, whether the healings were from God. "We saw what happened at Naomi's wedding," my cousin Samuel reminded me, "but now it seems that was just a foretaste. I've talked to people who've told me the most incredible stories—"

"Hearsay, Samuel. I know we saw the wine at the wedding ourselves, but all the rest is just stories, and you know how people exaggerate."

"There have always been stories about Jesus," Samuel reminded me. "Going back to before he was born."

I knew that to be true, though it was one of the things we rarely spoke of. Samuel's mother had been my father's sister and had told him about those strange times when we were just boys, before Jesus' birth, when Mary and Joseph were first wed. "You know Mary always held firmly to her story that there was something miraculous about his birth, no matter what anyone in the village said," Samuel reminded me.

"Oh, I don't need to be reminded of that," I said. "But really, Samuel, who believes any of that, except perhaps Jesus himself?" I could not, would not say more. I respected Mary as my father's widow, and it was not my place to tarnish her reputation, but Samuel read the things I would not say clearly enough on my face. "Anyway, it is a long way from a young girl's tale of seeing angels, to believing that Jesus really has the gift of healing," I added.

"But such gifts do exist, even if they have not been seen in Israel in many years," my kinsman pointed out.

Of course, we all knew that. We all knew the stories of miracles, though they came down to us from ancient times. Elijah and Elisha—I thought again of the comparisons that had already been made between John and Jesus and those mighty men of old.

And now John had run afoul of his King Ahab, Herod Antipas, and was in prison. And Jesus was in Capernaum, or perhaps in Bethsaida or Cana, preaching and gathering disciples and—healing the sick? Could it really be?

I struggled against believing it. *I will believe it when I see it,* I told myself. Even when I spoke with a woman from Bethsaida who told me she had been blind for ten years, since a fever took her sight, and that Jesus had touched her eyes and now she could see, I did not want to believe.

I see now, looking back, how hard I struggled against that belief, perhaps because I knew what it would mean. And also, I supposed, because there was a quiet voice in my head that said, *If God gave Jesus the gift of healing, why did He not give it to him in time to save Father, Rebecca, and my Rachel?* Where were Jesus' miracles when our family needed them? Even back then, I remember, Jesus had been good with those who were sick, had great compassion and was good at caring for them—I could admit that much. But no one had ever seen any miraculous healings when Jesus lived in Nazareth.

Several weeks passed. It had been winter when we heard news of John's arrest, and as the weather warmed toward spring and the flax harvest, we continued to hear news of Jesus in the villages around our north shore of the Sea of Galilee. He did not come home or send any word to us, beyond the greetings he had already sent by way of Simon. The stories of his "miracles" spread like fire through dry grass, and people never stopped asking me if they could be true, or when Jesus was coming home to Nazareth to perform some healings for us.

And then, one day he was there. It was the sixth day of the week, the preparation day, and I was in the synagogue alone, studying the scrolls, meditating on the scriptures I would share with those who gathered to worship on the following day.

When I returned home, the house and courtyard were a bustle of busyness as the women cooked, baked, and swept to prepare for the Shabbat hours of rest. Tabitha and Ilana were returning from the well, each with two large water jars, while Simon and Joseph cleared away the last traces of their day's work and Benjamin stacked wood for the fire. Joseph's wife, Abigail, removed round loaves of bread from the oven, while the small children toddled around picking scraps of wood from the work yard and delivering them to Benjamin at the fire.

I walked into the middle of this family chaos and stood there a moment, taking it all in. Within a few moments, I was leading the family in the prayer that welcomes the Shabbat as we all gathered around the fire. But I had barely sat down to enjoy the bowl of fish stew that Mary handed me, when her cry of joyful surprise interrupted me.

"Jesus! It's Jesus!" Mary cried, and we all looked at the courtyard entrance where a man in a travel-stained robe stood looking at our family dinner as if he were not quite part of the family. Which was, perhaps, appropriate.

But his hesitation lasted only a moment. The women and children rushed toward him, pulling him toward the fire, smothering him with embraces. Joseph, Simon, and I stayed where we sat for a moment longer, looking at each other. I tried to read my brothers' expressions. I knew that both of them, being Jesus' full brothers and younger than he, admired him and looked up to him. And yet, I also knew they had their doubts about Jesus' newfound ministry and the reports of his miracles. We were all of us concerned about the possibility that he might bring dishonor on our family. Yet they were glad to see him, and within a few moments they, too, had risen to their feet to welcome Jesus into the family circle.

I joined them. Of course I did. I would not sit apart from my family and show my disapproval of Jesus—not then, anyway. He was still one of us, and still to be welcomed when he came back home. I had questions for him, surely. I wanted to know more about what he thought he was doing, what his goals and intentions were, and why he was going about preaching and claiming to be able to heal.

But those questions could wait. It was Shabbat, and we were joining for our family meal, and Jesus had come home. Mary was so glad to see him that she was wiping away tears, and everyone was happy, laughing and talking and glad to see Jesus again.

I held out a hand in welcome to him, and he clasped it. "Good to see you, James. Are you well?"

"I am well," I said.

"I look forward to worshiping with you at the synagogue tomorrow," he said to me a little later.

"I think you have been doing more preaching than I have lately," I said.

"True, and some of it is in the synagogues. But I also preach in fishing boats and open fields, for whoever will listen to me."

In a sudden mood of generosity, I said, "When we go to the synagogue tomorrow, you should speak. You can read the Scripture portion and expound on it."

Jesus looked at me for a long moment. "Are you sure you want me to do that, James?"

It was good of him to ask. I didn't want to, not really, yet I thought it the decent thing to do. And perhaps the prudent thing. If my brother was making himself notorious by preaching all over Galilee, then people would think it strange if I did not invite him to speak in my own synagogue. It might suggest that I disapproved, and my open disapproval would cause a public rift that might bring shame on the family. After all, whatever Jesus was preaching might well be harmless enough. The miracles were another thing, something to worry about, but the message itself—surely it would be the same sort of thing John the Baptizer was preaching, repentance and judgment.

"Of course," I said. "Stay here with us tonight, and tomorrow you will read from the Scriptures."

"Thank you, brother. But I cannot stay the night unless my friends can stay too; it would not be fair to enjoy the hospitality of my family's home while my friends sleep in the fields."

Of course he was not traveling alone. Did he ever? When he went to fetch his friends—for, of course, hospitality dictated that we must not only sleep but feed the whole lot of them—there turned out to be a dozen or more. There were the men I already knew—Peter and Andrew, James and John bar Zebedee, Philip of Bethsaida and Nathanael the Judean—and there were more besides, a few I'd seen at Naomi's wedding and a few I'd never seen before. I even recognized a man called Levi Matthew, who I knew for a fact had been a tax collector who lived in Sepphoris among the Gentiles and shamelessly collaborated with the Romans. I had never thought to have such a creature sleeping on the floor of my courtyard, but they all rolled out blankets and bedrolls till the ground was carpeted with the ragtag men my brother called his friends.

Jesus took it upon himself to lead us all in a Shabbat prayer before bed, my entire household as well as his own friends. Finally they were all settled, family and unwanted guests, and I lay down on my own bed, wondering what kind of mischief Jesus could wreak in the Nazareth synagogue if I let him read the Scriptures the next day.

Chapter Ten

The women prepared the Shabbat morning meal, kept as simple as possible so that no one had to violate the laws regarding Shabbat work. I brought the cup and basin of water for the ritual washing, and Simon, Joseph, Benjamin, and I carefully performed the rite. I was horrified, but not truly surprised, to see Jesus and Peter already with bread in their hands, sitting on the ground enjoying a lively conversation as they dipped their bread in oil and helped themselves to figs with unwashed and unblessed hands. When Jesus lived at home, he had always observed the rituals, though I knew he cared little about them. Now, after months of living with John the Baptizer—who was rumored to eat insects when necessary—and living among who-knew-what kind of people, he had clearly abandoned any pretense of civilization. Some of his followers followed his example, eating their food without a ritual washing, while others took their turn after me, pouring the cup of water on each hand three times as they said the prayer of blessing.

I tried to hold my tongue, but as I found a spot for myself near Jesus and there was a pause in his conversation with Peter, I could not help saying, "Even on the Shabbat, you do not want to be purified before you eat?"

Jesus laughed. "I hope I am purified by the Spirit of God within me, on the Shabbat as much as any other day—or more." He lifted the piece of bread in his hand. "One ritual you'll notice I never omit is thanking the Father for this good food. Once I have accepted His gifts with gratitude, what more cleansing do I need?"

I didn't even try to hide my irritation as I answered, "You may think you have some special connection with God that keeps you free from impurity, but you are obviously teaching others to follow your example. What about these men? Is it right to lead them astray?"

"Who are you talking of leading astray, Rabbi?" Peter burst into the conversation. "Don't tell me you really think that in every little hovel in Galilee, men are pouring out little cups of water and washing their hands before every meal! Not everyone is a Pharisee, you know!"

"I know that," I snapped. I was developing a hearty dislike for the large, loud-mouthed fisherman who seemed to have no qualms about interrupting his elders and betters. He was right, of course; most of the simple poor followed few rituals and ceremonies, relying on Shabbat prayers and synagogue attendance to confirm their standing with God. "But if my brother is claiming to be some kind of holy man, he should be leading people to the Law, not to disregard it!"

"Ah, but what is the Law, James?" Jesus challenged. "How many laws are there? How many ceremonies and rituals must the people be burdened with?"

"The Law is no burden! The Law gives meaning to our lives; following the laws is how we know God."

"Which laws? The Commandments given to Moses on Sinai? The hundreds of other laws in the Torah or in the rest of Scripture? Or all the added laws the rabbis have contrived since the time of Moses, adding one restriction to another like a woman adding more and more bracelets and earrings to make herself more beautiful?" Jesus taunted me.

"The whole Law was given to Moses at Sinai—the written code on tablets of stone, and the oral law spoken directly to him by God and passed down through the priests and rabbis ever since! It is all a seamless whole, and you cannot tear out one piece without destroying the entire fabric!"

Around us, the voices of our brothers and of Jesus' followers created a ripple of murmurs, some agreeing with me, some with Jesus. Jesus cut across the debate now, saying, "Hush, James! Here comes Mother! We must stop our quarrel before she chides us like foolish children."

"Very well," I agreed. The arrival of thirteen unexpected guests had created enough extra trouble for Mary and the other women of the house, without having to worry about arguments breaking out.

Soon everyone had eaten—the unwashed along with the washed, though I had never expected to see such a thing in my house—and we made our way toward the synagogue. We were a large procession and attracted much attention among our neighbors, most of whom joined us on the way so that we arrived at the small building in a crowd.

As men, women, and children gathered on the benches around the small room, I moved to my usual spot at the front to light the lamps and open the service with blessings and prayers. "Amen!" the people shouted when I had finished chanting. Together, we intoned, "Hear, O Israel: the Lord our God is One Lord!"

I took the Torah scroll from its place in the ark, held it up before the people, and then placed it on the reading desk. One by one, I called up men from the congregation to read the appointed Torah portions for the day before I delivered the sermon. I had offered Jesus the chance to take on my usual role as prayer leader, which would have given him the opportunity to preach the sermon, but he said he would be glad to read the *haftarah,* the reading from the Prophets, instead, and to say a few words after that.

When my brief commentary on the Torah was finished, Jesus stood up and took the scroll of Isaiah from the basket. He unrolled it, found his place, and began to read in the clear, confident voice I knew so well.

The Spirit of the Lord is on me,
because he has anointed me
to preach good news to the poor.
He has sent me to proclaim freedom for the prisoners
and recovery of sight for the blind,
to release the oppressed,
to proclaim the year of the Lord's favor.

All the men around me nodded thoughtfully at the familiar words. This prophecy was often read as a prophecy of the Anointed One, the Deliverer upon whom so many of our hopes were pinned. The One who, when He came, would set us all free from bondage, lift us from poverty and oppression.

Yet hearing these promises spoken by Jesus made me uncomfortable. I could not have put into words exactly the source of my unease, but from the little I knew of my brother's preaching and teaching, he was proclaiming a message similar to John's—that the time had come for God to break into the world in an unprecedented way, that something new was arising. Was Jesus trying to foment rebellion, to stir the people to rise up and overthrow Herod and the Romans? There was no place in my synagogue for such talk; it was far too dangerous, as John the Baptizer had already learned to his cost.

I was surprised that Jesus ended the reading abruptly, cutting it off without reading the part about the day of the Lord's judgment. John's message had been all about judgment, but Jesus seemed to place his emphasis on the other parts of the text, on the work the Lord's Anointed would do among the poor, the oppressed, and those in need of healing.

Healing. The very kind of miracles Jesus himself was supposed to have performed in the villages around here. The feeling of discomfort grew sharper, lodged like a fist below my chest.

Jesus handed the scroll to me and stood for a moment looking at the people in front of him. "Today this scripture is fulfilled in your hearing," he said. "God's kingdom is finally at hand—not in some far future time, but right here, among you, right now. The kingdom of God is within you, among you, and all around you; and you can become citizens of that kingdom today!"

Again, the thoughtful nods, the smiles, as if they knew what he was saying. I wondered if they really understood. What did Jesus mean by "God's kingdom"? Was he talking about a revolution, about the nation of Israel being a kingdom again under a true Jewish king? If so, that was hardly in our midst right now. But perhaps he meant to suggest that the possibility was here, embodied in himself as the new, revolutionary leader.

"Today this scripture is fulfilled in your hearing." I played his words over and over in my mind as Jesus continued to speak. It almost sounded as if he himself were claiming to be the Lord's Anointed One, the Messiah who would lead the revolution and place himself upon David's throne to set Israel to rights. Indeed, judging by some of the things he was saying, perhaps he was talking about setting not just Israel, but the whole world, to rights. Why not? If a man is going to have delusions, they might as well be grand ones, and Jesus' were the grandest of all.

No. It could not be. His short homily came to an end, and as I looked at the faces of the men around me, I wondered if any of them heard what I had heard in Jesus' words. Did my lifelong resentment of my brother, my fear that he might shame our family, give his words a meaning he did not intend? Or was he, truly, mad enough to believe he was God's Messiah, a king of the house of David?

My father, of course, claimed descent from David's line; so did Mary's family. So did half of Israel, it sometimes seemed. Descent from a long-ago king meant little, even if the Lord had promised that king that his descendants would reign on the throne of Israel forever. The last kings we had had who could be called "kings of Israel" were the Hasmoneans, whose line had died out when my father was still a boy—and even they had been of a priestly line, not of the house of

David. Still, they had been Jews, and that foreign dog Herod, father of our tetrarch Herod Antipas, claimed his right to the throne by marrying a Hasmonean princess.

While I believed that someday a king of David's line would come to restore power to Israel, I found it hard to believe God would intervene so dramatically in my lifetime—and impossible to believe that my younger half-brother, who had been nothing but a carpenter and a troublemaker, should imagine himself in such a lofty position. Even John the Baptizer had not spoken such folly. He always described himself as a mere prophet, the forerunner of a greater One whom God would send.

Forerunner. I remembered the resentment John's disciples had shown toward Jesus, and John's own utter lack of the same resentment. How he seemed to take it for granted that Jesus would follow after him, would become greater than he . . .

Could John be a participant in this same delusion? Could he, in fact, have encouraged it in Jesus? Jesus had always been brash and disrespectful to those in authority, but he had never seemed obsessed with gaining power or position. This was something new, and I wondered if John might have planted the idea in his head.

I tore my attention away from my own troubled thoughts and back to the discussion that followed Jesus' reading. The first comments he had received were all approving. "Well spoken, well said, young Jesus," some of the older men around me nodded.

"What clever sons the carpenter Joseph produced," another said, gesturing toward Jesus and me. "Two learned rabbis in one family!"

The tenor of the talk went on like this for a few moments until another man said, "But surely if we heard rightly today, young Jesus is claiming more than the title of a rabbi for himself. Those verses from Isaiah speak of God's coming Deliverer, His Anointed One."

"May the Messiah come to us in God's good time," an old man said piously, but the first was not finished.

"Jesus, you said the scripture was fulfilled in our hearing today.

What did you mean by that?"

Jesus met the man's gaze clearly, levelly. "Only that we do not need to wait for God to send a deliverer in the future. If you would only open your eyes, you would see that your deliverance is at hand."

"Do you mean to drive out the Romans, you and your friends?" Our cousin Samuel gestured around at the group of men who had come with Jesus, swelling the numbers in our Nazareth synagogue. Several men laughed at the suggestion, but Jesus still looked calm and serious.

"Do you think the Romans are the true problem here? Cannot a Jew be corrupt and evil, and oppress his fellow man, as much as a Roman legionary would? Do you believe all of Israel is pure, and only the Gentiles lost in sin?"

There were some murmurs at this. Then Uri the potter raised his voice. "Are you setting yourself above us, Jesus? Saying you're better than the rest of us? We know who you are and where you come from—a carpenter's son, brother of James and Jude and all the rest of them."

"If he even *is* the carpenter's son," a quiet voice sniggered. I could not tell who among the men in the room had dragged up this old slander, but it was easy to see that the mood of the men was turning against Jesus. He raised his hands as if to command silence.

"Even the Scriptures say that a prophet is without honor in his own country," Jesus said. "Perhaps that is why God so often goes outside His own people to find those who are faithful. Do you remember the story of Naaman the leper who was cleansed by Elisha? Do you think there were no lepers in Israel? But whom did God choose to heal? A Syrian general, because he had faith! What about the widow who fed Elijah during the famine? She came from Zarephath! Were there no widows in Israel who could have fed and sheltered the prophet? Of course there were, but only the foreigner was faithful!"

"Are you saying God will take His blessing from Israel and throw it to foreign swine?"

"Do you set yourself up as a prophet like Elisha and Elijah?"

"What are you telling us? That you—you, Mary's bastard son, are God's chosen Deliverer? Why, I can remember when you were a child in short robes, running around Joseph's house!"

"Don't make yourself out to be better than you are!"

The voices rose, a clamor; the group of men suddenly turned angry. What had changed their mood? Jesus' audacious suggestion that God might choose Gentiles and heathen to do His work? Or his own gall in setting himself up as a prophet and maybe more? Whatever the cause, my fellow villagers were angry, turned in a few minutes from a devout group of worshipers to an angry mob.

They rose to their feet and moved toward the door of the synagogue. I waved my arms about and raised my voice, trying to bring some order to the madness, but no one paid any attention. "Why should we listen to any of the sons of Joseph the carpenter!" one man spat at me as he pushed past. It was as I had always feared; Jesus' madness was bringing shame upon our family name, upon me. I wanted no part in my brother's foolishness, but I did not want him set upon and beaten by an angry mob of his own neighbors either.

I tried to push through the group of men—now swelled by some women and children who had also left the synagogue—to find Jesus, to persuade him to come away quietly. I could no longer see him or hear his voice. There must have been fifty or sixty people in the crowd by now, most of them men and many of them angry. Hardly a fitting scene for a Shabbat morning!

Instead of Jesus, I found James bar Zebedee of Capernaum, a man I had known slightly through our family connections even before he took up with Jesus. "Where is he? Have you seen him?" I asked.

"Don't know," the other James said. "But he needs to get out of here quickly, or they'll do him harm. What kind of madmen are your townspeople? Everywhere else we've gone, the people have loved him!"

We were well away from the synagogue now. When I found the

front of the crowd, the group of the angriest men, led by Uri the potter, I found Jesus was not there either. The angry men looked about bewildered, trying to find the target of their anger.

"Where did he go, Rabbi?" one of the men demanded, seizing me by the arm.

I kept my peace and looked down at his hand, which he removed after a moment. "Forgive me, Rabbi," he said. "I did not mean to lay hands on you, but your brother must leave Nazareth. We cannot have him here, talking madness and making ridiculous claims."

"I quite agree," I said. "I will find him, and persuade him privately to leave, along with his friends." I threw in the mention of Jesus' followers because I could already hear rowdy Peter's voice raised in argument. But when I went back through the group of men, who grew progressively less angry the farther back in the crowd they were, and found Jesus' followers, there was no sign of Jesus. Peter was, indeed, in a vocal argument with two of my neighbors, and John bar Zebedee was involved as well, threatening to knock some sense into them if they didn't stop criticizing Jesus.

"The hand of God is on this man! He's filled with the Spirit—you should see what he does!" John shouted. "Heals the lame, cures fever . . ."

"Yes, we should see some of that! Funny we've seen nothing here in Nazareth!" one of the men, a farmer named Jabez, shouted back.

"He has!" a woman's voice cut shrilly through the men's growls. "He laid hands on me before I came into the synagogue! This pain in my back I've had for weeks—it's gone!"

"You believe what you want to believe," one of the men said to her, "but I see no miracles this Jesus has done for us here in his own town."

"How could you?" Peter challenged. "He came here only yesterday and look what you've done! Refused to hear his teaching, called doubt upon his authority . . ."

"What authority? What illegitimate carpenter has the right to call himself a prophet?"

I tackled John from behind just as he drew his arm back to swing at Jabez. Peter, seeing me, thought better of his own itching fists and took a step backward. "Stop this, all of you!" I commanded. "Where is Jesus?"

"Where is he? Where is Jesus?" The question echoed back through the crowd. But he was not with his friends, or with any of our family, nor among the knot of angry men who had propelled him out of the synagogue. Gradually, realization swept over us all: Jesus was gone. In the middle of the melee, he had somehow slipped away unseen, leaving turmoil and confusion behind.

When we finally admitted he was not to be found, I turned to Peter. "I don't know where Jesus has gone, but you lot had better be out of town before sundown, if not sooner."

"Sooner," Peter assured me. "We've no desire to stay and enjoy Nazareth's hospitality, or your family's. I see now why Jesus was in no hurry to come home."

"Watch your tongue," I warned.

"I'll watch my tongue if my Master tells me, and not otherwise," he shot back. "And he has a home with me in Capernaum whenever he wants a bed and a roof over his head. There's no need for you and your people to be troubled with him again."

He was gone, gathering his crew of unruly friends around him, before it hit me that Peter had called Jesus "Master." Master. They were not just friends; they were disciples, treating Jesus as a rabbi, a learned teacher. And if he'd implied what I thought he had while reading from Isaiah this morning, that might be the least of the claims Jesus was making for himself.

As far as I was concerned, Capernaum could have him.

Chapter Eleven

I'm sorry, Mother, but we have to do something. He's gone too far this time."

I sat next to my stepmother under the shade tree in the courtyard near the end of the day, as my brothers and son finished up their day's work and the women prepared the evening meal. Only Mary and I were at leisure: I because my duties were almost entirely those of a rabbi rather than a carpenter now, and Mary because of her advancing years. She was nearly fifty now, a few years my senior, and her hair beneath her veil was gray, though her face was not yet deeply lined. If anything had added white threads to her hair and lines to her face, it surely must be not just the passing years but Jesus' behavior in these months since returning to Galilee.

He had not come home again since his disastrous visit in the early spring. I know Mary longed to see him, and I would have made him welcome despite my disapproval. If he had come alone, without disciples. If he had come as a man visiting his family rather than a prophet coming to preach.

But he saw himself as a public figure, a family man no longer. He was concerned only about his calling as a prophet—and perhaps more, for there were many who spoke of him as Israel's Deliverer, a king waiting for his crown. The stories of the healings grew more extensive and impressive, and I met several people from other towns who claimed they had been healed by a touch from Jesus. It was no longer easy to deny that Jesus had some kind of power.

But what kind? I was by no means convinced that Jesus' healing ability, if it were real, was a gift from God. He could have been filled with God's Spirit, but if he were, would he set himself up as a prophet and rabbi, ignoring the authority of those he should have listened to? Would he not have observed the Law scrupulously and taught others to do so, rather than flagrantly ignoring it? I had even heard tales of his performing healings on the Shabbat, within the walls of a synagogue. And everywhere he went, he created conflict, arguing with fellow rabbis about everything from interpretations of the Law to what Israel's Deliverer would do when He came.

As for being the Deliverer himself, I had not heard that Jesus claimed that openly. But enough people said it about him, and he had never publicly denied it as John the Baptizer had done.

John was still in Herod's prison; nobody knew whether he would ever be released, or if he would be chained till he died. I could not help feeling a stab of pity for the man, little as I liked him or his message. It seemed more and more likely to me that Jesus would share John's fate. There were more than enough people, both in Galilee and in Judea, who would want to silence a man whom others claimed was a king ready to take the throne of David. Jesus went around preaching about God's kingdom, not Herod's or Caesar's; in some circles that would be enough to condemn him.

"It's becoming dangerous for him, not just embarrassing for us," I urged Mary. I had turned the thing over in my mind for weeks and decided it was high time to seek out Jesus and exert the authority of family over him. I knew he would not listen to or obey me if I went alone. But if I brought his mother, whom he loved and respected, and his other brothers, surely he would have to listen. I knew that Mary worried about him. She did not feel shame as I did but fear for the trouble he might bring upon himself. That was the tool I could use to move her to action.

"I spoke to a man from Chorazin who heard Jesus preach," I told her. "Not only is he traveling with those twelve men he had with him here—those are always with him—but he has dozens of others who trail around after him, not just men but women as well. Men and women all traveling together, living together, calling Jesus Rabbi and Master, leaving their homes and families behind. Women leaving their husbands to travel around with Jesus and his followers! Can you imagine what people are saying? He went to a feast in Sepphoris in the house of a tax collector who follows him, and half the guests there were Gentiles! He eats with Gentiles, with tax collectors, and with loose women; and he claims that all this shameless lack of discipline is of God. He preaches that this is what God's rule is like, everyone living together and sharing everything, disregarding the Law, and taking in all kinds of uncleanness. Yes, he heals the sick and casts out demons, but Mother, do you really think this can be of God?"

She remained silent, as she had throughout my entire diatribe, her still lovely face grave, her eyes cast down. Finally she looked up at me.

"I don't know, James. I simply don't know any longer. You know that I believe Jesus is special. He was given to me by God—no, don't deny it, James. You can never know the truth of what happened—nobody ever could, but me. But your father believed me, and now you must believe me too. His birth was miraculous; it was foretold. Whatever he is doing, James, it must be from God!"

I knew I could not shake her from that belief. And perhaps now, in her later years, it would be cruel to do so. Whatever sin she had committed in her youth, this tale of a Spirit-born child and an angelic messenger had so firmly fixed itself in her mind that I thought by now she believed it was the truth. How could I shatter that faith she had built to protect her own memories? Though I could suggest to my brothers—and had done so—that Jesus was mad or demon possessed, I could not say that to Mary. She was too firm in her faith, so I must focus instead on her concern for Jesus' safety.

"If God did indeed give Jesus a special task to do, surely He would not have Jesus killed or arrested before that task can be carried out, would He?" I pressed gently, taking her worn hand in mine. "At the very least, Mary, can't we agree that he is being very foolhardy in how he is going about his mission? He is not just drawing followers among the poor; he is also attracting attention from those in high places, those whose attention none of us want to draw. Do you want him to end like your poor cousin John?"

No. No, she did not want that; it was written on her face and in her tear-filled eyes. "So then, should we not go to him and ask him to come home?"

I pressed my point. "No, not ask him, but command him. Tell him that we come, as his mother and brothers, to bring him home, for his own safety. Before he goes too far and angers someone in power, and then pays for it as John has paid."

Her tears were flowing freely now, and she clasped my hand as she wiped them away with the edge of her veil. "I hate to do it, James. I fear that we may be turning him aside from the Lord's path, but, of course, you are right. He is being very foolish, and we must warn him. Bring him home, if he'll come, and keep him safe. He must be careful—I could not bear if he . . ."

Her voice broke, and she could not finish her sentence. But it was enough. I knew I had won.

Now instead of avoiding news of Jesus, I sought it out, asking my brothers and cousins what they had heard about where he was and what he was doing. Finally Simon, after a few days' work in Capernaum, came back and reported that Jesus was there again.

"Did you see him?"

"No, there was a crowd wherever he went. He wasn't even in town when I was there; he was outside town, preaching to huge crowds of people and healing the sick on the hills outside town. People streamed out of town every day to hear him. I don't know if he was coming back and sleeping in town at night or staying out in the hills, but sooner or later he'll come back to Peter's house—that's where he usually stays when he's in Capernaum, either there or at Zebedee's house. He always goes to the synagogue on Shabbat, so we may see him there." He paused, rubbing his sawdust-stained hands on his robe. "If you still want to go and confront him, that is."

I lifted my hands and then dropped them by my sides. "What else can we do, Simon? He is our brother."

"Yes, but he's a grown man and can make his own choices."

"Not when those choices affect the good name of the family— and put himself in danger! Do you think I feel good about bringing my brother home against his will as if he were a criminal? But better we, his family, apprehend him, than the soldiers of Herod. Do you want him to end like John the Baptizer?"

Simon frowned. "John's tale is not told yet. He might be set free, for all we know." When I said nothing, he sighed heavily and conceded, "Very well, I agree with you. I don't like it, but there's nothing else to be done. We must go find Jesus and talk some sense into him. We can go after our own synagogue service on Shabbat and be in Capernaum well before sunset. He will probably still be teaching or healing in some house there—that's what they say he does every Shabbat after prayers."

I shook my head. "No, not on the Shabbat. Capernaum is too far for a Shabbat journey." There were strict rules about how far one could travel on Shabbat without violating the holiness of the holy day, though many people disregarded them.

Instead, we started for Capernaum early in the morning on the first day of the week. I hoped to return the same evening with Jesus, though I found it hard to picture a scene in which he willingly returned home with us, giving up his preaching and his notoriety. We could have stayed a night there, but the only kinfolk we had were Zebedee's family, and while staying there would get us into the heart of Jesus' inner circle with Zebedee's two sons, it might be an uncomfortable visit if, as I expected, Jesus resisted our pleas to return home.

In the end, I thought no pleas would have any effect. We would have to command him to give up playing at being a rabbi and a prophet, and come home for his own good and ours. That was the value of having all four of us brothers—Jude, Simon, Joseph, and myself—as well as Mary. If he did not listen to me alone as the elder brother, I would have the weight of his other brothers to back me up. If he would not listen to any of us, surely he would respect his mother and agree to come with her.

We arrived midmorning at the village gates and asked if Jesus of Nazareth was in the town. There was no hesitation, no pause for the elders gathered there to seek information; they knew at once that Jesus was there. "He is at the house of Zebedee the fisherman," one said, and the others nodded vigorously.

"Stirring up trouble," said one.

"Bringing us the words of God!" another said, almost in the same breath, and they fell to quarreling as we passed on through and into the town.

The elders were, it seemed, divided in their opinion of Jesus' ministry, but they were right about where he was. And he had, as usual, a crowd around him. Mary and my brothers knew where Zebedee's house was, but we would have found it anyway by the fact that the courtyard was full of people and the road outside was thronged with more.

Among those waiting were many of the people usually hidden away: a sick woman carried on a bed, an old man walking with sticks, a younger man with one arm dangling useless by his side, a mother leading a blind boy by the hand. Mixed in among those seeking healing were the usual run of villagers, much the same in Capernaum as they were in Nazareth—the elders who were presumed to be wise (those who were not sitting at the gate), the rough working men, fishermen like Zebedee's sons or laborers like our own family, farmers from the fields around the town. And women with them, far more women than would normally mingle in a mixed crowd like this. Young and old, men and women—everyone was pressing into the courtyard of Zebedee's house to see and hear Jesus.

We ourselves could see and hear nothing; we could not even get close enough to spot where Jesus was, though I knew he must be at the center of the crowd. "This is no good," I told Jude. In the press of the crowd, Mary and our two younger brothers had disappeared, and Jude and I stood among the people of Capernaum, pressing in to hear Jesus.

"Hardly," Jude said. "We want to talk with him alone, not in front of a crowd. Can we send word in that we're here?"

When we got closer to the house itself, we could hear Jesus' voice, just his tones rising above the crowd, not his words. There was no point in trying to get through this crush of people to reason with him. We had to wait until we could get him alone.

Retreating into the street, we found Mary and our brother Joseph talking to an older woman about Mary's age. It was Salome, the mother of James and John, Zebedee's wife and Mary's kinswoman.

Mary turned to Jude and me, including us in the conversation. "I met Salome coming back from the well," she said. "She tells me Jesus has been here over the Shabbat and was going away today, but could not leave for the crowds of people who wanted to hear him and be healed."

"Not even all from Capernaum—they come from the country all round," Salome said. She looked proud to be the hostess of Jesus, proud to have her house be the center of all this attention. I thought that with such pride, she was unlikely to be sympathetic to our plan.

"Will he leave tomorrow, then?" Jude wondered.

"Tomorrow—or perhaps tonight. I think they may be going on to Bethsaida, or perhaps farther. My boys will be with him, of course." Again, Salome beamed with pride at her sons' involvement in Jesus' madness.

"James and John both?" Mary asked. "But James has a wife and children, hasn't he? And isn't it hard on Zebedee and all of you, if they leave off the fishing and travel around with Jesus?"

Salome frowned, the first crack appearing in her proud façade. "Oh, it's a hardship, no doubt," she said. "But what can you do? Jesus talks to people and says, 'Come, follow me,' and they uproot themselves and go off with him. Of course, they come home from time to time. And while they're here, they all pitch in and help with the fishing, not just my boys but Jesus and most of the others too—they all do their share to help out. It's harder in between times, just me and Zebedee now that we're getting older, and we do have James's wife and young ones to care for. But it will be worth it all in the end," she said, finishing her speech with a vigorous nod.

" 'Worth it in the end.' What do you mean?" Jude said.

Salome looked surprised. "Why, you're Jesus' own family; you should know better than anyone else what greatness awaits him! He won't always be a traveling preacher, you know. His gifts of healing, his miracles, the words he speaks—anyone can see the hand of God is on him. My boys think he's the promised Deliverer, that someday he will sit on David's throne."

"Hush!" I said, though in fact she had lowered her voice as she spoke the treasonous words. I saw no Roman soldiers in the crowd around us, but one could never be sure. "It is not safe to say such things, Salome! You put your own family, and ours as well, at risk with such words. And Jesus is in the greatest danger of all if people talk that way about him."

"Have faith, James," Salome said. "Great days are coming to Israel. Jesus says it himself—the kingdom is at hand!"

"Simon has gone into the house," Mary said to me, "to tell Jesus we're here. He hopes he can get Jesus to come out and talk to us privately."

"I would like to go in too," young Joseph said, "just to hear what he says. I got a little taste of it that Shabbat he spoke in our synagogue, but that turned to madness so quickly, it was hard to know what to think."

He slipped neatly through the crowd, leaving Jude and myself with the two older women. A moment later another woman joined us, an older woman like Mary and Salome but dressed in clothes far finer than they wore. This was no peasant woman but a woman of some means and class.

"Joanna!" Salome cried, addressing the other woman with greater familiarity than I would have expected, given the obvious difference in their status.

The other woman inclined her head graciously as Salome introduced us, but when she realized she was in the presence of Jesus' mother and brothers, the woman named Joanna flushed deeply as if she were in the presence of royalty.

"I am so honored, so very deeply honored," she said, holding Mary's hand as if she couldn't bear to let it go. "That I should meet the woman who gave life to him who has given life to so many—myself the least of them."

"Were you healed by Jesus?" Mary asked.

"Oh, yes. I lay at the point of death with a fever. Jesus came and touched me and healed me. My husband is a steward in Herod's palace in Tiberias. He forbade me to follow Jesus, but what choice did I have? Jesus saved my life, and I have some fortune of my own; if I can use it to help in his work, to bring his good news to more people, how could I stay at home?"

I stood gaping at her, and even Mary, though she smiled, looked shocked. For any married woman, much less a wealthy one whose husband was in a position of influence, to walk away from her home and responsibilities and use her own dowry money to support the work of a traveling rabbi was unthinkable. That she herself—and other unmarried women, too, apparently—would travel along with the rabbi and his male disciples, learning from him as if they were men yet living without supervision like loose women . . . well, such a thing had never been heard of in Israel. Indeed, I had never heard of such things even among the Gentiles, who kept their women in good order whatever other faults they might have.

I could not think of anything to say to such a woman, nor even think it proper to hold a conversation with her, so I drew Jude away with me, leaving the three women to talk. The crowd in the street had not dispersed, and it was no easier to get close to Jesus than it had been when we first arrived. The midday sun was now high in the sky, and I was hungry, tired, and irritated.

"How long can the man go on talking?" I wondered aloud. "No rabbi I've ever heard has had that much to say!" My mind wandered back to my old master, Rabbi Eli, in Jerusalem many years before. Yes, he could teach all day, I remembered, engaging his disciples in questions to help us learn the intricacies of the Law, or debating the finer points of Scripture with other rabbis. What kinds of questions did Jesus ask? With whom did he debate? What learning did he have to support such practice? Yes, he had read the Scriptures and thought much about their meaning, but without having sat at the feet of a learned master himself, how could he pretend to be a teacher, to take his place in that great river of tradition that passed on the Law, rabbi to pupil from one generation to the next? Like John the Baptizer, he came from outside that great stream and declared that God was doing a new thing—with him as its instrument, of course.

Finally, late in the afternoon, some of the people in the street began to go to their homes, and the crowd thinned. I saw that many of those who had come sick and needing healing must have gotten what they came for—the old man walked without his sticks, and the blind boy ran along beside his mother without needing her hand, pointing out things along the way and exclaiming with delight. I saw the joy in their faces, saw how deeply they believed that what had touched them was of God and was good. I saw how much they believed in Jesus.

And I? I could not share their joy, though seeing with my own eyes those who had been healed shook me to the core, I must admit. Could it be that God's Spirit really was working through Jesus? But if God were at work here, why would He reveal Himself through one who so blatantly disregarded all that I had been taught to respect? I thought of Joanna, who had abandoned her home and husband, and Zebedee's sons, who left their aged parents to fend for themselves while they traipsed around the country with Jesus. There was joy in this ragtag crowd to be sure, but where was order? Where was respect? Where was tradition?

As people moved in and out of Zebedee's house, I saw at last a face I'd been looking for—my brother Simon. With him was young John bar Zebedee. I hoped they had come to bring me to Jesus, or to bring Jesus to talk with me. But when they came to me, there was no sign of Jesus.

"Did he see you? Did you speak with him?" I asked Simon. My younger brother's face was clouded, and I could not read his expression. He shook his head, but said nothing, and John spoke for him.

"Jesus saw Simon, and he knew the rest of you were here. Several people told him that his mother and brothers were outside, waiting to talk with him." John's face wore that same pride I'd seen on his mother's face: delight at being part of the inner circle of this new movement.

"Well? What did he say? Is he coming out, or may we come in?"

John smiled; it was not a very nice smile. "When he heard you were here, he said, 'Who are my mother and brothers?' Then he looked around at all of us sitting there and said, 'Look, these are my brothers!' He pointed at the women and said, 'These are my sisters, these are my mothers. Everyone who hears my words and follows me—they are my true family.' "

I paused, letting the impact of the words sink in. "He—disowned his family? Admitted no ties with us?"

John nodded and looked to Simon. Simon finally met my eyes. "It's as John says, James. Jesus claimed that his true family is those who listen to him and travel with him, that he has nothing to do with the rest of us. He is . . . creating something entirely new, I think," he added, echoing the thoughts I'd had earlier. "Not only a new kingdom, but a new family—a new idea of what it means to be family."

"Rubbish!" said my brother Jude. Jude was no rabbi; he was a farmer, a quiet man who spoke little and when he did speak, said what he thought. He pushed between Simon and John. "Let me go talk to that insolent young pup! He'll learn what it means to deny his family. His mother! His own mother! Think how she loves him, how much she worries for him! How dare he say such a thing!"

Simon grabbed Jude's arm. "Hold it, Jude. It's not—it's not what you think. He's not barring us out; any one of us would be welcome to be with him, if we came willing to listen and follow."

"Follow him?" I echoed. "We came here to convince Jesus to follow *us*—to come home to Nazareth."

"That will never happen!" John declared with absolute certainty. "He knows what you're trying to do, to end his ministry, to pull him away from God's chosen path. No wonder he won't see you!"

"Hold your tongue, boy!" I said to John. He was a good ten years younger than Jesus, if not more—a boy who could barely grow a decent beard, who had abandoned his parents and responsibilities to chase around after a witless dream. My brother's witless dream.

"Very well then," I said. "If Jesus disowns us, we disown him."

"Do not be hasty, James," said a quiet voice at my elbow, and I turned to see that Mary was beside me. I had not heard her approach, but I could see from the sadness in her face that she had heard Jesus' words.

"He did not mean it as it sounds, Mother," Simon said again. "You should have been there; you'd have understood . . ."

"But she was not there, because he made it clear that none of us were welcome!" I reminded Simon. Joseph, our youngest brother, was with us now too. Jesus was still surrounded by a tight knot of people, cut off from us. Cut off by his own pride and stubbornness.

"No, Mother," I said to Mary. "I know you love Jesus, and he is your son, but this is unbearable. He cannot be a part of our family and behave this way. To me, he is dead from this day forward, as if I never had a brother. Come, if we leave now we can be home in Nazareth before nightfall."

They were harsh words, I knew, and they would hurt Mary, but not as harsh as the ones Jesus had spoken. I felt that severing all those ties would protect Mary, in the end, from more hurt, as well as protect our family from shame. It was too late to shield Jesus from the consequences of his actions; he had made it abundantly clear he did not want the protection of family.

"You can go," Simon said. "I am staying. For now, anyway."

"What?"

He shifted uneasily from one foot to the other. "I want—I want to spend more time with Jesus. To hear more of what he has to say."

"But he's told you he wants nothing to do with any of us!" I reminded him.

"No, that's not what he said," Simon countered. "He said his true family is made up of those who follow and believe. That's the family I want to know more about."

"Then you, like Jesus, are abandoning us?" I said, my voice cutting like an axe through wood. Simon looked as if I'd struck him.

Mary's voice interrupted me again. "Don't be so quick to cut limbs off the family tree, James. Simon has the right to follow his brother if he chooses."

I bit back the immediate response—who was she, a woman, to tell me what rights anyone in our family had or did not have? Instead, I said to Simon, "What of Ilana and your children? Are you going to become like these fools—" I gestured at John bar Zebedee, still standing nearby—"and leave everything behind to follow Jesus?"

"I—I don't know," Simon said. "I didn't mean to leave home for good—just to stay with him a little while and learn what it is he's doing, just to be a part of it."

"Be at peace, Simon," Mary said, gently usurping my authority again. "We will care for Ilana and the children till you return. Tell Jesus that I love him and pray for him."

"Tell him I think he's a fool who needs to give this up before he lands in Herod's dungeon," I said, wrapping my travel cloak around me and turning for the road without any more farewell to Simon.

Jude fell into step beside me, Joseph walking behind us with his mother. "Ah well," Jude said, his sudden temper dissipated. "Perhaps Simon will be able to influence him a little, make him be more cautious."

I laughed. "Simon, influence Jesus? You know any influence will be all the other way, Jude. I don't know when we'll hear of either of them again, but as for me, I'm heartily sick of the whole mad business."

Chapter Twelve

That was not the end of the matter.

Mary, Jude, Joseph, and I returned to Nazareth—Jude to his own wife and family, and Mary, Joseph, and I to our home, where we had to explain to Simon's wife that he would not be returning right away.

"But why?" Ilana asked, her eyes brimming with tears. "Why would Simon leave us, and why would Jesus ask such a thing of him? To leave his wife and children—it's just cruel!"

Mary put an arm around Ilana's shoulders. "You are not alone, dear one. You are part of our family, and we will all care for you till Simon returns." She drew Ilana away, toward Tabitha and Abigail, into their private women's world where they could talk and weep and discuss the strange ways of men.

Joseph and I were left staring at each other, bewildered. But there was nothing to say. We had talked it all out on the road from Capernaum to Nazareth, and neither of us understood Simon's decision, nor Jesus' harsh repudiation of his family. The latter I decided to put down to the arrogance he had always shown, and perhaps to the madness I suspected might have turned his brain.

But though I had declared him banished from our family, I could not banish him from thought and conversation, or even from my own mind. Nor could I stop the news of him that seemed to spread around Galilee like a noxious weed that would not stop growing.

I heard that he spent less time, now, in the towns and villages, because too many people crowded around, and there was not time or privacy to heal all the sick, nor places large enough to speak to all the people who wanted to hear him. He spent most of his time now on the seashore or out in the open fields or on hillsides, and people flocked there to see and hear him—even a few from Nazareth, despite all their skepticism about how the carpenter from down the road could be a prophet.

Rumors flew as quickly as news, making impossible to tell which was which. I tried to shield Mary from much of what I heard in the synagogue and marketplace, but news spread as quickly among the women as among the men. New prophets and rabbis, and possible revolutionaries, would normally have been men's business only, but this movement gathering around Jesus was different. He drew both women and men, as well as people from all classes. Mostly it was the poor who followed him, our own kind of working people and those even lower on the social scale—beggars and outcasts. But he also attracted some of the wealthy and influential, like the woman Joanna whom I had met in Capernaum.

However Mary learned of it, she heard some of the stories about Jesus and asked me if they tallied with what I had heard. Was it true that Herod had issued a command to arrest him? That Jesus had traveled across the lake to the Gadarenes and even into Samaria? That he had cast out hundreds of demons from a single man, that he had healed lepers, that he had even raised a dead man—or was it a child? Was it true that people were openly calling Jesus a king?

This last, at least, I knew to be true. I had heard men say it openly, even here in Nazareth. Even at our own village gate, a few were beginning to say, "Could he be the One promised by God? He is of the house of David, after all. We have waited far too many years for God to fulfill his promise to always have a king on David's throne. Will Herod's sons and their cursed Roman masters rule us forever?"

"From the house of David? Jesus, Mary's son?" one older man said with contempt, as I sat at the gate one day. Then he glanced at me. "Forgive me, Rabbi James. I would not slander your house, but it has to be said. Your honored father, may he rest in peace, was indeed of the line of David. But who has ever proven that Jesus was truly Joseph's son?"

There was a moment of silence, as if everyone were shocked to hear the slander that had been whispered behind doors for thirty years now spoken aloud. It was I who finally broke the silence. "You need not apologize to me, Zimri. The truth is not spoken of, even in our family, but I have always held doubts about Jesus being my father's son. My father was not the man to dishonor his bride before the wedding. I can never believe such a thing of him."

"But he was a decent man, and a kind one. To sacrifice his own good name to protect a sinful woman—now that, I could believe of him. That is what I have always believed, and so have most of the people in town," old Zimri said.

"What's past is long past. Mary has lived a good life and raised Joseph's children," said another man. "Surely the Lord has forgiven her sin, and such things are best forgotten."

"True enough, and they would be forgotten if Jesus were content to be a carpenter here in Nazareth, marry, and raise a family like any sensible man. But if he is going to go around Galilee making himself out to be a prophet and a rabbi, letting people style him a Messiah and claiming to be a king in the line of David, then it needs to be said loud and clear that he can claim no descent from David. Why, he could be anyone's son—the son of some Roman soldier who took advantage of Mary when she was a girl, for all we know! Such things have happened to our young women before. It is a crime and a shame, but what if Jesus were the son of a Gentile? He could be anyone!"

It was not the first time I had heard such suggestions, and privately I thought they might well be true, though I did not want to invite further speculation on Mary's past. If Jesus were not a true, full-blooded Jew, it would explain a great deal, particularly his strange tolerance of the heathen.

Mary's father was also of the line of King David, a fact nobody mentioned. It was hardly relevant in this discussion, since a would-be king could not claim royal descent through his mother's line. At any rate, a Davidic heritage was something many could claim. What few could claim was the power to speak so men would listen, to lead so they could follow. To attract the kind of fanatical devotion that might lead men to sacrifice their lives for the dubious chance to overthrow Rome and the Herodians.

All these things, apparently, Jesus had. And even in skeptical Nazareth, a few were willing to say, as one man now did, "Whatever his parentage, he is the son of a Jewish mother, he preaches from the Scriptures, and the Spirit of God is on him. That's more than any of Herod's brood have ever been able to claim. Isn't it time we had such a man on the throne of Israel?"

"Shut up, Eleazar!" I hissed. "Never mind what any of us thinks of Jesus. Such words, spoken aloud in the broad daylight, are treason."

Eleazar looked around at the small group of men gathered—five or six of us, all respected men in the town. "If we cannot trust each other, whom can we trust? We may not agree about Jesus, but surely we are all agreed about Rome and Herod."

Now others joined in telling Eleazar to be silent, to stifle his rash words. Of course we trusted each other; of course there was no spy in our midst. But still—one never knew for certain. We all knew of people who had been turned over to the authorities for speaking against Rome or against Herod. I had been still a young man when the Roman governor Varus took a bloody revenge on the rebels Judas and Zadok, but I remembered the bloodshed of those years, the two thousand crucifixions. Few people were as bold today as those Zealots. Few were as bold even as John the Baptizer, but it was possible to be arrested and perhaps flogged for careless words. We had learned in the last hundred years, most of us, to be a cautious people. Only fools like John and Jesus threw that caution aside.

Now, it seemed, there were more fools than wise men. "You may silence us here, Rabbi James, but such things are being said openly in Capernaum and Bethsaida, where Jesus has many followers. They talk of naming him King, and following him to Jerusalem to begin a revolution."

A chill shivered down my spine at those words. *King. Jerusalem. Revolution.* Deadly words, for Jesus and perhaps hundreds of others if they were fools enough to follow him.

"Then the men of Capernaum and Bethsaida are fools," I said firmly. "Such talk will not go unnoticed. No doubt Herod already knows of it, and Pilate, the Roman governor in Jerusalem, will hear of it soon if he has not yet. Believe me, nobody wants to attract the attention of Jerusalem."

"But there are men from Jerusalem in Capernaum already, asking about Jesus," someone said. "They were there when I visited a week ago. No doubt they will come to Nazareth soon, once they learn this is his home town."

I stood up, signaling an end to the discussion. "Jesus has not shown his face in Nazareth for months, and when he did come here, he was driven out of our synagogue," I said. "Any agents of Herod or the Romans will quickly learn that we have no sympathy for rebels here."

But my confident words could not quell the fears that troubled me. Every day I expected to see Roman soldiers tramping down our quiet village street, hammering at the gate of our house, demanding to question the brothers of the traitor Jesus.

When the visitors from Jerusalem did arrive in Nazareth, I almost laughed with relief. The men who had come to learn more about Jesus were no Roman agents, but Pharisees—learned men like myself, who were concerned to find out what Jesus was teaching and whether they should support or condemn the movement gathering around him. Four of them came to my house, and I welcomed them as honored guests. They told me that some of their fellows were still out in the wilderness with Jesus and his followers. "But we wanted to speak with you," one told me as we sat talking in the courtyard. The women and children ate in the far corner of the courtyard when we had guests, while Joseph, Benjamin, and I joined the Pharisees around the fire, enjoying the fine dinner that Ilana, Abigail, and Tabitha had provided for us

"When we learned that Jesus' own brother was a disciple of our honored Rabbi Eli, we knew we must meet you," said their leader, a man named Avram. "James the Just, we have heard you called, a title of great respect, indeed! But I recall now that you and I met many years ago, when we both studied under our teacher. I believe you left Jerusalem soon after I came there to study."

"Yes," I said. In truth I did not at all recognize the young man he must have been then, in this dignified rabbi who now sat before me. "Rabbi Eli, may God honor his memory and all his descendants, taught me almost all I know of the Law," I went on. "I have spent many years here in this quiet village, trying to further what I learned under his teaching. I wish I had been granted more years of study."

The men all nodded gravely; some of them had probably come from small rural villages, too, though likely in Judea rather than here in Galilee. But all of them had had what I had not: the opportunity to remain in the city, in that great center of learning, studying, and debating. While I taught village boys their letters so they could read a little Scripture on Shabbat in the synagogue, these men gathered their own young pupils around them in the porches of the Temple for learned discussions about the finer points of the Law. I yearned with all my heart to be among them, and I certainly did not want my brother's notoriety to cut me off from such society.

"What do you think of your brother Jesus and his teaching, Rabbi James?" Avram asked me.

I hesitated over my answer. "Jesus was always devout, as a boy," I said carefully, "and he has a great dedication to the Scriptures. But he was always willful, too, and inclined to do things his own way rather than following the counsel of his elders. He might have gone to Jerusalem and studied under one of the great rabbis himself. He reasons like a Pharisee, though I believe his leanings are more toward the school of Hillel than the school of Shammai, to which our revered master belonged. Instead, Jesus took up with John the Baptizer, a man as willful and independent as he is himself."

The Pharisees exchanged glances at the name of John, and one opened his mouth as if to speak, but Avram made a little gesture with his fingers, as if to put off that comment to another time, and said, "What you say fits with what we have seen of Jesus. We did not come to judge him harshly, you know, whatever his followers may say. They are quick to pick quarrels, just as John's disciples are—were. But we did not come to start any quarrel, only to learn and see for ourselves what kind of teaching Jesus was spreading."

"And? Now that you have seen?"

Again, they exchanged glances, and again it was Avram who spoke for the rest. "Truly, we do not know what to make of Jesus," he admitted. "In many ways he is one of us. He is, as you say, devoted to the Scriptures, and very learned. He teaches the resurrection from the dead, as we do. He preaches the rule of God and sends men back to study the Scriptures for themselves—and these are all good things. But the Sadducees say it is from among our Pharisee ranks that heretics like John and Jesus arise, and rebels like Zadok and Judas too. We must be careful, lest we be seen to be encouraging sedition."

"But his miracles!" another broke in. "We have seen these things for ourselves—the lame healed, the demon-possessed set free. Who could do these things if God were not with him?"

"Do not be so hasty to judge the work of God," Avram cautioned. He appealed to me. "Does not the Torah say that when Moses did mighty works before Pharaoh to show the power of God, the priests of Egypt were able to do the same works by the power of demons?

There are miracles, and then there is trickery."

"But I spoke myself with a friend of Jairus, the *hazzan* of Chorazin," said the younger man, whose name was Chaim. "Jairus's daughter was ill with a fever, and had actually been pronounced dead by the physicians, when Jesus came and raised her from the dead!"

"Oh, I have heard a similar story," I assured him, "but it was about a young boy from Nain, a widow's son. The man you spoke with was not present at this miraculous raising from the dead himself, was he?"

"No, but many have seen and reported it," Chaim insisted.

"Yes, as many saw and reported the incident at Nain," I reminded him. "That boy was supposed to have had a deadly fever too. Even if one story or the other is true, doctors do make mistakes. The poor child was surely not dead, but had merely lost consciousness and was fortunate enough to awake before being buried."

"I see you are a skeptic about your brother's so-called miracles," Avram said. He sounded approving, so I felt a little bolder about speaking my mind.

"I believe he has—some skill at healing," I said, unable to honestly deny what I had seen with my own eyes in Capernaum. "Whether it is of God, I will not judge. The wilder tales told about him—raising the dead, miraculously multiplying food, calming storms at sea—these are surely the gossip of superstitious people."

"It's what people want to believe," said my brother Joseph, who had been quiet until now. "They want a Deliverer, an anointed Prince, who can work wonders like Elijah, lead the people out of bondage like Moses, and rule justly like King David. They want to see all those things in Jesus."

"And they want to make him king," another of the rabbis said. He, too, had been quiet till now. "If anything, the ambitions of his followers are more dangerous than Jesus' own ambitions. I have heard him preach, and he does not call himself king or even Messiah. Indeed, I hear he has discouraged the people when they talk about making him king. But a man who commands the allegiance of the rabble as he does—well, such a man is dangerous whether he wants to be a king or not. He draws the attention of—" he lowered his voice, "those whose attention we do not wish to draw."

These were discreet men. There was no need to say more than that about our enemies; we all understood.

"That is our great fear," Avram admitted. "But there is still the question of Jesus himself to be dealt with as well. As I told you, I hardly know what to make of him. He enters into debate with us, and knows the Law as well as any rabbi I've ever seen. Yet some of his teaching is very strange—he teaches people to uphold the Law with one hand, and cast it down with another. He has no respect for traditions, or for purity. He calls men to repent and follow, but not to follow the Law—to follow him."

"He tramples upon the Law!" said another of the men. "He breaks the Shabbat and encourages his followers to do so! He does not follow our traditions or ceremonies—the very things that keep us distinct as a people, that allow us to continue being Jews even when we are under the rule of . . . of others. The traditions of Moses are far more important than the throne of David! Even if we never have a king of our own again, we will go on being God's chosen people as long as we keep ourselves holy and separate from the world. And this is exactly what Jesus doesn't understand! He talks of a kingdom of God that has room for everyone—the sinners, the unclean, the lepers, the tax collectors, even the Gentiles! He said that in the kingdom of God, the Gentiles will sit down with Abraham, Isaac, and Jacob and share the same meal! It's blasphemy!"

"Blasphemy is a serious charge, my brother, and not one to be tossed out lightly," Avram reminded him. "But, indeed, there is much in Jesus' teaching that we fear. He leads people astray. We have tried to warn him, but he is heedless of danger and argues with us when we try to make him see sense. He will bring the wrath of Herod and of Rome upon himself, just as John the Baptizer did."

Again, with the name of John, the rabbis exchanged glances. "What is it?" I asked. "Do you have some newer news of John's fate?"

"We heard just yesterday, as we passed by Tiberias," Avram said. Like me, they would not go into that Gentile city unless they had to. "We met travelers on the road who told us that John has been put to death—beheaded, we heard, as part of a celebration for Herod's birthday." He turned to spit on the ground as he said Herod's name, and I did, too, all caution gone for the moment. No matter what I thought of John himself, this was a slap in the face to all Jews. A Jewish teacher beheaded at a pagan birthday feast? It was unthinkable.

"Some of our fellows went back to seek out Jesus, to tell him the news," Avram said. "He must take warning from John's fate, be more cautious. This is not the time for any would-be Messiah to draw attention to himself. It could spell disaster for our whole nation—we have little enough freedom now, but things could be much worse."

I took the warning, but there was no reason to believe Jesus would take it, though I was sure he would grieve John's death. He might see it as a call to even more strident action, rather than to discretion. Discretion had never been his style.

But Avram was already thinking of something else, looking at the faces around the fire and the womenfolk as they came to clear away the remains of our meal. "I heard in Capernaum that Jesus had four brothers and three sisters," he said. "Do they all live here in Nazareth? Not all in this household, I can see."

"No, our sisters are all married and gone to their husbands' homes, and our brother Jude lives in the household of his wife's family," I said. "My brother Joseph lives here with his wife and children, and of course our honored mother, Mary, and my own children—and the wife and children of our brother Simon," I added with some reluctance.

"Ah yes, Simon. And where is your brother Simon?"

He was like a lawyer, asking a question to which he well knew the answer. If he had spent time among Jesus' followers, he would have known plenty about our family even before coming here, and had probably even met Simon. Two months had passed since our visit to Capernaum, and Simon had returned home to visit us twice in that time, but each time he had gone away again, saying that he wanted to learn more of what Jesus was teaching.

"My younger brother—is with Jesus," I admitted. "He wished to spend some time learning about his teachings—as you yourselves have done," I added.

"And what of you, young Joseph?" Avram pressed. "Or you, Benjamin? Do you admire your uncle Jesus and wish to follow him?"

My son, who, as befitted a boy of this age, had been silent all evening, looked startled to be addressed directly. "I follow my father's guidance in all things, Rabbi," he said.

"As well you should," Avram said, then turned back to Joseph. "And you, Joseph? With no father alive to guide you, which older brother do you follow? The wise James, who stays here in Nazareth and studies the Law, or Jesus?"

Joseph was silent for longer than I liked. Finally he said, "James is my eldest brother, and I am subject to him. I would not leave my wife and children to follow after Jesus, as Simon has done. But I—I confess that I have always trusted Jesus and would like to know more of what he is teaching the people. I understand why Simon has chosen to go with him."

"Of course you do, of course you do," Avram said. "But after our little talk this evening, perhaps you understand how such wishes could be dangerous? If more of those who were curious about Jesus would stay home, till their fields and catch their fish and follow their trades and obey the Law, we would not have so much to fear from our Gentile masters, would we?"

Joseph nodded silently, but I saw doubt etched on his face. Jesus was dividing our household. I feared for all of us, for the doom that might befall us. With all my heart I wished I were not caught in the middle of it.

For a long time now, I had wished Jesus would leave Galilee, go back to Judea, take his strange ideas and ambitions with him. Now I saw that he would not, that he was building something here and would not abandon it, even in the face of John's death—for I cherished no hope that this news would move him to caution. Instead, I wished I could be out of Galilee. I wished I could return to Jerusalem with these learned men, my true brothers. I wished I could abandon all the family ties that held me in Nazareth and devote myself to the study of the Scriptures in a place far from Galilee, far from Jesus.

I could not do it, of course. I was not such a man as Jesus' followers were, to abandon all responsibility for those who depended on me. But my heart wanted to be far from Galilee, and that night I prayed that if there were any way it could be possible, God would bring it to pass, that I might end my days in His service in Jerusalem.

Chapter Thirteen

My daughter Tabitha stood before me, her brown hair, heart-shaped face, and big eyes making her look the exact image of my dear wife when we were both young. Tabitha was only fourteen, younger than Rachel had been when we married. She was younger, to be truthful, than I generally liked to see girls married, although there were many fathers who felt differently. Had things been different, I might have waited a year or two.

Her hands clasped beneath her chin, she looked up at me with eager anticipation. "Do you have news for me, Abba?"

Despite my determination to discuss such a weighty matter with due seriousness, I smiled. She was fighting so hard not to look overly eager at the news of her prospective marriage. Since I had good news to share, I decided not to make her wait any longer.

"We have concluded the negotiations," I said. "The marriage is acceptable to Barak's father, and to me as well. We have agreed on a dowry and on a marriage date, six months from now. We can announce your betrothal at once."

Tabitha was usually a well-trained, reserved girl, but she could not restrain the impulse to launch herself into my arms with a happy cry. "Thank you, Abba, thank you!" I folded my arms around her, thinking of what a fortunate match this was. So many girls had to be forced into unhappy marriages, often with men much older than themselves, or with strangers with whom they had little in common. Tabitha and Barak had been childhood playmates, as he was the son of my cousin Samuel. As they grew to maturity and took on the roles appropriate for a young man and a young woman, they, of course, saw less of each other, but when they had the chance to catch a glimpse of each other at family gatherings, Tabitha always smiled and blushed when she saw Barak, and the few words they got to exchange were always pleasant ones.

All this, I must confess, Mary and Ilana had told me. Poor Tabitha had no mother of her own to look for such things, but her grandmother and aunts had filled that role well, and knew that she was fond of her young cousin—a handsome, respectful, hard-working boy just two years older than she. I had thought of nothing but the fact that I had a kinsman with a son of similar age to my daughter, and that it would be beneficial to strengthen the ties between our families. It was the women in the family who had told me that Tabitha's desires ran in the same direction mine did. Given the chance to make a good match that would also make her happy, I moved a bit more quickly than I might have otherwise.

Truth to be told, there was another motive. As I watched Tabitha dance away to tell Mary and the other women that the match was made and a betrothal party was to be planned, I wondered if I were being selfish in hurrying along my daughter's marriage. Once Tabitha was safely in her young husband's home, I would have one less responsibility, one less tie holding me in Nazareth.

In the weeks that had passed since the visit of Rabbi Avram and the other Pharisees, the dream of leaving Galilee and returning to Jerusalem had continued to tug at my imagination, though I did not see how it could ever be. Yet gradually, it seemed, events were falling into place.

Simon came home soon after the Pharisees had visited—this time to stay "at least for now," he told us.

"Have you given up on following Jesus, then?" I asked, more harshly than I intended.

He kept my gaze steadily. "Not at all, brother," he said. "I have followed him enough to know that what he says is true, and that the hand of God is upon him, perhaps in ways we cannot even imagine. But I have also realized that while he calls some people to leave everything behind and follow him, he calls others to go back to their homes and spread his message there. There is work for me to do in Nazareth, as well as my wife and children to care for."

"Did he reject you, then, as one of his disciples? Turn you away again—his own brother?"

Simon shook his head. "It is no good trying to make you understand, James, for you cannot. Your mind is closed to Jesus and all he has to say. If anyone is to open it, it will have to be Jesus himself. He has sent out many of his disciples, two by two, to go into different villages and preach and teach and heal, just as he does himself. But he sent me back here, back home to Nazareth. I can do his work here, until he comes here again himself."

"So you intend to take his part here, do you?" I challenged. "Your plan is to preach the same sedition and treason here in Nazareth, to stir up the same trouble, that Jesus is doing everywhere else? You'll have to think again about that, brother. I will not allow it."

"I'm sorry, James. Some things are higher than even an elder brother's authority. Whether you forbid me or not, I will continue to follow Jesus and share his message with others."

"So you are loyal to Jesus above me, even though I am head of this family?"

"Not loyal to Jesus above you, James. I am loyal to God's kingdom, and His call, above even the call of family."

I could scarcely contain my anger. He reminded me so much of Jesus then, of Jesus at the age of twelve coolly telling my father that he had thrown the whole family into consternation and upheaval because he was obeying the authority of his heavenly Father.

This was an idea that came straight from the lips of Jesus—that a person might owe allegiance to God that transcended the loyalty he owed to the head of his family, his clan, or the other authorities God had placed over him. It was an idea that, followed to its logical conclusion, would tear apart families and society itself. Now this poisonous idea that had begun in the heart of my own family was spreading to the rest of my brothers. I could see young Joseph, and even my own son, Benjamin, eyeing Simon with interest as he calmly stood his ground and told me he would not obey me.

This had to stop.

"Enough!" I roared. I so seldom raised my voice that it caught the attention of everyone in the house, including the women and children, who moved closer to see what the conflict between Simon and me was all about. I wanted to reach out and seize him by the front of his robe and shake him, but I held back. Violence would do no good here. I kept my voice raised, though, because I wanted everyone to hear this.

"If you defy my authority, Simon, then you are outcast to me just as Jesus is. You cannot dwell in this household and not respect your elder brother. You may be a grown man, but I am still the head of this family, and I say that you will lay aside this nonsense of following Jesus and spreading his message, or else you will pack your bags and leave this house. Go back to Jesus. See if he will take you in and feed you—yes, and your wife and children too!" I had no desire to punish Ilana and the little ones, against whom I held no grudge, but I had to make it clear to Simon that I was serious about this. He could not continue to reap the benefits of family, leaving me to care for his children, while refusing the responsibilities. "All of you will have to go if you do not agree to turn your backs on Jesus."

Simon looked at me for a long, grave moment. "I'm sorry you feel that way, James. I looked forward to returning home, but if you insist, I will leave again. Only allow me some time to prepare to depart with Ilana and the children, and we will be gone."

I heard a quickly stifled cry of protest and looked over to see Mary with her arms around Ilana, both women looking distraught. I knew I had caused Mary much grief by declaring that Jesus was cut off from our family—though in truth, I thought she should blame Jesus, not me, for that suffering. And now I was giving her even greater sorrow by banishing another of her sons. Where would this division and heartbreak end?

Simon turned to cross the courtyard to his weeping wife and mother, while I went in the opposite direction, out of the house altogether to the peace of the synagogue, where I could sit alone among the scrolls of Scripture and ask God why He allowed such trouble to come upon my family.

I found no easy answers that night. Instead, I found myself searching the scrolls for prophecies of a Messiah, looking for anything that might justify people's belief that Jesus was the One they had hoped and waited for.

When I returned home, I found the children in bed and the rest of the adults talking in low tones around the dying embers of the cooking fire. Simon, far from being an outcast, was part of the warm confiding circle—his wife, Ilana; Joseph and his wife, Abigail; and Mary. From the looks they gave me as I entered the courtyard, I realized that it was I, not Simon, who was the outsider here. They all sympathized with him rather than with me; they were all at least interested in the message of Jesus, if not ready to declare themselves open followers of his way.

I bypassed the family gathering and went straight to my bed, after going past the children's sleeping rolls to see that while Tabitha was sound asleep, Benjamin lay with his eyes closed, feigning sleep. I was sure he was troubled by the discord he had witnessed, but I did not know what I could say to him right now. At least he was here rather than down in the courtyard with the rest of them.

As I lay down, I contemplated the paths open to me. I could continue to assert my authority in this house where, increasingly, everyone disagreed with me. I could turn Simon and Ilana and their children out, and face the resentment of Joseph, Abigail, and Mary. How would it end? Would I send my last brother and his family away, too, if they chose to follow Jesus? What about Mary? I could hardly set an aging woman out on the streets, telling her to beg mercy from her son the wandering rabbi, who did not have a roof over his head and slept on the ground as many nights as he did in a house. How could I do that to Mary? Yet would she bend her will to mine? She was a woman, but a fiercely determined one.

There was, I realized, another path. One that freed me from all this conflict, from the difficult path of asserting an authority my family would not recognize. One that would ease my mind and give me what I wanted most. It would require a loss of honor, for I would have to back down from what I had said to Simon in front of everyone, but that, at least, could be kept within the family. I could couch my retreat in terms that would make it seem I had reconsidered and found a better way. I had only to consider what I would do about my own two children, for there was no way I would leave them in this nest of vipers where everyone was so quick to follow Jesus and disobey me. Once they were taken care of, I would be free.

So I sought Simon out in the morning and told him I had been too hasty, that I did not want to divide the family or turn him and his children out of doors. "I ask only that you do not stir up trouble if you can avoid it," I said, "while we see if we can find a peaceful way through this conflict that divides our family. With the news of John's death, we all know that the Herodians and perhaps the Romans themselves are watching Jesus and his followers. Speak of Jesus if you must, but be cautious and discreet, so that you do not bring trouble upon him."

Simon agreed to that, and we continued in an uneasy truce. But during the weeks that followed, I carefully dropped hints that I was dreaming of a return to Jerusalem—a long sojourn, in which I might study further with the learned rabbis there and deepen my own knowledge of the Law. I spoke of taking Benjamin with me, so that he, too, might enjoy the benefits of learning in the great city. And I began speaking to my cousin Samuel, Barak's father, about a match between my daughter and his son.

All this had unfolded over several weeks since the rabbis from Jerusalem had visited to find out more about Jesus. Now, with the marriage contract concluded and Tabitha in a flutter of excitement about her marriage plans, I was finally free to contemplate my own future.

I wrote a letter to Rabbi Avram, telling him that I wished to return to Jerusalem and dedicate my remaining years to the study of the Law. I would be bringing my son, whom I hoped could train to be a scribe.

That part of the letter was easy to write. I knew I should also add something about Jesus, but I was less sure what would be safe to say—to Avram himself, but also to anyone else who might read the letter before it found its way into his hands. After scratching several lines on a wax tablet and starting over half a dozen times, I finally transferred the following lines to my scroll.

> I share your concerns about that member of my family of whom we have spoken in the past. I do not think his enterprise will end well. He has turned his back on our family, and I no longer consider him my responsibility. My greatest prayer is that our land may continue to enjoy peace under the protection of God and our rulers.

That, I thought, struck the right tone of pious concern, while assuring him that I had no ties to Jesus—and, at the same time, mentioning no names that might incriminate me.

It was some time before his reply came, my letter winding its way in the packs of various travelers on the road south, and his making the same journey back. During those months, Jesus continued to preach and teach around Galilee, though he made no more visits to Nazareth. The tension in our household did not decrease, though I tried not to openly argue with Simon, or Mary or Joseph—who increasingly joined in supporting Jesus. Even Jude, I thought, was weakening, becoming convinced by the news he heard of Jesus' miracles, though unlike the others he had not gone to hear Jesus preach.

The miracles drew people's attention, but it seemed to be those who had heard Jesus preach, especially those who spent some time in his presence, who came back fully convinced that he was a prophet, a rabbi, and perhaps even Israel's Deliverer. I cannot tell you how many times in those last months at home the thought came to me that perhaps I, too, would go listen, just to hear what Jesus had to say. But I always pushed that thought firmly to one side. Had I not spent a lifetime listening to Jesus? None of his words ever made any sense. He might sway the ignorant rabble, but his honeyed words would never convince me to become his follower.

The sooner I got out of Galilee, I thought, the better.

Rabbi Avram's letter finally came, just a week before we celebrated Tabitha's wedding. He warmly invited me and Benjamin to stay with him and study with him whenever we came to Jerusalem, and he assured me that I could earn my bread there, as so many rabbis did, teaching young boys their letters and the basics of the Law.

As I had done, he added a few cautious sentences about Jesus, naming no names.

> That kinsman of yours should know that there are many in Jerusalem who know his name and hear of his doings with interest. It is not always good for a man's name to be known in high places.

I shuddered as I read his words, but I felt no obligation to pass the warning on to Simon or anyone else who might give it to Jesus. He had been warned enough. What mattered in this letter was that Rabbi

Avram thought there might be a place for me in Jerusalem. That was good enough for me. When the wedding feast was over—Jesus did not come home for this wedding—and Tabitha was settled happily with her husband's family, I told Simon and Joseph that I would take Benjamin to Jerusalem.

"When will you return?" Simon said.

"I have no plans to return. I want to study the Law, to raise my son to manhood there among learned men." I tried to keep bitterness from my voice as I said, "I am done with Nazareth, brother. My responsibility to my daughter has ended, my son will come with me, Mary has you and Joseph to care for her. The men of the synagogue can choose someone else to lead prayers and teach the boys—either you or Joseph could do it, or Eleazar ben Zimri, or our cousin Samuel. I have a chance to fulfill a dream, and I am going to take it."

Simon nodded. "All that you say is true, James, and you have every right to go to Jerusalem, of course. Joseph and I are more than able to take care of our mother. But is it really your dream that is drawing you to Jerusalem, or Jesus' dream that drives you out of Galilee?"

"Perhaps both," I admitted. "I have worked hard all my life to be a good scholar, a good Jew, a good carpenter, a good father, brother, and son. It is hard for me to live in a place where even those who have known me for years think of me first, now, as the brother of Jesus. If I agreed with his teaching, as you do, I might not care. But I am my own man, and I will not be known around Galilee as 'James, the brother of Jesus,' especially when Jesus brings shame on the family name and danger upon himself."

Simon only nodded and said, "We have spoken enough about this—it may be that we will never agree. I wish you well in Jerusalem."

I said my farewells to the rest of the household. I visited my sisters who still lived in the village, and my newly married daughter, and some of the men who had been my good friends for years. All seemed surprised and sorry that I would leave, but they all wished God's blessings upon me in Jerusalem. Then one morning after the spring rains, while the farmers gathered in the summer wheat, I packed my few belongings onto a donkey purchased for the journey, took my son with me, and set my face toward Jerusalem.

Chapter Fourteen

Both Benjamin and I fell quickly into the routine of our new lives. Rabbi Avram made me welcome as part of his circle, renting us two rooms in his large city house—he was a wealthy man—and finding me a few pupils. He also chose one of his scribes to become Benjamin's teacher. With such a patron to introduce me into Jerusalem society, I quickly ceased to feel like an ignorant northerner and began to consider the city my home.

Each morning I walked, sometimes in Rabbi Avram's company, to the Temple in the heart of the city. For so long the Temple had been a far-off, unattainable symbol of God's presence, to be visited only on rare occasions. Now it was my daily place of prayer, work, and study.

Each morning I went there to worship, observing the dawn sacrifice and joining other worshipers in prayers and psalms. Then I found my place in one of the Temple porticos, where I met my small group of students. We would unroll a scriptures scroll—a portion of the Torah or one of the prophets—and spend hours discussing it, as I patiently pointed out the many possible levels of meaning in the text. I recited to them the opinions of great rabbis of the past who had discussed this text, and they repeated my words, learning the opinions of these great men by rote so that they, too, could someday pass them on and apply them to their own study of Scripture.

So one day we might read the Law of Moses on the subject of divorce, for example, and I would recite for them the opposing opinions of the great rabbis Shammai and Hillel on the subject. I would coax forth their own thoughts and opinions, then explain why the view of Shammai was correct, and lead them in memorizing his commentary. In this way we worked through portions of the Torah each day and learned the teachings of the rabbis who had gone before us.

Generally I met my students in the morning and took a little light refreshment at noon, buying some food from one of the many stalls set up in the outer court of the Temple. It was somewhat disconcerting, now that I was there each day, to remember that the Temple was as much a place of business as of worship: the outer court was more like a bustling market than a place of prayer. I did not think this was right, but I purchased food there for convenience, as often as other rabbis did, from the little stalls and booths that vendors had squeezed in among the more official tables where people exchanged Roman coins for Temple shekels and purchased animals for sacrifice.

In the heat of the day, I might return to Avram's house for a rest, but more often I simply found a shady spot within the Temple precincts where I could read or rest. Later in the day, as the shadows lengthened and everything became cooler, I returned to the inner court to join one of the many groups of men who met to discuss Scripture and the events of the day.

By joining myself to the school of Avram, I identified myself as a Shammaite Pharisee; there were other groups and schools of thought among the Pharisees, one of the most influential being those who gathered about Rabbi Gamaliel, grandson of the Rabbi Shammai's great rival Rabbi Hillel. We discussed and debated among ourselves, but there was also debate with non-Pharisees, especially with the Sadducees, who held so much of the power in Temple circles, as most of the priests came from that party.

Lively debate often sprang up among different groups, with every man adding Scripture verses or quotes from the ancient rabbis to underline his arguments. These debates usually began with passages from Scripture and obscure points of law: What type of work was permissible on the Shabbat? Did God send angels to intervene in human affairs? But they often moved to events unfolding in the world around us: Was John the Baptizer right to have defied Herod, and should he be honored as a martyr for his death, just as the Maccabees and other holy men of the past had been? What about those who rose up in open revolt against the Romans, such as Zealots? Was it our duty to condemn them or support them? Should we pay taxes to the Romans and participate in their censuses? And most important of all, would God ever send us a Deliverer as He had promised to set us free from these foreign oppressors?

Of course, all these issues had to be addressed cautiously, often in very dry, scholarly language, to avoid the appearance of discussing anything treasonous. Even so, it was obvious to me that many of the learned rabbis in Jerusalem, as well as those who visited from outside the city, were impatient with our leaders' practice of always appeasing and obeying the Romans. They longed for leaders who would stand up for Israel.

I had been in Jerusalem only a few weeks when I first heard Jesus' name enter one of these discussions. We were talking about the Messiah, again, and one of the rabbis said, "Of course, the Galileans would have us believe the Messiah has come already." A ripple of laughter went around the group of men at the mention of Galilee; I was among men I did not know well that day and said little, so none of them knew I was a northerner. Mostly, in these gatherings, I listened and tried to learn, and I certainly did not want to say anything now that would brand me a Galilean, much less a relative of Jesus.

"You mean this Jesus from Nazareth?" said another. "A harmless fool! I've heard him speak—he doesn't even teach the Law like a rabbi. He tells stories, as if he were entertaining children! A storyteller, nothing more!"

"Don't be so quick to write off storytellers," another said. "These parables of his seem simple enough, but they are full of hidden meanings, and they are very subversive."

"Ah, but whom do they subvert? The Romans? Herod?"

"And ourselves!" another replied. "Have you not heard of Jesus calling the religious leaders of Israel a nest of snakes?"

"No, it was John the Baptizer who said that," another corrected. "Jesus says we are whitewashed tombs, beautiful on the outside but full of corruption within."

The tone was light, almost merry, as though none of them took Jesus seriously, but there were a few dissenting voices. "You write him off too easily," said the man who had spoken before. "Maybe he is a fool as you say, but a fool can be dangerous. The danger is not in his stories alone but in the crowds he attracts and the wonders he works. The Galileans will follow such a man anywhere—and don't be deceived, it's not just Galilee. He has followers even here in Judea, and if he were to come back here and work the wonders he has worked in the north, he would have hundreds of followers all over the land."

Amid the lively discussion that broke out in response to this, one dry, quiet voice cut across the conversation. Though the gray-bearded rabbi did not speak loudly, everyone hushed to listen to him. "Perhaps you write Jesus off too lightly in another way," he said. "What if there is truth in what he says? Is it so impossible that he *is* the One for whom we have waited?"

After a moment's silence, another of the men said, "I have great respect for you, Nicodemus, but not for the words you have just spoken. How could we take Jesus seriously as a Messiah? A Galilean? Surely you know that the prophet Micah says, 'But you, Bethlehem Ephrathah, though you are small among the clans of Judah, out of you will come for me one who will be ruler over Israel.' Our future Deliverer will arise right here in Judea, in the shadow of the Temple, in the town of King David."

Nicodemus simply stroked his beard as other voices rose around him. He was the most highly respected and influential man present, a member of the Sanhedrin, a wealthy man of great power and authority. When Nicodemus spoke, people listened. Many seemed shocked to hear him raise the possibility that Jesus might actually be the Messiah. Indeed, I was surprised myself to hear such words coming from an educated Jerusalem rabbi.

"He is a nobody!" one man said. "He wanders about the countryside, eats with Gentiles, has men and women together among his followers, consorts with the worst kind of sinners, and ignores all our teaching about righteousness."

"He has no learning!" another said. "Has he ever sat here among us, learning from his elders? Does he ever quote the opinions of the great rabbis of the past? Some call him a Hillelite, but I have never heard of him appealing to Rabbi Hillel for his authority. This Jesus speaks as if his authority comes straight from God."

"He is from a peasant family, carpenters or fishermen or some such," said another. "No noble blood, and even what bloodline he has is not pure. I have heard Galileans tell me on good authority he is illegitimate, born outside of the marriage bed."

Nicodemus continued listening as the rabbis piled one charge against another against Jesus. Finally he said, "In the prophet Isaiah it is written of God's servant, 'He had no beauty or majesty to attract us to him, nothing in his appearance that we should desire him. He was despised and rejected by men, like one from whom men hide their faces, we esteemed him not.' Yet it is also written in the same place, 'The will of the LORD will prosper in his hand.'"

"Are you saying you believe Jesus of Nazareth is God's Anointed?" one rabbi finally asked Nicodemus directly.

Nicodemus took a long time about his reply, stroking his beard. "Any man who says he thinks Jesus is the Messiah places himself at great risk," he said finally. "I would not take such a risk without more certainty, but I think we are too quick to condemn him. Do you want to be remembered as the rabbis who turned their backs on the Messiah when God finally sent Him?"

There was an uneasy silence until one of the Sadducees said, "If we do not condemn him, then Pilate will say that we are supporting revolutionaries. You Pharisees have traveled that road before, in our fathers' time, and we know where it leads. Do you want to see Roman soldiers desecrating this holy place? Thousands of crosses outside the city walls? Everything we have now"—he waved his hand to indicate the Temple, its greatness and glory—"could all be gone in a moment, torn to the ground. We cannot risk supporting anyone who defies the Romans."

"Then how will God ever send us a Deliverer?" Nicodemus asked. "You have just said yourself we can never risk following anyone who would truly set us free." With that he rose and walked out, leaving everyone with much to think about.

After that I heard similar discussions about Jesus among the Pharisees. A few, like Nicodemus, urged the rest not to judge him too hastily, but most were firmly opposed to Jesus—or to what they had heard of him. Most had never seen him or heard him speak. His great popularity had come only after he left Judea and went north, so he was not well known in Jerusalem, except by reputation.

Still, that reputation was enough for me to ask Avram and the other men who had met me in Nazareth not to reveal my family connection to Jesus. I warned Benjamin not to speak of it either. I had come south partly to escape talk of Jesus, only to find he was being talked of here too. But I thought I could at least keep myself apart from it, keep from being identified with him. And I had no idea how much support he really had in Judea, until I went to Bethany to visit my friend Simon.

Rabbi Simon, the son of my old master Rabbi Eli, still lived in Bethany. I had seen him once or twice on his visits to Jerusalem, and he had always invited Benjamin and me to come stay with him in Bethany sometime. Finally I decided, in the middle of summer, to take advantage of his offer.

Farmers outside the city were harvesting dates as Benjamin and I made the short journey to Bethany, where Simon welcomed us warmly. He looked older than when I had seen him last, and a little thinner and paler, too, as though he was not well. But he made no mention of poor health when we talked. We met his wife and two young daughters, and he asked about all my family and was pleasant and encouraging to young Benjamin. After we shared the evening meal, Benjamin went out into the village to meet a few lads his own age he had met earlier in the day, and Simon and I dug deeper into our conversation.

"And your notorious half-brother is still—notorious?" he said, delicately. He had not mentioned Jesus when talking about the rest of the family.

"Sadly, yes. I do not advertise my connection to him," I admitted, "for I would rather not have it known in Jerusalem."

"No, there are many of our brethren in Jerusalem who would be less likely to welcome you into their midst if they knew you were Jesus' brother," Simon chuckled. "On the other hand, there are many here in Bethany who would welcome you with open arms for such a connection."

"Truly? There are people here who admire Jesus?"

"More than just admire him; there are many here who count themselves his followers."

"Really? But Jesus has not even been in Judea since—how long? Two years, nearly, isn't it?"

"It has been nearly that long since John was first arrested and Jesus left for Galilee, although he and some of his closest followers have returned for a visit once or twice—at festival times, I think," Simon said. He paused, rubbing a hand across his face and over his head as if he were very weary. "But those who are loyal to him maintain their loyalty even in his absence. Tomorrow you will meet my kinsman Lazarus at the synagogue, and perhaps we will visit with him at his home in the afternoon. Then you will meet some devoted followers of Jesus, Lazarus and his sister, Martha."

The next day was Shabbat, and Simon had invited me to read the scripture passage and speak to the people. I read the portion from Genesis about Joseph's brothers selling him into slavery and discussed the views of some different rabbis who had commented on the story over the years. I ended by reciting the words of my old master, Rabbi Eli, "the father of your own good Rabbi Simon, who taught me in Jerusalem many years ago," I added by way of introduction. Rabbi Eli's words exhorted us to trust in God just as Joseph had done, for His will would be proved triumphant in the end.

This was what I loved—the feeling of being part of a great chain of tradition, of men who for centuries had read these scrolls, discussed and debated their meaning, and taught their students. Yet this was the very thing, it seemed, that people were willing to toss aside in their eagerness for Jesus. Though he preached Scripture, he preached it as though it were a new scroll he had opened that very morning, as if God had spoken to him directly. He stood outside that stream of tradition that I so valued, silencing all those voices of learned discussion and debate, those voices raised in prayer and faith throughout all the hardships of our people.

I wasn't the only one comparing my own preaching to that of Jesus. After the synagogue service, Simon and I walked to the home of his cousin Lazarus, where we were invited to take the noon meal. Lazarus, of course, knew from our previous meeting that Jesus was my brother, and he could not wait to turn the discussion toward his beloved teacher.

"You see, Rabbi James, you spoke well enough in the synagogue this morning—a fine little homily, as nice as anything I've heard over the years from Rabbi Simon here, or many another teacher. But you say, Rabbi so-and-so says this, and Rabbi such-and-such says that. This word means one thing, and this one means another, and it's all as dry as the parchment it's written on. No offense, you know. Now, when Jesus talks, he might start with a text from Scripture—'You have heard it said this way . . .' but then he goes on and tells you what *he* thinks about it, what message *he* has for us, as though he'd just been talking to God at the village gate that morning. Then he tells a story that drives home the point of it, and by the time he's finished talking, it's as if he's pulled aside a curtain allowing you to see into a whole new world."

I thought of Jesus standing in the synagogue at Nazareth and saying, "Today this scripture is fulfilled in your hearing," and of the power and authority with which he spoke. To me, that authority showed a brash disregard for tradition, but I could see how it might appeal to some hearers, especially those who were rebels at heart, who wanted to throw off tradition—or perhaps, those who were simply too ignorant to understand it.

"And what is this new thing he is preaching, Lazarus?" I pressed. "You have heard him speak, enough that you call yourself his friend and follower. Can you tell me what it is he is teaching?"

Lazarus paused for a moment. "That the kingdom of God has begun, here and now. That he himself is bringing it to us, and that it is a kingdom not of laws but of love. Not that it is lawless—" he added hastily, seeing me about to interject, "for Jesus says that God's Torah will never pass away till heaven and earth pass—but only that the heart of the Law is loving our neighbors, and that when we love one another and share what we have, God is among us."

"And what is this coming kingdom, then? Does it involve revolution? Overthrowing Herod, driving out Pilate and the Roman legions?"

Lazarus frowned. "Jesus never advocates war or violence. But I believe he is the rightful King of Israel, the One born to sit on David's throne."

I was about to ask how he thought such a thing might be achieved without war and violence, but we paused in our talk for a moment as Lazarus's sister and a servant came in to bring more food. Lazarus introduced us to his sister, whose name was Martha, and she smiled briefly at me as she inclined her head in respect: hers was a serious face that looked as if it were not much accustomed to smiling. She was not a young girl by any means, probably well into her thirties, and I wondered if she were a widow, to be living with her brother and keeping house for him. After she withdrew, I asked Lazarus about his family, as much to turn the conversation away from Jesus as anything.

"Father and Mother died some years ago, and none of us children have ever married," he said. That was strange in any family, unless there were some disability or deformity that kept people from marrying, and neither Lazarus nor his sister looked as if that were the case.

He sensed my unspoken question, and said, "To tell the truth, Rabbi James—"

Simon made an awkward noise, something between a cough and clearing his throat, and shot Lazarus a warning glance. Lazarus only smiled and passed him a bowl of figs.

"I have no shame to speak of it, cousin, not anymore. We are freed from our shame, thanks to Jesus," Lazarus said.

"Well, perhaps. But still, some things are not to be talked about—"

"Outside the family?" Lazarus finished with another smile. "But indeed, cousin, our family was the talk of the village for many years. Why should we not shout it from the rooftops when we have glad news? You see, Rabbi James, our family was in disgrace for many years. I have another sister, Mary, younger than Martha and I. When she was just a girl, she was possessed by a demon. We do not know why, for we were always a devout family, and she was not a bad girl—a bit willful, perhaps, but nothing to deserve such a punishment as came upon her. Under the influence of her demons, she behaved—well, in ways that were shameful to the family. To the community. In the end she went away, into Galilee. We heard no more of her for many years, but the taint of having such a child in the family—it shadowed over us. It kept my father, and later me, from being able to make a good match for Martha. As for myself, well, the few families who would have accepted me for their daughters were not families I wished to join. And so we have kept apart, nursing our private shame. We treated our sister Mary as though she were dead."

"I am sorry to hear it," I said.

"It was a heavy burden to bear, for Martha more than for me, because women are cruelest in their talk about such things. Some hinted that if her sister was demon possessed and immoral, Martha might be no better. Anyone who knows Martha knows that nothing could be further from the truth."

I cast a discreet glance across the courtyard at Martha, who now sat in the shade taking a brief moment of Shabbat rest. She was an attractive woman, and certainly seemed, from the brief glimpses I'd had of her, to be a model of womanly modesty and deportment. What a shame her life had been blighted by her sister's disgrace!

"But you spoke of your shame being ended," I prompted Lazarus. "What has happened to your sister Mary?"

His face brightened. "She returned home, just a few months ago," he said. "For the first time since she was a girl, it was as if, when I looked at her, I actually saw her, rather than the spirits that filled her. Her eyes were clear and she was in her right mind. She said she had met Jesus, and he had cast out all her demons and had forgiven her sins. Now she is one of his most dedicated followers. What a joy it was to see her healed!"

"So, is she here in Bethany now?"

"No, she returned to Galilee. She is one of those who travels with Jesus wherever he goes." Amazingly, Lazarus, who had spoken of the shame his demon-possessed sister had already brought upon the family, seemed to see no shame in the fact that she was now traveling around the countryside, an unmarried woman in a largely male crowd. The women among Jesus' followers puzzled me. The married women who had followed their husbands I could understand to some degree, but unwed women like Lazarus's sister Mary, or those like Joanna who had left their husbands' side to join this ragtag band of disciples, were a mystery to me. Their behavior seemed to suggest either the worst kind of immorality—like the camp followers who traveled with armies into battle—or else as if they were aping the roles and privileges of men, studying under a rabbi. The whole thing was very strange, yet Lazarus seemed quite at ease with the idea of his sister traveling in such company. I could only assume that after what they had been through with her, being a disciple of Jesus was mild by comparison.

Simon, unlike Lazarus, seemed anxious to steer the conversation away from the missing sister. No doubt as a kinsman of much higher social standing, he found the family disgrace particularly galling. But though we stopped talking about Mary, we could not stop talking about Jesus. He intruded his way into every conversation, despite my discomfort with the subject. Lazarus loved to talk about his would-be Messiah, and even Simon, though no disciple, was curious. They both wondered if Jesus would return to Judea.

I shrugged. "I am not the man to ask," I said. "I have had little contact with my family since coming to Jerusalem, and none at all with Jesus." I did not want to tell these men, friendly though they were, about the depth of the rift between Jesus and me. But their interest in him made me uneasy, as if I could feel his long arm reaching down from Galilee to trouble my Jerusalem life.

Chapter Fifteen

A messenger arrived at my lodgings one evening with a travel-worn scroll that he said came from my brother in Galilee. When I unrolled it, I saw that it was from Jude.

> Joseph, Simon, and I are coming to Jerusalem for Tabernacles. Simon urged Jesus to come with us, but he says his time is not right. I do not know what he means by that. Women and children are staying home.

It was a cryptic missive, but then Jude was never one to write long letters. His message gave me time to prepare for my brothers' arrival, though I did not need to arrange for sleeping quarters at Avram's house since we would all be sleeping in booths during the festival. Benjamin and I simply planned to build a somewhat larger sukkah than we would have done if it were just the two of us. I was glad Jude was coming, and Simon and Joseph as well, despite the division between us; festivals are always times for family to come together, and it would be good to have some of mine with me in this far place.

But the few words about Jesus worried me. Was he trying to warn me that Jesus might come and cause trouble? I fervently hoped he would not. If, by saying his time was not yet come, he meant that he was not yet ready to incite his followers to revolution, then I hoped it would be many, many years before the "right time" ever came.

Of all the festivals, Tabernacles has the truest family time, especially in the countryside, where farming families celebrate the end of harvest. My memories of sleeping outside under the leafy canopy of the sukkah my father built went back to my earliest childhood. Even during the years in Alexandria, we had gathered with other Jewish families to build our booths outside the city and observe the feast.

Memories of feasts past wove together in my mind as Benjamin and I wove the palm and willow branches together to make the booth we would share with my brothers. I remembered Benjamin's earliest childhood, when his mother was still alive. Tabitha was a baby at Rachel's breast and Benjamin a child on my lap as we gathered with my father and Mary and the rest of the family, watching the stars come out one by one before retreating inside the booth to sleep. I cast back for my own earliest memories of Sukkot and those were bittersweet, too, for I could remember my own mother who, like Rachel, had been taken from us too early. She loved Tabernacles, I remember, unlike some of my friends' mothers who complained about the discomfort and inconvenience of sleeping outdoors. My laughing, red-haired mother would lean back, supporting herself on her wrists and raising her face to the sky, and say, "Joseph, we should become nomads! We should sleep in booths always!"

Then another memory surfaced, long buried, of later years when she was gone. This must have been one of our Egyptian Sukkots, for I remembered that Mary was there with my father, Jesus was a little boy, and Rebecca just a baby. I remembered the smell of the sea air in Alexandria, so different from home.

I must have been—what, thirteen, fourteen? Perhaps a little older, but not much more than that. Jesus was running about and talking a great deal by then, precocious for a child of his age, everyone always said. One night we sat in the booth, and I recall watching the sun set through the palm branches. Jesus sat down beside me, his head against my arm, and said, "Why are we sleeping outdoors?"

So I began to tell him the old story, even though I knew my father and Mary had told him before. How once our people had lived in this land, in Egypt where we were, not as strangers like we were, but as slaves. How they, like we, had had a true home in another land far away that God had promised to lead them to. How Moses, the great deliverer, led them out, and how they wandered forty years in the wilderness, sleeping in tents and shelters made of boughs or animal skins. How God brought them at last to their true home, the land of promise, and commanded them once every year, when they went to the fields to gather in their harvests, to sleep in booths to remind themselves that God had brought them from a place of wandering to their homeland.

"But where is the homeland?" Jesus asked.

I pointed to the northeast, generally toward where I thought Israel was. "It's the land of Israel, where you were born. We come from a place called Galilee, and someday we'll go back there."

"So we'll be like Moses' people, going home?" Jesus asked.

"Yes—someday." I did not know then my father's plans, although after his last Passover visit to Jerusalem he had told us of the horrific violence in Jerusalem, the rebellions against Herod's son Archelaus. My father had determined then that if we went home, it would not be back to Bethlehem, where we had lived for a time after Jesus' birth, nor anywhere in Judea as long as Archelaus ruled there. He spoke of our old home of Nazareth, in Galilee, a land that in those days was more peaceable than Judea, under the rule of King Herod's son Herod Antipas.

"I would like to be like Moses," Jesus said. "To be a great leader and lead God's people to a new land."

I had laughed—I remembered that now—and brushed his hair with my hand. "Perhaps someday you will, little brother."

Such harmless words they seemed then, but how deep the roots of his ambition had gone! I wished I could enjoy the pleasant memory—

I had so few of Jesus from boyhood—without thinking about his present-day ambitions and the people who saw him as a new Moses or a new David. How he had loved those stories as a child! Most little Jewish boys do, of course, but few grow up to imagine themselves messiahs.

The day before the feast began, my three brothers arrived in Jerusalem and found their way to my lodgings. I embraced all three warmly and asked after the women and children, determined that our disagreements over Jesus would not keep us apart or become the main focus of our time together.

We went to the Temple service for the first day of the feast and watched as the priests performed the morning sacrifice on the altar, then poured a pitcher of water over the altar, praying for life-giving rains. With the other worshipers we recited the Sukkot prayers as we paraded around the court bearing our branches of willow, palm, and myrtle. Then we joined the throng of pilgrims dancing and singing in the streets as we returned to our own sukkah.

Perhaps because they were trying to be discreet around me, there was no mention of Jesus, though I got plenty of news from home: Naomi was expecting a baby, Tabitha was happy and well settled in her new husband's home, Joseph's and Abigail's new baby was a healthy boy, the harvest in the village had been good. Of course they came, as we always did at festival time, with the little money they could scrape together and a list of things the women hoped they could find in the Jerusalem markets.

During the daytimes my brothers visited the Temple and the city with me, and each evening we retired to the sukkah. On the second evening, I heard the first mention of Jesus' name, not intended for my ears, when Joseph quietly said to Simon, "I think Jesus is in the city."

It was Jude who responded; like me, he had overheard. "What? He said he would not come!"

"If he did, he would not have told you, Jude," Joseph said. It was the first hint of tension I'd seen between my brothers since their arrival. "He knew you were mocking him, trying to bait him to come here for the feast."

"Mocking? Certainly not," Jude said. "I only told him the plain truth—if he wants to spread his message and gather more followers, he needs to be in Jerusalem during the feasts. That's when people from all over Israel can hear him and judge for themselves what they think."

"Yes, and that's when he can attract attention from those who want to bring him down," Simon said. "He's wise to stay away, I think. And Jude, he doesn't believe you have his best interests at heart."

Jude shrugged. "It's not my fault if he doesn't trust me. Anyway, you say he's come after all, so perhaps he listened to me."

"I'm sure I saw Judas Iscariot in the market today," Joseph said. "And I heard a tale from some man who claimed his neighbor's wife was healed of her deafness by a Galilean rabbi with the gift of healing."

Simon nodded. "Those two signs surely point to Jesus. I wonder if he is in the city but trying to keep his presence a secret?"

I hoped they were wrong, that Jesus was not in the city. But the next day at the Temple, we found the outer court more crowded than was usual even for a festival. Seated on a rough block of stone right there in the Court of the Gentiles, amid money changers and booths selling animals for sacrifice, sat Jesus. His strong, clear voice carried well even in that busy place, and that was a good thing, for a hundred or more people had pressed close to hear him speak.

Joseph and Simon immediately joined the group around Jesus. Jude and I hung back, watching and listening.

Of course, the unusual sight of a rabbi teaching out here in the outer court soon attracted the attention of the learned men who occupied the inner courts, and I was not surprised before long to see a group of Pharisees, including my friend Avram, approach the crowded circle of Jesus' hearers. They listened to what he had to say, but withdrew again after a time into the inner court, shaking their heads and talking amongst themselves.

I followed them, leaving my brothers behind to listen to Jesus. I attached myself to Avram, and he acknowledged my presence with a glance. I hoped he would respect our longstanding agreement not to reveal my relationship to Jesus among the other rabbis.

"If he wants to present his teachings, to talk about his view of Scripture, he belongs in here, in the inner courts, with us!" one of Avram's associates insisted as I caught up to the group.

"No," Avram said firmly. "This is the one place he does *not* belong. He is not one of us; he will never be one of us. We should not encourage any illusion that he ever could be."

"Then what is he?" responded another. "If we do not allow him to call himself a rabbi, a Pharisee, are we agreeing with those who would make him a prophet? He is another John the Baptizer, but a dozen times worse!"

I kept quiet as the men debated Jesus' teaching. It was clear that what most wanted was for them to get him out of the Temple precincts, to make him stop teaching there—ideally, to get him out of Jerusalem altogether. But there were no laws in place to stop anyone from speaking or assembling in the Temple's outer court; indeed, it was the place where anyone, including women, children, and even Gentiles, might wander freely. There was no reason Jesus could not speak there, if he chose to—no legal reason, at any rate.

"If we cannot get rid of him because he is in the wrong place, surely the content of what he is teaching is enough to ask him to leave," Avram said. "At least John the Baptizer spoke out by the riverside, where people had to leave the city to hear him. This Jesus brings his Galilean heresies right into the Temple itself. I have heard that he speaks outright blasphemy—that he places himself on the same level with God!"

Of all the slanders I had ever heard against my brother—including a good many complaints I had against him myself—this was one I had never heard, and it chilled me to the bone. Jesus, whatever his faults, had the greatest reverence for God. I could not believe he would say such a thing. But it was a serious charge. If men of influence here in Jerusalem could interpret anything Jesus said as blasphemy, then he was surely not safe.

"I could tear apart this would-be Messiah using the Word of God as my sword," Avram said, "but I refuse to do it out there in the public court among Gentiles and women and the lowest of the common people. Perhaps you are right after all," he added, turning to the other rabbis. "Let him come in here and meet us, those who truly know the Law. We will show this Galilean who is wiser!"

Avram's suggestion met with a chorus of approval. "The day grows late, and soon it will be time for the evening sacrifice," someone said. "Let us go from here and issue this Jesus an invitation to debate us here in the inner courts tomorrow."

"I will do it," Avram said, but when the other rabbis had dispersed, he drew me aside and said, "Do you want to talk to Jesus privately, and tell him that we want to debate him here tomorrow?"

I hesitated. I did not want to do anything that might draw public attention to my family connection with Jesus—especially not if there was a chance he might be charged with a crime as serious as blasphemy. Yet with that threat hanging in the air, would it not be wiser for me to speak to him privately before any of the other Pharisees approached him? I knew concern for the family's honor carried no weight with him, but surely he cared as much for his own skin as any man. He would not risk a charge that carried the penalty of death under our law, would he?

Jesus and his band of followers came to our camp that night, swelling our numbers, making the night loud with laughter and song. I took him aside from the others and tried to talk some sense into him, but it was hopeless; he was as recalcitrant as ever.

His debate with the Pharisees the next day was disastrous, although very well attended. Often when two learned teachers, especially those who were known to have very different views on important issues, met to discuss the Law, large crowds of rabbis, scribes, and students gathered to hear them. Today was no exception; in fact, if anything, due to Jesus' notoriety, the crowd was larger than it had ever been. Unlike yesterday's ragtag crowd in the outer court, this group consisted entirely of Jewish men learned in the Scriptures. A harder group for Jesus to impress with his storytelling and his miracle working, I thought.

All my brothers accompanied me to hear Jesus as he sat across from Avram in one of the shaded porticos that bounded the Court of the Israelites. Where we sat revealed the division in our family: Simon and Joseph sat near Jesus and those of his male followers who had joined him, while I sat among the Pharisees with Jude and my son Benjamin. I could not help noticing, though, the admiration with which Benjamin's eyes turned upon his uncle Jesus, and I feared it was only loyalty to me that kept him from openly declaring himself Jesus' follower.

Outside the circle where we sat, on the edges of the group, stood a ring of Sadducee priests, curious to hear the outcome of this debate among Pharisees. Most of them thought of Jesus as one of our number, despite the fact that he claimed no such label.

"Well, today's debate will end the division in many minds," I said quietly to Jude as we took our places. "When he is forced to answer questions from men who know the Torah well, he won't be able to rely on the showy illusions that impress women and beggars. Surely this will reveal him for what he is—a shallow man of shallow tricks."

Jude nodded, but said nothing, watching Jesus and the group of gathered rabbis with his customary quiet observance.

The very first question Avram threw out to Jesus was a challenge. "Jesus of Nazareth, in Galilee you teach the people the Scriptures, and the common people say they are amazed at your wisdom. But where does this wisdom come from? What rabbis have you studied under? Who was your teacher? For you are unknown to us here in Jerusalem."

"My teacher is the One who sent me," Jesus said. "What I teach does not come from myself, but from Him."

"The One who sent you? Do you mean the Lord Himself?"

Jesus nodded. "If you doubt whether my teaching comes from God, test it and see. Live by my words, and see whether they lead you toward God. That will tell you whether my teaching comes from Him or from myself. I claim no earthly master."

"No, we know you are very arrogant in declaring yourself to have no teacher and master," another Pharisee spoke up. "You want men to honor you for your own wisdom, rather than honoring your teachers."

"I seek no honor for myself; I never have!" Jesus responded. I could see the quick temper that I knew was in him flaring, then as quickly reined in, brought under control. "I seek only the honor of God who sent me. I do honor my teacher and master, because God is my Master and my Teacher, and I am always true to Him. Why do you not honor the Law of your own master, Moses? Why are you trying to have me put to death?"

At this, a murmur of protest broke out around the room. "You're a madman!" one of the younger Pharisees said. "Who is trying to put you to death? We have invited you here to debate your teachings, but all you want to talk about is yourself!"

"I have come to teach the teachings and to do the will of God who sent me," Jesus said. "If you knew my Father, you would know me."

"Your Father!" Avram echoed in a shocked voice. "Now we come to the heart of the matter. You have claimed God as your only Teacher and Master; do you now claim Him as your Father as well? Are you making yourself equal with God?"

"These are dangerous words for a carpenter from Galilee," said another. "People are calling you a Messiah, but we know all about you and we know you are no Messiah."

"You think you know all about me and where I come from," Jesus countered, "but you don't truly know. If you knew me, you would know my Father also."

"Are you not a child of Abraham, like all of us?"

"You call yourselves the sons of Abraham, but you lie and deceive and cheat the people—you are sons of Satan!" Jesus said, his voice still controlled but his tone deadly. "Abraham would be ashamed to claim such children as you. Moses would be ashamed of his so-called pupils, who have made the Law into a chain to bind the poor, a burden to lay upon the backs of the people!"

"You are calling us children of Satan? If Satan is in this room," Avram said, his voice as cold and terrible as Jesus' had been a moment before, "then I know in whom he dwells. You claim to cast out demons, but I say you are casting out demons by the spirit of the devil himself!"

Jesus laughed, and his laughter broke for a moment the terrible tension that was in the air. "Would Satan give me his power to cast out his own demons? No house can stand if it is divided against itself—the devil is no such fool. But look to yourselves and your own divided house! God's judgment will fall upon you if you do not repent, turn from your wickedness, and trust the One whom He has sent."

And so it went on, the debate sometimes touching on points of the Law but more often returning to a personal attack on Jesus and his outrageous claims. I said nothing, but listened carefully. I noticed that Jesus never claimed the title of Messiah, though he said often that God had sent him; he called God his Father but did not claim to be equal with God. But when others asked him if he was the Messiah or if he thought himself equal with God, he did not deny those charges either; each time he sidestepped them neatly, deflecting the attack onto his attackers. But these were men learned in the Law, used to the intricacies of debate. They could hear the words Jesus was not saying as well as the ones he did say. The spoken words alone might have been enough to condemn him, but the unspoken words would surely invite stoning.

The "debate" ended with Jesus and his followers rising and sweeping out of the place amid disgruntled muttering from the rabbis. Nobody felt that anything had truly been resolved; and certainly those who had hoped it would end with Jesus humbly admitting his errors and submitting to their authority were bitterly disappointed. But then, anyone who hoped it would end that way had never really known Jesus.

My brothers Simon and Joseph left with Jesus' followers, and Jude and Benjamin left a few minutes after, along with most of the gathered Pharisees. But I stayed to talk to Avram and a few of the other leaders.

"This is enough," Avram said. "This proves everything I have been saying—the man is dangerous and must be stopped sooner rather than later."

"Why?" Nicodemus protested. "What did he say that you can prove wrong from the Scriptures?"

Avram sighed impatiently. "We have been over this a thousand times, Nicodemus. I can sit down and teach you from the Scriptures why the Messiah will not be an untutored Galilean carpenter, but that is hardly the point. The real point is that every claim he makes for himself—and the claims that others make for him—brings us into danger with Rome. We have already had men here from Pilate asking us about Jesus since he arrived in Jerusalem, asking if he poses a threat. Anyone who can stand up in the outer court of the Temple and gather a crowd of hundreds is someone the Romans will want to take down. If we are seen to support him, we will fall along with him. That is why I recommend we move first, to take him into custody and show Pilate and his men that we are no supporters of Jesus."

There were murmurs of agreement, though Nicodemus, as usual, voiced a contrary opinion. Avram cut him off with a quick gesture. "No. We have been patient long enough; it is time. This cannot be allowed to go on."

"Your pride is hurt because he insulted us personally," Nicodemus said.

"Of course I resent his insults!" Avram shot back. "Not because of pride, but because he defies every authority God has set over men to keep them in place. His attitude breeds rebellion—and we do not need rebellion here! No more false messiahs, no more Zealots! We learned our lesson in the days of Archelaus. You know the emperor in Rome would be glad for an excuse to raze this city and our Temple to the ground, destroy our people, and reduce us all to slaves! That is the fate Jesus will bring down on us if we do not stop him now!"

"Very well then, what do you propose to do?" someone said.

Avram opened his mouth to speak, then grew cautious. "I must think and take counsel," he said. "Let us go now for the evening sacrifice and talk more of this later."

His words were innocent enough, but I saw his glance dart to Nicodemus and then to me. Avram did not know for certain whom he could trust. Nicodemus was suspect because of his obvious support for Jesus, and I because Jesus was, after all, my brother. I could not blame Avram for his caution. In fact, a part of me was glad of it. Better I did not know exactly what he had planned for Jesus.

My own plan was to warn Jesus to get out of Jerusalem and back to Galilee. But I did not see him that night. He did not return to our camp, and I saw none of his close disciples. Simon and Joseph came back to the sukkah with us—it was the next-to-last night of the feast—but they both claimed no knowledge of where Jesus had gone.

"We looked for him after the evening sacrifice," Simon told me as we sat in the doorway of our sukkah that night, listening to the sound of singing and tambourines drifting through the night. "I asked anyone who might know, but no one had seen him; even some of his disciples claimed they didn't know where he had gone."

"Perhaps he has already left Jerusalem," I said.

"I hope so," Simon said. He stirred the fire's embers with a stick. One flame quickly flared, then died down again. "You and I may disagree about Jesus, James. The more I listen to his teaching, the more I believe he really is something more than our brother, the carpenter from Nazareth. But we are agreed in wanting no harm to come to him, and if I saw him, I would tell him to leave Jerusalem and get back to Galilee as soon as he could."

None of us saw Jesus that night, or most of the next day. In the early afternoon we went back to the Temple for the final hours of the celebration of Tabernacles. The outer court was crowded with pilgrims. We were about to continue on through the women's court when I realized the people were stirring, and a crowd was gathering at one end of the courtyard. My heart sank as I looked over to see Jesus standing on a step, just beginning to speak.

"Are you thirsty? Come to me, and I will give you living water! As the prophet says, 'Come, all you who are thirsty, come to the waters; and you who have no money, come, buy and eat!' Don't you want to drink of the water of life so you will never thirst again?"

A ragged cheer went up from the crowd, and Jesus continued, "Are you hungry? Will you eat the bread that God has sent from heaven, as He sent the manna to your fathers in the wilderness? The bread that fills you so you will never be hungry?" Again, another cheer from those listening.

"Do you walk in darkness? Then walk in darkness no longer, for I am the Light that has come into the world to light your way! Do you want to walk in the light? Do you want eternal life, so that you will never see or know death?"

Amid the happy cries of the common people came a harsh, commanding tone I knew very well: Avram's voice. "Are you promising people they well never die now, Jesus? You are greater than our father Abraham, then? He died, and sleeps with his fathers; so will we all, in our time."

Jesus paused in his oration and shaded his eyes against the sun, looking out into the crowd. "Ah, one of the children of Abraham!" he said, spotting Avram in the crowd, laughter edging his voice. "Tell me this, Rabbi. Your father Abraham, whose name you bear, was honored because he obeyed the voice of God and went off to a far country. Yet you, when you hear the voice of God coming from a Galilean teacher, ignore it and try to silence it! If you are Abraham's son, why not do Abraham's works, and trust God?"

"Are you saying we are not sons of Abraham?" another voice cried from the crowd.

Again, Jesus looked for the speaker and identified him before answering, though his words were pitched for all to hear—the common people, the curious listening Gentiles, the learned Pharisees and Sadducees among the crowd, even the Roman soldiers watching with interest from the sidelines. "I tell you the truth; you are not sons at all, but slaves! Everyone who lives a sinful life is a slave to sin, and only God's truth can set you free! Throw off your chains of sin, turn from slavery, and become God's true sons by following Him and the One He has sent! Take pride in God's truth, not in being children of Abraham—for before Abraham ever was, I AM."

Among the ripples of sound in the crowd, both of approval and disapproval, I heard it. The word *blasphemy,* uttered first quietly by one voice, then taken up by another. Jesus had spoken the sacred name of God, the "I AM" that God had told Moses was His name, and used it of himself.

"This man makes himself greater than Abraham, greater than Moses—equal with God Himself!" Avram called out, not to Jesus but to the crowd. "This man is no teacher or rabbi. He is a rebel and blasphemer! Men of Israel, we must not stand for this!"

I could see the division in the crowd, between those who supported Jesus and those who were angry at him. *This could become ugly,* I thought, imagining the rabble pitted against the Pharisees. A few men began to tussle here and there, but just as quickly others moved to separate and quell them. The Temple police quickly stepped forward from their positions, swords drawn. "Would we fight in the very Temple courts?" someone cried, and I saw that it was Nicodemus. "Whatever your quarrels, we do not resort to violence!"

"No, not violence, but justice!" Avram contended. "Justice must be carried out!" He looked around for Jesus—we all did—but Jesus was no longer standing on the steps where he had been.

It reminded me of that day in the synagogue at Nazareth when the crowd had turned against Jesus, only this crowd was several times larger. Confusion spread quickly as one man asked another, "Where is Jesus? Where did he go?" It was an easy crowd to get lost in, and I knew Jesus' skill at slipping away when he did not wish to be found. By now he was probably in the crowded streets of Jerusalem. I wondered if he would evade capture, or if Avram had men on his trail.

Apparently he evaded capture. No more was seen of him in Jerusalem that day, but later in the evening as my brothers and I took down our sukkah, Jesus appeared in our camp again.

I went over to talk to him. "So, you escaped today without being stoned for blasphemy," I said.

He smiled and spread his arms wide. "It seems I did." At my stern expression, his smile spread into a broad grin. "Stop worrying, James. I will not be captured or stoned or executed until it is God's will for that to happen. If the time is not right, then nobody can hurt me."

"I admire your confidence, even if it is misplaced," I said. Then my even temper snapped and I said, "You're being a fool, Jesus. You need to get out of Jerusalem, now."

"I am going, this very night."

"A very good plan. Get back to Galilee, or better yet, to some place far from here. Even Galilee is not safe for you now, not with Herod watching you like a hawk."

"Oh, I am not going to Galilee, or very far at all," Jesus said. "I'm going to Bethany, to visit some friends there. Would you like to come with us?"

Chapter Sixteen

I still am not certain why I went to Bethany with Jesus and his friends. Perhaps because the rest of my family was going. Perhaps because I already knew Jesus' friend Lazarus, and I was curious about the devotion Jesus inspired among followers who had known him only briefly a few years before in Judea. Were they drawn to him for the same reasons the Galileans were, or did they see a different Jesus, follow him for a different purpose?

I will admit that I was drawn to find out more about Jesus' teaching— not, like Simon and Joseph, because I wanted to become a disciple, but because I truly believed now that he was in great danger. I wanted to find out how I could prevent harm, if there was any way I might turn aside the fate I saw coming toward him. For surely if Jesus were to suffer, the whole family would suffer along with him.

Besides curiosity and fear, I was eager to see my Bethany friend, Rabbi Simon, once again. He had not come to Jerusalem for many months, though he had once been a familiar figure in the inner court, discussing and debating with the other rabbis and teachers of the Law. I wondered where he was and why he had not come to Jerusalem during the feast to debate Jesus along with the other rabbis.

Benjamin, Jude, and I traveled the short distance from Jerusalem to Bethany separately from Jesus and his large, noisy crowd of followers.

I had heard people speak of Jesus' "twelve disciples," and I knew that there was an inner circle of men who followed him all the time and participated in his ministry. But anyone who pictures Jesus traveling with an orderly file of a dozen disciples at his heels has completely failed to understand the nature of Jesus' movement. It included everyone—whoever was able to come with him, for as far and as long as they wanted to.

Along with those twelve closest followers and my brothers Simon and Joseph, there were at least another twenty people following Jesus to Bethany—men, women, and even little children whose parents had brought them from Galilee to Jerusalem for the feast, and others who had joined the party in Jerusalem. I saw women walking along and talking with the men, mingling freely; I saw at least two Gentiles. Jesus himself, the last glimpse I caught of him, was strolling through the town gates of Bethany with someone's small child riding on his shoulders, chatting to a young woman who walked beside him with uncovered head and shameless unbound hair. Whether she was the mother of the small child, I could not tell: she might have been a common harlot, for some of the company Jesus kept was entirely disreputable.

We waited till they had entered the town. Then, instead of following them to the house of Lazarus, I went with Jude and Benjamin to the house of Simon the Pharisee. Our departure from Jerusalem, at the first light of dawn, had been so early that I had had no time to send a messenger ahead, but I was sure my friend Simon would welcome us as he had done in the past.

I was wrong. A servant at the door told us he was sorry, but the master was not well and could not see us. I told him to bear my name and my greetings to his master and my sorrow at hearing of his sickness. I hoped that Simon's illness was nothing serious, and that upon hearing who it was who had come to visit, he might rouse himself enough for a short visit.

Instead, Simon's wife came to greet me, her face shadowed and grave beneath her veil. "Forgive us, Rabbi James," she said. "When I heard it was you at the door, I did not wish to send a servant to turn you away. You must know that my husband honors you greatly and would not close the door to you, except that his illness is very grave."

"Mistress, I am very sorry to hear it," I said. "What is it that ails Rabbi Simon?"

She looked away. Like any modest married woman, she would meet the eyes of a male visitor only briefly, but I saw in her demeanor that there was more than the usual reserve here. She was uncomfortable talking about her husband's illness for some reason. "It is—a fever," she said at last, but I sensed there was more to this "fever" than she was willing to say.

"What do the physicians say? I hope it is not a sickness unto death."

"We . . . do not know yet," she said. "I will give your regards to my husband."

"Tell him I will pray for him."

She lifted her eyes to mine just for a moment. "Only one person's prayers could do him any good now," she said, raw honesty breaking through her careful façade. "If you could convince Jesus to come to him—but no. My husband would not want it known that . . ." She shook her head and withdrew from the doorway. "I am sorry, Rabbi James. I will tell my husband of your visit."

After she had gone, I went back to Jude and Benjamin, whom I had left standing in the street, and told them that Rabbi Simon was ill and could not see us, much less invite us to stay with him.

"Should we go back to Jerusalem at once?" Jude asked.

"Or can we go see what Jesus is doing?" Benjamin suggested.

I sighed. "We might as well go to the house of Lazarus. Everyone else is there, and at least I can keep an eye on Jesus. I'll be a happier man when he's on the road north, far away from Jerusalem."

But when we reached Lazarus's house, Jesus showed no signs of being ready to leave. He was well settled in, sitting on a bench in the courtyard with people gathered all around, both men and women—those who had come with him from Jerusalem this morning, and others, from Bethany, who had come to hear him.

Among the women who joined the men in listening and talking to Jesus was the same unveiled woman who had been talking to him earlier as they entered the town. "But Lord," she said now, raising her voice in question just as a student might do when being taught by a rabbi—a shocking role for a woman. "How can we know if God truly forgives the sinner? I have heard teachers who say that some sins are too great for even God to forgive."

Jesus looked at her with a warm smile. "Do you know what it is like in heaven when a sinner repents? You know women who have lovely headpieces and bracelets of coins?" When she nodded, he went on, "Imagine a woman has such a headdress—ten gold coins, her marriage dowry, worn on her wedding day and then saved carefully for special occasions. One day she takes it out to admire it, only to find that one of her coins is missing; she has only nine! Can you imagine how horrified she would be—a poor woman with only those ten pieces of treasure to her name?"

The woman next to Jesus—I could see now that she was quite a striking beauty—nodded. "Of course! She would be frantic!"

"She would search all the house, sweeping every corner, lighting a lamp to peer into the dark places where she seldom looks. And if she finds it? What will she feel like then?"

"Why she would rejoice, of course," the woman said.

"She would celebrate, tell all her friends, show the coin around with great joy. 'Look at this beautiful treasure that I thought was lost, and have now found!' And I tell you the truth—that is exactly how God our Father celebrates when one sinner repents and turns to Him. He throws a great party, for each of us is a priceless treasure in His eyes."

All around, his listeners smiled and nodded appreciatively, and some added comments or questions to continue the discussion. But the beautiful woman gave a small, thoughtful smile, and said, "Thank you." It was not hard to see that this question of sin and forgiveness cut very close to her heart.

Then, looking at her, it came to me who she must be, and the family resemblance I had not observed before suddenly seemed obvious. She was so familiar and at home here in this courtyard as well as with Jesus, that I realized she must be Mary, that notorious sister of Lazarus. The demon-possessed girl who had been set free by Jesus. Looking at her now, I could see her resemblance to Martha, though all that in Martha was reserved and womanly was shameless and untamed in this woman. It was not hard to believe that under the spell of her demons, she had allowed men to use her in immoral ways; for any man but the most rigidly moral—like myself—would be drawn to such a beauty. I thought how foolhardy, how dangerous it was for Jesus to have such a woman, with such a reputation, near him. It was one more weapon for his enemies to use against him—the charge of immorality among his followers, if not against Jesus himself.

Without realizing it, I had drifted to the edges of the courtyard, near the women's quarters. When I looked over, I saw that Martha stood nearby, her arms crossed, looking impatient.

"Look at her!" she said.

"Is that your sister?" I asked.

"Yes, that is my sister. After the life she's lived, don't you think she would want to cover her head and stay in the women's quarters? There she is, out flaunting herself among the men, for all she says she's saved and living a holy life for God now."

Her sentiments echoed my own exactly, but I did not know how to say that without insulting her sister. So I said simply, "Still, you must be glad to have her home."

"Oh, she's not staying," Martha said with a surprising edge of bitterness in her voice. "She's not Mary of Bethany anymore; they call her Mary of Magdala, for the town where she was living in shame when Jesus found her. She'll be here as long as Jesus is here, then off to Galilee again. Not that it makes much difference to me—as you can see, she's no help with the work of the house when she is there, out with the menfolk!"

Again, I hardly knew what to say, but the irritation in her tone so exactly matched what I often felt about Jesus himself that I said, "One would think, if he is as caring and compassionate as he is supposed to be, he might send her back here to give you some help in the kitchen, rather than encouraging her to play a man's role."

Martha looked up at me. "Yes! That's it exactly! If she doesn't come in here soon, I may not be able to keep still about it any longer." Then, as if realizing what a lengthy conversation she had just had with a man she barely knew, she slipped back to her work in the kitchen.

She must have reached her breaking point, too, for a little while later I saw her in an earnest conversation with Jesus, looking as if she were chiding him, though I might have told her how little success she'd have with that. At the same moment, I was talking to James and John bar Zebedee, trying to convince them of the very real danger to Jesus if he stayed in the area of Jerusalem.

"What he said in the Temple yesterday was as close to blasphemy as a man is likely to get, and still live," I reminded them. "I know these men, these Pharisees. They do not speak idly, and many of them feel Jesus has gone too far and must be stopped before he draws down the wrath of the Romans, if not for the sake of the blasphemy itself. You must warn him."

John shrugged. "He knows the danger. He says no one can harm him before God's appointed time."

"And do you have any idea what he means by that?" I challenged. "Is there some appointed time at which God will say that it is acceptable for the authorities to arrest Jesus, and he will meekly submit to being thrown in prison, maybe even put to death as John the Baptizer was? Is he waiting for the perfect moment for all that to happen?"

"Of course not!" John said. "He is waiting for the right moment to come into his power, to take his place as Israel's rightful king."

"Shut your mouth!" I warned him. "It's that very kind of talk that will get Jesus arrested and all of those who follow him thrown in jail—or worse."

"That's your fear, isn't it, James?" Another voice joined our conversation—that loud and uncouth fisherman of Bethsaida, Peter bar Jonah. "Don't pay any mind to Jesus' brother, lads; he's not concerned about our Lord—or about us either. He's concerned for his own skin, afraid his precious Jerusalem friends will find out he's related to Jesus and some shame will spill over onto him!"

It was close enough to the truth to anger me, so I turned on Peter. "At least I don't claim to love and follow Jesus and then urge him on to actions that will end with his head on a Roman spear!"

Peter opened his mouth to reply, but before he could, Jesus was there between us. "No quarrels, now, friends," he said.

"Lord, this so-called brother of yours is attacking you, telling us you must stop preaching, or the Pharisees will turn you over to the Romans!"

That wasn't precisely what I'd said, but I had no time to explain, for Jesus put a hand on my shoulder and laughed. "Peter, have I not told you before that my true family are those who choose to follow me? James and I were raised in the same household, but he can choose to call me brother or not—and right now I think he would rather not." Then his face grew serious. "But right now, it is to you I need to speak, James. Lazarus tells me he has a kinsman here, Simon, who is very ill."

Peter, looking disgruntled, shot me one last look of pure anger and moved off with the other disciples—his true brothers, I suppose. I said to Jesus, "Rabbi Simon is, indeed, very ill, though his wife would not tell me what his sickness is. She did say," honesty forced me to admit, "that if you were willing to see him, he might welcome your visit." My heart was still divided over Jesus' gifts of healing. I could not deny they existed, but I was unsure that they were truly of

God. Still, if Simon was really so ill, I did not think it was my place to stand in the way.

"Will you take me to his house?" Jesus asked.

After a quiet word to Lazarus, who wanted to accompany us, we left the rest of the group in Lazarus's courtyard. On the way we passed several of Jesus' female disciples, carrying baskets and bundles of food, on their way back from the market. I recognized the woman Joanna, whom I had met in Galilee, and some of the others looked similarly well off; no doubt they were buying food out of their own purses to share with this mob. "Go bring this to Martha, and some of you help her prepare it; she's half-mad with fretting," Jesus told them as they passed.

"Of course she would be, Rabbi," Joanna answered. "What man, even our Lord and Master, would understand a woman's troubles when faced with a houseful of unexpected guests?"

Jesus laughed and said, "You may be right," and sent them on their way back to the house. A dozen reproofs rose to my tongue, but I decided if I had the advantage of a few minutes' walk with him, I would stay with the most important subject: the very real threat Jesus faced if he stayed in Jerusalem, or even if he continued to preach publicly in Galilee.

But Jesus simply waved all my fears away, telling me, as he had told others, "When the time is right, I will return to Jerusalem and face whatever is to be faced there. My Father will lead me, and I trust His leading."

"It's that very kind of talk—calling God your Father—that will get you dragged out of the Temple and stoned to death."

"But if God created us all, is He not the Father of all of us?" Jesus said mildly.

I was glad to see Simon's house ahead: I could not tolerate another five minutes of conversation with Jesus.

The same servant who had answered my knock before came again. This time I said, "Tell your mistress that Rabbi James has come again and has brought Rabbi Jesus with him, whom the master wished to see."

The servant's mouth was open to refuse me entry again, but when I mentioned the name of Jesus, his eyes widened. He stared for a moment, then beckoned us in to wait in the courtyard while he scurried away to find his mistress. A few moments later he returned, obviously with orders to bring us to Simon's chamber.

Simon's house was one of the finer ones in a village such as Bethany, one of the few that would have had separate sleeping quarters for the master and mistress, unlike the common houses where master, mistress, children, servants, and often animals as well slept in a single room. Simon was sitting on his sleeping couch, awaiting us. He did not look frail, thin, or wasted as I'd expected; he did not have the burning eyes of the fevered nor the hollow cough of the consumptive.

But his illness was apparent at a glance, nonetheless. It was evident in the ravaged face, in the skin on his hands and arms. Even the smell in the room proclaimed the presence of the most feared and hated of all diseases: leprosy.

Everything became clear to me now. Simon had ceased going out of his house, ceased communicating with friends, ceased allowing anyone to visit him, not only because he was sick but because he dared not allow anyone to find out the nature of his illness. Even a doctor could not be consulted, for any physician would recognize leprosy at once and send Simon to a priest, who would pronounce the dreaded words and banish him from his family and community. He would be forced to live outside the village, among the poorest of outcasts, the lepers who could not even beg for their bread, for they were banished from all human contact. Simon's wealth and rank would not protect him from this fate if he were known to have leprosy, but it did allow him to hide in his house and keep his condition a secret, with the complicity of his wife and at least one servant.

It was not a manly way to react to such a situation—the noble thing would be to admit the illness and take his banishment boldly—but it was understandable. From the moment his leprosy became known, life as Simon had known it would essentially be over.

Even as I thought this, as my eyes met his, my compassion was replaced with the fear every man feels in the presence of the word *leper*. How much more terrifying the presence of the leper himself! I drew back to the doorway of the room. Beside me, Lazarus did the same.

But not Jesus. Jesus, to my horror, crossed the room and sat down on the bed beside Simon. The servant cried out an involuntary "No!" and even Simon himself drew back as if to protect Jesus from too much contact.

But Jesus reached out and took Simon's sore-covered, leprous hand in his, and would not let it go when Simon tried to draw back. "My old friend Simon," he said. "You have borne a heavy burden, haven't you?"

Simon nodded. "Yes, yes, Lord."

Jesus smiled. "You call me Lord now; you never did before. Do you believe I can heal you?"

I could see desperation and honesty struggling on Simon's scarred face. "I—I want to believe it," he finally confessed. "I need to believe."

"Wanting to believe is the first step to faith," Jesus said. "Simon, that mustard seed of faith has made you well. Be healed!"

There was nothing more, just those words. I saw or heard nothing to indicate a miracle had taken place. Then Simon drew out his hand from Jesus' grasp and held it up before his face in wonder, and we all saw that it was free of the leprous sores that had afflicted it a moment earlier. The hand Jesus had touched was healed.

Then, when he held up the other to compare, we saw that it, too, was whole. I looked at Simon's face before he touched it himself, and saw that there, too, the sores had gone; his skin was healed. In a moment he was pushing back the sleeves of his robe, checking for sores, and calling at the top of his lungs, "Hannah! Hannah! You, boy, go fetch my wife! Bring her here so she can see this!"

Only after a moment did he remember Jesus and look back at him. "Is it really true?" Simon asked, a sob catching his voice. "Am I healed?"

"You are healed, Simon. Today is the first day of your new life."

Once again the two men joined hands, this time Simon grabbing Jesus' hands in his newly restored ones. "Jesus, Lord, Master, forgive me for doubting you! Forgive me for—" he hesitated again, looking at Lazarus and me. "Pardon, friends," he said. "I would speak alone with Jesus; there are things I need to talk to him about."

Lazarus said, "We will leave you with pleasure, cousin. It is good that God has healed you."

"I am glad to see your suffering ended," I said, and bowed farewell as Lazarus and I left the room.

"Go back to your house and tell all my friends I will be along soon," Jesus called to Lazarus. "I must spend some time with a man whose body has been healed, and who now longs for healing for his soul. Isn't that right, Simon?"

The rest of their words were lost as we descended to the lower level of Simon's house and went out into the street.

Chapter Seventeen

The months between the Feast of Tabernacles and the Feast of Dedication were quiet: a welcome relief after the madness of Jesus' visit to Jerusalem. Benjamin and I parted ways from the rest of the company at Bethany. We returned to our work in Jerusalem. Jesus and his followers and the rest of my brothers went, presumably, back to Galilee.

Rumors and opinions about him continued to fly around Jerusalem, so I was never really free from the shadow he cast over my life. And, as I had feared, his visit to the city had ended my hope of keeping our family connection a secret. Many now knew me as Jesus' brother, and I was constantly being questioned about him. Did I believe he was the Messiah? Did I know what his plans were? Did I know where he was?

This last became a most pressing question as fall moved toward winter, for the reports of travelers from Galilee told the Jerusalem rabbis—who were very interested in Jesus' movements—that he had not been preaching and teaching openly in that region since he had left for Jerusalem in the fall. Everyone had a theory about where Jesus was. Some said he was in Galilee, but in hiding. Others said he was in Jerusalem, again, hiding. Some said he had gone into Samaria, or some of the Gentile regions; others said he had left the land altogether and gone to Egypt or some other far place.

A letter from my brother Jude at home shed no light on Jesus' disappearance; he said that Simon and Joseph had gone home to Nazareth as well, and that none of them had any idea where Jesus was, nor was there any word of him in Capernaum or Bethsaida, where many of his followers lived. His closest followers, the twelve disciples and a few others, were likewise hard to find; the sons of Zebedee had made a brief visit home to Capernaum but then had gone away again.

I thought that by disappearing for a time, Jesus was showing more prudence than I usually gave him credit for. I tried to bury myself in my work and think as little about my brother as possible. I also turned my mind to the task of arranging a marriage for my son, Benjamin, who now, at seventeen years old, would soon be ready to take a wife.

I considered, of course, taking him back to Nazareth to find a bride from among our own people. But I had no desire to return to Galilee just then, and because Benjamin seemed happy with his training as a scribe and his life in the city, I thought it might be best to find him a bride in Jerusalem or the surrounding area. Perhaps he and I would make our lives in Judea from now on. I asked Benjamin what he thought about it.

"I would be glad to stay in Jerusalem and marry here, Father, if that is your wish for me," he said.

"You are content to stay, then? You don't long to return to Nazareth?"

No, he did not. I was glad his will and mine accorded well together. When I asked about finding a wife, he seemed to have no particular thoughts on the subject, no young woman among the families of his friends and fellow scribes he admired. This, too, I thought good, for it meant that his eyes and mind were not wandering from his work as those of so many young men did, seeking distraction in a pretty face. It was easier to negotiate for a marriage if the boy had not formed any kind of an attachment, although he would not have the advantage his sister had had, of making a match with someone she already knew and admired. But that was hardly necessary. I had barely met my Rachel before our wedding day, and I had loved her as dearly as ever a man could love his wife, so much so that more than ten years later, her loss still haunted me. If I chose wisely for Benjamin, God might bless him with the same happiness.

But when I went to my master, Rabbi Avram, to talk about possible brides for my son, I found his manner oddly cool. He and I had studied and discussed Scripture together much as we always had since Jesus' last appearance in Jerusalem, but now that I thought on it, the friendly dinners we used to enjoy together before that time had ceased. Though I rented rooms in his house, we did not always eat with Avram's family; the household was large and the household servants often brought food from the kitchen to our rooms. I knew Avram was very busy—he had a seat on the Sanhedrin now, and spent as much time at politics as he did at prayer. But as I sat with him in his courtyard discussing my son's marriage, I sensed that there was more than busyness behind the fact that I saw him so rarely at home now.

"Are there any girls of marriageable age you might recommend?" I asked. Avram's own youngest daughter was fourteen or fifteen and not yet promised to anyone, but I would not aim so high as to propose a match between my house and his. There were others, though, I knew—daughters of some of the other Pharisee rabbis. Yet he shook his head and said, "No, I cannot think of anyone."

"No one at all? What about Rabbi Chaim's daughter?"

"The little one? No, I am sure she has just been betrothed."

"The sister of Levi, then?" Levi was one of my students; his father was a prominent scribe, and Avram knew the family well.

His brow furrowed. "Ah . . . no, there has been no contract made, but I know her father has someone in mind for her, a cousin. You know it's best to keep such things in the family. Why do you not send to your own people in Galilee for a bride? Surely there's a girl up there that Benjamin can marry."

"I had hoped for a young woman from Jerusalem, or at least a Judean," I said.

"Well now, that may not be wise. Marriage is a way to strengthen the bloodlines and family ties, after all, and all your ties are in Galilee. Surely it's best if you keep it that way."

Anger began to rise in my chest. "Pardon me, my master, are you suggesting I aim too high in seeking a Judean bride for my son? That we ignorant northerners should go back to Galilee and marry among our own kind?"

Avram sighed heavily. "No, no, of course not, James. It is—no, it's not that. I just do not think there are many families in Jerusalem, certainly not among the Pharisees, who would be eager to make an alliance with your family just now."

"Ah. You mean, because of Jesus."

Avram said nothing, toying aimlessly with his phylacteries as he stared off into the distance. He did not confirm or deny my statement, but said after a moment, "I have heard he is in Judea again, that he is coming to Jerusalem for the feast."

"You have heard a rumor. I hear a dozen every day, about Jesus and what he is doing. What is it to me? You know I'm no follower of his, and neither is my son. Why should Jesus' disrepute tarnish my hopes of making a good match for my son?"

"It's family, James. You understand. Whether you agree with Jesus or not, he is still your brother."

"Is he?" I said bitterly. "Half-brother at best, and sometimes I think—"

"Yes? You think what?"

I hesitated, reluctant to air our family's shame before this learned man. But he had already told me my family was not good enough to join with his or any of the other Pharisee families he knew. I was tired, so tired of the shame of being labeled as Jesus' brother.

"I am the son of my father's first wife, who died when I was young," I explained. "Jesus' mother was already with child when my father married her, and though my father gave her his name and called Jesus his own, there has always been much gossip in Nazareth . . ." I let my voice trail off; the implication was clear enough. I felt bad about slandering Mary, but she and her son had certainly caused enough trouble for me. What would a Galilean peasant woman care if a Jerusalem rabbi thought she had once been a wanton woman in her youth?

The information interested Avram more than I had thought it would. "So, you think Jesus is not your father's son, then?"

"I cannot be sure," I confessed. "I tell you only what the gossip of the village was. My father Joseph was glad to spread the cloak of legitimacy over Jesus and his mother, but you notice Jesus never calls himself the son of Joseph."

"No, he is far too busy claiming God as his Father!" Avram said. "What does he mean by that, I wonder? Only that we are all sons of God because God created us all? Of something more, unique to himself?"

Again, I hesitated, then said, "Mary has always believed—or at least, told others—that there was something special, something miraculous about Jesus' birth. I think she truly does believe God is his Father, rather than Joseph; and I think she somehow made my father Joseph believe it too. They both treated him as if he were something more than an ordinary child."

"A son of the gods!" Avram laughed. "Something the heathen poets would dream up! But might a young girl dream up such a story to cover her disgrace, her shame? It is ingenious, and if Jesus were raised to believe such a thing were true, it would explain a great deal about his—well, his delusions."

I nodded. "Yes, I suppose it would."

"It would also mean you are not Jesus' brother, except as your father adopted him. And it seems he has cut those ties, turning his back on your father's name. No doubt he is the product of some youthful folly on the part of his mother."

"Or even something more shameful," I added. My former reluctance to share our family's private matters was overcome by the fact that Avram seemed once again to be treating me as something like an equal. I was anxious to encourage the idea that Jesus and I shared no common blood. "I have heard some suggest that Mary was taken by force as a girl—perhaps by a Gentile, maybe even a Roman soldier."

Avram nodded. "Indeed, it may be so. She would not be the first Jewish girl to suffer such a terrible fate. She was fortunate indeed that your father was willing to cover her shame—but what madness it has led to!"

I wanted to say, "Does this mean you'll help me arrange a marriage for my son?" but I held my peace. I realized Avram had greater things on his mind than my family troubles. Discrediting and silencing Jesus was of paramount importance to him, and I was not surprised when, along with all the other rumors flying around about Jesus, I soon began to hear people saying that Jesus was illegitimate, possibly even half-Gentile. "So much for all those who say he is the son of David, hey?" said one rabbi, a man who was apparently unaware of my relationship to Jesus. "Some house of David!" He spat on the ground.

Yet, strangely, despite Avram's rejection, I received an inquiry about a marriage contract soon after that—and from the family of a respected Pharisee too. It was my old friend Simon of Bethany, whom I had not seen since my visit with Jesus. Simon wrote to invite me to come to Bethany and discuss a possible union between our families.

Simon had a young daughter, a little above the usual age for marriage, perhaps sixteen or so. He had been waiting to make the right match for her, and then, of course, the growing worry about his leprosy and his need to hide it, had consumed all other concerns. Now Simon was apparently as hale and healthy as when I had first known him and anxious to make this alliance.

How strange the world is! The fact that I was—in name at least—the brother of Jesus, had prevented me from marrying my son into any of the Pharisaic families to whom I had hoped Avram would grant me introduction. But that same relationship was, I soon realized, the main reason Simon was anxious to make the match. He had become an ardent follower of Jesus since his illness and healing, and he was eager to ally his family with ours.

"You realize I am no disciple of my brother," I reminded him.

"James, James, how can you still doubt? After seeing in this very room how Jesus healed me, can you still question that his power comes from God?"

"The power . . . I do not know," I admitted honestly. I had toyed with the idea that, as some suggested, Jesus' healing powers came from the devil, but I found it hard to believe that something satanic could do so much good. Yet might the devil not do some apparent good, healing a few hundred sick people, to accomplish the greater cause of bringing down the nation of Israel, destroying God's people? For it seemed to me that this would be the ultimate end of Jesus' madness.

"I do not know about the miracles, or where his power comes from," I began again, "but I am still convinced that this movement he has started cannot be of God, and that it will end in evil rather than good for our people. Enough people talk about making him king, and Rome cannot ignore it. Already we hear of threats against him. I cannot support him, brother or not, while he is a danger to our people. One man may rise or fall, but protecting the people of God—that is what matters."

Simon laughed, a low throaty chuckle. "Hasn't saving the people of God always been God's job? Can we not trust Him with that?"

"Of course, but in every generation He has raised up faithful men to do His task."

"And how do you know Jesus is not the one He has sent us in our day? Perhaps instead of destroying the people, Jesus is the one who will save us."

"Truly, Simon, I cannot see how."

"No matter. I believe in him because I cannot do otherwise. You do not—yet. Still I honor you as a godly man, and I want to be joined to your family. I have a daughter who is ready for marriage. Now I think, Rabbi James, you are not looking to take a young wife yourself, are you?" He chuckled again.

"No! Certainly not," I assured him. "If you wish to make a marriage between our families, it is my son Benjamin who will be the bridegroom."

"Ah, very well. I'm sure Raina will be happier with a young husband than an old man like her father, eh? Although, you are not so very old yourself, James; perhaps you should think of marrying again. If you don't want a young bride and another brood of children, maybe a nice older woman. A widow, perhaps, to keep you company into your old age? The Lord did not make man to be alone, you know."

I was uncomfortable with his levity, although I had been relaxed enough in his presence on previous visits. The fact Simon now counted himself a follower of Jesus was the dividing line, the reason why I was no longer comfortable with him. But the marriage was still a fine alliance for Benjamin and for our family, so I went ahead and haggled out the details of the agreement with Simon, had a quick look at his daughter who seemed healthy and comely, and went home to tell Benjamin that the arrangement was concluded.

But more news awaited me back in Jerusalem. As I told my son about the marriage contract, he also had news for me. "Did you know that Jesus is in town?"

"What? Have you seen him?"

"No, but I heard—"

"Ah, never mind what you heard; it's another rumor, that's all. The city is full of rumors about Jesus."

"It's no rumor, Father! He was in the Temple today. I spoke with three or four men who saw him. There was a blind beggar there, claiming he'd been healed by a touch from Jesus, and several rabbis who debated with him about the healing, trying to find out if it was true and if it was the work of God or not."

I sighed and rubbed my forehead. "And where is he now, do you know?"

"Nobody knows. Jesus is good at hiding when he doesn't want to be found. I suppose he came for the feast."

It was the Feast of Dedication, one of the feasts not prescribed in the Torah, a newer feast, like Purim, that celebrated the work of God in these later days. The rededication of the Temple and the miracle of the oil that did not burn away was the basis for an eight-day feast. The fact that it was winter, and not one of the major feasts like Passover or Tabernacles, meant that far fewer Jews from the countryside made the journey into Jerusalem for this festival, but there were still some who came, and the number of people in the streets and in the Temple courts was greater than usual. I still was not sure about the veracity of Benjamin's story, but arriving at festival times seemed to be Jesus' pattern.

So I was not really surprised the next day when I went to my accustomed place in the inner court to meet my students and found them all talking about Jesus.

"I hear he is coming here today, to the inner court, to debate with the Pharisees," one young man said to me.

"Aren't you a kinsman of Jesus, Rabbi James?" another asked me. I nodded briefly to concede that it was so, without specifying exactly what the relation was. "Then why do you not follow him?" the boy persisted.

"We must judge every man's teaching on its own merit, not simply by whether we like the man or have a tie of kinship loyalty to him," I said. "Weigh the words of Jesus as you would those of any teacher. Compare them to the teaching of other learned rabbis who have studied the Scriptures. You will find that what Jesus teaches about the Torah does not accord with what our fathers taught, while the claims he makes for himself come dangerously close to blasphemy."

One of the young men stood up and looked toward one of the porticos where a group of men was gathering. "With your permission, Rabbi," the boy said, "if you wish us to judge Jesus' teaching for ourselves, we have our opportunity. He is here now."

We all moved toward the group of men, and, indeed, I could hear the unmistakable voice of Jesus in their midst. The crowd around him was a mixture of his own followers, easily distinguished by their rough, travel-worn clothes and Galilean accents, and the rabbis of Jerusalem. Among them I could see Avram as well as several others I knew were deeply opposed to Jesus. These same men had spoken about having him arrested the previous time he was in Jerusalem, but now they were once again debating with him. No doubt with so many of his followers around, they did not want to run the risk of starting a riot, as had almost happened in the outer court during Tabernacles.

It was not Avram but another teacher, a Sadducee, whom I now heard challenging Jesus. "Come, stop playing games with us," the man said. "If you think you are the Messiah, why not declare it openly?"

Several voices, both those of Jesus' detractors and his followers, took up this call. Jesus responded, "Declare myself? I have already done so! I've spoken to you through actions, not words—the works I've done are my declaration. If those aren't enough for you to believe, then it's because you aren't the sheep of my flock. I am the Good Shepherd, and my sheep know me and recognize my voice."

"Sheep!" someone called back in derision.

"That's the rustic northern preacher for you, making us all out to be sheep and goats," another said.

Jesus continued, "Perhaps you learned rabbis don't know much about shepherds, but our forefather King David did, for he wrote that the Lord is our Shepherd, and we want for nothing. As for me, I am like a shepherd who guards and protects his sheep, who will even lay down my life for them if need be! Sheep need to be protected from thieves who would come in to steal and attack and kill. I have come to bring them life—a full, more abundant life, and eternal life to come."

At the mention of eternal life, there were some disgruntled murmurs: the man who had first questioned Jesus was a Sadducee, while many in the group were Pharisees. Belief in eternal life, in a resurrection for God's faithful at the end of time, was one of the dividing lines that separated our two parties.

"Yes, eternal life!" Jesus said, seizing upon the division among his critics. "The sheep who follow me as their shepherd will live forever and never die. No one can snatch them out of my hand. They are my Father's flock; He has given them to me and will protect them, for my Father and I are one."

"Blasphemy! Stone him!" cried a voice, and others took up the call.

"What do you want to stone me for?" Jesus called out, not a trace of fear in his voice. I was near enough to see him by this time: he looked as calm as ever, as if he were having a pleasant discussion with some friends in the marketplace rather than facing down a group of men in authority who thought he ought to be stoned for blasphemy.

I knew there was no chance they would actually stone him. Even if Jesus were judged guilty of blasphemy, the Roman authorities would never allow us to carry out our law in such a barbaric fashion. There were limits to our freedom, and the Sanhedrin well knew that no matter what our Torah said, we could not always enforce our own ancient laws.

"For what do you want to stone me?" Jesus repeated. "For healing the sick? For giving sight to the blind? For preaching the kingdom of God? You have all seen the deeds I've done; which of them has deserved death?"

"Not your actions, but your words!" Rabbi Avram called back to him. "You are a man, and yet you put yourself on a level with God Himself!"

"Does not the Scripture say, 'You are all gods, you are sons of the Most High'?" Jesus shot back. I knew the psalm he was quoting: it was a text that rabbis would debate and argue over for hours, yet he tossed it into the debate as lightly as a man tossing a handful of pennies on a tabletop. "If the people of God can be called 'gods,' how much more the one whom God has sent to you? Why accuse me of blasphemy for claiming to be One with my Father? Why not look at my actions instead? Am I doing the works of God? If you trust what I do, then you will believe what I say—that God the Father is in me, and I am in Him."

A clamor of voices rose up at this, but Jesus turned to his followers. "Come, let us leave this place," he said, and they followed him out to the outer court.

"Why did you not call the Temple guard to seize him?" an angry scribe demanded, watching Jesus and his group leave.

"What, and have a riot on our hands as soon as that rabble outside found out?" Avram countered. "He's a hero to them! We cannot arrest him openly."

"If we don't, the Romans soon will," said another.

I returned to my rooms that night deeply troubled, wondering what would happen to Jesus and what, in my heart, I truly hoped for. If he quietly disappeared, there would be no public shame or humiliation for his family. If only he could simply go away, or be silent. Two things I knew Jesus would never do.

I found Benjamin quiet that night as we ate our evening meal in our private rooms. He, too, had been among the crowd in the inner court and had heard Jesus speak, but he seemed to have no desire to discuss the debate as he had done on other occasions. A silent supper suited me, too, and I soon fell into a troubled sleep.

The next day I went back to the Temple as usual, but there was no sign of Jesus, nor any word of him. Yesterday's debate was on every rabbi's tongue, but no one had any fresh news of Jesus. Some said he had left Jerusalem to avoid capture.

Perhaps he would stay away for a few months more—another blessed oasis of peace. Yet I sensed these reprieves were nearing an end. Matters were coming to a head, and soon I would no longer be able to ignore my divided feelings about Jesus.

I didn't realize how soon that day was until I walked into the house and went to my room. It was empty. *Benjamin must,* I thought, *still be at the Temple.* It took a few moments for me to realize that a bag was missing, as were Benjamin's few robes and his traveling cloak. It took even longer before I saw the piece of parchment laid in the corner where his bed was usually unrolled. It contained just eight words:

Father, forgive me. I have gone with Jesus.

Chapter Eighteen

I stood holding the scrap of parchment for a long time, as if frozen, unable to grasp what I had in my hand. Benjamin? Benjamin had left me with a note eight words long and gone to follow Jesus?

I had known he admired his uncle and was interested in Jesus' teaching and ministry. I had done my best to steer him in the right direction, to teach him why I believed Jesus was misguided. But what shocked me the most was not that Benjamin had decided to follow Jesus. What I could not get over was that he had done it in this way—secretly stealing away, leaving only a note behind. Defying my authority behind my back.

Of course, if he had told me he wanted to go with Jesus, I would have forbidden it. He was seventeen years old now, almost fully trained as a scribe, but he was still my son, still under my care and authority, and yes, I would have forbidden him to go. All his life, Benjamin had been a dutiful boy. Never had I seen in him the least spark of the defiance that had marked Jesus as a boy, the determination to do his own will (or, as Jesus saw it, God's will) no matter what he was told. No, Benjamin had always been subject to me, in everything from our decision to move to Jerusalem, to my choice of a bride for him. He had never questioned me, certainly never disobeyed or defied me.

Now it was as if all his youthful obedience had crumbled. Perhaps this was why he had stolen away—he was, at heart, a good boy, and did not have it in him to openly defy me. He knew that I would have forbidden his going and decided to avoid the confrontation. It was the strategy of a weak man, but perhaps also of one too kindhearted to openly flout his father's authority.

Or, I thought now, the strategy of a boy with a father so harsh he could not be reasoned with or appealed to. Benjamin might see it in that light. I had never thought myself harsh or unyielding as some men were with their families. Now that my son was nearly a man, I talked to him, I consulted with him about decisions. I did not go ahead and choose a wife for him without first talking the matter over with him. I was never a man to thunder and beat my fist on the table, to command obedience from those under my rule. Yet Benjamin must have seen something of that in me, to shrink from this confrontation and leave in this underhanded manner.

No matter the reason, he was gone. Gone away with Jesus. And I had to bring him back.

The first problem was that I had no idea where Jesus had gone, and I was unlikely to find out that night. I lay down to an uneasy sleep, wondering who in Jerusalem might know anything about Jesus' whereabouts.

In the morning I went back to the temple, but instead of going to my usual spot, I sought out Nicodemus, the one Pharisee who seemed to have a fondness for Jesus and his teaching. I knew no rabbi in Nicodemus's position would dare to openly declare himself a disciple, but I also knew from our debates and discussions that he was not hostile to Jesus as so many of the learned men in Jerusalem were. He might have a clue as to where Jesus had gone.

But when I found him and posed my question, he shook his head. "Rabbi James, why do you ask me about Jesus? He is your brother; if anyone would know where he is, you would be more likely than I."

"My brother Jesus knows I do not follow him or his teachings, and he would not be likely to tell me where he goes," I said simply.

"What, and you think I am a disciple? Do I look like a Galilean?" Nicodemus said.

"Rabbi, I know you are no Galilean fisherman, but I also know there are many here in Jerusalem, and all over Judea, who are friendly to Jesus and listen to his message."

"And you think I am one such? Who has told you this?"

I realized that it would be difficult to make much progress with this inquiry when Nicodemus did not trust me. He was afraid, on one hand, that I might expose his friendship with Jesus to the other Pharisees, and on the other hand, that if he let me know anything about where Jesus had gone, I might make trouble for Jesus.

I spread my hands wide, as a man does to show he is carrying no weapons. "Rabbi Nicodemus, I do not come to you as a Pharisee or as a Galilean or even as Jesus' brother. I come to you as a father. My son Benjamin has gone off to follow Jesus, and I must find him and be assured that he is safe."

"And talk him out of his folly and bring him back to Jerusalem, no doubt," Nicodemus said.

I did not comment on that. "Would you not worry if your only son had gone away and you did not know where he was?"

His expression softened only a little. "I am sorry, but I know nothing of where Jesus has gone. I have listened to his teaching, it is true, but I am not privy to his secrets."

"Very well then. You can do no more for me. Thank you." I turned to go.

I was several steps away from him when Nicodemus called out. "Rabbi James!"

"Yes?"

"I know of another family whose son has gone away with Jesus."

When he told me the name, I knew it. The boy was John Mark, a friend of Benjamin's who, like my son, was training to be a scribe. His father had been a merchant, and his widowed mother was a woman of some means with a large house in Jerusalem. When I called upon her, she said that her son Mark had left with Jesus and his followers, but she did not know where they had gone. Unlike me, she was not distraught over this; she, too, was a believer in Jesus and had given Mark her blessing to follow him.

She gave me the names of a few other followers of Jesus, but all of them claimed they knew nothing of where he had gone after the Feast of Dedication. Meanwhile, I was being bombarded with the same question from Avram and others in Jerusalem who were anxious to know where Jesus was. The arrest they could not make in Jerusalem at the feast, among all Jesus' supporters, was still very much on their minds. If he could be captured in some quiet place, without many people around, and brought to justice, it would be simpler for everyone.

Avram did not spell this out for me; he did not have to. "I know your son has gone with Jesus," he said. "Your other brothers may be with him too. Can you really have no idea where he is? Or are you protecting him?"

"Protecting him from what?" I snapped. My temper was short: it was at least the fourth time Avram had asked me this question, and this after days and days of my own fruitless inquiries among Jesus' friends in the city. "What do you have in mind for him, Rabbi? Stoning for blasphemy? A quiet assassination at the hand of some murderer? Or do you want to hand him over to Herod or to Pilate for them to deal with?"

"I don't know!" Avram replied, as impatient as I was myself. "All I know is, we are under pressure from all directions to do something about Jesus. And what can we do if we do not know where he is?"

"If you do not know where he is, what threat does he pose?" I countered. "You say everyone is concerned that he and his followers will start a revolution and bring down the wrath of Rome, but how will Rome even notice if Jesus and his followers are nowhere to be found?"

Avram's eyes narrowed. "Wherever he is, whatever he is doing, he is either making trouble or preparing more," he said. "You seem very anxious to protect him all of a sudden. Are you warming to your family messiah?"

"No! I am a father concerned for his son!" I said, temper flaring again. There was no point discussing this further with Avram.

"We have men looking for him, too, and we will find him," Avram assured me, in a tone that did not encourage me at all. "And if you find him before we do, you might want to warn him that he will be safer in the hands of his fellow Jews than in Roman custody. Better he lets us capture him than Pilate."

But I thought that if I did see Jesus again, I would not give him that message. I was by no means sure it was true.

It took some time, but eventually rumors about Jesus began to trickle back to Jerusalem. People told me they heard he had gone over the Jordan, into the wilderness where John the Baptizer had begun his ministry. It made sense: it would be hard for anyone who wished Jesus ill to capture him in the wilderness with a large band of followers around him. And perhaps it made sense to him in another way too; he was coming full circle, going back to where he had begun his ministry alongside John. Coming back to the beginning in preparation for—what?

Were Jesus and his followers really about to mount a revolution, march into Jerusalem and attempt to overthrow the Roman governor, perhaps overthrow our own Jewish civil and religious authorities too? Every time I had spoken to Jesus over the past year, he had talked about the time not being right. Was the time finally right? Right for what?

One thing I knew for certain: if there was going to be violence, I wanted Benjamin far from it. I wanted to get him away from Jesus before the Roman legions came down in their full force and crushed Jesus and his disciples, as they crushed every would-be king and messiah eventually.

But I could not go hurrying off into the wilderness beyond Jordan without a guide or a clue where Jesus was. So I went to Bethany.

I had not been there since I had arranged Benjamin's marriage to Simon's daughter, nor had I sent any word to Simon of Benjamin's disappearance. I had, I suppose, cherished hopes that Benjamin would come home, safe and chastened, before Simon even needed to know he had run away. Home in time to celebrate a betrothal and continue with the life I had planned for him.

But it was too late for that now. I would not get my son back at all unless I found Jesus in time, and I hoped that someone in Bethany could lead me to him.

I could tell that Simon's feelings were mixed when I told him of Benjamin's flight. Being sympathetic to Jesus' movement and message, he did not disapprove of Benjamin's decision as another might have done. But the manner of it, yes, I could see that it concerned him. "I thought you said he was a steady, obedient young man," he said.

"He always has been—until this happened," I said. "This is what I cannot fathom about Jesus' message, Simon. If it is truly good, if it is from God, would it not lead people to greater loyalty and obedience? Would it not create more order in the family, in society? But instead, ever since he began preaching up in Galilee, I have seen families torn asunder—including my own. Wives leave their husbands and travel about with his disciples like immoral women; sons defy their fathers' authority; men abandon their families. What kind of kingdom is this that he preaches? A kingdom of no rule, no order, no respect? People say that he preaches about peace, but all I see is division and discord wherever he goes!"

Simon nodded. "You know that I believe his power is from God because he healed me," he agreed. "But those same things you speak of concern me as well. If he is really to gain any kind of power—the power we all dream of the true Messiah having—he will need wise counselors, older and steadier men who can set his feet on the right path."

I shook my head. "You speak in dreams, Simon. Long before any of that could happen, Jesus would be nailed to a Roman cross. You know what they will do to anyone who calls himself King of the Jews or sets himself up as a deliverer. That's why our own leaders want to arrest him—to silence him before the Romans can do it, and bring half Jerusalem down with him."

Simon opened his mouth to reply, but I cut him off, for once forgetting the respect I owed him as my better. "I have no patience for this talk, Rabbi Simon. I need to bring my son back—soon, before any evil befalls the followers of Jesus. Do you know where he is?"

"I only know what everyone is saying, that he is on the east side of the Jordan," Simon said. "But Lazarus has been out to see him. If you told him of your concern for Benjamin, he might take you there. I make no promises, you understand, but it would be worth your while to ask."

Lazarus, too, was suspicious of me. "As it happens," he said, "I was going there to see Jesus—sometime soon. This Shabbat, perhaps. But I hardly know if—I don't know if he would want me to bring you."

"I thought he said that anyone who came to him would never be cast out," I told Lazarus with a wry smile, and he laughed.

"Yes, but are you coming to him, or coming to spy on him?"

"I am coming to find my son and make sure he is safe," I said. "In truth, yes, I will urge Benjamin to come back to Jerusalem with me, because I think Jesus and his followers are in great danger, and I want my son far away from it."

Lazarus looked up from the bucket of plaster he was mixing; I had interrupted him at his work. "Rabbi James, if your son has given his life to following Jesus, I doubt you will convince him to come back, for he will not care much for his own safety. When you say that Jesus' followers are in danger, that makes me want to go to him and stay with him, rather than to stay away. All of us would be willing to face prison or death for him."

Would they be so willing, I wondered, *if prison or death were harsh realities rather than mere ideas?* It is easy to say one would die for a cause; harder to bear the reality when it comes.

Finally, Lazarus said I could travel along with him and his sisters. "When all is said and done, you are Jesus' brother, and I do not think he would keep you away. But you must swear—no, you must promise not to tell his enemies where the place is."

Mary, who had come up beside us without my notice, laughed. "You caught yourself, Lazarus! You were about to make Rabbi James swear to secrecy, till you remembered Jesus says not to swear by anything!"

I went back to Jerusalem and packed a few belongings, glad that Avram was not at home to question my departure. I told his household steward that I would be gone for a few days, and sent word to my students as well. On the morning of the fifth day of the week, I went to Lazarus's house in Bethany.

Lazarus had warned me we would walk much of that day, camp overnight, and continue our journey on the preparation day so we could reach Jesus before sunset on Shabbat evening. He and his sisters planned to stay for several days with Jesus.

Traveling with Lazarus's family put me in a curious position, for they were all—even Martha, in her quiet way—eager to see Jesus again, to be among his followers, while I was a hostile outsider. I kept my hostility, and my doubts, to myself as we walked through those barren hills by the river, looking for a shallow ford where we could cross to the other side.

Lazarus and Mary were both talkative, but Martha was quiet, which I found appropriate in a woman. Still, as the day went on, even she became a bit more relaxed around me. She was an attractive woman, past the first flush of her youth, of course, and not extravagantly beautiful in the way of her sister Mary, but there was a quiet dignity to her well-formed features and downcast eyes that I admired. What a shame such a woman had remained unwed—an unusual fate for a Jewish woman! I imagined she must resent her sister deeply for the ignominy Mary had brought upon the family and the way it had shadowed Martha's own life.

We crossed the river after a night camping on its banks, and late in the afternoon on the second day, after passing through miles of trackless wilderness following the winding path of the river, we saw a small village. But this was no ordinary village—or rather, it was quite ordinary in one way, a small cluster of mud-brick houses such as one might find anywhere in this Perean wilderness. But around it had sprung up a second village, a village of tents, as if a company of desert nomads had chosen the fringes of this village as their campsite.

But the inhabitants of the tents were no desert nomads but the followers of Jesus. No doubt Jesus himself was staying in one of the makeshift shelters. I saw the sons of Zebedee; I saw Matthew, the tax collector from Galilee; finally, I saw my own half-brother Simon, walking along talking earnestly to a couple of strangers.

I was alone on the road by then: Lazarus, Mary, and Martha had already gone to find Jesus. I called to Simon, and fairly ran down the road toward him. His face brightened to see me, but I spared no time on pleasantries.

"Simon, is Benjamin here? Do you know where he is?"

"Of course, brother. Benjamin came from Jerusalem with Jesus and was already here when I arrived. Do you want to see him?"

"Of course I want to see him! Am I permitted to? Or is he under orders not to speak to his own father?" I had not realized how upset I still was until I heard my own angry voice and saw its reflection in Simon's puzzled face.

"Simon, surely you know I didn't give Benjamin permission to come here with Jesus!" I snapped. "He stole away in secret! I have been mad with worry for him."

"James, there's no need to worry. He is perfectly safe with us."

"I wish that were true," I said, hurrying along the road behind him.

I expected fear or guilt or shame to cloud my son's face when I saw him again. But Benjamin was sitting on a rock by the riverside with several other young men about his own age, including his friend Mark, and looked glad to see me. "Father! You've come!" he said with a happy cry, and scrambled down off his perch to greet me.

"Benjamin!" Despite my anger and worry, I was glad to see him safe and well, and I clasped him in my arms, forgetting for a moment to chide him.

He did look appropriately sorry as he took my hands in his and said, "Forgive me, Father, for leaving the way I did, without seeking your permission. I was afraid you would not give me leave to go, and I knew that God was calling me to come and follow Jesus."

"Do you have any idea how I've worried? The nights I've lain awake fretting over you? Jesus is in danger, Benjamin—both from the Romans and from our own people. If he is arrested and punished, some of his followers will be at risk, too, especially his close disciples and his family. Do you think I want to see you in Roman chains?"

"But—but what about you, Father? You're here now; aren't you facing the same risk as the rest of us?"

I saw the light of hope in his eyes and had to crush it. "Benjamin, I am not here as a follower of Jesus. I still think his so-called mission is as misguided as I ever thought it was, and I still believe he is a deluded fool. I came to bring you home, to safety."

The light drained from his eyes. "I am sorry, Father, but I cannot leave now."

"Not even if your father gives you a direct order? Benjamin, as your father and head of this family, I forbid you to remain in the company of Jesus any longer. Return with me to Jerusalem."

It was pointless, as I knew it would be. But it was the only weapon in my arsenal, and Benjamin had obeyed me all his life. All his life, until now. Now he simply stood there shaking his head, his brown eyes brimming with tears, and repeated, "I'm sorry, Father, I cannot."

"Not cannot, but will not!" I said, my voice harsh and rough. I was holding back tears as well. "Do you take your uncle Jesus in place of your father now? Do you owe him the allegiance of a son? Will he adopt you?"

"No, Father, that's not it at all!" Benjamin said. "It's not about my obeying one father over another. God is the Father of all of us, and Jesus tells us that our greatest loyalty must be to Him, no matter what our earthly parents say . . ."

"Ah yes, Jesus is very good at telling people what God thinks and what God wants, isn't he? I think I need to have a talk with him."

"I'm sure that would be a good idea, Father," Benjamin said. "He's down by the river now."

I left Benjamin without another word. I was glad he did not offer to come with me, for what I wanted to say to Jesus I did not want to say in my son's presence.

I found Jesus at a noisy spot along the riverbank where women stood up to their knees in water beating clothes on the rocks while small children splashed and played around their feet. Jesus and John bar Zebedee were the only men present. John sat on a rock at a slight remove from the whole scene, but Jesus was in the center of everything, his robe hiked up above his knees and the hem of it damp, standing knee-deep in the cold, muddy Jordan water. He held something in his hands, some garment he was wringing out; apparently he had joined the women in the task of washing out clothes. But he was easily distracted by the children playing around him and was, as I came upon the scene, engaged in a laughing tug-of-war with a boy of about four or five who was hanging on to the end of the same wet piece of cloth. I stood surveying this bizarre scene, trying to imagine if any would-be messiah or king had ever looked so inappropriate for the part.

Finally John saw me and spoke to Jesus. Jesus looked up. Like Benjamin, his face was alight with welcome, although I could not believe Jesus was so naïve as to think I had come to be his disciple.

"James! Welcome!" he called. I picked my way through the grass and reeds along the riverside till I was close enough to say, "Jesus, I need to talk to you."

"Of course." He handed the garment to one of the women and waded out of the water, the sopping wet hem of his robe still slapping around his knees, his lower legs bare like a fisherman's. He led me over to a large rock where he sat down, and, after a moment's hesitation, I joined him.

"This is about Benjamin, of course," I said. "I cannot believe that you claim to be a teacher of the Law, doing God's work, yet you teach young men to disobey their fathers. Is 'Honor your father and your mother' not one of the commandments?"

"I follow the same Ten Commandments you do, James, and I hope all my followers honor their earthly parents. But honor is not always the same thing as obedience, especially when a boy has grown to manhood. Benjamin must answer to a higher authority than yours."

"A higher authority—you mean God. But you feel free to interpret God for your followers, to tell people you were sent by God. So what you really mean is that Benjamin must obey you!"

"I invited Benjamin to follow me, and he chose to come. I am sorry he did not feel able to tell you face to face. That is why I'm glad you've come—so that you can see for yourself what we are doing here, and that Benjamin is well and happy with us."

"That is not why I came! I came to bring my son home! You don't listen, Jesus, when I tell you that you are in danger, but you are! And I don't want my son in the middle of it."

Jesus had been looking out at the river, but now he turned back to me, his face grave. "James, if I don't listen when you say I'm in danger, what am I doing here in the wilderness, rather than back in Jerusalem or up in Galilee? I've come here because I know there is danger, and it's not the right time yet for me to face it."

"Hiding out in the wilderness won't protect you forever. Many people in Jerusalem know you are here."

"Of course they do! People come here every day from Jerusalem, from all around." He gestured at the tent village that had sprung up. "They come; they listen. Some like what they hear enough to stay. All our brothers are here now, and their wives, and even my mother."

"Mary is here?" I thought of that long-ago day in Capernaum when we had tried to see Jesus and he had turned us away, saying that his disciples were his true family. Yet he seemed glad enough to have his mother and brothers here now.

"Stay with us, at least for a while, James," Jesus said. "You do not have to believe—only listen, and judge for yourself."

I had no choice but to stay through the Shabbat, at least, for I could not travel during the sacred hours. So I found the tent where my brother Jude was staying, and he was kind enough to offer me a bedroll and food.

"Why are you here, Jude?" I asked. "Surely you have not been taken in by Jesus' message like the rest of the family?"

He shook his head slowly, thoughtfully. "I came because Simon, Joseph, and their families, and even Mary, all wanted to come. Even my own wife urged me to bring her here. And I stayed because—well, it's hard to explain. But I guess maybe I have been taken in by his message, after all." Taciturn as ever, Jude would enter into no more discussion than that, but answered my questions with, "Wait and see. Wait till you've been here a while, and then see what you think."

The next morning I joined the rest of Jesus' followers on the riverbank for the strangest Shabbat service I had ever attended. There, in that synagogue without walls, well over a hundred people sat on the grass and on rocks while Jesus perched on a little rise of land and pitched his voice to carry over the crowd.

The hymns we sang and the prayers we prayed were familiar ones, the beloved psalms and prayers we all knew from years of Shabbat worship. But then Jesus began to speak, and it was nothing like the homilies I gave in the synagogue on a Shabbat morning, or like the teaching of any other rabbis I knew. Nor was it confrontational like the way he had addressed the crowds at the Temple in Jerusalem, where he knew his enemies were hanging upon every word. Here he was among friends; even those who were not avowed followers were here because they were curious and interested, not because they wished him harm. His tone was relaxed and easy, though he spoke loudly enough for us all to hear.

"How happy it makes God to see people turning away from their old lives and beginning again!" he said. "God, your Father, is like a shepherd who has a hundred sheep. As he brings them back to the sheepfold, he counts and sees that there are only ninety-nine. One is missing. Won't the shepherd leave the ninety-nine sheep who are safe in the fold and go out and search for his lost lamb? Won't he search high and low, on mountains and cliffs, through the rain and the dark night, till at last he finds it? Picture him then, placing the lost lamb on his shoulders and carrying it home, calling to everyone, 'Rejoice with me! I have found my lost sheep!' "

A ripple of laughter ran through the crowd at the picture of a shepherd so in love with his one sheep that he called everyone to come celebrate its return. Jesus laughed, too, but he said, "That is exactly what God is like! He rejoices just that way, and the angels in heaven along with Him, when even one sinner repents and turns to Him."

I scanned the crowd as Jesus spoke, trying to see who these people were who had come out into the wilderness to hear him and declare their allegiance to him. Like John when he had preached and baptized in this same spot years earlier, Jesus attracted all kinds of people, many of them curiosity-seekers. But those who stayed with John and followed him, his disciples, were almost all young men. Jesus, by contrast, drew young and old, men, women, and even children to come follow him. I knew that not all these people were staying here permanently; some, like Lazarus and Martha, would come for a little while as their lives and their work permitted, and then return home. Others had made a complete break with their past lives, it seemed, and did nothing but follow Jesus about.

When he spoke of the joy in heaven over the repentant sinner, I looked at Lazarus's sister Mary of Magdala, who sat nearby. I remembered Jesus telling her a similar story once, about a woman and her dowry coins. Her face shone as she listened to Jesus, and I thought that for one such as Mary, whose past life had been a wreck of sin and demon possession, this news that Heaven rejoiced over a repentant sinner was good news indeed.

But what of someone like me? Or—I looked at her, sitting as always in the shadow of her sister—Martha? How did Jesus welcome those who had lived lives of goodness and duty, following the Law, obeying the rules of family and community? The truth was that though many among his hearers clearly felt like they were the lost sheep, I felt no such thing.

"Another story, then?" Jesus said, in response to something someone near him had said. "All right, the same story, but in different words, perhaps. A man had two sons. The oldest was good and dutiful, but the younger was rebellious and willful. He said to his father, 'Give me my share of the inheritance now. I don't want to wait till you die.'"

A few in the crowd gasped, for to say such a thing was flagrant disrespect to one's father—almost the same as wishing his father dead. But, as Jesus went on to tell the story, the father acquiesced to this strange request, and the younger son left home with his money and, predictably, went on to squander it all on sin and luxury, as served him right.

So far, it seemed a harmless tale of wrongdoing and punishment, for the rebellious son ended up penniless, rejected by his worldly friends, feeding swine and envying them their slop. The son came to his senses, as anyone would expect, and saw that he had done wrong, and determined to go home to his father and repent, asking for a servant's position in the house since he had thrown away the privileges of a son.

"But on the road home, while he was still a long way off, his father saw him and ran toward him, taking him in his arms," Jesus said. Again, surprise from the listeners—at least, those who had not heard this particular story before—at the image of the dignified old man picking up the skirts of his robe and running. Running, to meet his worthless son who should have come home groveling and ashamed!

Yet I felt a twinge of sympathy for that father, thinking of my own reunion with Benjamin the day before. Angry as I had been at him for running away, I had still been overwhelmed with joy and relief to see him well and safe again. No doubt the father had worried for that worthless son, and wept over him, and in the moment of reunion his joy overcame wisdom.

But the story continued on, Jesus piling detail on detail to make it ever more incredible. "The father would not even allow his son to apologize but called the servants and asked for the best robe to cover his rags, and the family signet ring for his finger. Then he ordered them to slaughter the fattest calf for a feast, to celebrate his son's homecoming!"

This was simply too much! Reinstated as a son? Given high honors? Celebrated rather than being punished for his wrongdoing? If this was Jesus' picture of God, it went far beyond the woman finding her coin or the shepherd finding his sheep. This father was so loving, so generous as to be foolish. It was one thing to say God rejoiced over the repentance of a sinner, but another to depict Him as not even remembering or caring about the sins of the past. Yet as Jesus described that homecoming party, I remembered a text from the scroll of the prophet Isaiah: "I am He who blots out your transgressions and remembers your sins no more." Could God really be so generous, so prodigal in His love and acceptance?

The story was not finished. "As the celebration went on, feasting long into the evening, family and servants rejoiced because the lost son had come home. But one remained outside—the older son. The father went outside and found him and said, 'Why are you not inside enjoying the feast?' The older son burst out in anger, 'All these years I've worked and slaved for you, and when did you ever throw a party for me? And now this worthless boy comes home, having spent your hard-earned money on drink and prostitutes, and you welcome him back like a conquering king!' "

The elder son's words echoed my own thoughts so neatly that I caught my breath. Why, this older son was just like me—a sensible man, one who understood duty and loyalty. He was offended by his father's foolish generosity just as I was offended by the picture of God that Jesus' story was painting.

"The father said to his older son," Jesus went on, " 'Son, you have always been with me, and all that I have is yours. But your brother was dead, and is alive! He was lost, and is found! Come in, and celebrate with us!' "

Jesus did not tell the end of the story; that is, he did not tell what the older son did or said. As he often did with stories—in the little experience I'd had of listening to him, and the accounts of others—he simply let the story sit on the listeners' hearts, allowing them to draw their own conclusions. Now he said only, "Never doubt that God rejoices when you turn to Him, nor think that He will turn anyone away. And He invites us all to join in that celebration."

Judging by the smiles on people's faces, they loved the story, appreciated the hope it gave them. In the faces around me I saw only one as troubled as mine, only one that wore a frown. It was the face of Martha. I did not question, just then, why my eyes were so often drawn toward her; I only noticed that Jesus' story had left her troubled, too, and I had an unaccountable urge to talk about it with her. An impossible urge, in the everyday world we both inhabited—but here, in this strange world Jesus had created about him, where women discussed the Scriptures with him like disciples, and Jesus himself went down to the river to help the women wash clothes—perhaps

anything was possible. We broke for the midday meal, and I promised myself that if the moment arose, I would find a time to talk to
Martha about Jesus' strange story.

Chapter Nineteen

During the noon meal, everyone ate in small groups, sharing whatever they had. I wondered how Jesus managed to feed all this company, so far from a large town or market. Lazarus and his sisters had brought food with them from Bethany; we ate some and gave the rest away. I had never seen anything to confirm the tales of Jesus miraculously multiplying food, but however it worked, everyone seemed to have enough.

While we ate together, I had no opportunity for the private conversation I had imagined with Martha. Everyone joined in the conversation, but while Mary was voluble and excited, Martha was quiet. She added to the conversation only when Lazarus said he had to return home within a few days to complete a job he had been given, plastering a new house in Jerusalem, and asked his sisters if they wanted to stay with Jesus or return home to Bethany. Mary was unsure, but Martha said quickly, "I want to go home with you."

During the meal, I noticed Jesus moving from group to group, spending a little time with each. When he reached our circle, he waved away the offer of some bread and figs, saying he had already eaten more than enough. "James," he said to me, "Benjamin is looking for you. He has something important to discuss with you."

While Jesus stayed and chatted, I went to find my son. He was eating with some of the other members of our family but excused himself when he saw me coming.

"Father, I don't want to repeat the mistake I made when I came here, making a decision without your knowledge," he said, his young face earnest and serious. "I am going to be baptized this afternoon, baptized as a follower of Jesus. I wanted to tell you before it happened."

Tell me. Not ask my permission, but simply let me know that he had already reached this decision. "What do you mean by being baptized?" I said. "Is Jesus baptizing people now, as John did?"

Benjamin took a deep breath, apparently relieved I wasn't thundering and forbidding him to be baptized—as if forbidding would have made a bit of difference! "Jesus has always taught that baptism is a symbol of beginning a new life, just as John taught. He and his disciples used to baptize people here in the Jordan in the old days. Now that we're back here, Jesus has called for those who want to begin a new life in God to be baptized."

I did not know what to tell Benjamin. "You are a good Jew, raised to observe the Law. The Temple ceremonies provide for the forgiveness of sins and a new start. There is no need for Jesus' baptism or John's baptism to declare your intent to begin a new life—but I suppose there is no harm in it, either. I only worry about anything that draws you further into Jesus' circle, worry because it will mean trouble for you in the future."

"I believe it will mean glory for me in the future," Benjamin said, and whether he was talking about the resurrection, or about some imaginary future when Jesus would become king and honor those who had been loyal from the beginning, I really did not know. But I did not forbid him—perhaps because I did not want to put him in a position to disobey me again.

Sure enough, a little while after the noon meal was finished, Jesus began circulating among the people again, calling everyone down to the riverbank. When we had all assembled, he said, "Most of you remember John's baptism here in this river. Many of you were baptized then, some of you by John himself. I told you this morning how your heavenly Father rejoices when a sinner turns away from his old life and begins a new, eternal life in Him. Going into the water of baptism and rising again shows that the new life is beginning. Who will come and be born again?"

People began to move toward the river. Several of Jesus' closest followers—I noticed Peter, Andrew, and the sons of Zebedee among them—were already wading out into the water, not to be baptized but to baptize. Jesus himself remained on the riverbank, speaking to people as they approached, helping them down into the water, but not baptizing.

"Why does he not baptize them himself?" I asked Lazarus, who again sat near me.

"He never has," Lazarus said. "In the early days I think it was because he did not want to be seen as a rival to John. Now, perhaps he is afraid that anyone he baptizes would set himself above others, think he was better because he was baptized by Jesus himself. He talks about how there are to be no hierarchies or distinctions between us, how all are equal in God's eyes."

Now Benjamin was coming down the riverbank, ready for his baptism. Nor was he alone. Most of my family was with him—all three of my brothers and their wives, our sister Naomi and her husband, and Mary as well. Jesus spoke quietly to each one as they passed him, but he made no special mention of them nor showed them any particular favor, not even his mother.

Though I thought I would not be able to look at anyone but Benjamin, I found my eyes drawn as much to Mary. She walked down into the water with her head uncovered, as did all the women being baptized, and I saw that all her long dark hair was now gray. But her face, despite the lines, was the face of that girl my father had brought home to marry, that girl I had resented so much when I was a child. Her serious eyes were wide, and I could see joy all over her face as she moved toward John bar Zebedee, who embraced her warmly before plunging her beneath the cold, muddy water and helping her to rise again.

What a strange journey her life had been! Somehow she had managed to convince herself that her child, conceived in who knew what kind of sin, was a divine gift, and she had raised him with that belief. Now she came to him—her own son—as a humble disciple, receiving no special honor, being submerged in dirty water by one of his followers as a sign of allegiance.

I was so caught up in studying Mary that I almost missed the moment when my son Benjamin was baptized by Peter the fisherman. He looked up at the watching crowd as he emerged from the water, and I knew he was looking for me, hoping for a sign of recognition, of approval. But I could give him none. The only gift I had to offer was that I had not forbidden him to do this, had not severed the ties between us irrevocably.

Many people, like Benjamin, had apparently arranged beforehand to be baptized today, but others were coming on the spur of the moment, responding to Jesus' call. All our family had gone through the waters now, and other followers were coming, when to my surprise I saw Martha approaching Jesus. I had never seen her without a veil covering her hair and obscuring her face, and I am ashamed to admit that my first thought was how lovely her hair was. Then I wondered why she had chosen to be baptized now, when she had counted herself a follower of Jesus from his earliest days in Judea.

Later that day, sitting in front of a tent with my son and my brother, I had a chance to ask her. I saw Martha and Mary passing by on a path, and went over to speak with them, asking about their plans to return to Bethany. Mary, as I had hoped, stopped to speak to the women of our family, leaving me to walk with Martha back toward Lazarus's tent.

"You were baptized this afternoon," I said. "I suppose I ought to congratulate you."

She darted me a sideways smile, her beautiful hair once again covered by her veil, her face in shadow. "I know you do not accept Jesus' teaching, Rabbi James, so I am sure you do not accept his baptism."

"Still, I can recognize when someone makes a decision, a step that is important to them. Can you tell me—if I'm not too bold to ask—why you decided today to be baptized?"

She was silent a moment as we walked along, and I thought that after all I had been too bold, presumed too much. Then she said, "I have followed Jesus since Lazarus and I first heard him preach, back when he was still with John. After Mary was delivered from her demons, I knew for certain that Jesus was the Messiah, and I trusted him to set Israel free. But at the same time—oh, Rabbi James, I cannot tell you how I resented my sister! How angry I was at her for being so . . . oh, I cannot explain it. She has had a harder life than I have, I know, and yet, once she met Jesus, everything seemed—too easy."

"Like Jesus' story about the two sons."

"Yes!" Martha dared to meet my eyes for a moment then looked away. "He told that story for me, I know. I am like the older brother, resenting how easily Mary repented and was welcomed back. I didn't understand. And then, this morning, after he told the story, I finally saw."

"Saw what?" I asked, almost eagerly, as if she might somehow have the key that would help me understand all the mysteries Jesus had brought into my life.

"How great God's love is. How it is big enough for Mary *and* for me—how much He loves us all. I see it because of Jesus; the way he loves is the way God loves. I truly believe that now—and then I knew I had repented. Not of the kind of sins my sister committed, but of pride, of thinking I was better than she was."

A wave of emotion I could not name swept over me, and I struggled to find the right words. "If following Jesus has brought you some peace, some happiness, then I am glad for that," I said. "I only fear that in the end, all of you who follow him will trade that peace for something far worse."

"It's a risk I am willing to take," Martha said. We had reached Lazarus's tent, and I said Goodbye but stood quiet for a moment, looking out at the river before turning back.

"She is a good woman," a voice behind my shoulder said, and I turned to see Jesus. I had not heard him come up behind me.

"Yes, she is," I agreed. "It's a shame such a good woman—" I was about to say something about her being corrupted by the loose morals of Jesus' group of followers, but it seemed unnecessarily harsh. I changed my mind and instead finished, "such a good woman never had the chance to marry and have a family."

Jesus smiled. "Some might say what a shame it is that such a good man as yourself, widowed so young, has never taken another wife to keep him company in his old age."

I shrugged away from Jesus' hand on my shoulder. It was one of the things that made me most uneasy about him: we could be at odds over almost everything, yet have these sudden moments of camaraderie warmed by all that we shared—our family ties, our common past—and he almost managed to draw me into that warmth with him. Then I would remind myself, as I did now, of everything that he was doing, of how firmly I was opposed to his mission, and pull away.

"When you were younger, you never let me arrange a match for you," I reminded him. "Why should you try to arrange one for me now?"

Jesus only laughed. "Martha and Mary and their brother are returning home to Bethany in a day or so," he said. "Lazarus has work he must attend to. Are you going with them, or will you stay with us a little longer?"

"I . . . I suppose I will go back with them when they go," I said. I had not realized they were returning so soon.

"You might stay a little longer," Jesus suggested. "Benjamin would like it if you did—and so would I."

"You don't know what danger you're leading these people into, my son included," I said, but Jesus simply waved a hand, brushing away my warnings. I started to protest, but he said, "I know it all, James. I know the danger from the Romans, from Herod, from our own people. It doesn't frighten me."

"Why not?"

"I know I am doing what I was sent to do, and if the time comes that I'm arrested or imprisoned or even executed, then that will be the right time."

"That's rather hard on those who follow you, isn't it?" I countered, still thinking of Benjamin, but also of the rest of my family, and of Martha and Lazarus.

"They have made their choice. But it's true some of them haven't truly counted the cost," Jesus admitted. "They are still looking for something different from what I came to bring."

"That's what I struggle to understand. What did you come to bring? What are you trying to accomplish here?"

Jesus smiled. "I can't tell you, James. I can only show you. That's why I want you to stay—so that you can see what I mean by God's kingdom."

The strange thing is, I did stay. And in a way, I did see. I told Lazarus that I would stay a while longer rather than returning to Bethany with him, and gave him messages to send on to Jerusalem for me. I said only that I would be out of the city some time longer, but I wondered what Avram would think. Would he believe I had capitulated, followed the rest of my family at Jesus' side?

Certainly that was what Benjamin thought, though I urged caution, told him I was only there to observe and see if I thought it safe for him to stay. He ignored my cautions. I think he was so taken with Jesus and his message that he truly did not believe that anyone, having once heard it, could reject it.

Even stranger than my decision to stay was the fact that, over the days that followed, I truly did begin to see a little of what Jesus was trying to do. There in that isolated spot on the east side of the Jordan, he had created, among his followers and the curious who came to listen and look, a kind of kingdom of God in miniature. It was a strange kingdom, with many of the features I had already noticed and always disapproved of among his disciples: the lack of respect for traditional authority and the structures of family and community, the freedom of women to mingle and participate with men on an equal basis, the lack of concern for the rituals of our faith.

But honesty compelled me to admit, as the cool winter days unfolded, that there was much to admire there as well. Everyone shared the work equally, whether it was putting up shelters, building fires, preparing food, or whatever needed to be done. Anything that came into the little community was shared equally by all. And this sharing, with the loss of those same social hierarchies I had mourned, meant that no one was given special preference. There were no divisions between rich and poor, master and servant. As I had seen before, Jesus' own family was given no special treatment, nor was Jesus himself. Far from setting himself up as a would-be king or lord, he shared equally in the work with everyone. Only when he spoke or taught did he assume a mantle of authority; then it was as if he really believed God were speaking through him, and the others listened to him as if this, indeed, were true.

It was strange, but it was also, in some ways, beautiful, as if this entire community had been drawn together in an attempt to live out the most basic principle of Jesus' teaching: love one another.

What was most clear to me during those weeks was that the kingdom Jesus was trying to build had nothing to do with the power structures of Herod or the Romans. He did not talk about revolution, nor call men to arms: he called them instead to love and to give and to share. He seemed to envision a whole world of little communities like this one, of people willingly laying aside wealth and power and influence to come together and love and serve one other.

It was a mad dream, of course, and even half his own followers didn't seem to grasp what he was after. Perhaps I saw it more clearly through the eyes of an outsider, a stranger. As I talked to Jesus' closest followers over the days I spent there, it seemed to me that only a few saw what I saw, that Jesus was establishing a kingdom that had nothing to do with thrones and governments and had everything to do with people living together in peace and generosity. Many of them, even the Twelve, who had been with him longest and worked with him most closely, still dreamed of Jesus declaring himself Messiah and seizing David's throne by force, though Jesus himself never spoke of such things.

There was rivalry, I discovered, between the two sets of brothers—James and John, the sons of Zebedee, and Peter and Andrew, the sons of Jonah. I knew Zebedee's sons better through our family connection with them, and young John tried to make a confidant of me and enlist me to his side in the power struggle.

"Peter claims that because his brother Andrew was the first to follow Jesus, they should have precedence when Jesus sets up his kingdom," John told me earnestly one day as we worked side by side to put up a shelter that had collapsed one windy night. "But it's only because Peter is so loud and bold, he thinks everyone will listen to him. He's just a fisherman, no better than my brother and me; indeed, we've all fished side by side for years."

I listened to his diatribe, watching his serious young face. He was still half boy, really, not many years older than Benjamin, with the passion of the young. "What do you hope to gain?" I asked. "If you do win out over Peter and Andrew and earn the positions closest to Jesus, what do you think that will mean?"

John hesitated, suddenly unsure of himself. "Well, when Jesus becomes king, we will—we will have positions of honor in his ruling council. We have been with him long, and we are blood kin to his mother. You will be honored too; your family will be royalty! But those of us who followed him from the first will have the first places. It's only right."

"And this business of Jesus becoming king—how is it to happen, do you think?" I asked mildly. "What is he doing to prepare to take the throne?"

Again, John seemed momentarily at a loss for words. "He speaks of waiting till the time is right," he said finally. "When the time is right, God will give the kingdom of Israel into Jesus' hands."

There were others among Jesus' disciples who had the same expectations of worldly power and success, but much clearer ideas about how to achieve those goals. I spoke one day with a man called Judas Iscariot, who had been among Jesus' followers since the early days. I had never met the man before, but I recognized his keen mind at once. He had some skill with business, and kept account of the money that was earned or given to Jesus' cause, making sure that everything was apportioned equally. He also had a shrewd politician's mind, and when I spoke with him about Jesus' ultimate victory, he was far less willing to leave it all in God's hands than John had been.

"Jesus has everything he needs to lead a movement that could seize power in Jerusalem," Judas told me one day as we walked back from the nearby village with some supplies we had bought there. "He has popularity all over Judea as well as in Galilee, and when he speaks, men listen. They are willing to lay down their livelihoods, leave their homes, and follow him! He has followers from all walks of life, the rich and the poor; his message appeals to everyone. If he were to focus his efforts on creating a movement that would topple the government we have now, I truly believe he could gather enough support to overthrow even Herod, perhaps drive out the Romans."

"You really believe it?"

"I do. I haven't followed him for three years for nothing. I know what he's capable of."

"But do you think that is what Jesus really wants? Is that his plan?"

Judas sighed heavily. The question obviously frustrated him. "Jesus is a great leader, but he is also a dreamer," he said. "What he has here— this little camp of followers, all working and sharing and praying together—sometimes I think that is all he wants. And he says ridiculous things—talks about sacrifice and laying down his life—when he should be talking about marching into Jerusalem in triumph! He needs someone to guide him, to force him into action if need be. I sometimes think if no one forces his hand, he will never take action."

"What do you mean by forcing his hand?"

Judas got a faraway look, which I took to mean that he did not intend to share his plans with someone whose loyalties were as unclear as mine. "Something that will force him to show his power," was all he said.

I thought of Rabbi Simon of Bethany, telling me that Jesus needed wiser men to provide him guidance. He seemed to share the same view as Judas did: anything was possible for Jesus if only the right men could be allowed to control him, to steer him in the direction they wanted him to go. I laughed inwardly at that. They would have had to grow up in the same household as Jesus to realize how unlikely it was he would ever let anyone control or even guide him. He had gotten through more than thirty years of life firmly believing he took orders from no one but God.

I gave another quiet laugh at the thought that any movement with Jesus as its figurehead could ever succeed against the Roman army; but that was a bitter laugh full of dark memories. Did nobody recall the uprisings of the past, Rome's bitter revenge?

Even if Jesus had no military or political ambitions of his own, the threat from Rome was still real. Jesus' followers in Judea and in Galilee numbered in the hundreds, perhaps even thousands by now, and while many of these were fair-weather followers who would drift away at the first sign of trouble or challenge, there was definitely a hard core of those who would fight to make him king. The presence of such a movement was all the Romans needed to crack down and eliminate the leader. Despite all Jesus' talk of peace and love, it was easy to find things he had said—the same sorts of things any Jewish teacher might have said over the past two hundred years—about obeying God above any earthly lord—or to point to the fact that his followers often called him "lord" and "master." The Romans had crucified would-be rebels for far less.

And if the Roman threat was real, then the threat from our own leaders was just as real. I knew the Jerusalem religious leaders. The Sadducees, comfortable in their positions of power, had no desire to be associated with any kind of rebellion or uprising. As for my own faction, the Pharisees, they had supported rebels too often in the past. The Pharisees I knew had grown cautious, anxious to avoid any taint of scandal. Jesus was clearly a devout Jew, however unorthodox; some of his teachings and practices might even lead people to identify him as a Pharisee. It was vital to the leaders that they distance themselves from Jesus so that the Romans would not suspect they were supporting him. And the best way to distance themselves was to show the Roman governor that they had already taken steps against Jesus, such as putting him and some of his key followers in prison.

I thought John bar Zebedee's dreams of sitting on Jesus' ruling council were just that—dreams. But he was right about one thing. Those closest to Jesus—the disciples who had followed him longest and his own family—would be accorded special status. Not the status of rulers in his government, but the status of fellow prisoners when either our own rulers or the Romans felt ready to attack this little enclave. I did not intend to be here when it happened, and I did not want Benjamin here either.

Still, I lingered. I gave up trying to convince anyone, even a sensible man like Judas Iscariot, of the very real danger facing Jesus and his followers. I simply lived day to day with them. Despite the dissension and quarreling among some of his disciples, despite the fact that they were often at odds about what the goal of this movement really was, still, there was so much good here that I had no difficulty seeing why people were drawn to it. Drawn to Jesus, with his stories and his healing and his warmth that attracted men as they might be attracted to a campfire on a cold night.

There were plenty of those, too, both campfires, and cold nights, as the weeks of winter unfolded. Jesus had come to the Temple for the Feast of Dedication, and I had crossed the Jordan to find him a few weeks later. Now it was almost time for the flax harvest and the celebration of Purim. While new followers continued to arrive and some others had to return to their homes, I stayed, not sure what I was waiting for. Benjamin still refused to return to Jerusalem with me, and I suppose it was the hope that I might convince him that made me linger.

One day as I sat debating a passage of the Torah with a few of Jesus' followers, a man ran into the camp, clearly out of breath and exhausted from running. "Where—is—Jesus?" was all he managed to say. Andrew got up and offered to take the man to Jesus, and the rest of us, our discussion broken, drifted along in his wake, all curious to see who had sent Jesus such an urgent message.

We found Jesus sitting outside the tent of a widow with two young children, telling stories to the children. The messenger dropped to one knee in front of Jesus. "Master," he said, still struggling to get his breath. "I have come—in great haste—from Bethany. One you love there—Lazarus—is ill and—on the point of death." He drew one deep breath as Jesus, startled, set aside the little boy on his lap and got to his feet. "His sisters, Martha and Mary, told me to come get you," the messenger went on. "They ask you—to come heal him."

Jesus stared at the man for a moment, then said, "Thank you. Thank you for bringing me this message." He looked down the road the man had come along; as if he could see all the way to Bethany, see Lazarus on his sickbed. My friend Lazarus had been well and healthy when he left Jesus' camp just a few weeks before, so this surely must have been some fever that had come upon him suddenly. Such an illness could kill a strong man within a few days. Despite all the skepticism I had ever had about Jesus and his healing powers, I was overwhelmed with gratitude now that Martha and her sister had seen fit to send for Jesus. I wanted to go with Jesus to Bethany, to offer some comfort to Martha if I could and to see Jesus restore Lazarus to health and strength.

Already those around Jesus were discussing the journey. "It's two days' walk to Bethany; we should leave at once," Peter said.

"This fellow said he got here in a day," someone said, pointing to the messenger who was being led away for water and rest.

"Yes, but we're hardly going to run all the way."

"If Jesus takes only a few of us, we could travel quickly," Peter said. "We might get there in a day and a half."

"Jesus would be mad to go to Bethany," put in another voice. This was Thomas the Twin, a quiet disciple who, despite having been with Jesus a long time, was more reluctant than most to talk about his hopes for the future. Though he said little, I thought Thomas had a better grasp of the dangers facing Jesus than most of his followers did. "Bethany is on the doorstep of Jerusalem, and the entire reason we are here in the wilderness is that Jesus has enemies in Jerusalem. If he goes there with only a handful of men, what's to stop them from arresting him—and all those with him?"

"How can you think of such a thing when Lazarus is dying?" snapped Peter.

Amid all the voices, one was silent—the voice of Jesus. He stood among his bickering followers looking troubled, and gradually they, too, fell silent, turning to him for a decision. "Do we leave at once, Master?" Peter said.

"No," Jesus said abruptly, and turned away. "I need time alone with my Father, to pray."

"Do we have time?" Peter countered, the only one who dared question Jesus so directly. "The message said Lazarus was at the point of death!"

"There is always time to pray, Peter," Jesus said, and walked down the path away from the rest of us.

As soon as he was gone, the disciples fell into their usual bickering, arguing about whether they should go to Bethany or not. I left them and went down the same road Jesus had gone, following at a little distance. I did not wish to interrupt him at his prayers, but I was curious. I could see both sides of the argument. Lazarus was a good friend and a devoted follower in dire need. But going so close to Jerusalem was dangerous for Jesus. Yet when had Jesus ever thought of his own safety? He had always acted impulsively, especially when he believed he was following God's call, to preach or to heal. Why was he suddenly debating whether to go to Bethany?

From a bend in the road I watched him, though he did not see me. He was in his own world, kneeling over a tree stump, face in his hands, pouring out his heart to God, whom he called his Father. I was too far to hear his words, but from every line of his body, I could sense how deeply troubled he was. Jesus, who had always seemed so certain about every decision, was agonizing about whether to go to Bethany.

As soon as he returned to the camp that evening, with night shadows falling, people surrounded him. "Will you leave at once for Bethany?" "Do you suppose Lazarus is still alive?" The messenger who had brought the news added to the clamor, saying, "Lord, Martha was most insistent you come at once."

"Yes, yes, I know," Jesus said. "But I will not leave tonight. The time is not right." As he always had, he fell back on that mysterious saying: "The time is not right." He moved to some inner schedule the rest of us could not understand, and I knew that many in the camp were frustrated that night that he was not already on the road to Bethany, while others thought the very idea of going was madness.

Mary, Jesus' mother, was in the former group. She was very fond of Lazarus's sister Mary of Magdala, and when I visited her tent the next morning, she was fretting. "I wonder if that poor man even survived the night, James?" she asked me, although neither of us had any way of knowing. "I hope Jesus leaves at once this morning; Mary and Martha trusted him to come right away, and I cannot understand why he delays."

"I have never been able to understand why Jesus does anything," I said heavily. "Just when I think I have figured out what he's about, he does something completely different. I suppose he will leave for Bethany this morning, though, to get a full day's travel in."

But he did not. Whenever anyone asked about his plans to go to Bethany, or urged the seriousness of Lazarus's illness, his answer was always the same: not yet, not yet. If anyone asked, "Then when, Master? When will you go? Will you go at all?" he simply refused to answer.

The whole day passed like that. By the following morning, nearly two full days now since the messenger had come, people had stopped asking Jesus about going to Bethany. Finally Peter said, "Lord, what about Lazarus?"

Jesus, who was usually so busy, was sitting idly by the embers of a dying fire, poking them with a stick. He looked up then, stood up, and as if the question had just occurred to him for the first time, said, "Get ready. We are going to Bethany. Lazarus is asleep, and we must wake him up!"

Everybody nearby looked at each other in confusion. Nobody had any idea what Jesus meant, nor why he had suddenly made the decision he had been putting off for two days.

Finally John ventured, "I suppose if Lazarus is sleeping, that's a good sign." I had noticed before that many of Jesus' followers seemed to believe he had some supernatural knowledge, that he could foretell the future or know what was going on far away. Which is probably why everyone took it seriously when Jesus' next words were, "Lazarus sleeps the sleep of death; he has already died."

I was skeptical. There was no way Jesus could possibly know that; no one new had come into the camp since the messenger from Bethany, and I did not credit him with divine knowledge. Most likely he was guessing, based on simple common sense. After all, Lazarus had been near death three days before, when the messenger first left Bethany. Now Jesus was speaking with his usual authority to make people think he knew things he could not know. But Jesus' face was shadowed and sad, and I thought that he really believed Lazarus dead.

Why, then, the delay? And if Jesus really thought Lazarus was dead, why risk going to Bethany now, of all times?

"Not too many may travel with me," Jesus said. "There is no need for haste now, but we do not want to travel too slowly, either. The Twelve—all of you will come. And . . ." He hesitated, his eyes scanning the group. "James. You and Benjamin come. That's enough. The rest stay here. I will return soon."

"He may never return," I heard Thomas say, aside, to Andrew as we prepared to gather our belongings and go, "not if he ventures so near Jerusalem. But we may as well go and die with him as stay here."

"Thomas, ever the optimist," said Andrew.

The mood in the camp, and among those chosen to go with Jesus, was as somber as Thomas's words indicated. There was confusion, too, for no one understood why Jesus was acting as he was. I was glad, though, that he had chosen Benjamin and me to go with him, no matter what his motives. I wanted to visit Lazarus's resting place, if he truly was dead, and to offer my condolences to his sisters. And then, so close to Jerusalem, it might be easier to urge Benjamin to return home with me.

Jesus made no especial haste about the journey; we camped for the night at the same spot I had camped with Lazarus and his sisters, weeks before. It was hard to imagine Lazarus, who had been so vital and lively a short time before, lying cold and still in death. Harder still to understand why, if Jesus really did have the power to heal, he had not prevented such a thing. Those who believed most fervently in his powers claimed they had seen him heal at a distance, with just a word, even when he was not in the presence of the sick person. I doubted that, as I doubted so many of the tales about Jesus, but it was strange that he had not at least made the effort, for such a dear friend.

Late on the second day of our journey, we could see the houses of

Bethany in the distance. A slight figure stood outside the town gates as if waiting for someone. As we drew closer, I could see it was a woman.

I expected the impulsive, emotional Mary, but it was Martha who came toward us as we approached, her face so grieved I could tell at once that Jesus was right: Lazarus was dead.

She stopped in the road in front of Jesus and held out her hands as if pleading. "Lord, if you had been here, my brother would not have died," she said.

Jesus moved toward her, and I wondered how he might possibly explain his delay. He began to say "Martha—" but she cut him off.

"Even now, even now that he's been dead four days, I know God will do anything, anything if you ask—" her voice broke off and tears streamed down her face.

"Martha, your brother will rise again."

"I know, Lord. I believe in the resurrection, and I know my brother will rise on the last day," Martha said, brushing away her tears with the edge of her veil, struggling for composure.

"The resurrection?" Jesus' voice was stronger now, as if he was preaching. Other people were coming out of Bethany now, joining our little group on the road. "Martha, I AM the Resurrection and the Life. Whoever believes in me, though he dies, he will live again eternally. Do you believe this?"

Martha turned her tear-streaked face up to his, no longer hiding behind that womanly modesty I had so admired in her. I remembered she had told me how for so long her faith had been reluctant, hemmed in by her pride and bitterness. Now it shone out of her eyes, despite the pain and grief there.

"Jesus, I believe you are the Messiah, the Son of God, the One sent from heaven to save us!"

Jesus smiled at her. "What a confession of faith! Thank you for that, Martha. Now, where is your sister?"

But Mary arrived at that moment, attended by a group of the

women of Bethany. Among them I saw Simon's wife, and his daughter Raina, who was betrothed to Benjamin.

Mary, so much more demonstrative than Martha, fell to her knees at Jesus' feet. Her words were the same, though she held nothing back in pathos or reproach: "Lord, why were you not here? If you had been here, Lazarus would not have died!"

Jesus bent in the dust before her, put a hand under her chin and lifted her weeping face toward his. "Show me where he is buried."

Together, the sisters led Jesus to the burial ground on the edge of town. Following them, our little group who had come with Jesus mingled with the mourners from Bethany. I found Rabbi Simon there and saw other men with him. Most were from Bethany, but I saw a few from Jerusalem, whom I knew—other Pharisees, many of them hostile to Jesus. Was it coincidence or condolence that brought them to Bethany this day? Or had they gotten word that Jesus might be there?

Simon looked surprised to see me. "James, where have you been? In the wilderness with Jesus all this time? Has he made a believer of you after all?"

"No," I said shortly.

"I will admit, my own faith in him is shaken," Simon said. "Their whole family has been so loyal to him. He healed me when I did not even believe in him; why didn't he do anything for Lazarus? If he could heal a leper and open the eyes of the blind, why would he not save Lazarus?"

"He seems sorry enough about it now," one of the other men said, pointing to Jesus. We had reached the burial ground, and Jesus stood with Mary and Martha in front of a rough-hewn rock tomb. All three, Jesus as well as the women, were wiping away tears.

"See how much he loved him?" Simon said. "Then why didn't he—"

Jesus' voice, loud and commanding, rose above the murmur of the group. "Roll away the tombstone!" he said.

A ripple of shock ran through the bystanders. What did Jesus plan to do? I thought of those tales in Galilee of Jesus raising a person from the dead. They had been easy to explain away, those stories, though in one case the boy had been on his bier, being carried to the burying ground. Skeptics like myself had said that Jesus had only healed someone who was close to death, so far fallen into unconsciousness that those around believed him or her to be dead. Yes, his powers of healing were undeniable, but the boundary between life and death was another matter altogether. No one but God had power over death.

"Lord, he has been in the ground four days!" I heard Martha protest. "The stench—"

"Didn't I tell you to believe and see what God would do?" Jesus said. He gestured to a few of the men, and they put their shoulders to the tombstone, grunting as they moved it aside. Indeed, an unpleasant odor drifted out from the dark cleft in the rock: Lazarus's family, like most, used a family tomb, and his body would be only the most recent of the many dead laid there.

Jesus looked, not at the tomb, but up to the sky, raising his arms in prayer. "Father, I thank You for hearing me," he prayed aloud. "I know that You always hear me, but I thank You now for the benefit of these people here, so that they will know that You have sent me here." Then, with little change of tone, but looking toward the tomb, he shouted, "Lazarus, come out!"

Gasps and cries of horror. This, I thought, was the moment where I finally became convinced that Jesus was no clever charlatan, nor any well-meaning, misguided holy man. No, he was clearly mad. He was about to try to call from the dead a man already buried four days ago.

My eyes were drawn, like everyone's, to the entrance of the tomb, which yawned dark and foreboding. Then Simon said, "Look!"

Something—someone—was moving inside that tomb. I saw it myself now, as the whole crowd surged forward, heedless of the smell. Something white—something that struggled toward the tomb entrance blindly, like an infant struggling out of the birth canal into the light of life. A human figure, crawling, trying to stand, obscured by the tight bindings that wrap the bodies of the dead.

The same men who had rolled away the stone shrank back in terror, but Martha and Mary ran forward, into the mouth of the tomb, and helped the struggling figure to stand, guided it out into the light.

"It can't be!" someone near me said, echoing the cries all around.

"Unwrap him!" Jesus commanded, and the women began with the cloth around the figure's head, peeling it back to reveal Lazarus's familiar face. He looked—well, he looked like himself, healthy and whole, though shocked and disoriented. As his sisters continued to unwrap the grave cloths, Jesus moved forward and embraced Lazarus. No one could hear what he said, but even if he hadn't spoken softly, I doubt we would have heard, for the response of the crowd was a roar.

Many people were cheering, shouting "Alleluia!" Some were turning to their neighbors saying, "I told you! Didn't I tell you Jesus could do anything?"

But a few disgruntled voices around us, including one of the men I recognized from Jerusalem, said, "It's a trick. The whole thing was a ruse; no man can raise the dead!"

"A trick?" It was Simon's voice that responded. "Friend, I can assure you this is no trick! Lazarus is my kinsman; I was at his bedside when he died. Most of the people in this community saw him laid to rest in this very tomb four days ago, and all can tell you this is the very same man! There is no trickery here; we are in the presence of God's own Messiah!"

"No trick, you say? If it were a trick, Rabbi Simon, you would be in on it! You want us all to believe in this Messiah of yours. Perhaps you planned this whole show!"

Simon was laughing, "How could I? You're mad. You see a dead man raised to life before your eyes and still find reason to doubt. I am going now, to welcome my kinsman back!" He moved through the crowd to throw his arms around Lazarus, leaving me in the little circle of doubters and skeptics.

I drew back from them, and back from the far greater crowd of believers celebrating this astonishing miracle. I knew in my heart, as Simon had protested, that this was no trick. True, Lazarus was such an earnest disciple that he would probably have been willing to play at dying and rising if he thought it would bring more people to believe in Jesus, and Mary certainly would have gone along with such a plan. But Bethany was a tight-knit village, and people talked about what they saw. Such a thing could not have been kept secret, and the grief on the sisters' faces when we arrived had been all too real. Besides, I could not imagine Martha having been party to such a deception. I knew that she had truly lost her brother and truly rejoiced to see him alive again.

But if it was all true, what did it mean? Why, what Jesus' followers were claiming already—that he could do anything. Heal the sick, raise the dead, maybe even restore the throne of Israel. It meant that he had a kind of power from God that had not been seen in the holiest of prophets since ancient times. It meant, at the very least, that hundreds more people, hearing this tale, would come to believe he was the Messiah.

What did I believe myself? I could not fathom it. I was too confused to even attempt to sort out my thoughts. But I knew one thing for certain—the controversy that had been swirling around Jesus, the danger he had faced in Jerusalem during the last two feasts, was coming to a head. Nobody in Jerusalem was going to be able to ignore reports that Jesus could raise people from the dead. Passover, the biggest feast of the year, was just a few weeks away. What a time to declare a new king of Israel!

What a time to destroy a would-be king!

The group—swelled, now, by almost everyone in Bethany, who had poured out of their homes to stare at Lazarus and hear the tale— moved away from the burial ground and back through the gates of the village. The village square was turning into an impromptu celebration: someone had already set up a table and was bringing out food and drink, while on the far side of the square someone struck up a tune on the lyre. A group of young men formed a chain and began to dance around Lazarus, as if it were his wedding. I saw Benjamin among them; the sight of him, the thought of him dancing at his own wedding to Simon's daughter, spurred me into action. I threaded my way among the crowds and pulled Benjamin from the line.

"Benjamin, we must go home—back to Jerusalem. At once."

"Father, why? This is a wonderful day! And how can you still doubt Jesus, after what you've seen?"

"After what you've seen, how can you still doubt there will be trouble here? What do you think is going to happen when the Romans hear that this Jewish prophet is raising the dead and people are calling him King of the Jews?"

"But Father—"

"Your father is right, Benjamin." I looked up to see Jesus beside us. "I will not stay here long. I must take my disciples and go to a solitary place for some time; and you must go to Jerusalem with your father, as he asks. Great things are about to happen, Benjamin, and everyone must decide where he stands."

"I stand with you, Lord!" Benjamin said. "I want to go with you."

"I will see you soon, Benjamin, but there is work for you to do among my friends in Jerusalem," Jesus said. "I have many friends there, and you must tell them that I am coming back—when the time is right. You must prepare."

"Yes, Lord," Benjamin said, and Jesus turned his gaze to me.

"You heard what I said, James. The time is coming when every man must decide where he stands."

I met his eyes. "I stand for the God of Israel and the people of Israel, as I always have. You know that, Jesus."

"I do, my brother. Go back to Jerusalem now, with my blessing," said Jesus.

So, in the midst of that happy celebration, I prepared to take my leave, as did Jesus and his disciples. Benjamin went to say his farewell to the family of his future bride, while I went to embrace Lazarus and tell him how glad I was to see him alive and well.

"It's a strange business, James," Lazarus said. "Everyone keeps asking me what it was like to die and rise again, but I have no memory of it at all."

"You need rest," I said.

"That's what I have been telling him," said Martha, who had appeared near us carrying a huge basket of bread to share with her joyful neighbors. "Are you leaving us, Rabbi James?"

"I am going back to Jerusalem," I told her. "But I am sure I will be back in Bethany soon." I smiled at her and added, "I am happy for you, for Lazarus's—recovery."

Her face was alight with smiles, but she dropped her eyes modestly as she said, "Praise God for what Jesus has done. I hope we will see you again, Rabbi."

I hoped I would see her again as well—hoped it more than I wanted to admit. But I would have been glad to step aside forever from this whirlpool of controversy that Jesus created all around him, happy to sidestep the questions and debate I would hear about this day when I returned to Jerusalem. I thought of Jesus' words about every man deciding where he stood, and I realized I myself still had many decisions to make. But one thing was clear that Jesus and I agreed on: a crisis was coming. And I had to be ready to face it.

Chapter Twenty

"Can you tell us, at least, where he is?" Avram demanded.

I shrugged. "I can tell you where he was before Bethany. He was in Perea, on the east side of Jordan. I think he has gone somewhere else now, not back to the same place. Wherever he is, he has at least a hundred and fifty followers with him, all fanatically loyal."

"Armed?" Avram asked.

"I don't think so. Jesus preaches a message of peace and tells his followers not to carry a sword. But not all of them agree with this message, and there could well be some who are armed. The point is, you will have a hard time capturing him."

"You spent a long time there across Jordan," Avram said, watching me closely.

I had been back in Jerusalem three days now, back in the house of my old friend and master. We were talking now, not at the house, but in the Temple, where Avram spent most of his time. I knew he would be suspicious about my long absence in Jesus' camp and perhaps think that my allegiances had shifted.

Had they? I did not think so. I could hardly deny what I had seen with my own eyes at Lazarus's tomb—a tale that was already spreading around Jerusalem like wildfire by the time I met with Avram. But I still found it hard to imagine that God could work through a vessel as unconventional as my brother Jesus; and I could see only ruin, rather than good, coming from his mission. Ruin for Israel. And as I had told Jesus, Israel was my first loyalty.

"You say you were there at Bethany too?" Avram prompted. "With this man—what's his name? Simon's kinsman?"

"Lazarus," I said. "I knew him too—know him, I mean. The man was dead and in the tomb, and I saw Jesus call him out. He was alive afterward. I spoke with him."

"Trickery," Avram said. "I talked to men who were there, and they say it must have been some kind of trick. The man and his family are followers of Jesus; they colluded with Jesus to make it look as though he were dead and then came back to life."

"I . . . don't think so," I said. When I was in Bethany, surrounded by believers, I had been so sure it could not be a hoax. But now, facing Avram, I found it hard to remember why I had been so certain. It was possible, wasn't it?

My mind was so confused, so troubled, by all that I had seen and thought these last weeks. I had to find something to cling to, some clear path to carry me through this wilderness of confusion.

"I don't know about Lazarus," I said. "But I know what people think about it, and that's enough. They think Jesus is the Messiah, the promised Deliverer, a king of the line of David. Some of them are calling him the Son of God. You hear these things yourself. Passover is coming, and Jesus has spoken about coming back to Jerusalem 'when the time is right.' What do you think it all means? What do our leaders think?"

"The Sanhedrin meets tomorrow," Avram said. "Everyone, from every party and faction, agrees that something must be done about Jesus. And if, as you say, he is talking about returning for Passover, it must be done soon."

I still had two pupils left who had waited for my return rather than studying with other rabbis during my absence. I met with them that day after I spoke to Avram, but rather than study the passage of the Torah I assigned, they, too, wanted to talk about nothing but Jesus. The fact that I was Jesus' brother, that I had spent time with him across the Jordan, and that I had been at Bethany when Lazarus was raised, all seemed to be common knowledge.

I did my best to turn aside their questions and turn their minds back to the Scripture, but I left the Temple that day feeling weary. Benjamin joined me for the evening meal but excused himself soon afterward to go visit his friend John Mark, who had returned to Jerusalem a week or more ago.

I sat alone that night, trying to concentrate on the scroll of Isaiah. But every verse I read reminded me of Jesus—verses I had heard him quote or preach about, verses that might apply to his own idea of himself as Messiah, sent of God, servant of the Lord. I went to bed early that night, hoping for a peaceful sleep and untroubled dreams.

The next day was the meeting of the Sanhedrin to discuss the issue of Jesus. I was very far from being included in such lofty circles of power, though some of their meetings were open for scribes, students, and other interested parties to watch. This meeting was held in private, but my friendship with Avram, strained though it was by recent developments, allowed me a little insight into what went on. I waited eagerly to dine with him that evening so that he might tell me what had passed.

"The debate was lively," he admitted to me. "Few on the council would come out and say they support Jesus, except Nicodemus, but there are many who would rather wait and see. They say that while he might be deluded, or a madman, he is our deluded madman, and we should protect him from the Romans, from Pilate. I think some believe that they can control the movement that will rise up around Jesus, use him as a figurehead to unite the people and perhaps gain a little more independence for Israel."

"But that is the very opposite of what will happen once the Romans get wind of any such movement!" I pointed out.

"Of course. You know that; I know that; all sensible men know that. And a majority of the Sanhedrin, if not all of them, acknowledge that. They know—we all know—that Jesus has to be stopped before the Romans intervene, lest they accuse us of supporting him. Indeed, most of us think the best course would be to arrest him ourselves and hand him over to Rome, so that they can see our hands are clean and we have no intent to rebel."

"Hand him over to Rome?" I echoed. I had not imagined that the Sanhedrin planned such drastic action. I had thought their goal was to arrest Jesus and perhaps some of his key followers, imprison him so that they could show the Roman authorities they were taking the threat of rebellion seriously. Then what? Perhaps Jesus could eventually be released under threats of further action, in the hope that he would give up preaching and teaching in public. If the Romans got hold of a would-be King of the Jews—or king of any land where Caesar held sway—they would put him to death on one of their crosses, those hideous torture devices reserved for non-Romans who threatened the Pax Romana. Surely the whole point of the Sanhedrin arresting Jesus would be to avoid such a fate?

Tentatively, I outlined those thoughts for Avram, but he shook his head. "There are those who agree with you; and because the man is your brother, I can see why you would think that way," he said. "Perhaps I thought so once myself, but not anymore. Things have gone too far. Raising men from the dead? Being called the Son of God? This is blasphemy under our law, and treason under the Romans' law. The treason gives them a reason to want him dead, and the blasphemy gives us an excuse for doing so. If we move quickly to capture Jesus, try him, and turn him over to the Roman governor for execution, everyone will see clearly that the Sanhedrin, the Jewish nation, does not want rebellion. That should keep Pilate from taking the kind of revenge he took at the time of the aqueduct riots." A few years earlier, the governor had used money from the Temple treasury to build a new aqueduct, and many Jews had been killed when his soldiers savagely put down the resulting protests. We all knew Pilate was no friend of our people.

I licked my lips, which had become suddenly dry. "What of Jesus' followers? Those close to him? Would you turn some of them over to the Romans, too, to make an example?"

Avram steepled his fingers, looking down at his hands instead of at me. "As few as possible, James, as few as possible. None at all, unless they resist and try to defend him. That's why a quiet arrest would be so much better—get him apart from his followers, and we may be able to take him without bloodshed. Perhaps no one will have to die but Jesus."

We were both silent for a moment, contemplating this. "I am trusting you a great deal to tell you all this, James," Avram said at last.

"I know. Thank you."

"The man is, as I said, your kinsman, and I know many of your family follow him. I trust your love for our nation is great enough that you will not betray us—perhaps even help us? Remember, our goal is to shed as little blood as possible—no one's but that of Jesus, if we can manage it. To show the Romans we want peace, not revolution."

"I don't think Jesus wants a revolution," I said. "It seems a shame for a man to die for a throne he never pretended to want."

"What Jesus wants may not be the most important thing here," Avram pointed out. "It's what his followers want, the words they use, and what the Romans see and conclude from it. That's what counts." He breathed deeply. "I am troubled about it, too, James, for while I disagree with almost everything Jesus says, it is a heavy thing to put a man to death, especially a fellow Jew and a fellow rabbi. But Caiaphas, the high priest, said something last night that set my mind at rest. He reminded us that it is better for one man to die, if by his death he can save the whole nation. Jesus' death will save us from Rome's wrath, James. It's a hard truth, but it's the only way."

I nodded, not so much to indicate agreement as understanding. There was so much here to think about, and I found that despite all my own differences with Jesus, the idea of supporting his death was a hard one. The ties of family still held me more tightly than I had thought—and perhaps they had been strengthened by the weeks I had just spent in Jesus' company. The vision I had caught there of God's kingdom as Jesus and his followers tried to live it as a community of equality, ruled by love—did appeal to me. At least, parts of it did. It was a beautiful ideal.

But completely impractical. And dangerous. Nobody could ever live that way for long. The bickering and ambition I'd seen among even Jesus' closest disciples showed how any such experiment would end, and long before Jesus' followers had a chance to turn on each other and tear his dream apart, the iron hand of the Roman legions would descend. Not just upon Jesus and his followers but, if Avram was correct, upon all Jews. Such things had happened before; anyone who thought they could not happen again was a fool.

So, the Sanhedrin's solution: throw Jesus to the Romans like a bone to a pack of snarling dogs, distracting them so they would not attack us. Use him as a scapegoat, a sacrifice. All my life I had battled Jesus. Could I, now, take the final step of lending my support to a scheme to have him put to death?

What would Benjamin say if I told him I had sat and listened to such words? If I warned Jesus, would he finally heed my words and flee—perhaps leave the country altogether? Where did my allegiance truly lie?

"With God," I reminded myself, but could not be content with that. I had to add, "With the God of Israel." God, people, and land were tied together in a bond that could not be broken. Our people had lost so much since the Romans came; we were a conquered and occupied nation. It was all very well to dream of a new David or Solomon who would restore a lost golden age, but Israel was ruled by practical men like Avram, men who knew what survival cost.

This time, Jesus might be the one to pay the price for our survival as a people. Was the price too high?

I said nothing about the conversation with Avram. Not to Benjamin, certainly, who spent nearly all his free time now with Mark and other followers of Jesus. Not to Avram himself, or anyone else in the Temple. I spoke of it only to God, in long, agonizing prayers that I poured out in hopes of finding a solution. What was God calling me to do?

For the moment, I decided, nothing at all. I did my work. I taught my few pupils; I studied the Scriptures; I discussed and debated with other rabbis. I stayed silent in discussions about Jesus, and I would not allow my son to draw me into conversation about him, or to bring me to meet other Jesus followers. I did not go back down to Bethany. I waited—for Passover, for a crisis to come, for my way to become clear.

Then, one day, a fortnight before Passover, things became clearer. A message came from Rabbi Simon in Bethany.

> James, my honored friend, Jesus has sent word he is coming to Bethany before going to Jerusalem for Passover. I am holding a feast in his honor at my home six days before Passover. Lazarus will be a guest of honor as well, and many of the men I invite from Jerusalem will have the opportunity to see Lazarus in the flesh and know what Jesus did. I hope that you and your son will be my guests on this occasion.

I looked up from the letter to Benjamin, whose smile had broadened as I read the message aloud. "Jesus is coming to Jerusalem for Passover, Father. Something is going to happen. I know it; it's in the air. I want to be there, at Bethany, with him. Before he enters the city. May we go?"

My heart felt heavy. If I sat there at the feast at Simon's house, whose side would I be on? I would be surrounded by Jesus and his followers, including my own son and my brothers. But I ought to have a seat among Simon's skeptical guests from Jerusalem, fellow Pharisees, no doubt, who were plotting Jesus' downfall.

If I went to that feast, I would feel disloyal to both sides. I would be an imposter to everyone, hiding my true feelings, which were as conflicted as the Sea of Galilee on a stormy day. And though women were kept separate from the men at such feasts, directing the servants from behind the scenes, still there was a chance I might see Martha. I knew now that what I felt for her was more than respect and admiration—or rather, an admiration that, if it were allowed, might deepen into much more. But how could that be allowed, when we might stand on opposite sides of a huge chasm? Jesus spoke of peace, but his presence as often brought division as unity.

"I cannot go," I told Benjamin. "I have been feeling ill lately. No, nothing serious, just some stomach trouble, but a feast would be a bad idea. I want to rest and be well in time for Passover. You should go, though. Simon will be your father-in-law soon enough, and you should take him our greetings and honor."

I could see Benjamin did not believe my flimsy excuse, but he was so relieved that I allowed him to go that he was not about to protest. "I have meant to ask you, Father, when do you and Simon plan to announce the betrothal?" he added.

Since we had made the marriage arrangement, weeks had stretched into months—months filled by the turmoil of our journey into the wilderness beyond Jordan, then by the drama of Lazarus's death and resurrection. Now my thoughts were entirely overshadowed by what might happen to Jesus in Jerusalem during Passover and what part I would have to play in it all. Planning a betrothal celebration was the furthest thing from my mind. I wanted to say, "When all this trouble has died down, my son, when things are peaceful again," but what would it take to win that peace? Did I mean, "When I have colluded in the murder of your beloved uncle, whom you follow as your Master and Messiah"? Would Jesus' death permanently sever me from the rest of my family, including my beloved son?

It was easier to say, "After Passover, Benjamin. When the feast is over I will visit Simon again, and we will plan the announcement. Until then, go to his dinner and bring him my highest regards."

The stories I heard afterward about that dinner made me glad I had not attended. I heard many times the tale of how Mary of Magdala had burst into the men's dinner, shameless and with unbound hair like the loose madwoman she had once been, throwing herself at Jesus' feet with tears and anointing him with costly ointment. I could only imagine the shame Martha, and no doubt Lazarus and Simon and all the rest of the family, must have felt at her unseemly display. Yes, I was glad I had stayed away. But, in fact, long before I ever heard the story of what happened at that feast, I had far greater troubles to worry about. The next day Jesus came to Jerusalem, and after that there was no turning back.

Chapter Twenty-One

The night after Simon's feast, Benjamin stayed in Bethany. Early the following morning, before I had finished my morning prayers, I heard footsteps racing up the stairs toward my room. Benjamin and Mark stood there, breathless and excited as only young men can be when they have run a long distance with important tidings.

"Father, you must come! Jesus is riding into the city from Bethany—everyone is there—it's going to be like a royal procession!"

"What are you talking about? A royal procession?" This sounded terrible, worse than my worst imaginings of how Jesus might reappear in Jerusalem.

"He sent us to Bethphage, with John and Peter, to borrow a donkey, sir," Mark explained, still a little out of breath. "They went back, but Benjamin wanted to come get you."

"You need to be there, Father," Benjamin insisted. "Whatever you think about what Jesus is doing—you must see this."

I agreed. If Jesus was about to make some kind of royal proclamation, I needed to see what was happening. I hastily threw on my cloak and followed the boys out into the street.

The streets of Jerusalem were still quiet. A few early risers went about their business, shopkeepers opening their shops, priests on their way to the Temple. The clear, crisp morning air carried no hints of cataclysmic events today. Only the feverish excitement of the young men beside me hinted that anything out of the ordinary was happening.

But out on the road that led from Jerusalem to Bethany, we had not traveled far before we saw a commotion in the distance. A crowd of people, all moving toward us. Even from far off, we could hear voices raised in song.

We moved quickly; they moved slowly. The boys ran ahead of me, leaving me to plod in their footsteps. Soon they mingled with the happy crowd, which, I could see now, was comprised of friends and followers of Jesus. Many were those who had come with him from Galilee—including the Twelve, our family, and some of the women disciples. I recognized Judean followers, too, and soon saw Lazarus, Martha, and Mary in the group. I saw no sign of Rabbi Simon. Had he decided it would be imprudent to associate himself with Jesus in such a public way?

Dozens of people crowded the road, but it was the figure in their midst that drew my eye—but not because he looked lofty and commanding. Jesus sat on a young donkey, his head hardly raised above those of the crowd. There was something deliberate in his movements; he sat with great dignity, though he still turned to talk and laugh with the people walking nearby. I had never seen him astride a horse or a donkey in his life that I could remember: he had planned this moment carefully. Was he really going to allow his followers to declare him king, to begin the bloody revolution that could end only in his own death and the death of hundreds of innocent people?

It seemed contrary to everything I knew about Jesus and what he wanted, but I thought of Judas Iscariot, who was surely not the only one among Jesus' followers who thought their Master could be carefully steered into taking the right political gambles. Had Jesus given in to their pressure? Or did he have, as he usually had, some secret agenda of his own that none of the rest of us could even guess at?

Whatever the reason, one thing was sure: there was going to be no more talk about how "the time is not right." Jesus had obviously decided the time was right—and to march on Jerusalem very publicly, attracting as much attention as possible. I joined the procession, keeping apart from the happy holiday atmosphere, watching closely. I saw people running back and forth down that same road I had just come with Benjamin and Mark, saw other travelers on the road who were not part of Jesus' party notice what was going on. Word would spread through Jerusalem quickly, I knew.

Sure enough, we were barely in sight of the city walls when I saw men on horseback. Roman soldiers, obviously. But there were many others too—people on foot, coming out to see Jesus, to join the procession.

People waved palm branches in the air, shouting, singing. "Blessed is He who comes in the name of the Lord! Hosanna! Hosanna to the King!" I heard all around. Seeing the soldiers on either side of the road, I found those words chilling. The Romans made no move toward Jesus, just lined the road on either side, their captains mounted, hands on sword hilts. But the crowd of people—men, women, dozens of little children—swarming around Jesus paid no heed to them and kept on shouting and singing. More and more people joined the crowd, pouring out from the city. I saw people tear off their cloaks and throw them in the road for Jesus' donkey to walk over.

To the watching Romans, it must have seemed a parody of a kingly procession. I had heard of their Caesar's triumphs, had seen the processions when Herod Antipas visited Jerusalem, or when Pontius Pilate and his soldiers marched through the city. Compared to their grand conquerors riding on warhorses or riding in gilded chariots, the image of a would-be king plodding into town on a donkey must have seemed faintly ridiculous. And, indeed, the donkey was an apt mount for Jesus in that way, for he had never admired or emulated the wealthy or powerful, embracing instead the life of the poor.

But the Roman soldiers would not have read our Scriptures,

would not know that Zechariah wrote: "Rejoice greatly, O Daughter of Zion! Shout, Daughter of Jerusalem! See, your King comes to you, righteous and having salvation, gentle and riding on a donkey, on a colt, the foal of a donkey." Our own leaders, the members of the Sanhedrin, knew that text well. They knew that by entering the city this way, Jesus was claiming the name of King. As for the Romans, all they needed to see was a growing crowd of Jews hailing a man they called king and lord. That was more than enough for them.

I kept to my place on the edge of the happy crowd, so far unmolested by the watching Roman soldiers. Flowers, palm branches, and cloaks now lined the road over which Jesus moved. The air was full of festival celebration, though the Passover Feast was still days away.

Some of the people coming out of the Jerusalem gate joined the procession at once, shouting praises to Jesus. Others lined the road on either side and watched. Among those more cautious watchers, I found a group of Pharisee rabbis I knew, and as I had expected, Avram was among them. He hurried up to me. "James, this is a disaster!" he said. "Could you do nothing to stop this display?"

"It began before I even got here," I said.

"Look at the Romans! How long do you think they'll let this go on?" he stormed. "Can't you talk to Jesus?"

"He would not listen to me."

"He must listen to someone! Come with me, at least," Avram said, and began plunging through the crowd of supporters toward Jesus.

It was hard to read the expression on Jesus' face. He smiled and spoke to people in the crowd as he passed, and looked as if he were enjoying this triumph, or at least the air of celebration that surrounded it. But there was sadness in his face, too, or perhaps apprehension. I wondered if he actually was worried, for once, about the consequences of his actions.

Avram, with several of the other rabbis, got close enough to speak to Jesus. I joined them, thinking I could at least add my voice to theirs.

"Jesus, you must put a stop to this!" Avram said, reaching out to pluck the edge of Jesus' cloak. Jesus turned to look at him.

"Some things, once started, cannot be stopped," he said. "What do you want me to put a stop to, Rabbi?"

"These people," Avram said, waving an arm, "shouting and praising and calling you king! Can you not see the Romans are watching? It will mean disaster, not just for you but for all of us!"

Jesus actually laughed, right in the face of that venerable Pharisee. "I can no more stop them than I can stop the will of God, Rabbi. If I were to tell these people to be silent, then the rocks along the side of the road would cry out in their place! You cannot stop the work of God when the right time has come."

We were at the Mount of Olives now, looking down over the Kidron Valley at the city below. Avram looked aghast at Jesus' brashness, but I had to try once more. "Jesus, please. Make them stop; make them realize what can happen. It's not too late to . . ."

"It's much too late, James," said Jesus. "I have told you before I will be ready when my hour comes, and now it is upon me. Oh, Jerusalem!" He reined in the donkey and looked out at the broad vista of the city spread below him.

The sadness I had seen hints of in his face seemed to overcome him for a moment, and he put a hand against his brow. I thought this might be a good moment to press him, take advantage of his momentary weakness, urge him to disperse the crowd and leave the city quietly. But even while the people around continued cheering and Jesus sat silently looking down at the city, several of his followers moved closer to him, pressing in to hear what he had to say.

I moved away, joining Avram and the other rabbis in a little huddle by the side of the road. "This is a disaster," Avram said. "I expect those soldiers to attack at any moment."

"They won't," another Pharisee said. "They're watching closely, and they're concerned, but they don't want a massacre, which is what will happen if they start attacking a crowd of unarmed people."

"If they really are unarmed," Avram said dourly, looking over the crowd of Jesus' followers.

"I think most of them are," I said. "But it would take only a few to resist, and . . . no, I can see why the Romans don't want to deal with this."

"It's impossible to arrest Jesus in a crowd like this—for the Romans, or for us," Avram said. "We have to find him alone, catch him off guard when he's not surrounded by hundreds of supporters. We want this to be quiet and simple."

Whatever had caused Jesus to hesitate for a few moments on the hill had apparently passed, for he had moved on and the crowd moved with him. "Where is he going?" Avram wondered aloud.

I knew the answer without even thinking. "Where else? He would go to the Temple." True, Jesus had spent much of his ministry avoiding the centers of power, living among the poor, doing their work and sharing their simple lives. But when in Jerusalem, he had always preached and healed in the Temple courts. The Temple was the heart of our faith, the symbol of God's presence among His people. Whatever Jesus was doing here today, it would lead him to the Temple. What he might do there, no one could predict. Though, despite my disbelief, it was beginning to seem more and more likely that at the temple he would go through some kind of ceremony, declaring himself as king or allowing someone to place a crown on his head.

I knew what Avram would say. Things could never be allowed to get that far.

I lost sight of Avram and the other rabbis as we moved toward the Beautiful Gate, the gate in the wall that led directly to the Temple Mount. The crowd squeezed around Jesus, more and more people joining. Shouts and songs filled the air. At every street corner I saw Roman soldiers, watching and waiting.

Ahead of us, the Temple gleamed, its massive stone walls rising into the sky. The river of men, women, and children flowed toward its steps. I could barely make out the figure of Jesus on the donkey near the head of the crowd, and then they began to surge up the steps of the Temple itself. I could see Jesus no longer, only the backs of all the people following him into the Temple.

I hurried along behind the growing crowd, wondering what I would find when I got to the outer court. But none of my speculations prepared me for what was actually happening.

The outer court was the bustling public square of the temple. Although it was inside the walls, it was not a sacred space like the inner court. Here was where the Temple money changers exchanged Roman coins for Temple coins, merchants sold sheep and birds for sacrifices, and various other businesses—some more closely related to the Temple services than others, some more legitimate than others—flourished around the edges of the official money changers' tables. Above and behind everything was the constant sound of builders working on the greatest construction project in Israel, for Herod's Temple had not been completed in Herod's lifetime, nor would it be for many years.

I had spent enough time in the Temple this last year that the chaos of the outer court barely troubled me anymore. The bleating of sheep and calls of birds mingled with a tapestry of human voices. Most spoke the familiar Aramaic or Greek, but I heard many accents and dialects and even other languages. Jews from all over the Roman Empire came to Jerusalem for Passover, the greatest feast of the year. And not only Jews—Gentiles were permitted in the outer court, even Roman soldiers, though the Temple had its own Jewish police force, who were allowed into the inner courts. Our Temple was considered one of the wonders of this part of the world, far greater than many of the Temples of the pagan gods. It was unusual because there was no great gilded idol at its center—only a people's endless dedication to their unseen God. I could see a little cluster of Greek visitors now, easily recognizable as non-Jews. Nearby lurked a couple of good Jewish beggars and a good Jewish pickpocket; truly, the outer court of the Temple attracted all kinds of life.

In the midst of this scene now came Jesus and the crowd that surrounded him—that ragtag mass of people. Men, women, and children, the sick and lame, Jews and Gentiles, all pressed close to hear him and be healed by him.

Watching around the edges were the Temple police, the priests and rabbis, waiting for the moment when Jesus would make some announcement or incite his followers to rise up, to overthrow the authorities and make him king. But there was no such announcement, only a throng of people cheering and celebrating, and Jesus in the midst of them, looking about him thoughtfully.

As the afternoon grew later, the crowd thinned, and Jesus and his followers left the Temple with far less fanfare than had heralded their arrival a few hours earlier. I breathed a sigh of relief. Perhaps the day would pass without any confrontation after all.

I slept more peacefully in my bed that night. Benjamin had returned home, though we had barely finished our morning meal when he said he was going to the Temple to see if Jesus was there.

"Was he in the city last night?" I asked as I put on my phylacteries and prayer shawl, preparing to accompany my son.

"I think he returned to Bethany," Benjamin said. "But he is coming back. Today will be a great day, Father. I'm sure something is going to happen!"

Something did. When we arrived in the bustling outer court, a crowd had already gathered—gathered around Jesus. But today, no one was pressing close to him at all. People were backing away from him, some in terror.

Jesus, whom I had never seen lose his temper in his life, stood in the center of the outer court beside a toppled table. In his hands he held a knotted rope, which he swung over his head, not hitting anyone but scaring a number of the money changers who scurried away as Jesus tipped over another table. Coins clattered to the ground and rolled at the feet of the men running away from Jesus.

"Get out of here!" Jesus roared, in a voice I had never heard him use before. "All of you! Take your filthy money out of my Father's house! This is to be a place of prayer, but look what you've turned it into—a den of thieves!"

Despite the clamor of the animals and the falling tables, a kind of hush had fallen over the courtyard since Jesus bellowed. Nobody— not the merchants, not Jesus' followers, and certainly not the rabbis and priests watching in horror from the fringes of the crowd—had any idea what Jesus would do next.

He continued to turn over the tables, knocking over a few cages of birds, which burst open, sending doves shooting into the sky above us. He broke open the door of a sheep pen, sending Passover lambs scurrying loose among the crowd. "Get out!" he shouted again, and the merchants scurried away, some grasping for coins to tuck into their pockets as they ran.

Some of the crowd ran, too, including a few I knew were cut-purses. The priests and rabbis scurried away into the inner court, but most of the common crowd surged back around Jesus. Apparently, they had decided that wreaking havoc in the Temple court was almost as good as being crowned king, although to give Jesus' followers credit, I did not see any of them joining in the chaos or tipping over tables themselves.

I hurried away into the inner court, looking for Avram. But the first rabbi I saw was Nicodemus, besieged by a group of other rabbis and priests all trying to shout him down.

"What has he done?" Nicodemus was shouting. "What more than any of us has said a dozen times? Have *you* not deplored the trade in the outer court? Haven't *you* said it makes a mockery of a place of worship?" With each *you*, his finger stabbed toward one of the men standing around.

"It's a necessary evil!" someone else responded, and I recognized Avram now, stepping up to confront Nicodemus. "Unfortunate, yes, but nothing compared to the sacrilege Jesus has committed out there!"

"Sacrilege?" Nicodemus shot back. "Why, are the sheep merchants sacred now? Is the table of a money changer a holy place?"

"No, but the Temple is a sacred place!" Another voice chimed in, this one with authority that everyone listened to, for it was Gamaliel, the great rabbi, grandson of Rabbi Hillel, a powerful voice among the Pharisees. "This is about more than Jesus' righteous indignation over the traffic in the outer court. This is about his entire disregard for our religion, our customs, and our Temple! He claims to be sent from God, yet he desecrates the very place where God had chosen to dwell among us!"

"Yet he has not done the one thing you were so afraid he would do," Nicodemus argued. "You all thought he was coming here today to declare himself a king, and there has been no sign of a coronation."

"There might be by now, for all we know," one of the priests said. The babble of noise from the outer court had grown, and drawn nearer. "He has brought that whole rabble into the Court of Women," Avram said. "Probably Gentiles and all!"

"As I said, a desecration! No respect for the Holy Place!" Gamaliel said. "Do we need any more evidence to convict him under our law?"

"No!" Avram said. "The Romans may be waiting for him to declare himself a king, but we have no need to wait. He has already committed blasphemy over and over. We can try him, condemn him under our own laws, then hand him over to the Romans for sentencing. It will show them we are serious about quelling rebellion, and stop them from making any moves against our Sanhedrin."

"Yes, yes, Avram, your same old tune," Nicodemus said.

"Lest you forget, it is Caiaphas's tune too," Avram retorted.

"Where is he, anyway?" Gamaliel asked, and several of the men hurried off in search of the high priest.

"Do you know what he said, what Jesus said?" another of the rabbis put in. "Someone spoke to him about respecting the Temple, and he said, 'If you tear down this temple, I myself will rebuild it in three days'!"

Chapter Twenty-One

"What madness! The man is delusional!" another said.

"But his delusions could be the death of us all if we don't put a stop to them," Avram warned. "This procession yesterday, this riot in the outer court today—all this is just the beginning."

"Listen!" someone else said, and we all turned toward the entrance. The crowd was flowing from the Court of Women into the inner court, where only Jewish men were allowed to go. Yet this was a mixed crowd, a rabble of men and women and children. The lame and sick were here, though those with such afflictions were barred from inner courts as well. I even saw a group of Greeks I had noted earlier among the crowd.

Jesus was at the head of the disorderly mob, carrying a small child on his shoulders. His rage had ended; he was, as usual, laughing and talking with those around him. Some people were singing. As I watched, a woman leaning on a crutch hobbled toward Jesus. He stopped walking and turned to her, placed a hand on her shoulder. Another wretched soul begging for healing, no doubt. Before long the lepers and the madmen would be here too—if they weren't already.

The other rabbis had surged toward Jesus, protesting this new sacrilege, but Avram drew me aside. "Do you need to see any more, James? Isn't it clear not only that we must act quickly but that Jesus has given us every excuse for doing so?"

I nodded, unable to speak but sure he was right.

"Then you will help us?"

Near the entrance to the inner courts, Jesus was carrying on a lively debate with the rabbis and priests who were anxious to hurry him out of there. His followers milled around, that strange mixed bag of people who would normally never set foot in this holy place. Some were singing, "Blessed is He who comes in the name of the Lord!" setting the words they had chanted on the road yesterday to a well-known hymn tune. Little children danced and clapped around their elders' feet. It was a scene at once beautiful and horrifying.

I turned to Avram. "Help? What do you want from me?"

"You know what we need, James. What we have always needed." His hand gripped my arm like iron as he drew me away from the others, away from Jesus, into a solitary portico where we could talk without others hearing. "We need someone who can lead us to Jesus when he is alone, when he is not surrounded by an army of followers. You are his brother. Invite him for a private conversation. Anytime during the festival, but the sooner the better. Get him to arrange to meet with you, and then get a message to me, letting me know when and where. We will send men to take him away quietly. There will be no fuss, no violence."

I stared at him, at this wise, kind man who had done so much for me. He was asking me to betray Jesus, to turn him over to the Sanhedrin for trial and punishment. Not to a quiet imprisonment or exile, as I had once imagined, but to a body of devout Jewish men who would in their turn give him to the Roman authorities, branding him a rabble-rouser and a traitor to the empire, so that they might show that their own hands were clean. Avram had explained it all so clearly to me, so many times. Now he was laying out for me what I had not understood before: my own part in the drama. The role he had given me to play.

"I—I cannot," I said. "He will not come. He will suspect something."

"From you? Is he suspicious of you?" Avram pressed. "Tell him it is you and your son who wish to meet with him, or one of your other brothers. They are his followers, are they not? He will not suspect that. Perhaps on the night of the Passover Feast—invite him to eat the feast with you."

"At your house?" I said, mockery in my tone.

"Of course not. Find another place, with some of your family who are here."

"No. Too many people," I said, drawn into the plot against my will.

"Yes, perhaps." He stroked his beard. "And sooner is better, as I said. Surely you can get word to him, can you not? He would come if you asked him."

"I don't know. I don't know." I wrung my hands. "This is a heavy thing you are asking, Avram. He is my brother."

"Yes. But is not your first loyalty to God and Israel?"

"Yes. Of course. But I must think. I cannot . . . this is a heavy thing," I repeated. "At least give me time to think . . . time to pray."

"Time may be the thing we do not have," Avram said. "Think quickly. Pray quickly. Give me an answer tomorrow."

I left the Temple then. I did not stay to see if the priests were successful in driving Jesus and his followers out of the inner court, or how long it took for the money changers to slink back to their tables, or even whether anyone tried to declare Jesus king. I went home, away from it all, and did what I had told Avram I would do. They were no empty words. I drew my prayer shawl over my head and I prayed, begging God Almighty for wisdom, for guidance. I blocked out the noises from the street outside and existed only in a world of prayer and inner turmoil. Someone hammered at my door and I heard voices. I stayed silent, waiting for one of Avram's servants to tell my guests I was not at home. It seemed incredible that I lived in the house of a man who wanted to put my brother to death, that I ate at his table and called him master and friend. And he considered me an ally in his cause. Was I? Whoever was at the door went away. Still I prayed, and still the path before me was no clearer.

Afternoon turned to evening. The shadows grew long. Benjamin did not return home that night; no doubt he was with the rest of the family, the rest of Jesus' followers, wherever they were staying. Inside the city or outside? Had the Romans already made an attempt to arrest Jesus?

I did not know. And I did not sleep, until the night was far gone and sheer exhaustion forced me into a land of uneasy dreams in the hours just before dawn.

I woke to the sound of Benjamin and his friend Mark in the other room. I eased myself off my bedroll and began to dress, listening to them talk.

"So where is he going today?" Mark asked.

"To the Temple again, so he says," Benjamin replied. I heard the scrape of spoon against bowl as he ate his breakfast. He must have risen well before me; perhaps he had gone to the kitchen for food or perhaps he had already been out in the street to buy something from a market stall, which might be where he had found Mark.

"To do what?" Mark asked now.

"The usual things—preach, teach, and heal the sick."

"The usual things? After yesterday? How can things go on as usual?" Mark wondered. "Won't they arrest him as soon as he sets foot inside the Temple?"

"If they didn't arrest him yesterday, why would they do it today?" Benjamin countered. "I tell you, Mark, more of the priests and rabbis are on our side than we realize. Many Pharisees, some Sadducees, and some priests. Even a few with seats on the Sanhedrin! Jesus has friends in high places."

Foolish boys, I thought. Little did they know that it was not Jesus' friends in high places who were protecting him—he did have a few, including Nicodemus—but rather the lowly rabble that followed him, and the fear that any attempt to seize him might erupt into mob violence. Nor did they know how easily that safety might be shattered.

Their conversation hushed as I joined them. Though the three of us said the morning prayers and broke bread together, the tension in the room was obvious. They still did not know whether to trust me, whose side I was on. Little wonder, when I did not know myself.

I went with them to the Temple, still turning my dilemma over in my mind. I thought now, as I walked beside my son, less of the good of the nation or the will of God, and more of the bonds of family. To betray a brother, even a half-brother or a brother by adoption, was unthinkable. But if the Sanhedrin did not act swiftly to silence Jesus, then the Romans might exact a far more bloody vengeance. Their tendency to crucify not just the ringleaders of a rebellion but dozens of followers was well known. If I did not betray Jesus, I might be betraying Benjamin, my other brothers, and many others who would fall by the Roman sword or die on Roman crosses. The words of high priest Caiaphas echoed in my mind: *"Better one man should die . . ."*

But if I lured Jesus into the presence of those who would arrest him, my family would surely know it was I who betrayed him. Benjamin would know. I would lose my son.

Yet he might live and be safe. Better for him to live safely and hate me, than for him to die at Roman hands.

So my troubled thoughts chased each other like a pack of quarrelsome dogs, growling and snapping but finding no peace.

Jesus was already in the Temple—in the outer courts again, where I noticed a few of the money changers and other merchants had set up their tables again, though the hustle and bustle was far less than normal during Passover. Jesus sat well away from the money changers, and as usual a large crowd surrounded him, the same motley assortment of folk that he had paraded into the sacred precincts of the inner court the day before.

Benjamin and Mark moved forward at once, pressing close to Jesus to hear his words, but I hung back, on the far fringes of the crowd, so that I could not even hear his words but could only watch.

He was telling a story, or making some discourse about something, but he could hardly get through it for interruptions: every few minutes a sick person would push through to the front of the crowd, and he would stop speaking to talk to the person, lay hands on him or her. Or someone would ask a question, and whether the question came from a disciple seeking more wisdom or an adversary challenging him, Jesus took the time to answer each one. He even broke off, once, to answer a question from a small dirty boy, a beggar child perhaps, who could not have been more than ten years old—then called the child to sit up next to him on the step where he perched, putting an arm around the ragged child as he continued.

I looked away after that. I could not continue to watch him, not with the conflicting images that crowded my head. Jesus as he had been two days ago, riding at the head of a crowd ready to declare him king. Jesus as he might be tomorrow, broken on a Roman cross—if I cooperated with the Sanhedrin. If I issued that private message to meet me in some lonely place so that we might talk as brothers. I could even hint that I was thinking of becoming a follower at long last.

I had the power to end it all—this chaos that disrupted our religion, that mocked our laws and the God-ordained distinctions between people, and that made a beggar child as valuable as a high priest. I had the power in my hands to bring an end to this terrible, beautiful kingdom Jesus was building.

I got up from my seat, skirting the edge of the group around Jesus. Also on the fringes were the Temple police, watching closely, and many rabbis and priests. I did not see Avram, so I went into the inner court looking for him.

I found him near the Nicanor Gate, and he drew me aside, looking glad to see me.

"I see Jesus has returned to the Temple today and is preaching openly," I said.

"You know all the reasons we cannot arrest him here, James," Avram said. "And you know my solution. Are you ready to carry it out?"

"No. I cannot."

"Cannot? You mean you will not."

"Cannot or will not, it makes no difference. This is too great a sin for me, Avram—even for the greater good of our people. I cannot betray my brother, knowing that you mean to hand him over to the Romans, that he may die."

Avram looked at me for a moment, his jaw tense, his eyes smoldering. Then the fight seemed to go out of him, and he shrugged and turned away.

"Very well," he said. "Don't think you have saved him by defying me. If you will not do it, we will find someone else who will."

Chapter Twenty-Two

Avram was right. They found someone else.

I did not know it was Judas Iscariot who betrayed Jesus—not till long after, after Judas had killed himself, after everything. But even before I found out about Judas, I knew there would be someone. Jesus' followers were loyal, but in even the most loyal group there is always someone who can be swayed. Perhaps by the promise of money; perhaps by the belief that he is doing the right thing. Perhaps Judas, who had such clear visions of what he wanted Jesus to accomplish, even deluded himself that he was still working toward that goal, forcing Jesus into a corner, giving him an opportunity to show his power.

Who knows? If I had been the one to betray him, people would have speculated for years about what led James the Just to betray his own brother. No one can see into a man's heart except himself and God; and sometimes, I think, we do not even see clearly into our own hearts.

For the rest of the week before that Passover, I avoided Jesus, avoided his followers or any of my family, avoided even the Temple. Even in the house, I kept to myself and stayed away from Avram; that was not difficult, since he was at the Temple most of the time. I knew what he and the others were planning, and I knew that by refusing to help them, I had placed myself outside their circle. I still wrestled with whether I had done the right thing, but I felt a sense of peace. I did not know what would happen during the feast, but I did not think that peace would have been there if I had chosen to betray Jesus.

On the day of the feast, Benjamin asked me to join him at Mark's home. I had made no plans, for whom could I enjoy the feast with? My own family would all be with Jesus and his followers, and I could not dine here in the house with Avram's family and students. "Is that where Jesus is going to be—at Mark's mother's house?" I asked.

"Jesus and the Twelve are eating the feast there; Mark's mother has a separate room upstairs set aside for them. Jesus said he wants to share Passover alone with the Twelve. The rest of us—Mark's family, our family from Galilee, some of the others—are going to have our feast downstairs, in the courtyard. Grandmother will be there," he added. "We would all like it if you joined us."

Part of me wanted to, but I had a sick feeling of dread in my stomach. Avram had said something would have to be done before Passover. Tonight was the feast. If something was going to happen— violence, a confrontation, an arrest—I wanted to be as far away as possible. I did not think I would be fit company for anyone tonight, celebrating this feast that reminded us of God's care and deliverance, His love for His people.

"I cannot," I told Benjamin. "Give my regrets to your grand-mother and your uncles, and to Mark and his mother."

"But where will you eat the feast, then?" Benjamin said, obviously worried about me.

"I would rather be alone."

"You cannot ignore the Passover meal," he pointed out. "Nor can you eat it alone." His face cleared suddenly. "I had another invita-tion," he said. "From Raina's family—her father invited me to eat the feast with them. He said you could come too. I sent a message to say I had plans already, but I know they will welcome us. Why not go to Bethany?"

Bethany. While the thought of eating at Mark's home with Jesus and my family filled me with dread, something pulled me in the direction of Bethany. There, too, I would be surrounded by followers of Jesus. It was likely Lazarus, Mary, and Martha would celebrate the feast at the home of their wealthier kinsman, but the distance from the city made it feel less oppressive. And it was fitting for my son to share the feast with his future in-laws. He was right, after all—as a devout Jew, I could neither ignore Passover nor keep it alone. And I will confess that the thought of seeing Martha again, sharing this occasion with her, appealed to me even in my troubled state.

Best of all, if trouble was coming tonight, I would have Benjamin out of the city. "I would like to go to Bethany," I told him. "I am sorry you would have to break your plans with Mark, though."

Benjamin assured me he did not mind, though I knew he wanted to be close to Jesus. He had the same feeling I did, the same feeling many of us did, that something momentous was happening this Passover. Unlike me, he thought of it as something joyous, something that drew him into Jesus' presence instead of making him want to flee. I hoped someday he would thank me for getting him out of the city for these few days, for I was confident Simon would invite us to stay through the preparation day and the Shabbat hours. If he wanted to go to the Temple to see the Passover sacrifice, I would remain behind. As far as I was concerned, the farther I was from the Temple this Passover the better.

Benjamin sent a message to Mark, and we each quickly packed a bag, put on our cloaks, and headed out of the city. It was strange to leave Jerusalem just as so many streamed in through the gates. We struggled against the flow of the crowd, but I felt relief with every step that took me away from the city. Benjamin, I knew, had mixed feelings. We talked little on the road to Bethany.

As I hoped, Simon welcomed us warmly as his unexpected guests; as I had also hoped, Lazarus and his sisters joined us. Unlike a formal dinner such as the feast Simon had invited us to earlier in the week,

Passover was a family affair. Usually the whole household shared the feast together, even the youngest children joining in the readings and prayers that reminded us of the great Exodus from Egypt, that powerful story of deliverance.

As I listened and took part in the readings this Passover night, my heart was strangely stirred. I thought of the Roman soldiers lining the roads into Jerusalem as Jesus rode past, of the Roman governor, Pilate, in his palace overseeing all we did. Our people were in bondage in our own land today as much as we had ever been in Egypt in the time of Moses. No wonder people longed for a new Moses, a Deliverer who would set us free.

And perhaps, I thought, as I passed the scroll to Simon and he took up the reading, perhaps we were all in a deeper bondage, our lives overshadowed by something darker and more sinister even than a Roman legion. There was, after all, a darkness in every human heart, a bondage to sin and selfishness that led people to commit a thousand sins and acts of cruelty every day. Sin led the rich to keep the poor in bondage; sin kept us from ever building the true Promised Land whether the Romans were there or not. I thought of Jesus' camp on the far banks of the Jordan, and I wondered if he had a broader vision of Israel's captivity and the kind of exodus we needed. I had never, not even when he rode on the donkey, been able to see him seeking David's crown and toppling Herod and Pilate. No, he was after something else. Only he would never have the opportunity to pursue that dream, whatever it was, for by tomorrow, or by Shabbat at the latest, he would no longer be free. I knew it in my heart.

I looked up to realize the reading had ended and everyone was eating. Only Martha gazed at me, her steady kind eyes watching me from beneath her veil. When I looked up and met her glance, she flushed and looked away. I averted my eyes, too, wondering what she would think of me if she knew I had almost agreed to trap Jesus.

The feast ended late at night, long after the formal prayers and readings had given way to conversation and singing, and the last fragments of unleavened bread had been dipped in the wine and eaten, the platter of lamb scraped clean. Simon, of course, invited Benjamin and me to stay the night, and I gladly accepted.

I slept more soundly than I had the past few nights, no doubt relieved to be out of Jerusalem and away from my troubles. That, I suppose, was why I was still asleep on a pallet in Simon's courtyard when I was awakened by urgent, troubled voices. Before I opened my eyes, I could identify Simon, Benjamin, and Lazarus, and at least one other. Mark? Could it be he, here in Bethany instead of in Jerusalem? If he had made the journey in the early hours of this morning, it could only be because he had tidings. And I could guess what those tidings were.

"In the early hours—before dawn, even!" I heard Mark say, before he lowered his voice and the rest of the words were lost.

"The Sanhedrin?" Simon echoed. "You must be mistaken, surely; they cannot meet at night . . ."

"We must go to Jerusalem!" Benjamin's words, at least, were clear. I was glad Simon was at his side to say what I wanted to say, even as I struggled into my clothes.

"We must stay well away from Jerusalem!" Simon cautioned. "Whoever was behind Jesus' capture will be looking for his followers too. Many of them will doubtless flee here, to Bethany. Going to Jerusalem now would be the most foolish thing we could do."

I was already crossing the courtyard to join them by the time Lazarus said, "My sisters will both be determined to fly off to Jerusalem as soon as they hear this news."

"Don't be such a fool as to tell them," Simon said. "What can women do; what can any of us do? I'll send word to Nicodemus— he sits on the Sanhedrin and is friendly to our cause. Joseph of Arimathea—there's another, although he's kept quiet about his loyalties until now. Friends in high places—they are the only ones who can help Jesus now."

"It may be too late for that," John Mark said. "By the time I left the city, Jesus had already been brought to Pilate's palace."

Simon shook his head. "The Sanhedrin to meet at night, to turn Jesus over to Pilate—I cannot fathom it! What are they thinking?" He turned to me. "Have you heard Mark's tidings, James?"

"Jesus has been arrested?" I said, and they all nodded. "It is hardly a surprise," I reminded them. "There have been many threats, especially after his ride into the city and his demonstration at the Temple a few days ago. Has anyone else been arrested?" I asked Mark.

"Not yet," he said. "Jesus and the Twelve, and a few more of us, left my house after the Passover dinner and went to the Garden of Gethsemane. Jesus was much troubled and wanted to pray alone. He took Peter and the sons of Zebedee with him and went off by himself, while the rest of us waited in the Garden. This was—" he paused to calculate. "It must have been about midnight, or a little after. Some of us were asleep, and we heard an uproar, a commotion." He went on to tell how Temple police had arrested Jesus in the Garden and taken him to the house of the high priest.

"Was there any violence, any commotion when he was arrested?"

"Very little," Mark said. "There was some struggle; a few people attempted to stop the soldiers from arresting him in the Garden. Peter drew a sword, I think, and he may have attacked someone, but I heard Jesus tell him to put it away. He ordered everyone not to resist, and I think most of us just ran. I know I did." He blushed. "One of the soldiers tried to grab hold of me, and I lost my tunic in the scuffle. I ran away with nothing on! I always thought I would be braver, that I would defend Jesus. But when you're faced with armed men with swords and you have nothing but your bare hands, it's not so easy to be brave."

Benjamin was frowning, no doubt thinking he would have been braver in Mark's place. But I nodded, and so did Simon, with the wisdom of older men tempering the bravado of young ones.

"Do you know where everyone is?" I asked Mark. "Where my brothers are, and our mother Mary?"

He shook his head. "I think a few people followed Jesus to the high priest's house, but I don't know who or what became of them. I went back to my mother's house; some of Jesus' followers were sheltering there. I think I saw his mother, but I can't be sure. They talked of barricading the doors, in case soldiers came. When we heard Jesus had been taken to Pilate, I left the city. I don't think I'm the only one; several people fled the city. Some are talking of going back into the wilderness beyond Jordan—or even all the way to Galilee. As for me, I came here. I knew you would all want to hear the news."

"Did everyone desert him?" Lazarus said. "No one stood by him?"

Mark eyed him warily. "It sounds easy, Lazarus, to talk of standing by Jesus when you're safe here in Bethany. You don't know what it was like in Jerusalem last night, this morning. Besides the Temple guard who arrested Jesus, there are Roman soldiers everywhere. Even before they brought Jesus to Pilate, the governor had word that there was a disturbance, a possible rebellion. Nobody feels safe. Don't blame people for trying to get to safety, to protect their families. What can any of us do for Jesus now?"

Simon began to talk, again, about appealing to men in power who were friendly to our cause, but I knew it was too late for that. The Sanhedrin had done exactly what Avram had told me; he had outlined the plan for me, step by step. Jesus had been arrested in secret. Someone must have led the Temple guard to the Garden, known he would be alone there with just a handful of sleepy followers. He had been tried in secret, accused no doubt of blasphemy under Jewish law, then delivered to the Gentile authority under a charge of sedition and treason. From there, the wheels of Roman justice would roll forward—and crush Jesus. And our own leaders would do nothing— or rather, they would do everything in their power to demonstrate to Pilate and, through him, to Caesar, that they did not support Jesus or any uprising in his name. He was being thrown to the Romans as a bone to angry dogs, sacrificed to those who kept us in bondage, on the feast celebrating our freedom.

The day turned into madness. As Simon had predicted, Mark was not the only follower of Jesus to flee Jerusalem and seek refuge in Bethany. Others, including some of the Twelve, arrived throughout the day; all went either to Simon's house or to Lazarus's. Some traveled in the opposite direction: Martha agreed to stay after Lazarus gave her a direct order, but Mary of Magdala defied her brother and insisted on going to Jerusalem, weeping wildly and swearing she would not leave Jesus to face his fate alone. John bar Zebedee escorted Mary back into the city late in the morning to see what was happening, despite warnings from the rest of us.

Simon sent messengers to the men he trusted in the city—Nicodemus and Joseph of Arimathea, among others—and we waited, tense and unhappy, as noon passed and the afternoon wore on.

"We should return to Galilee," I said to Benjamin at one point. "Perhaps if we go into Jerusalem tomorrow—no, tomorrow is the Shabbat. The day after, perhaps. We can find your grandmother and the rest of the family and be back in Nazareth by the end of the week."

Benjamin looked at me as if I were mad. "For over a year you've shown not the slightest interest in returning to Galilee, and now you say we should go there at once?"

"It's far from Jerusalem, far from Pilate's jurisdiction. If his men want to come looking for the rest of Jesus' family, they won't find us here."

"No, they'll find us in Nazareth, where Herod rules. Herod is no friend of Jesus either, so why should we be any safer there?" Benjamin challenged. "I don't want to run to Galilee and hide."

"You may be glad of a place to hide before this is all over."

We did not know it then, but it already was all over, in one sense, anyway. As the evening shadows lengthened toward sunset, another traveler arrived at Simon's house. It was Andrew, Peter's brother, and I could tell by his grief-stricken face, before he even spoke, that the news was not good.

"The Lord is dead," he said abruptly.

"Dead? What?" I echoed.

"Dead. The Romans crucified him at noon. They had a great display of crosses set up outside the city, at the Hill of the Skull. A little Passover reminder to our people of who their rulers are, I suppose. Jesus was crucified with a rabble of brigands and rebels."

"No!" Benjamin cried. I could not bear to look at my son's face, but I could hear the pain in his voice. "No, it can't be! He can't really be dead!"

"He is dead, Benjamin," Andrew said. "I saw his body, taken off the cross and carried to a tomb."

"He was buried?" Simon put in. Usually the bodies of crucified criminals were flung into a common pit to rot.

Andrew raised his eyes briefly to Simon's. "Yes. Nicodemus and Joseph saw to that. The tomb belongs to Joseph's family, and they asked Pilate for the favor of burying his remains."

"Were you there when he died?" I asked. "It seems—quick, for a crucifixion." I knew men could hang on crosses, writhing in agony and gasping for breath, for many hours, even days, before death released them.

"Our priests wanted the bodies down before Shabbat," Andrew said, a trace of bitterness in his tone. "They are very careful about observing the Law, yet they were the ones who captured the Lord, handed him over to the Romans, and testified against him—even when Pilate might have released him! They were determined he would die; they have always hated him."

"You were saying—about taking the bodies off the crosses," Benjamin prompted him.

"Yes. The Romans broke the legs of the other convicts, so they would strangle and die more quickly. But when they came to Jesus, he was already dead."

"You're sure he was dead?" Benjamin asked. I could hear the naked hope in his voice; perhaps it was not true, perhaps Jesus would escape and return.

"I wasn't there myself," Andrew admitted. "Of the Twelve, John bar Zebedee was the only one to stay at the cross—John and some of the women, including Mary, your grandmother," he added to Benjamin. "I heard it all from John, how the soldiers saw that he was dead and stabbed him in the side with a spear to be certain. If he wasn't already dead, that would have killed him. But he's dead now, and at least he's buried in a decent grave. Some of the women are going after Shabbat is over to anoint the body."

"That's foolhardy of them," Simon said. "They should stay well away from his grave—everyone should. Men like Joseph and Nicodemus have power and money to protect them, but the rest of you—the family especially—should get into hiding as soon as you can. I think Rabbi James is wise to say you should all get back to Galilee."

We talked endlessly through that night and into the bleak Shabbat beyond. A few more refugees drifted out of Jerusalem to Bethany, while others returned to the city, where, Andrew told us, Mark's house was still being used as their refuge. Joseph of Arimathea and Nicodemus were apparently willing to take the risk of burying Jesus' body but not of sheltering his followers or family, so the home of Mark's mother had become the safe house for those who chose to stay in Jerusalem. Many did not. Some came to us in Bethany, while others fled farther afield, heedless of the laws against traveling on Shabbat.

"I still cannot believe it," Benjamin said as he laid more wood on the fire in Simon's courtyard, late on the night after Shabbat. Mark was still with us, as were Lazarus and Martha and a few others. "How could he die? I truly believed he was the Chosen One, sent from God, just as he always told us he was. How could he die with his mission still incomplete?"

"Any man can die," Simon said gently. His wife and daughters sat with us, too, young Raina sitting as near Benjamin as she dared, trying to offer some comfort for his deep grief. He hardly seemed to even see her.

"No, Jesus was something more!" Benjamin insisted. "He was going to deliver our people, to bring peace, to bring a new era of hope . . ."

"All our hopes have turned to ashes now," Lazarus said.

"But how can it be?" Martha burst out. It was so rare for her to speak in mixed company that I knew she felt driven to say this. "Lazarus, you should know better than anyone else! Jesus raised you! He had power over death. How could he let himself be captured and crucified? Is the power of Rome greater than the power of God?"

Lazarus simply shook his head. He had no answer. There were no answers.

I felt for them, my friends and family, in their grief. I had never believed, as they had, that Jesus was anything more than a mortal man who meant well but made terrible mistakes. I had no shattered faith to struggle through, as they did, and my loss was a more personal one. For all the resentment I had had against Jesus in my younger days, for all the conflicts I had had with him in our manhood, still he was a part of my family. As I had come a little closer, these last months, to seeing what his dream was and what he lived for, I realized I did, indeed, grieve his death. I mourned the loss of a truly good man. Though I disagreed with the choices he made, I saw now that beneath his bravado and arrogance he truly had a good heart. If only he had heeded my many warnings! But he never had. It was almost as if, in the end, he did not fear death but welcomed it.

My only consolation was that I had played no part in bringing him to his death. And my only concern now was safety for the rest of my family, especially Benjamin. It was possible that with Jesus dead and buried, the Romans would consider the whole incident closed, but one could never be sure. There might still be reprisals.

"All we can do is remember him and be cautious," I said now. "Make sure that no one else suffers and dies for his cause. He would not have wanted that, surely."

"We can do more than that," Martha said. "We can honor his body properly, pay tribute to him." She turned to Lazarus again. "Brother, if the women are going to the tomb in the morning, you know Mary will be among them. I want to be there too."

"No, Martha! We are safe enough here; don't tempt fate by seeking out Jesus' tomb!" Lazarus said sharply.

"You would not let me go before his death, so that I could stand by him!" she shot back, more anger in her voice than I had ever heard. "Mary defied you, and she was there. Only the women and John, you heard as well as I did. All the rest of you men were too frightened to stand by him at the last. I obeyed you, because I always have obeyed. But now—now that he is dead, all I beg is the chance to go anoint his body! Please, Lazarus! Do this much for Jesus, who gave you back your life!"

His face softened as he looked at her, and I guessed he was thinking what I was: poor Martha, she asked so little. Compared to her sister, who blazed through life like a shooting star, going her own way and doing her own will, Martha was always dutiful, always served and obeyed. Now she begged this one boon of her brother, to be near the body of Jesus one last time.

"If Lazarus will not take you, I will," I heard myself say. When Martha turned to look at me, I added, "I want to go back to Jerusalem anyway, to find my brothers and my stepmother and bring them all back to Nazareth. You can stay here if you wish, Benjamin, in your father-in-law's house. But I think everyone else will be safer back in Galilee."

"What watch of the night is it?" Martha asked.

"Just past midnight," said Lazarus. "Come then, sister, let us go home and pack a bag. James and I will both travel with you into Jerusalem. We may be going to our deaths, but I have faced death before and come through." He laughed, a fragile sound in the darkness of that courtyard. Then he stood up and offered his sister a hand, and the three of us made ready to travel in darkness into the city.

Chapter Twenty-Three

Jerusalem felt, in those pre-dawn hours on the first day of the week, like a city under siege. There were more guards on the walls than usual, though I did not know whether that was because of the disturbance around Jesus' arrest and death, or simply because it was Passover, with the usual influx of foreign pilgrims and the possibility of trouble.

We made our way through streets empty except for occasional patrols. The Passover Feast had ended, but many pilgrims stayed in the city throughout the Days of Unleavened Bread. At first I led Lazarus and Martha toward my own house—Avram's house—then thought better of it. I had no desire to meet Avram, and it would be best to seek out Jesus' disciples at the home of Mark's mother. Lazarus would find his sister there, and I might find my stepmother and brothers. I hoped I could persuade my family to return with me to Galilee before anyone decided it would be wise to arrest all of Jesus' relatives.

The house looked dark and hushed, and there was no reply to our knock. It seemed for all the world like a house deserted.

"They aren't here," I said, but Lazarus shook his head.

"They are here, but they're frightened," he said. "In hiding." He leaned in closer to the door, tapped again, lightly but insistently.

"Mary! Rhoda! Peter! Is anyone there? It's me, Lazarus! The one Jesus raised from the dead!"

Still the house was silent, though I thought I could hear faint movement beyond the door. I added my voice. "I am here too—James, Jesus' brother. Are my brothers inside?"

Again I thought I heard something—a faint rustle, the murmur of voices. Then a girl's voice, close to the door. "What did the Lord say we must become like, to enter the kingdom?"

Lazarus hesitated a moment and looked at me, but Martha pushed forward. "Like little children!" she hissed into the crack by the door, and after another agonizing moment, it swung open an inch or two, then far enough to let us inside.

Beyond the silent outer wall, the large courtyard was full of people, people sitting or lying in the dark, huddled together. Not a single lamp was lit in all that house, yet almost everyone was awake.

"You came from Bethany? Is Mark with you?" asked a woman's voice in the darkness.

"No, he stayed behind," I said to the young man's mother.

"Wise boy," one of the men said. "I wish I were in Bethany right now. Or back in Galilee where I belong." I recognized the voice; it was Peter of Bethsaida.

I was about to ask if my brothers were there, but Martha interrupted. "Is Mary of Magdala here? Is it true some of the women are going to the tomb?"

"As soon as it's light," said another voice. In the moonlight I could now pick out a few faces. But of course I would have known that voice anyway; it was my stepmother Mary, her voice hoarse from crying. "Come to the tomb with us, Martha—it is the last gift we can give him."

"You're fools to go out there, especially with Pilate's soldiers guarding the tomb," Peter said. "None of us should put a foot outside this house unless it's to flee the city."

"We are safer than you men would be, Peter," Mary said. "Neither the Temple guard nor the Romans will think to arrest women;

they do not think we could have any part to play in great events. They set a guard on the tomb for fear someone might steal his body, but they would expect men, not women, to do such a deed. Martha, your sister is not here," Mary went on. "She was with us when we brought his body to the tomb, but she went to stay with a friend somewhere else in the city yesterday, during the Shabbat. She said this friend could get her some ointment and spices for the burial, and she would meet us at the tomb at dawn."

I started to speak, but someone hushed me. "We have to stay quiet. They are searching for us."

I was not certain this was true. I had seen many soldiers in the streets but no evidence of a search for Jesus' followers. However, I shared their fear and found a spot where I could crouch uncomfortably against a wall until dawn came.

By then, five or six of the women, including Martha and my stepmother, were putting on cloaks and veils, getting ready to go out in the street. I wondered if one of us men should go with them, for protection, but then thought that perhaps Mary was right that they would be safer on their own. Anointing the bodies of the dead was a woman's rightful task, and surely even Jesus' enemies would not prohibit our women from doing so.

Jesus' enemies. *Our* enemies. *Our* womenfolk. How easily I had slipped into the habit of thinking of myself as one of them! I never had been, not while Jesus lived, but grief at his death had bound me to them. I had had my opportunity to take my stand on the other side, with Avram and the other religious leaders. In refusing the chance to betray him, I had cast my lot with the believers, even though I had never believed.

Now even the truest believers were shattered, lost, not knowing what to hope for. The night sky lightened toward dawn; people, tired of hiding in silence without sleep, began talking in hushed tones. My brothers Joseph, Simon, and Jude were all there, with their wives and children. I urged on them the importance of getting back to Galilee.

Chapter Twenty-Three

"If we stay here, are we in danger?" Simon asked me.

"There is no way to be certain," I admitted. "I think the Sanhedrin wanted only to be rid of Jesus. As long as his followers disperse quietly, there may be no trouble from them. But I know they would be more comfortable if we were all back in Galilee, out of their territory. As for the Romans, they have been known to hunt down the families and followers of men accused of treason, to wipe out whole clans. I do not know what they might do, and I certainly do not trust them."

As I spoke, I saw that others besides my own family had gathered around, particularly the Galileans. All of the Twelve were present in the house except Judas Iscariot. The sons of Zebedee pressed close, asking my opinion about what we should do next.

"Today many of the Passover pilgrims will begin to leave the city, though some will stay for the rest of the festival," I went on. "Travelers will be on the roads in every direction. It will be an excellent time for us to slip away, not all in one large group but in several smaller parties, without attracting any notice."

"What of those of us left here in the city?" Mark's mother began, but a harsh voice cut her off.

"Why are you all listening to James, asking his counsel as if he were our leader?" It was Peter. I had never liked the man, and he had never liked me. Whatever veneer of politeness had covered his behavior to me while Jesus lived was gone now, and his anger was evident. Someone reminded him to keep his voice low. "This James is a man who never believed our Lord while he lived, despite being his kinsman!" Peter went on, more quietly but still with anger. "He was never a disciple! Why, Joseph and Simon and Jude have better claim to being brothers of the Lord, for at least they followed him for a while. But this man? I don't even know why you're here," he said directly to me.

"Peter, be quiet," his brother Andrew urged, a hand on Peter's arm.

"He speaks truth," I admitted. "I was not a follower of Jesus, as you all were. I am sorry for his death, but my first concern is to get my family safely out of the city. You can take my advice or leave it, as you please."

"I will take it," said John bar Zebedee. He turned to Peter. "James may not have been a disciple, but he is a rabbi and a wise man. He knows the rabbis and priests and what they are likely to do. Why should we not listen to him?"

"Because I don't trust him!" Peter snapped. Then he deflated a little. "Of course, I don't trust anyone now. You notice that little toad Judas is nowhere to be seen. I'll swear till my dying day he was in the Garden with the soldiers that night, when they came to arrest Jesus."

"You can't know that for sure, Peter," another said. Someone else chimed in, "But it's true we've not seen him since Jesus was arrested."

Our hushed bickering was interrupted when the door flew open. There stood my stepmother Mary with Martha and the other women who had made their way to the tomb just an hour or two before.

"Something is wrong at the tomb! His body is gone!" burst out Salome, the wife of Zebedee.

"The great stone was rolled away, but there was nothing inside," Martha said.

"I thought the tomb was guarded," Peter said.

"There was no sign of the guards," Mary said. "But I saw someone there. Someone—not an ordinary man. I thought—"

"Hush, Mary," Martha said, not disrespectfully but as if to soothe her. "No talk of angels or visions now. The tomb was empty; that's all we know."

"But we did see someone!" Mary insisted. "I have seen an angel before, you know, and I wouldn't mistake one for an ordinary person. He spoke to me. He asked why we were looking for the living among the dead! He told us Jesus was alive!"

"It's her grief that confuses her," Salome said. "It's true the tomb was empty, and we saw someone there, not a Roman soldier, but I don't know about angels. It's my opinion that someone has stolen his body after all—but who?"

"Was anyone else there—any of our people?" John bar Zebedee asked. "Mary of Magdala was supposed to meet you there with spices. Did she come?"

The women looked at each other, a little shamefaced. "We ran away," Martha admitted. "Mary could have been on her way, but we were terrified. We wanted to get back and tell you what we had seen."

"I was not terrified!" my stepmother Mary insisted. "I believe the angel spoke the truth. Do you not remember Jesus saying he would destroy the Temple and raise it up in three days? Or that as Jonah was in the belly of the fish three days, the Son of man would be three days in the earth? Today is the third day. He is alive!"

Most of us agreed with Salome and Martha—that the body must have been stolen, and this latest grief had turned Mary's mind so that she was imagining angels and heavenly messengers. It was something, I was quick to point out, that she had always done where Jesus was concerned.

At least, that was what we all told ourselves until another frantic hammering came at the door. It was Mary of Magdala. She, too, was flushed, out of breath, and excited as the other women had been. Her story was the same: the tomb empty, the stone rolled away, the guard gone.

"We will be accused of stealing the body," Peter said. "It's what both the priests and the Romans said we'd do. Even though we haven't gone near the place, that will be their next accusation."

"Come with me and see it!" Mary of Magdala insisted.

The other women told her they had been there before her and seen the same thing, but they all agreed some of the men should go. Peter and John followed Mary to the tomb, and the rest of us waited, tense, for their return, talking over the possibilities of this new development. Who could have stolen the body when the tomb was closely guarded? Where were the Roman soldiers now? Was there someone, indeed, perhaps some of Jesus' other followers, who would claim Jesus had risen? Or was someone trying to make it look as if his disciples had stolen the body, as an excuse for more arrests?

I was sure of one thing: the need to leave Jerusalem was more pressing than ever.

Peter and John soon returned, telling the same story as the women: the empty tomb, the guards missing, even the linen grave cloths in which his body had been wrapped were neatly folded and laid aside.

"Someone *unwrapped* the body and then stole it?" I echoed in disbelief.

"What thief would do that?" Jesus' mother Mary said. *It is going to be hard for her to get over her grief at losing her best-loved son if she clings to the desperate hope that he is still alive,* I thought.

"Where is my sister?" Lazarus asked.

"She stayed behind—there at the tomb," Peter said. "I'm sorry, Lazarus, we should have brought her back with us. She said she wanted to be alone, to weep and pray."

"Come, Martha," Lazarus said. "Let us go find Mary, and the three of us will return to Bethany. We're safer there."

But before he could gather his few belongings, Mary of Magdala entered the courtyard again. She looked completely different from when she had come the first time. Yes, she was once again flushed and out of breath from running, but instead of fear, her face glowed with an elation that was almost otherworldly.

"I have seen him!" she announced.

"Seen who?" several people replied.

"Jesus, of course!" she said, as if we were all fools. As if seeing a man who had died the day before yesterday was the most natural thing in the world.

"Mary, you're mad; you're sick with grief," Lazarus said, putting his arm around her. But the other Mary, my stepmother, moved to her other side, holding her arm. "You saw him?" Jesus' mother prompted.

"Mary, you can't have seen him. We were there just before you; there was no one there," Peter said.

"After you left, he came!" Mary said. "I wasn't looking at him. I had my face in my hands, weeping, and when he spoke I thought he was the caretaker of the garden. He asked why I was crying, and I told him someone had stolen the body of my Master, and I didn't know where it was. Then he said my name, just in his own voice as he always did, and I turned and—oh, it was him! It was Jesus! I could never mistake him for anyone else!"

"But Jesus is dead, Mary," Martha said.

"No! You saw the tomb yourself," Mary of Magdala said, "all you women, and Peter and John too. You know he's not there anymore. And if you remember everything he said to us, you know that he spoke of death, and of rising from the dead too—only we didn't listen. Lazarus! If anyone should know that Jesus has power over death, you should! Won't you believe me?"

"How did he look?" some people asked; and "What did he say?" others put in. I couldn't tell if they really believed Mary, or if they were testing her story. *Surely anyone who would believe such a tale is more than ready to delude themselves,* I thought. Of all the madness ever spoken about Jesus in his life, this tale of his rising from the dead was worst of all. It would play directly into the hands of Jesus' enemies on the Sanhedrin, who had suspected his followers might claim a resurrection to keep his name and his movement alive. Just the excuse they and the Romans would need to arrest the remaining Jesus-followers.

Mary's words tumbled over themselves in her eagerness to speak. "He looked—like himself, but—but more. That's all I can say—more. You'll understand when you see him. He told me to tell you, 'I am returning to my Father and your Father, to my God and your God.' "

A moment's silence greeted Mary's statement. Then the entire room erupted into argument, a few obviously eager to believe she spoke the truth, everyone else decrying her, saying it could not possibly be true.

"Come back with me!" Mary urged. "Come back to the tomb, and we'll see if he's there again."

"Absolutely not. We'd be fools to leave this house!" Peter said.

"I intend to leave, but only to gather my things and travel north," I said. "It's time to leave Jerusalem."

Most of those gathered in that house agreed with me. "I'm taking my sisters back to Bethany at once," Lazarus said.

"My wife and I will return to Emmaus," said a man named Cleopas, while a fellow called Zacchaeus announced his intention to pack everything right away and get back to Jericho. Peter, Andrew, James, and John said they would return to Galilee and go back to fishing—but not today. "We'll spend the night here and begin the journey in the morning," Peter decided.

My brothers agreed that they and their families would join me in the journey north. "But first, I must go to Bethany for the night," I told them. "Benjamin is still there. I hope he will come with us, but at least I must say Goodbye to him."

I needed, too, to return to my room in Avram's house, to gather my belongings. I suppose I could have left it all behind. As for clothes and other things, I might not have cared, but my scrolls were there, a lifetime's collection of carefully collected wisdom. I could not leave them behind. In the chaos and confusion of these past weeks, and especially of these last few days, how could I leave behind the only thing I knew that mattered, the only things I could still grasp—the Law of God as revealed in the Torah and the Prophets? I did not think I would return to Jerusalem.

All around us, people were doing what we were—making plans for departure, hearts heavy with disappointment and shadowed with fear. Only a few repeated Mary's story over and over, wondering if she was truly mad again—"She was a madwoman before, when Jesus first cast the demons out of her"—or whether there was any reason for hope.

Hope was a commodity in short supply that day, as people drifted away from the house in pairs and small groups, carrying their bags and bundles, blending in with the crowds of Passover travelers leaving the city. Mary of Magdala repeated her bizarre tale to anyone who would listen, but most, apart from our mother Mary, simply shook their heads and turned away, unable to bear the hope in her eyes. The elder Mary refused to leave Jerusalem with me and her other sons. "Perhaps I will come later, when James and John and Salome go back to Capernaum," she said. "But now I want to stay here, to find out if he is really alive."

"He is not, Mary. You know this in your heart."

"What do you know of my heart, James?"

I turned to go. There was no talking sense to her.

We finally agreed that my brothers would go on to Bethany with Lazarus and his sisters, while I would return to my rooms, gather my scrolls and a few other belongings, and join them in Bethany by nightfall. We would spend the night there and begin our journey north the next day. I hoped Benjamin would be with us, but if he chose to stay in Bethany as part of Simon's household, I was sure he would be safe there. The dreams I had had for him of a scholarly life in Jerusalem—would those come true? Or would his association with the family and followers of Jesus of Nazareth taint his career forever?

No way to know. I walked through the busy streets of the city in the mid-afternoon sun. Travelers everywhere were moving out to the city gates with packs and bundles on their backs, laden donkeys and handcarts. No one noticed me; no one was talking about a man rising from the dead.

But someone had talked; rumors were spreading, for I found Avram in the courtyard, looking displeased when I arrived.

"James. At last, you have returned."

"Only to collect my goods and pay you my rent," I told him. In truth, I had hoped to leave the rent money without having to face my old friend again.

"Going back to Galilee?"

"Yes," I replied shortly.

"Good. The best place for all Galileans. We would have had much less trouble if your brother and his rabble had stayed up in the north where they belonged."

"That trouble is settled now, though," I said. "You got what you wanted."

He shook his head sadly. "To turn over a fellow Jew to Roman authority? Hardly what I wanted, James."

"That's not what I heard. I heard you practically had to coerce Pilate to have him executed."

Avram shrugged. "Pilate put up a show of reluctance. He hates our people—did not want to do anything to accommodate us. He tested us to make sure we really wanted an end to Jesus' revolution. Believe me, if we had not acted as we did—"

"I know. You have told me before—Rome would have acted. Anyway, you have your Pax Romana now."

"No thanks to you, James," Avram reminded me. "But peace? I don't know. The man was crucified and buried, but now his body is gone, and there are rumors all over the city. Some women are claiming to have seen him alive; others are claiming that they have seen visions of other dead men—ancient prophets long dead—walking about the city and the Temple. Some say the earthquake on the day he died was a sign of Heaven's displeasure. I had hoped Jesus' death would silence his followers, but now I am afraid of a movement that will keep going even in his absence."

"You have nothing to fear from these people," I told him. "From our people, I should say, because like it or not, they are mostly my kinsmen and countrymen. They are frightened; they are in hiding; they will scurry back to their homes. Don't soil your hands with anymore Galilean blood . . . the thing will die out of its own accord."

"Do you promise me that, James?"

"I can tell you I will do nothing to keep the talk of Jesus alive, anyway."

"I hope you are as good as your word."

"I am. I always have been." As I bade farewell to Avram for the last time that day, I meant what I had said. I fully intended to go home, never return to Jerusalem, never speak of Jesus again outside the family circle. I meant to do everything I could to make sure stories of his death and supposed resurrection died down as quickly as possible.

That was what I intended, before I walked into my own room and saw Jesus sitting at my writing table.

Chapter Twenty-Four

Of course I did not believe it was Jesus. A man sat in my room, at my table. Then he turned to face me. His smile brightened the room, and he said, "James!" in that old, delighted voice.

I just stood there. I did not speak, nor did I fall to my knees as Mary said she had done. I think I pressed my hand to my chest, to make sure my heart was still beating, that I was still living in the same ordinary world I had inhabited a moment ago.

But no. I had crossed over. I was living in the land of those who saw visions, who were visited by the dead.

Jesus stood up and crossed the room to me, and I took an involuntary step backward—not in fear or horror, for there was nothing frightening in his aspect, but—simply because I had to.

I had, of course, seen a man raised from the dead already. I was there when Jesus called Lazarus forth, and I have been asked, many times in the years since, to explain the difference between the two. I will try my best now, hanging on to that moment of strangeness when the risen Jesus stood by my writing table and held out his hands to me. I could still see, on both hands, the wounds made by the nails that had bound him to the cross; they had healed, but the scars were still livid against his brown skin.

The best way I can put it is this: when Lazarus came out of the tomb, and the grave clothes were unwrapped, he looked exactly like himself. The same Lazarus who had died a few days before had been raised again, healed of the fever that had killed him but otherwise the same, with all his human weaknesses and frailties. Raised, I knew without doubt, to die again some few years down the road: as frail and fallible and mortal as any of us.

The Jesus who stood before me that day was—not like that. Not like the old Jesus I had known all my life.

Oh, I recognized him. The same face, the same features, even the same smile. But he was not—and this is where words fail me, as they had failed Mary of Magdala a few hours earlier. He was more alive than he had been before, more alive than I or any other person I had ever seen. It was as if his body hummed and glowed with vitality far beyond that normally given to humans. It was as if—

Forgive me, I cannot tell it except by comparisons. Have you ever seen a drawing or a mosaic of a human figure? Our people do not make such decorations, of course, because the Torah commands us not to make images, but I have seen them on the walls of Gentile homes when I worked as a younger man in Sepphoris or Tiberias. I have seen these flat images painted on a wall or picked out in stone, recognizable copies of human beings but obviously not alive, not able to move about and breathe for themselves.

When I saw Jesus on the third day after he died, it seemed to me that I, and every other man I had ever seen, was a painted image on a wall, and Jesus was the only true, living human being I had ever seen. He was the Real; all the rest were mere copies.

I try to say all this in words now, but then it overwhelmed me with sudden and absolute knowledge. Tears sprang to my eyes. I had not thought it was possible for him to be alive, but here he was—not just alive, but glorified. *This is what we will all be like in the resurrection at the last day,* I thought.

"It is true, James. *I AM.* Lay aside your doubts."

When he said the words "I AM," something flashed, some fire in his eyes, and I knew that I was looking at more than a man, more than even a resurrected man. All the tales Mary had told and believed— angels at his conception and birth, fathered by the Holy Spirit, foretold in prophecy—all my life I had thought these the ravings of a deluded woman who had fed her son her own delusions till he believed them too. Now I saw, unveiled, what she had seen all those years ago and believed for so long.

"Mine eyes shall see the King in His beauty," I said.

"They shall behold the land that is very far off," Jesus said, finishing the quotation from Isaiah. "But it is not so very far off now, is it, James? And you will help bring my people there with me."

Then I found that I was kneeling, after all, kneeling on the hard floor before him. Kneeling before Jesus! I thought of the old tale of Joseph, son of Jacob, dreaming that his brothers would bow down before him, and how at last they did bow before him in Egypt. I would never have thought I could bow before Jesus. But this was not my arrogant little brother. Or rather, it was he, and what I had mistaken for arrogance and bravado all those years were simply the moments when Divinity shone through his humanity and he could not restrain or hide it. He had always spoken with authority, and I had resented it. Now I saw that authority like a naked sword before me, and I bowed.

"Forgive me, Lord," I said, bowing my head. I called him Lord, because he was my Lord. "Forgive me for never believing in you. Forgive me for—all my wrongs. My pride. I almost betrayed you— they tried to persuade me to give you up. Forgive me for even thinking of it!"

I felt his hands, solid and cool and real, on the top of my head. "Peace, brother," he said. "All is forgiven, and all will be well. Now rise up, for I have work for you to do. I cannot tarry here forever, and my people will be like sheep without a shepherd. They will need someone to lead and guide them."

"I?" I looked up at him, almost feeling I had to shield my eyes as from the sun. "I can have no part to play—why would they trust me? They have their own leaders, Peter and the sons of Zebedee . . ."

"Of course, and there is work for you all to do. They have had the benefit of learning from me these past few years and will have much to teach others, when I have driven out their fear and frailty. But you, James, have gifts of your own—James the wise, James the just. My people will need those gifts, until I come back again."

"You will come again, though? You will not leave us here?"

"I will come, James. Do not fear." He took both my hands in his, clasped them tightly, and then . . . he was gone. He disappeared.

If I told you I had been in a room with a man I knew had been dead, and had talked to him and touched him, and then he vanished from my sight, surely you would ask if I had been dreaming or in a vision. You would wonder if he had ever really been there. I would have asked the question myself, the day before.

But that day, I did not ask it. I did not doubt, even for a moment. He had been there. He was gone, but he would come back. He had promised.

Epilogue

Here I am at the end of my story, which is the beginning.

I had intended to tell you more. I thought the story I had to tell would be of what we did in Jerusalem after Jesus died and rose again, after He disappeared from our earthly sight and returned to His Father. After the Holy Spirit came and filled us all, and we began to build the kingdom He had taught us of, a kingdom without crowns or thrones or swords, a kingdom where all are welcome and all are equal in His sight.

But it seems the story I had to tell you was the story that came before that one. It was the story of how I had Jesus, the Son of God, before my eyes every day for years—but I never saw Him. How my own pride, my sense of what was right and wrong, blinded me to the Truth that lived in my own house all along. How I never really saw Jesus until I saw Him risen, and that changed everything. That changed me.

Despite the changes the Spirit brought to my life, I suppose I am still the same man in some ways. Still stubborn, still proud, still tied to our old ways. I have to struggle against the desire to hold back when the rest of the church wants to move in another direction, and I do not think I am always in the wrong.

There have been struggles, just as there were when Jesus was among us. The Spirit transforms, but we are still tempted by our sinful natures. We jockey for position and power, though we know we should not. Peter and I did not always share power easily, in the early days. It was as Jesus had said—Peter was a natural leader among the original Twelve, but many people deferred to me because I was an educated man, a rabbi, and the brother of Jesus. While Peter and many of the others were illiterate fishermen from the north, I knew my way around Jerusalem. I knew the men in power—though many of them were my enemies, now—and I could debate with the learned rabbis. Some turned to me as a leader, others to Peter; and it seemed for a time we might split Jesus' followers into factions. But we both knew that would not be His will. We met and prayed together about it and found we could work together if we both laid aside our pride.

In the same way, we sought solutions to many of the problems that threatened us in those early days. We were constantly under threat from those outside, for while many flocked to hear the message of Jesus in those heady days after Pentecost, the same powers—both our own leaders and the Romans—who had sought to silence Jesus in His life, now wanted to put down the growing movement of His followers. But though we dealt with arrest, imprisonment, and even death, our greatest dangers came from within as we struggled to build His community, His church, here on earth, and waited for Him to return.

We dealt with dissension and deceit among our own people, with quarrels among the Hebrew and Greek widows who felt that food was not being distributed equally. We discovered the need to choose deacons and deaconesses to share the work of the apostles, and we dealt with the growing changes that came as Gentile converts to the message began to overwhelm the numbers of Jews.

I suppose this was the hardest struggle for me, for I believe, as I have always believed, that we are God's chosen people, and it is His Law and the land He gave us that keeps us separate and special. I thought that Jesus came to revitalize Israel, to set us free from the bondage to sin and be the nation God meant us to be. But in my study of the Scriptures, as more and more Gentiles were baptized into the faith of Jesus, I came to see that what God had meant us to be was a light to the Gentiles, a city set on a hill, as Jesus Himself said, that would draw all the world to us.

Even so, it was a struggle to accommodate all these new converts. I felt that their men should be circumcised as we were, that they should observe all our ceremonies and rituals; and that if they did not do these things, we should maintain the separateness that had always kept our people apart from the rest of the world.

Oh, how Paul railed at me for that! Paul—now there is another whole book I could write, about that intense little man who turned our world upside down, taking the message of Jesus to the farthest corners of the empire. We had many other missionaries, of course. While I stayed in Jerusalem, guiding the church there through the harshest times of persecution, apostles and new converts went all over the empire spreading Jesus' message. But no one else had the energy, the power, the sheer ambition of Paul; and no one else, I think, could have done what he did. He sits in chains in a Roman prison now; I can pay him at least that much tribute.

But oh, the conflicts we had! If I thought my struggles with Peter in those early years were contentious, they were nothing to what I went through with Paul a few years later. How many times, in my arguments with him, did the word *arrogant* flash across my mind! Every time it did, I thought of how I had given Jesus that label for so many years. Not that Paul was very much like Jesus in temperament, and his arrogance was certainly not divinity bursting through his humanity as it had been with Jesus. But having misjudged Jesus for so many years—for His whole life, really—I was cautious against judging others too hastily. Though I really did think that Paul was often brash and outspoken, I reminded myself that the confidence born of God's Spirit can often make people outspoken, and sometimes even arrogant, and it does not mean they are wrong.

Still, it has been difficult. I am an old man now. Nearly thirty years have passed since Jesus died and rose and went away. I did not expect to have to carry on so long without Him—and I did not expect, myself, to live so long.

But there are blessings to a long life. I have seen my children and grandchildren grow up, and every one of them is a follower of the Way of Jesus. And I have found love and companionship in my second marriage, for yes, after Jesus left us and returned to the Father, I asked Martha to be my wife. She was past the age of childbearing, and truth to tell, while some men might have been disappointed by that, I was relieved. I had had my child-raising years long before, with Rachel and then for many years without her, and I did not want to begin all that again. I wanted, instead, to begin this new work, to be part of bringing to birth this new community of those who followed the Way of Jesus. This was the new life I wanted to nurture, and I was grateful for a dear comrade like Martha who shared my faith and my dreams.

I have spoken of the challenges and conflicts we Christians have faced among ourselves, but I would leave you with the wrong impression if I spoke only of that and not of the joy we have found together, worshiping and praying, studying the Scriptures to try to understand how Jesus' life and His words, His death and resurrection, all fit into the writings God gave us so long ago. When we meet to share the common meal of bread and wine that reminds us of His body and blood, then I know a deeper communion than I have ever known with anyone. I begin to understand, then, why Jesus said that His followers were His true family, and not those of us who shared His blood and were raised in the same household. The bond that really matters is the bond of faith, the bond we choose.

Most people among our fellowship now call me "James, the Lord's brother," though a few still call me "James the Just," a nickname of which I confess I am a little proud. I do not call myself "the Lord's brother," but only an apostle, one who saw Jesus after He was risen and carried that message to others. I never refer to Him as "my brother" but only as "the Lord Jesus." Because the truth of it is, I did not really know Him, all these years that He was my brother. We grew up in the same house, shared the same work, ate the same bread. But my heart was closed to Him, and I never truly loved Him as a brother.

My heart did not open, I did not truly see Him, until I saw Him risen and knew Him as my Lord and my God. So when I think of Jesus now, that is how I think of Him—the Divinity that had always been veiled suddenly unveiled, glorious and risen, love and light shining out of Him.

I have thought so much about the past these days, dwelling on the early years, on the time when Jesus was among us. This is strange, because I set out to think about the future. I have been trying to write a letter to send out to the churches. Like the letters Paul and Peter have written (though Peter dictates his to Mark, having never learned the knack of putting pen to parchment, though he eventually learned to read the Scriptures a little). All of us, those of us who knew Jesus and walked with Him, are growing older now, and we have to face the possibility that some of us may die before He returns. What will we leave behind for those new followers who come after us? Mark and that Gentile doctor, Luke, have already taken on the task of writing down some of Jesus' words and works, and I hear others are doing the same. Paul and Peter and John bar Zebedee have written letters to the churches about doctrine, reminding them of what we believe, interpreting our Hebrew Scriptures for these new Gentile converts, helping them to make sense of the stories of Jesus in a world that is becoming increasingly hard.

I want to add my own few words for these troubled times. I travel much less than the other apostles, and people often ask what messages I would like to send to these far-flung believers I have never seen, as well as to our own faithful little company here in Jerusalem. I have led the church in Jerusalem for nearly thirty years now, and have never traveled farther than Antioch twice, and once to Ephesus, where my stepmother Mary lived in her last years with John bar Zebedee. Yet the world is full of people who are my brothers and sisters, because Jesus binds us together.

We are, as Paul once wrote, pressed on every side. When I read the psalms now and hear the voice of David crying out against his enemies, I think I know a little of what he felt. Our fellow Jews have become less and less tolerant of those of us who follow the Way of Jesus, forcing us out of the synagogues, making a wall of separation between us—and many would still like to see us wiped out altogether. But to be fair to my fellow Jews, they are under their own pressures from the Romans, whose rule grows harsher every year. Judea sits ever more uneasily under the domination of the Roman Empire, with dozens of little uprisings springing up, only to be harshly stamped out, till I cannot help but believe that it will all come to a head in some great conflagration not too many years down the road. Jesus Himself used to warn of this, to speak of enemies standing in the Temple and the whole place being torn asunder, and I fear in my deepest heart that this is true.

So our believers here in Judea and Jerusalem are persecuted by their fellow Jews and living in fear of the Romans, who persecute us all; outside Judea, the Gentile Christians find that they, too, are being persecuted. This wicked emperor in Rome, Nero, blames the burning of his city on Jews and Christ-followers, and drives our people out, and no one is safe anywhere. We look for Jesus to return as He promised He would, and we cling to His gift of the Spirit and the community we find in loving each other, breaking our bread together, and telling His stories, reading the Scriptures, and praying in His name.

So that, I think, is what I will say to the believers when I write this letter. Stand firm in the face of these hardships, for they will make your faith stronger. Ask God to give you greater faith, and it will be given. Live in the light Jesus gave us, sharing everything with one another. Don't make divisions among yourselves based on who is rich or who is powerful; see the beggar on the street as being as valuable as the emperor in Rome (perhaps more!). And don't allow your pride, your harsh words, your quarrels to tear you apart. Watch your words. Live with grace and love. Love each other as you wait for Jesus to come. In the end, what else is there to say?

I will keep it short. I have wasted too much time already dwelling on the past, though to tell the truth it has been a joy to remember the long road that led me to that glorious meeting, when I saw my risen Brother Jesus face to face and knew Him in all His glory. Mine eyes have seen the King in His beauty, and I have known true joy because of that.

I am an old man now, and I have seen many days. I am ready to rest until He comes to call me. On that morning I will share in the glory of His resurrection, and I will be alive as He was, and is, alive.

Author's Afterword

W hy write a book about James, the brother of Jesus?

I remember as a young person being surprised to learn that the epistle of James was written by a man who described himself as "the brother of the Lord." All the stories I'd heard in church about Jesus' family had concentrated on the little trio of Mary, Joseph, and Baby Jesus; but, of course, when I began reading the Gospels with more attention, I noticed many references to the rest of Jesus' family. His brothers and sisters are mentioned, the brothers by name (see Matthew 13:55); we learn that His brothers questioned His decisions and didn't believe in Him (see John 7:1–5); we find that His brothers and His mother decided He was crazy and they needed to bring Him home—and that they received a stinging rebuke in return (see Mark 3:20, 21, 31–35).

Clearly, Jesus had siblings, and just as clearly, His relationship with them wasn't always easy.

Where did these siblings come from? This is a big point of debate for Christians. Those who follow the Roman Catholic tradition say that Mary remained a virgin even after Jesus' birth, so they believe that the brothers of Jesus mentioned in Scripture must be stepbrothers from Joseph's earlier marriage, or even that they were not brothers at all but cousins. Protestant Christians tend to believe that Mary and Joseph had a normal married life after Jesus' birth, so they could have gone on to have younger children. For the purposes of my story, I imagined both possibilities, so Jesus' brothers and sisters in this story include older and younger siblings—if for no other reason than that the dynamics of a blended family make for a more interesting story!

But why James in particular? Well, it seems that the brothers of Jesus weren't very supportive of His ministry and weren't counted among His followers during His lifetime, yet very soon after Jesus' resurrection and ascension, in the book of Acts, we see Jesus' brother James taking a key role in leadership of the early church (see Acts 12:17; 15:13; 21:18). How did James go from one who failed to recognize his Brother Jesus as Messiah during Jesus' earthly life, to someone who was a leader among the apostles? That's the kind of unanswered question that gets storytellers curious.

A hint of a possible answer is provided in Paul's account of Jesus' resurrection in 1 Corinthians 15. He lists all the different groups of people to whom Jesus appeared after rising from the dead, with an addendum that we don't find in the Gospels: "Then he appeared to James, then to all the apostles" (1 Corinthians 15:7, NIV). The fact that Paul makes a point of mentioning James separately suggests to me, and to many biblical scholars, that Jesus made a separate post-Resurrection appearance to James. If James had had doubts about whether Jesus was truly sent from God, surely seeing Him risen from the dead would have dispelled those doubts and made a believer out of James!

When I started working on this book, I honestly intended to write about that time period after Jesus' resurrection, and about James's role in the early church. But as I began to study the little the Bible says about him and think about what kind of man he must have been, I became more interested in writing about his relationship with Jesus. How could a man have grown up in the same household as Jesus, been raised by the same parents, had close contact with Him throughout His life—yet not have accepted Jesus as the Messiah until after His death and resurrection?

Writing about Jesus

In all the books I've written imagining the lives of biblical characters and the world they lived in, one thing I've usually avoided is writing about Jesus.

As a writer, I've never felt equal to the task. Depicting the sinless perfection of the Son of God is a challenge for any writer, so while I've often had ideas for stories about some of Jesus' disciples and various characters in the four Gospels, I've steered clear of writing them because I didn't think I could depict Jesus in a way that was both believable and reverent.

Then, a couple of years ago, I wrote a short Christmas book called *Yosef's Story*, about Joseph, the husband of Mary and earthly father of Jesus. In that story, I imagined James as an eleven-year-old motherless child, reacting with confusion and a little resentment to the arrival of his father's new wife and an unplanned baby brother. I realized this James was a character I wanted to explore further.

It became easier for me, as a writer, to imagine Jesus through the eyes of someone who *didn't* accept Him as Savior, King, and Messiah. Someone who still saw Him as the annoying younger brother who was too smart for His own good, who wouldn't conform to society's expectations. The guiding text for me here was Jesus' own statement in Matthew 13:57 (also cited in Mark and in John, as if to underline how important this concept is): "A prophet is not without honor except in his own town and in his own home."

It's so much easier to be impressed with someone who comes from outside with a new plan, a new program, or a new message. But when someone from your hometown, or your home church, or your own family is the one preaching a new message, it's easy to be disdainful. To say, "Oh, he's not such a big deal; why, I knew him back when . . ."

This, I thought, is how Jesus' brothers must have seen Him, how the people of Nazareth must have seen Him. They were expecting God to *send* them a Messiah, not to raise one up from right in their midst. And exploring Jesus' life and teachings from James's skeptical perspective made those teachings take on new life and meaning for me.

Where did the story come from?

When I write about Bible characters, people almost always ask where I got my information. While the Bible gives us four versions of the life of Jesus written by Matthew, Mark, Luke, and John, Jesus' early life before the beginning of His public ministry is only briefly alluded to by Luke. Even during the years of His ministry, many "behind the scenes" moments weren't recorded by the Gospel writers. For example, it's intriguing that Mark tells us that Jesus' family was ashamed of His public ministry and wanted to end it—but why? What kind of family meeting led to the decision to confront Jesus publicly, and how did His mother and brothers feel after He turned them away?

There's an old hymn, rarely sung now, which alludes to the years of Jesus' youth in these lines:

> The hidden years at Nazareth
> How beautiful they seem!

Somehow I'd absorbed this idea that Jesus' early years must have been quiet and idyllic. I was surprised, then, to turn to the chapter in Ellen White's book *The Desire of Ages* dealing with Jesus' youth and young manhood, and find that it was titled "Days of Conflict." In that chapter, she explores the conflicts between Jesus and His brothers hinted at in the Gospels—conflicts fueled by Jesus' unwillingness to follow many of the traditions of religion that were so important to His brothers.

In focusing these conflicts on the character of James, the brother who later became most prominent in the Christian church, I did some research into early church traditions about James, such as the fact that he was known by the nickname "James the Just." The epistle of James also gives us some clues to his character: he is a man deeply concerned about the practical side of religion, about justice for the poor and equality within the Christian community. The leadership role we see him playing in the book of Acts indicates that he must have had substantial leadership ability and perhaps more experience in that area than the disciples did. Paul's report of his own conflict with Peter and James (see Galatians 2:11–14) suggests that even after James became a follower of Jesus, he remained a traditionalist at heart, a devout Jew who found it hard to accept the changes that Gentile converts brought to the new Christian movement.

I tried to incorporate as many of these elements as I could into my portrait of James (though in the case of extra-biblical church traditions, I felt free to pick and choose), but ultimately, the Gospels were my guide in writing this story. This story follows the outline of Jesus' ministry as presented in the four Gospels—but from the point of view of someone who has a hard time believing that Jesus can possibly be the Messiah!

Why does James's story matter?

Although I love exploring and imagining the lives of people from the past, especially the biblical past, just for their own sake, I always find myself thinking of a particular story, "Why is this relevant to me as a Christian today?"

Two background characters in the gospel story who fascinate me are James, the brother of Jesus, and Martha, the sister of Mary and Lazarus. In this book I have brought them together, although the Gospels don't tell us whether they knew each other. By introducing James and Martha, I was able to explore an idea that's very important to me in my own Christian walk.

You see, I've attended a Seventh-day Adventist church faithfully since the Sabbath after I was born. I was baptized at thirteen and have rarely missed a church service except when ill or traveling (and then only if there wasn't another Adventist church nearby to visit!). Like many of you reading this book, I'm a lifelong Christian who is deeply familiar with the Christian way of talking, thinking, and doing things.

Like the family of Jesus and his neighbors in Nazareth, we who spend our lives in "churchy" settings can become so familiar with Jesus, so accustomed to His words and the stories about Him, that we lack the ability to see Him with fresh eyes and recognize how startling His claims really are.

We're familiar with Paul's road-to-Damascus conversion, and with similar stories of life-changing conversions in our own time. We can all appreciate the tale of the thief or the drug addict who comes to Jesus and has his or her life transformed.

But what about the conversion stories of good, religious people who are set in their ways and need to be shaken up and challenged? People like James or Martha—or me? Or, perhaps, you? In this story I've imagined James as a man who is absolutely confident that he is a good man and that what he's always done and believed is right. He resists the radical message of his Brother Jesus because he knows that message will turn his world upside down—and, eventually, it does.

I need my comfortable religious worldview shaken up. I need to see the risen Christ with new eyes, and to allow Him to turn my world upside down. I wrote James's story because I'm like James— smug and self-righteous and sure of myself. I need to be humbled and healed and surprised by Jesus. If that's what you need, too, then I hope the story of James, as I've imagined it in these pages, has touched you.

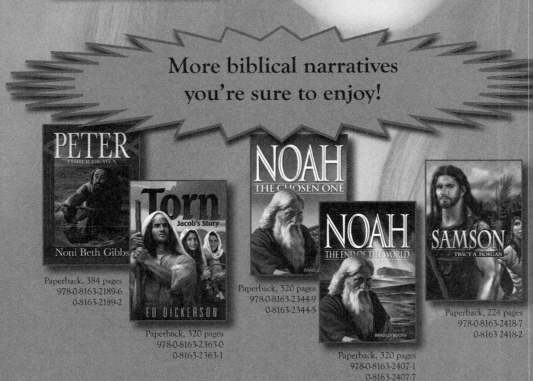